THE HOLLOW INSIDE

THE HOLLOW INSIDE

BROOKE LAUREN DAVIS

BLOOMSBURY
NEW YORK LONDON OXFORD NEW DELHI SYDNEY

DAVIS,
B.
2021

BLOOMSBURY YA
Bloomsbury Publishing Inc., part of Bloomsbury Publishing Plc
1385 Broadway, New York, NY 10018

BLOOMSBURY and the Diana logo are trademarks of Bloomsbury Publishing Plc

First published in the United States of America in May 2021 by Bloomsbury YA

Text copyright © 2021 by Brooke Lauren Davis

Bloomsbury books may be purchased for business or promotional use. For information on bulk purchases please contact Macmillan Corporate and Premium Sales Department at specialmarkets@macmillan.com

Library of Congress Cataloging-in-Publication Data
available upon request
ISBN 978-1-5476-0611-5 (hardcover) • ISBN 978-1-5476-0612-2 (e-book)

Book design by Danielle Ceccolini
Typeset by Westchester Publishing Services
Printed and bound in the U.S.A. by Berryville Graphics Inc., Berryville, Virginia
2 4 6 8 10 9 7 5 3 1

All papers used by Bloomsbury Publishing Plc are natural, recyclable products made from wood grown in well-managed forests. The manufacturing processes conform to the environmental regulations of the country of origin.

To find out more about our authors and books visit www.bloomsbury.com
and sign up for our newsletters.

6/21 Pur

To Mom and Dad—there are some bad parents in this book but you guys are the best.

THE HOLLOW INSIDE

Chapter 1

MOM ASKS ME TO rob the house at the bottom of the hill.

At least, she says it like a question, but it doesn't feel like one. She looks at me with her dark eyes leveled right at mine, and whenever she does that, I can never think of any answer but *yes*. She knows I can't.

Maybe that's why it feels a little unfair. Not that I'm going to say anything about it because—well.

We were painting this fortune-teller's house a few weeks ago in exchange for gas money, somewhere on the Texas side of the Rio Grande. She was a fiftysomething woman with hair red as a cherry lollipop and twining roses tattooed up both her arms. She sat on her front porch steps, drinking something clear with olives in it while she watched us work. And she went on and on about souls.

"Every soul is born with a match, see? We don't get any say in who ours is. Or if we're born in the same country, or even in the same life. Most people don't find their match, but once you do, you've got no choice but to stick with them."

I huffed at that. I told her, "Only rich people have time for falling in love."

"Did I say anything about love? Souls are a different thing altogether. There's an old story about how humans used to be born with four arms, four legs, two faces, two hearts. What a sight." She spit an olive pit into the grass. "But the gods thought we were too powerful, so they split us in two, and now we're doomed to wander the earth looking for the missing part of ourselves. And if you're lucky enough—well, maybe *lucky* isn't the word." She leaned her elbows on the step behind her, closing her eyes and tipping her head back to expose her neck to the sun. "Finding your match doesn't mean you've even got to like each other. But you have to stay together. You've got no choice in that."

Most of the time, I think all that hair dye she used had started melting down her brain.

But other times, late at night, when I fall into the thoughts I don't want to think, I wonder what I'd do if I ever lost Mom.

And that's why I tell her that I'll rob the house at the bottom of the hill.

———

Mom's eyes look black but aren't. I used to think they were. But once she let me look closer, I realized they're actually the same blue as a bruise—the same blue as the web of veins that I can always see through her temples and pale wrists. Her skin's got a blue tint to it, too, which always makes her look cold. Makes you want to rub her hands between yours and blow on them, even on a day as hot as this one.

Her blue-black eyes skitter over the narrow road and across her rearview mirror to make sure no one's around. Then she pulls off into the grass next to a gravel driveway that winds back around a hill. I can just see the peaked roof of the little house on the other side.

We both crawl up the hill while the sky blooms into an orange dawn. The grass is slick with dew that dampens the front of my shirt, and blades of it cling to my hands and knees.

We lie flat on our bellies and peer down at the little house. No movement for the first hour. I make attempts at whispered conversation while we wait. Things like, "How did you sleep?" and, "The days are getting long, aren't they?" and, "Have you ever been so hungry, you start imagining little creatures in your body feeding on you from the inside? Just sucking everything right out of you until you're just bones and skin?"

She doesn't answer me. Not once. Even when I let my voice get too loud, she only cuts her eyes at me. And that's enough to make me swallow whatever else I had to say.

I start to nod off, but when Mom's breath hitches, my focus snaps back to the house. There, up in the left corner window—a light. A minute later, another one flicks on beside it. Then another, below.

They walk into the kitchen one right after another. The family. I shrink a little lower behind the crest of the hill. Mom's a string pulled tight enough to break.

A gust of wind whips brown curls around my face, and I push them back down with both hands. Mom already thought to gather her long, black waves at the base of her neck. I cut my own hair a month or so ago, just below my chin. When I showed Mom for the first time with a grin and a shrug, twirling the rusted scissors around my finger, she said, "It looks like you used a butter knife."

I thought keeping it short would be practical, but now it keeps fluttering over my eyes. Mom glances at me with an irritated twitch in her jaw before I dig a red ribbon from my back pocket and tie it into a headband.

Then she turns her blue-black eyes on me in full force, and they ask the question that isn't a question.

I nod.

She flips onto her back to scoot down the hill. She's going to hide the van, and I'm supposed to sneak into the house after the family leaves.

"Wait," I say.

She doesn't.

"What if they don't go?"

"You wait until they do," she says, eyes on the road below. She doesn't stop to squeeze my hand or ruffle my hair or give me a soft smile and whisper something nice.

Those are rewards. I haven't done my job yet.

When I turn back to the house, I can see them sitting down to breakfast together—a man, a woman, and two girls with hair like cinnamon. The younger one sits on her father's lap, and the older one swirls her spoon in the air while she talks. Breakfast is a simple spread of toast, cereal, and orange slices. But all I've had to eat today is a handful of stale barbeque chips, and my mouth waters.

I don't have to wait long. The man leaves in a white pickup truck. I press myself flat against the hill when he passes, holding my breath, my cheek against the cool grass.

The girls are next. Their mother slips behind the wheel of a minivan, and her daughters climb in with backpacks on. It must be a school day.

I haven't stepped foot in a school in more than seven years. But I nearly finished the fourth grade before I left, and I've gotten by just fine in my opinion. Haven't needed to recite the presidents or use long division even once. Mom teaches me what she knows.

I wait a few more minutes to make sure there's no one else in the house. But when I make my way down the hill, I still keep low in the tall grass, a trash bag balled up in my fist. The front steps creak under my weight. There are initials carved into the wood—T. L. M. and J. M. M. Maybe the girls'.

The front door is locked. I could check for others, but Mom has told me over and over again that getting it done fast is more important than getting it done right, so I shatter a window with a fist-size rock from the flower bed.

I empty the fridge first, and then I check the bedrooms upstairs, dumping clothes out of drawers and tearing through closets. There's a fifty-dollar bill in a makeup drawer and a twenty rolled up in a jar by someone's bed. The little girl has a plastic piggy bank heavy with coins that I tuck under my arm.

I'm walking out of her room when I hear the lock on the front door rattle.

I won't admit to Mom later that I freeze. My mind and body tense up, and I know that I'm being pretty damn useless, but I can't do anything about it as the door swings open, and a man stands tall in the doorway. The man I watched eat breakfast. Our gazes lock, and for the span of a few seconds, neither of us moves.

Like an idiot, I run back into his daughter's room, thinking I'll just climb out a window. But from the second floor, I could break my leg.

As I turn to face him, he mounts the top of the stairs, and I brace myself for him to attack me. But he holds very still in the doorway. He has a baseball cap on—Atlanta Braves.

"Now just hold on," he says. He raises his hands.

I obviously don't have a gun, or I'd be waving it around in his face and shooting holes into these pretty walls right now. So I don't know why he waits.

Maybe because I'm young. Maybe because I'm a girl. Maybe because he has daughters.

"Just—let's talk about it, okay? I'm Clint. Clint Mitcham."

I tilt my head at him. He takes that as a good sign and lowers his hands. Then he steps into the room and asks, "What's your name?"

My name.

Well. I won't tell him that. I won't tell anyone that. Not the one I was born with. Anyone who ever knew it forgot it a long time ago anyway.

My new name is Phoenix.

Mom told me it's a bird from old stories that catches fire when it dies. It burns down to a pile of ash, and then it crawls out as something new.

But I don't give Clint that answer. Or any other answer.

He takes another step forward. I hold still while he takes one more. He even manages a slight smile when he reaches for me, like he'll squeeze my shoulder.

With a growl from deep in my gut, I charge headfirst into him.

His fall vibrates the whole staircase. Wood splinters under his bulk, and the sound makes me sick to my stomach.

He's stone-still when he gets to the bottom. I hurry down after him, hold my hand under his nose, and feel his hot breath on my skin, just to make sure he isn't dead. Blood leaks from the corner of his mouth. His arm is splayed behind him at the wrong angle.

I could call an ambulance and be clear of the house before anyone got here.

But Mom's voice circles in my head, *Get out get out get out get out get out.*

I leap over Clint Mitcham and run through the open front door.

The van idles at the bottom of the gravel driveway, a hulking white box that has probably never seen a car wash. Not in my life-time, anyway.

I sprint toward it, the trash bag knocking hard against my hip and the plastic piggy bank rattling under my arm. The sun is higher now, bearing down on me—exposing me. But I don't see another soul.

Mom watches me on the way down through her half-lowered window, her face blank. I could have a pack of wolves on my heels and her face would look the same.

I toss the trash bag and piggy bank through the open door before I tumble in after them. The tires screech under us, and I almost pitch right back onto the asphalt before I slam the door shut.

The thin, yellowed mattress that takes up the back end of the van breaks my fall, but the lid popped off the piggy bank when it landed, and hundreds of shiny little coins vibrate with the hum of the road. I don't bother to gather them up, just lie down on top of them and feel them cold and hard against the sweat-slicked back of my neck while I gulp down air.

Mom turns in her seat to look down at me.

I watch her blank face break into a grin. And I can't help grinning back.

I don't forget about Clint Mitcham, but he's just a blurry after-image on the insides of my eyelids by that afternoon. If I took the time to feel bad about every Clint Mitcham in my life, I'd have driven the van off a bridge a long time ago.

———

The fortune-teller told me one other thing that I'll never be able to scrub from my mind.

After we finished painting her house, while Mom was taking a shower inside and I was cleaning trash out of the back of the van, the woman snuck up behind me and grabbed my wrist, clamping it tight in her bony hand.

"You can feel it on her," she whispered to me, glancing back at her house. Nervous.

"What?"

"The evil."

I snatched my hand back. "You're drunk."

She shook her head, red curls swaying. "Not that drunk, honey. I'm not saying she *is* evil. I'm just saying she *has* it. Maybe it was done to her. Whatever it was, it's living in her skin now. The pain."

I looked her up and down with a scowl and went back to gathering trash like I didn't know what she was talking about. Like I didn't feel it, too.

"Whether it was her fault or not," she told me, "it's not good to live with that burrowing in your bones. It rots you. Turns you mean."

"Don't worry about us."

But she didn't seem to hear me. She was watching her house again. Like she could see the bad energy curling like black smoke through her windows.

"You could stay here, if you wanted," she said. *Without her*, she didn't have to say.

I took a deep breath and eased it out through my teeth. "What about all that talk about souls? Sticking together?"

She caught her lower lip between her teeth and thought that over for a while. I went back to clearing out the van, until she said, "Stay with her then, if you feel like you have to. But listen—I know you want to save her. I know you think it'll be as simple as sucking the poison out of a snakebite. But it's not going to work, because she *is* the snake. Do you understand? Stop drinking her poison, or you'll wind up dead."

I turned to the fortune-teller. And maybe she was worth her salt, because her face fell, like she already knew what I was going to say.

I spoke in scissor snaps so she'd know there'd be no changing my mind.

"Then I'm dead."

Chapter 2

IT'S DARK WHEN WE pass over the state line from West Virginia into Ohio. We drive through a faded little town, the kind of place that pops up out of nowhere in the Appalachian foothills— crooked houses, peeling paint, and boarded-up windows. Where the only signs of life on a Saturday night are at the bar and a gas station with two pumps and a flashing sign for seventy-nine-cent Polar Pops. Dust clings to everything. Our tires kick up clouds of the stuff, and I wonder if it sticks to the tongue of every person who lives here. Maybe that should depress me, but I've always liked places like this—permanent as roots a hundred feet deep.

I'm taking my turn behind the wheel, careful to keep the red needle on the speedometer hovering right at thirty-five. Getting pulled over would be just the kind of attention we don't need— especially because I don't technically have a license.

I thought Mom was asleep on the mattress in the back, but she grabs my shoulder and points to a parking spot. "Here."

While I pull in, she rifles through the trash bag we keep our clothes in, then tosses me a T-shirt and jeans. The shirt hangs on me, and the pants don't quite cover my ankles. I think I found them somewhere in Tulsa, that time we broke into a storage shed.

We get dressed in the back of the van, our elbows knocking against each other. Then I hop out and use the gritty mirror on the driver's side to adjust the red ribbon controlling my hair. I took it from someone's sewing drawer in Birmingham.

Mom wears a black dress with a lace neckline that I stole for her from a stranger's closet in Indianapolis. Black like mourning, but the color has always looked alive on her, like she's wrapped in a cut of midnight sky. The glow of a naked bulb mounted to a telephone pole—someone's hopeful attempt at a streetlight—casts hectic shadows over her pretty face. The night is warm, and cricket chirps and dragonfly wingbeats make the air pulse with its own heartbeat. Mom and I smile at each other in the dark.

Then she turns on her heel and strides off, boots crunching over gravel, and I trot behind her like I'm attached by a rope, a boat being towed to shore.

The Haggard Colonel is full to the brim, with people standing in the doorway and flowing out onto the street. The band set up in the corner is made up of men with white T-shirts tucked into their jeans, their gray beards hanging down past their belt buckles. They play mostly Toby Keith covers. There's a nice, warm light draped over everything, like we've stumbled into a sepia-toned photograph.

Mom twists all the way up to the bar and asks for two beers— beers that I'm not old enough to drink yet; I'm only sixteen.

But the bartender doesn't notice me anyway. He's too busy

drawing his eyes over the fine lines of Mom's collarbones while he pours amber liquid into two tall glasses. I can't tell if he's closer to my age or hers. She turned thirty-one a month ago. We celebrated with a cake I made out of whipped cream and graham crackers.

Her hair falls in deep-black waves down her back; her dark eyes are quick and wide, and her teeth flash sharp when she smiles. I think she's probably the most beautiful woman most people have ever seen, but they're usually too startled to know exactly what to do about it.

We find two empty stools against the wall and shout at each other over the din of the crowd. "When I saw that man driving back up the hill—" She clutches her heart while she laughs and stamps her foot against the low rung of her stool. "Well, I thought we were done for. He was so *big*, too. I would have loved to see his face when he saw a little thing like you running at him."

The deeper her laugh is, the quieter it becomes, like it gets lost somewhere in her chest before it ever passes her lips. Her body shakes with it. I laugh, too, and tip my head toward hers, the way you lean into a lit candle when you want to breathe the smell in deep.

The bartender comes over to ask if we'd like refills on our drinks, which are still almost full. People grumble over the bar he abandoned while he gets lost somewhere in the blue-black of her eyes. We both washed our hair in a gas station bathroom sink yesterday with shampoo I snatched off a grocery store shelf, but he doesn't need to know that.

Everything down to the food in our stomachs, we took from somebody else—little bits of other lives stolen and sewn together to make us who we are. And I know that's the real reason Mom looks so happy. Because tomorrow, everything changes. Tomorrow, we start making a life of our very own.

Because we have a plan.

A plan for a new beginning, a plan to stanch old wounds, a plan to soothe the pain that the fortune-teller said is trying to rot my mother's bones.

A plan to set things right.

The bartender tries to ask her where she's from, but Mom turns her back on him and raises her glass to me.

"To tomorrow," she says.

"Tomorrow."

Her laugh is a hopeful magic, and her arms are tight when she wraps them around my neck.

Chapter 3

MOM ISN'T MY REAL mother.

I knew my birth mother, but not for very long—she ran off when I was two, though she left traces of herself behind in my own face. I have her high cheekbones and dimpled chin. The scattering of freckles across the bridge of my nose mirrors the photos I've seen of her. I mostly take after my father, with his brown curls and dark eyes. But he said the way I was always a little flushed at the cheeks was all me—like I was born angry, and had always been angry, and always would be angry.

My father's name was Jonah, and he was a big man who smelled like cut grass and summer breezes—he owned a landscaping company in Virginia. He told me all the time that I was tall as a sapling and quick as a water strider. He said he'd bet all his money that I'd play basketball for Virginia Tech, and he practiced with me on the lowered hoop in the driveway every afternoon, until I was six years old.

Until one day my father came into the kitchen after school, towing a woman behind him by the hand. He told me her name was Nina.

Nina's face was completely blank, like she was on autopilot, just moving where she was expected to move and saying what she was expected to say. Like she'd been that way for a long time.

But the moment she spotted me sitting at the kitchen table, her face sparked with a sudden smile. Like I was a pleasant surprise—like an A on a spelling test you didn't study for, or a gift for no reason, or the first ice cream truck of the summer.

And when someone looks at you that way, it's impossible not to smile back.

Nina started sleeping in my dad's room and making breakfast for me every morning. He worked long days in the summer and collapsed into bed whenever he finally got home, so I spent most of my time with her. I played basketball in the driveway while she sat in a lawn chair and drew pictures of me.

I loved them so much I hung them all over my room. I remember one of me wearing a queen's crown and another of me spinning a basketball on the tip of my finger (which I practiced doing for hours a day with no success). My favorite one, I kept next to my bed—the one where she gave me a pair of beautiful, flaming wings. Just like the ones on the bird tattooed on her forearm.

Nina let me watch movies my dad said I wasn't allowed to see, let me rest my head in her lap while she stroked my hair, and covered my eyes when I got scared. And I pretended to be scared more often than I was, because I liked the feel of her warm skin on my face and the way she cradled me close and whispered, "I'll hurt anyone who tries to hurt you, you hear me?"

I remember asking her once if she knew where my real mother went, and she smiled and said, "I'm right here."

"But I didn't come out of your stomach."

"No. You sprouted in the woods like a wildflower, and I picked you and took you home."

I was old enough by then to know that wasn't how things worked, but I liked the way the story sounded. I dreamed it so many times that it became more real than the wisp of smoke where my birth mother had been.

It was the mother-daughter tea party that my Girl Scout troop put on that clinched it for me. All the daughters were bundled up in pink dresses with puffed-up skirts, looking just like the pastries on the tiered trays at the center of the tables. But Nina and I showed up in matching black dresses she'd bought for us, with elegant bows tied at the waist.

The other girls were clearly unimpressed, but I ignored them. I hardly spoke to them at all. Nina and I spent the entire party focused solely on each other, giggling behind our hands at our own little jokes that no one else was allowed in on. The woman I'd brought was the most beautiful, the funniest, the most interesting one there. What else did I need?

It was us against everyone else.

From that day on, I didn't tell people she was my father's girl-friend. She was just Mom.

After she had lived with us for three years, it was easy to believe that she had always been there. She took me to school and picked me up, helped me with my homework, taught me card games, how to ride a bike, and how to skip rocks.

Dad was a sleep-deprived shadow that slipped into my room

late at night to sing me to sleep, only to slip back out and wake me up a few minutes later with the sound of his yelling through the walls. Mom didn't yell back. Her replies were a muffled whisper that never lost its calm or its nerve.

Until the night I woke to her shaking me, just a few days after my ninth birthday, and her voice shattered into a million quaking pieces. "We need to go," she said, fingers digging into my narrow shoulders. "Now."

"Where's Dad?" I asked.

"He doesn't want us anymore."

"What do you mean?"

"He wants us to leave. He's going to—" Her eyes snapped to the door, like she'd heard something. Her voice dropped to a whisper. "I won't let him hurt you."

She pulled me out of the bed and toward the door, but I pulled back. "Why would he—"

Then she switched on the light, and I saw the blood dripping down her chin—stark red against the glow of her pale skin. The kind of shock you never forget. "Please, sweetheart. Please."

I started to cry, but she held her hand over my mouth and snuck me through the kitchen and into the garage. We climbed into the big, white van with his company logo plastered on the side, weed whackers and push mowers rattling when she started the engine.

When the kitchen door banged open, and his huge shadow lurched toward us, I screamed.

Mom screeched the van in reverse, and I closed my eyes and latched my hands to my ears when we crashed through the garage door, metal roaring around us and trying to grind us to a stop, but she jammed the pedal to the floor until we shot free.

We careened down the street, and I looked back in time to see my father run out of the house and down the driveway. He was barefoot, sprinting toward us, screaming something.

Then the van rounded the corner, and I never saw him again.

———

We didn't stop to rest until we were two states away from him. Mom parked at the edge of a Walmart lot, then leaned the driver's seat all the way back and cradled me on her lap, my wet cheek pressed against her strong heartbeat. I started at every noise, certain he'd found us. That streak of red blood dripping down Mom's face flashed in my mind every time I tried to close my eyes. But she wrapped me up in her steady arms, tighter and tighter, until nothing in the world could tear me away. "I'll keep you safe," she promised. She pressed a kiss to the crown of my head, whispering against my hair, "You're my girl now."

Chapter 4

I'M HALF ASLEEP AND more than a little drunk when we drive into Jasper Hollow, Ohio. It's one o'clock in the morning. I'm sprawled on the mattress watching the tree-covered hills through the windows, the moon hanging low and casting a blue, haunting light that tumbles down the slopes.

Jasper Hollow is a small town in southeastern Ohio, smack in the middle of Hocking County. Even though I've never been here, I know that it pools in the bowl between three mountains, named for the three daughters of the founder, Will Jasper, in 1851—Mattie to the east, Pearl to the north, and Clara to the west. And that there used to be a heated debate that raged between the towns-people and everybody else about whether they're actually mountains or just really big hills.

I know because Mom told me. And she knows because she lived at the base of Clara Mountain until she was sixteen years old.

I climb up into the passenger seat just as we clatter over an old covered bridge, the only way in or out of town. The car goes dark inside the tunnel. But just before we come out on the other end, we jolt to a stop.

Mom's hands are bone-white on the wheel. I pry one free and hold it. Her fingers are cold and still in mine, but I hold them. I don't say a word or even look at her face. I just roll down the window and let the warm, heady smell of the woods fill up my chest.

My mother never feels anything halfway. She's either plunged in the deepest depths of the ocean or flying up, up, up into the stars. It's not hard to tell which one she's feeling now, a few feet from being in her hometown again for the first time in fourteen years. She can't make herself drive forward just yet.

It takes her a few minutes to come back to herself, but finally, her hand tightens on mine, and she laughs, a little unnervingly. Then the van lurches forward.

The road is one long curve around the base of a mountain that rises until it disappears into the black sky. There are little pin-pricks of light that could be houses or could be stars.

Mom turns off the road suddenly, into a gap in the trees that she must have known was there. The van jolts over thick roots so hard that I grip the edges of my seat. Branches crack like warning shots. The coins from the busted piggy bank rattle and roll in the back.

Then the ground levels out, and the trees open up into noth-ing, and I'm so sure we're about to hurtle over a cliff that I grab Mom's arm. She laughs quietly before she cuts the engine and climbs out.

I blink until the blackness becomes a little less black, and I see a glassy pond and the cabin on the other side. But the cabin is not going to be any good to us, because a tree fell and split it right down the middle. The glass is busted out of the windows, and a door swings and shrieks on one hinge.

Mom looks it over with her hands on her hips for a while before she crawls in through one of the broken windows, glass crunching under her boots.

The closer I get to it, the more I start to understand what the fortune-teller said—about getting a bad feeling from certain people or places. She used the word *evil*. Which felt dramatic at the time, but that's the only way I know how to describe the sensation that radiates from the cabin. Evil. Or maybe just *dread*.

I only lean my head through the window long enough to pick up the smell of mold and a dead animal or two. "No way in hell I'm sleeping in here."

She whirls on me. Earlier, at the bar, she looked like magic. But now, in the dark of the cabin, she's wraithlike. A ghost.

"You'll do what I tell you to do," she snaps.

I freeze, as still as I would be if I came across a wolf in the woods. I have to be very careful about what I do next. If it's the wrong thing, her skin will flush red and her voice will lower to a hiss, and she'll talk about disloyalty. About my secret plans to abandon her like everyone else has.

I've pushed too far before. Sometimes, it takes a few hours for her to forgive me. Other times, days.

Slowly, I climb into the cabin to stand beside her.

I watch her shadow for a few tense moments, holding my breath. Then she goes back to searching the cabin, opening drawers and turning over rotted furniture. I'm relieved when she finally tells me to go set up the tent outside.

Making camp never takes me long anymore. I have a fire going by the time Mom's footsteps shuffle in the dirt behind me. She grabs a pot from the back of the van and a can of beef stew. Soon the thick broth is bubbling over the fire.

It smells better than it tastes, but I wolf mine down while it's hot. Mom sits across from me on the ground; her pretty dress is bunched up around her hip bones, and dirt clings to the lace, but she doesn't seem to notice. She stares into the depths of her chipped bowl, stirring slowly.

"It's okay," I tell her. "To be nervous."

Her dark eyes flick to my face.

I don't know why I said it. If anything, she seems too calm, aside from the incident on the bridge. She can't feel as blank as she looks—not here. Not in the same place as the person who took everything from her.

Not the night before we take everything from *him*.

"I'm just saying that you've been waiting for this for a long time."

She tilts her head at me. I look down into my bowl and scrape the bottom with my spoon, even though I've already scoured every drop.

"So maybe that feels like a lot of pressure."

She pauses. Then asks, "For me, or for you?"

I don't know what to say to that, so I smile and shake my head like she's said something funny before I take my bowl to the pond to rinse it.

But when I crouch by the water, I set the bowl aside and plunge both of my hands in up to the elbows. I splash my face until all I know is the clarity of coldness, dripping down my cheeks and into my shirt.

Mom kneels down beside me and rinses her bowl, then takes mine and does the same. Without looking at me, she says, "I wouldn't send you if I didn't think you could do it."

I don't answer. But I can't stop myself from thinking, *What happens if I can't?*

I keep my mouth shut because I don't think I want to know the answer. The best one I could expect would be that she'd forgive me.

The worst—

Well. I won't think about that.

———

I climb into the tent and curl up inside a quilt so soft and cool, I sigh when I feel it close around me. I don't remember where we took this one from, but I bet they were sad to lose it. I would be.

We need it more than they do. The justifications didn't use to come so easily to me. I used to linger over things like that for days—that the quilt might have been made by somebody's favorite grandmother. That there's a little girl somewhere who has nightmares when she sleeps without it. Or maybe a woman who liked to press it close to her face because it smelled like her dead husband.

But Mom told me that other people don't dwell on things that way. They usually don't give the hurt they might be causing others a second thought. *It was a quilt nobody had touched in years*, she'd probably tell me, if I said something. *They forgot they even had it.*

And if Mom says it's okay, then it's okay.

I listen for her now. I can hear the leaves shuffle under her feet as she paces from one end of the clearing to the other. Then the night goes quiet, and I wonder if she's inside the cabin again.

I try to put myself in her head, in this place.

I've heard the story of how her life fell apart so many times. And you can't tell it without this cabin.

I don't know how long I've been asleep when Mom finally crawls into the tent. My eyes open blearily, and I lift the edge of the quilt for her.

I feel her hair first, tickling my face as she settles in. I stacked three blankets between us and the bottom of the tent, but no matter how many I use, the ground will always be hard under our backs. Even after seven years on the road, I remember what it was like to sleep in a real bed well enough to miss it.

But once she finally stops fidgeting, she curls her head against my neck, and I don't mind the ground so much.

I press my face to the soft crown of her hair and let my eyes close again, all my nerves about tomorrow dissolving in the soft rhythm of her breath. Because she said she wouldn't send me if I couldn't do it.

And if Mom says it'll work, then it'll work.

Chapter 5

I SLEEP MORE THAN ten hours. I can't remember the last time I did that. Living outside means always being ready to fight off whoever's trying to steal your stuff while you're asleep, and usually just a subtle shift in light is enough to wake me.

Maybe it's being in Jasper Hollow. From the moment we got here, there's been a layer of calm settled over everything. It feels safe. But I know better. It's like how right before people freeze to death, they start to feel warm and sleepy—if I let myself be lulled by the promise of peaceful rest, the cold will stutter my heart to a stop.

Metaphorically, anyway. It's got to be close to a hundred degrees inside this goddamn tent.

I crawl out and blink several times. In the thick of the woods, summer is everywhere—in the honey light and the branches heavy with lush, green leaves and the insect wings zipping past my ears. The humidity is a solid thing, a blanket that could smother someone to death.

Mom is already dressed in a gray cotton dress, her arms folded over her chest while she stares out over the pond. She turns to me when I emerge from the tent, and before I can ask her what she's thinking, she says, "Time for a bath."

The pond doesn't know it's summer yet, and it's ten degrees below frigid. My teeth chatter hard enough to rattle my brain while Mom kneels on the muddy bank behind me and rubs shampoo into my hair. She uses a harsh brush on my back and arms, scrubbing my skin raw. I told her I could do it myself, but she has a clear idea of how things have to go today, and she wants to control as much of it as she can.

I snatch my towel from the low branch I hung it on and wrap myself up tight as Mom starts to pick through the tangled mess of my hair with a comb.

"This is a pretty spot, in the daylight," I say.

She doesn't answer.

"It doesn't look like anyone's been up here in a long time."

Silence.

"Are you—"

But then she gives a sharp tug on a tangle, and I clamp my mouth shut.

When she finishes, she pulls open the back doors of the van and disappears inside. I wait, dirt turning to mud between my bare toes.

When she climbs out, she pushes a pile of clothes into my arms. I dress quickly while she watches, her hands braced on her slender hips and an impatient scowl turning down the corners of her mouth. I fumble into a pair of dark jeans and a plain white shirt, my hands unsteady and my balance thrown off under the weight of her gaze.

I can tell right away that these clothes are different. The jeans fit snug over my waist and hips, and the bottoms hit me right at the ankles, the way they're supposed to. The shirt is soft and doesn't hang shapelessly off my shoulders.

"Where did you get these?"

"A boutique the next town over. While you were sleeping."

Alarm flashes in my chest for just a second when I realize that I slept so hard, I didn't even notice she left me here alone. But I'm still too distracted by the clothes to say anything about it.

I'm used to wearing things bought for other people, too big in some places and too tight in others. This is the first time in a long time that I've worn something that fits. Something that's *mine*.

Mom steps back and studies me up and down, like I'm something she's sketched and she wants to make sure all the lines are just right.

I'm used to it being the two of us against everyone else, but all at once, I feel like I'm standing on one side of a wall of glass with my clean hair and new clothes, and she's staring at me from the other with her dirt- and sweat-smeared face and a dress so old that threads dangle from the hem like cobwebs.

I've got a job to do. And I have to do it alone.

The weight of it settles on my shoulders while Mom goes back to the van to rummage some more. She returns with a camera in her hands.

I stole the camera from a park bench a few months ago while the owner had her back turned. It's a nice one, heavy when Mom slings the strap around my neck. I thought we might be able to pawn it, but Mom had another idea—it would be part of my costume instead. My new identity in Jasper Hollow.

"What's your name?" she asks me, moving around me in a slow circle while I stand still, back straight, eyes forward. Like a soldier.

"Phoenix Ann Mallory."

We made up the middle and last names, but Mom told me to keep Phoenix. She taught me that the key to lying is sticking as close to the familiar as you can. And I'm about to tell a lot of lies.

"And why are you in Jasper Hollow?"

"I'm a sophomore from Ohio State studying photography, and I'm doing a summer project on rural landscapes."

A front that will let me move freely around town and watch everyone from behind the safety of a lens. To be Mom's eyes and ears without letting anyone know she's back. Because if they found out she was here—

She wouldn't exactly be welcomed back with open arms. And there's one person in particular who wouldn't be happy to see her.

The man who ruined her life.

I've never actually laid eyes on him, but I've seen pictures. And the more she told me about him, the more he started to become tangled in all the other stories I heard growing up—he is the wolf at the door, the bandit who strikes in the night and takes everything, the dragon guarding the tower with molten breath that melts skin from bones. The fortune-teller told me that she sensed evil in Mom, but it was just an echo of everything this man has done to her—this man I've never met and has become my definition of evil.

His power is in the way he draws people to him, Mom told me once. *He's handsome but approachable. He has a face people want to trust. A strong voice. And just the right words. Always just the right words. Once he's got you, he could bury a knife in your gut, and you'd die telling everyone that it was your own fault.*

And now, it's my job to get as close to him as I can.

I'm here to learn about him. To watch him and everyone in town who knows him. I'll tell people I'm staying in the motel we passed on the way into town, but instead, I'll be sneaking off into the woods every night, feeding Mom the information she needs.

To destroy everything he's built.

To make him suffer the way she suffered.

To wreak complete havoc on his life so Mom can get back the one she lost.

This is not about revenge, Mom has told me so many times, though I see she hungers for that, too—the chance to hurt him the way he hurt her. *This is about exposing the truth.*

We're going to do whatever it takes to scare him into confessing what he did to her.

Of course, Mom tried to tell everyone herself, all those years ago. But no one believed her. There wasn't any evidence. No witnesses. No proof. Nothing but her word against his—and everyone chose his. Which means the only way to clear Mom's name is to get the truth from his own lips.

And maybe it won't take us long—maybe he'll know what's good for him and give quickly under the pressure we put on him.

But I've got a feeling that he won't.

How far is this going to go? I asked Mom a few weeks ago, just as the plan was starting to come together. She'd been sitting in the back of the van, the doors thrown open to the fading, windswept day. Her sketchbook was propped on her knees, and she intermittently glanced at the view as she drew.

As far as it needs to, she said.

She held up a finger before I could respond, silencing me so she could concentrate on the last flourishes of her sketch. Frankly, I didn't see anything there worth drawing. We were facing a run-down gas station, a plain bank building, and a strip mall where almost every storefront had faded *CLOSING SALE* signs taped to the windows. Concrete cracked into spiderweb patterns. Cigarette butts skidded in circles with each gust of wind. Even the air was stale as corpse breath.

When she was finished, she showed me her sketchbook, and it turned out that she hadn't been drawing the view at all—or rather, not the one in front of us. She had drawn what it would have looked like without the buildings and the parking lot. Just the grassy hill rising behind the bank, the trees that probably used to be in the same spot where the crumbling asphalt was now. Not the world as it was, but the way it should have been.

It's not up to us how far we take things, she said. *It's up to him. We'll stop the moment he gives us what we want. If he lets things get out of hand . . .* She shrugged. *Then that's his choice.*

She stared intently at her drawing, tracing her fingers over the unwavering lines she had made. *His life is in his hands. Just as it always has been.*

Which I took to mean that whatever we end up doing to him, it's his own damn fault.

Chapter 6

MOM EASES THE VAN out onto the road. My stomach feels like it's turned to liquid, and I can feel it churn with every bump on our way back down Pearl Mountain. All I've seen so far is the woods, but now, it's time for my first glimpse at the heart of the town. Jasper Hollow has always just been a story to me, but I'm about to experience the real thing.

Mom told me it isn't unlike the hundreds of other forgotten towns we've driven through—boarded-up windows and neglected homes. Defined by how poor it is, not to mention a steady rate of suicides and opioid overdoses. *The only things Jasper Hollow has to hold on to are black-and-white photographs of how good it used to be*, she said. *Once the paper mill went under, anybody with promise moved on. I've watched more than one person drive away from this town for the last time, flipping the bird to the rearview mirror.*

I asked her why she cared so much about coming back to such

an unremarkable place. Her mouth had responded in a strange way, with a smile, but a tight one, like she tasted something sour. *Because it's mine*, she said.

But when the van rounds the bend in the road, the Jasper Hollow she described to me isn't what we find.

She slams on the brakes. A car behind us almost rams right into our bumper, and the driver lays on his horn. But for a handful of seconds, Mom doesn't even seem to register the sound. She's too busy staring.

We're facing a large roundabout with a massive tree at its center that Mom told me once was called Harriet's Oak, named after the founder's wife. But that's the only detail from her stories that seems to ring true. Instead of a scattering of dying businesses, we're surrounded by brightly painted shop fronts, all crammed together and clamoring for space like there's no better place to be, their flower boxes overflowing with blooms, their doorways packed with customers.

There are people everywhere—strolling along the uncracked sidewalks, following their dogs around ornate streetlights that gleam like new, lounging on freshly painted benches around the oak tree, drifting between shops and restaurants, sampling local wines and cheeses, browsing antiques, and cooing over hand-carved wooden statues and soy candles and custom jewelry.

"Mom?" I say.

The guy behind us is still blaring his horn. People are starting to look over. Our first day here, and we're already drawing too much attention.

"Mom," I say again, grabbing her arm and shaking it.

She's leaning far over the steering wheel, staring through the dirty windshield.

"We have to move," I say. "We have to—"

When she finally turns to me, I can't find a single emotion on her face. It's gone completely blank—a wall that I've never been able to find a door through.

"Get out," she says.

"What?"

The horn is starting to make my ears ring.

"*Now*," she says.

There's no time to argue. People are outright staring now. I fumble with the door handle, and as my feet hit the ground, before I can swing the door fully shut, the van rockets forward. The horn stops. Peace is restored, and everyone looks away.

I stumble out of the road and onto the sidewalk as my mind catches up to what's just happened.

Dropping me off to look around was always part of the plan. I wasn't expecting a pep talk or anything, but I thought she'd at least put the damn car in park before she shoved me headfirst into this new world.

It was probably just the shock of this place not being what it used to be. It was probably just that she wanted some time to herself to process it. Probably.

Introduce yourself. They like to chat. That was her only instruction for me, and I'm not going to get any more clarification now. I brace my hands on my hips, camera hanging awkwardly around my neck, and assess my options.

My gaze is drawn to a storefront painted a soft, inviting blue.

Cursive gold letters say *Sugar House Bakery*. As good a place to start as any—that's what I tell myself. But if I'm being honest, it's the smell that draws me in.

When I open the door, a warm, sweet mixture of aromas tickles my nose and tugs me toward the display case before I've even had time to take note of my surroundings, my mission forgotten for the moment.

I have to refrain from pressing my nose to the glass between me and the rows and rows of desserts arranged on glossy white plates—coffee cake, brownies, bread tied into knots and sparkling with cinnamon sugar, bars of swirled fudge and peanut butter, golden-brown croissants, cookies decorated in swirls of frosting, and cupcakes as large as my palm.

It's been a long time since I've been in a bakery. My only recent experiences with dessert have been the crushed boxes of Zebra Cakes that I've shoved down the front of my pants at grocery stores.

"That one," I say, tapping my finger to the glass like a little kid. With a pair of tongs, the boy behind the counter grabs the biggest cinnamon roll from the display, which is dripping cream.

And then I see the price, mocking me in swirly handwriting on a little chalkboard plaque.

"Seven dollars?"

I've been in this town less than ten minutes, and I've already gotten careless—revealed that I'm different from everyone else here because I can't just hand over a ten-dollar bill without guilt or regret or fear.

I shake my head and tell the boy behind the counter, "Never mind. I'll just have a coffee."

I'm sure no one is really paying attention to me, but my

disappointment is palpable. I'm embarrassed. I try to soothe the burn in my cheeks by telling myself that it'll probably be the best coffee I've ever had, compared to the ninety-nine-cent cups Mom and I sometimes get at gas stations.

Just as the boy is about to put the cinnamon roll back in the display case, a voice from behind me says, "I've got it, Jake."

The guy who spoke offers me a shy smile before he steps around me and says, "I'll take one of those, too. And a coffee."

I stare, gripping the edge of the counter. Hard.

Because I recognize him. His name is Neil. And he's the son of Ellis Bowman—the man I'm here to find.

I've seen photos of Ellis before, and this boy's resemblance to him is unmistakable. The low light of the bakery makes his golden hair glint like a crown. His curls hang loose, just past his ears. His chin is dimpled, his shoulders broad, his teeth pearly as he gives the boy behind the counter an easy smile and asks him about his plans for summer vacation.

I suppose I shouldn't be that surprised to run into him here. Both of his parents used to work in this bakery, according to Mom. And I know that if I'd grown up near a place that smelled this good, I'd probably be here every damn day. I should have been prepared for this possibility, but I wasn't.

I'm not supposed to recognize him, and I'm sure as hell not supposed to be staring, so I wipe the flustered look off my face while his back is still turned. I snap out of it too late to politely decline his offer to pay for my order, but by the time he turns back to me, I think I've managed to rearrange my features into something more appropriate. Though I can't quite manage a smile.

"Thank you," I say. "You didn't need to do that."

35

He gives me a lopsided smile. "Are you new around here?" he asks.

I remember the camera and grab onto it like it's a life preserver. "I'm a sophomore from Ohio State, and I'm doing a summer project on rural landscapes," I say.

I'm afraid I sound like a bad actor reading from a script. But he accepts my statement with a nod—he has no reason not to believe me.

"Awesome," he says. "Bucks had a decent season, didn't they?"

Bucks? I draw a complete blank.

He laughs while I stutter for a response. "You know . . . the Ohio State Buckeyes? Not a football fan, are you?"

"Not really," I say, fighting to tamp down another blush warming my cheeks. I'm already messing this up. I shouldn't be this nervous. But my hands are shaking when he hands me my coffee, the mug jittering on the saucer.

I think he's going to walk away from me and that'll be the end of it, but as he moves toward a table, he says over his shoulder, "I'm headed to OSU in the fall myself. Haven't decided what I'm studying yet, though."

He looks at me, and it takes a few beats for me to realize he wants me to follow him. I sit down across from Neil, and a man in a blue apron comes behind us, carrying out the cinnamon rolls. His name tag says *Tim*. He has silver hair and a neatly combed mustache, and he pats Neil on the back, glancing between us before he gives him a conspiratorial smile. "Who's your friend?"

"Well—" Neil tilts his head at me. "She's a photography student from Ohio State—"

Tim grips Neil by both shoulders now, practically shaking

him. "Well, did you tell her that you're on your way to being the next Buckeye football star?"

Neil blushes and looks down at the table, but his smile gets even bigger. "It's just a partial scholarship—"

"A football scholarship to a Big Ten school!" Now Tim really is shaking him, so hard that the table rattles. "A D1 athlete hidden in little old Jasper Hollow."

Tim's chest is puffed with pride. But Neil stammers in response, apparently too shy to handle this much praise—a notable difference from what I've heard about his father.

"So," Tim says, taking mercy on Neil by turning his focus back to me. "Tell me more about this photography student from Ohio State."

Neil says, "She was actually just about to tell me her name."

Now it's my turn to stammer. Up until yesterday, I made it my business to avoid attention. To slip around the edges, take what I needed, move on before anyone realized I'd been there at all. I survived by making sure no one knew I existed. But it's time for a new strategy.

And now, all eyes are on me.

"Phoenix," I say. "Phoenix Mallory."

"Phoenix," Neil repeats, nodding, like he's testing it out. "Well, Phoenix. Welcome to Jasper Hollow. My name is Neil, by the way."

Dammit. Because I already knew his name from what Mom told me, it didn't occur to me that I should have asked.

Tim shakes my hand, then leaves us to take care of other customers, and Neil and I are alone.

I've never considered myself very lucky, and yet here I am.

Less than five minutes in this town and I've found a connection to Ellis. A wealth of the information I came here for, sitting right in front of me.

But just because I've gotten a windfall doesn't mean I know what to do with it. How to capitalize on it. I can still say the wrong thing, make him suspicious, lose his trust, and this opportunity could quickly turn into a disaster.

What I *do* have experience with is talking my way out of some tight corners. You get good at it, after you're caught with stolen goods in your pockets a few times. *Oh, I was just on my way to pay for this* or, *It's a Christmas gift. I had to hide it from my Mom until I got to the checkout.*

I say, "This is such a beautiful town. Are you from here or just visiting?"

"Lived here my whole life," he says.

I lean back in my chair with a wistful sigh. "It must have been heaven, waking up to these views every day."

"Never get tired of them," Neil agrees.

"I'm sure it's really breathtaking from the houses up on the mountains. But it would also be nice to live closer to town. . . ."

I'm trying to lead him subtly into telling me where he lives, but he just smiles and nods along until I ask outright, "Does your house have a nice view?"

I wince internally, hoping that I haven't pushed too far. But then he says, "Yep. I've been blessed with one of the nicest, if I do say so myself."

He points over my shoulder, and I turn to look out the bakery's windows. One of the mountains looms beyond it, and about halfway up, there's a house. "Kinda hard to miss," he adds with a laugh, like he's a little embarrassed.

He's right. It's big and white, looming over the whole town. Poised in the perfect place for everyone to keep an eye on the Bowmans and for them to keep an eye on everyone else.

When I turn back, I study Neil for a moment. Sure, he has a strong resemblance to his dad. But that doesn't necessarily mean he likes him. Maybe he knows what kind of man his father is. Maybe he's the Bowman black sheep, ready to blow the lid off his own family's scandals. Maybe he'll be on my side.

"It must have been the perfect childhood," I say, hoping he'll divulge that it was anything but.

To my disappointment, he agrees. "Pretty much."

"No complaints, huh?"

He takes a bite of his cinnamon roll. "Nothing that comes immediately to mind."

I shake my head. "Jasper Hollow just seems so . . . quaint. Too good to be true, you know?" I keep my tone light, like I'm joking when I add, "There's got to be *something* wrong with it."

"Oh, there is." He crooks his finger, and I lean in so he can tell me in a conspiratorial whisper, "We have a lawn statue bandit."

I frown. "A what?"

"A *lawn statue bandit*," he repeats, very seriously. "All summer, any kind of statue anyone puts out in their yard is gone by the morning. Gnomes, Virgin Marys, flamingos—you name it. Nobody knows who's doing it, or why. They've never left a ransom note behind."

He can't help the slight smile that curls one corner of his mouth. I fight the urge to roll my eyes, but I play along. "How . . . upsetting."

"My thoughts exactly," he says. "But there's been this argument going for months about what it all means. Some claim that the bandit is doing the town a favor, ridding us of a plight of tacky lawn decor. Others claim it signifies the deterioration of morals in modern society. Lots of great, philosophical points on both sides. It's all anyone's been able to talk about on the community Facebook group all summer. According to my mom anyway."

"You're kidding."

He leans back in his seat, unleashing the grin he's been fighting. "I wish I were." He adds, "Seriously, though, I know what you mean about Jasper Hollow seeming too perfect. We've all got our own problems under the surface, I'm sure. And I know that this town wasn't always as nice as it is now. But ever since I've been around, it's been a great place to grow up. I've got a good family. Good friends. What more could you ask for?"

I nod, hoping the disappointment isn't plain in my voice. "Sounds wonderful."

A moment later, his phone buzzes, and he excuses himself, taking the last bite of his cinnamon roll. "Gotta run," he says through a mouthful. When he swallows, he adds, "Great to meet you. Hope I see you around."

When he's gone, I drop the pleasant expression and let my face settle into its usual scowl. I down the rest of my coffee, mulling over the conversation.

I gave him opportunities to complain about his dad, but he didn't take the bait. Maybe he just didn't want to share any bad blood between them with a stranger, but I don't think so. When he said that he had a supportive family, his voice never wavered.

And as nice as Neil was to me, if he considers himself his father's ally, that makes him my enemy.

———

I meet Mom at the designated pickup location outside of town just as the sun is starting to set, streaking the sky in bands of orange and blue.

She hardly glances at me as she starts the drive back up Pearl Mountain to the clearing. Like she's already primed to be disappointed in me. But I'm eager to prove her wrong.

"I met Neil Bowman," I say, my voice too loud in the confined space.

Mom casts a look sideways at me, her expression flat. "Oh?"

"In Sugar House Bakery. He was there."

She waits for more.

I lean in close. "I found out where he lives."

I'm about to tell her when she cuts me off. "It's that monstrosity on Clara Mountain, isn't it?"

I feel my face fall. "How did you know?"

She sighs. "Because he moved into it right before I left town. He's wanted all his life to be significant. And that place is—significant."

Now that she's ripped a hole in my sails, I sit in silence the entire bumpy way back up Pearl Mountain, dreading the question that I know will come next.

And when she puts the van in park and cuts the engine, she turns her dark eyes on me and asks it. "What else?"

I don't have anything else. Unless she'd be amused by the lawn statue bandit story Neil told me. Somehow, I doubt that.

I try to play it off. "It was a short conversation. He got a phone call and had to go. But it's an opening, isn't it? A way in."

"Who was the call from? Did you listen in?"

"He walked away from the table before he answered it."

"You didn't follow him? Didn't try to see where he was going next?"

When I don't answer her right away, she nods. Let down. But not surprised.

She doesn't need to say a word. I feel everything that she's thinking. That she's second-guessing my value in this plan. That if she weren't so recognizable, she would just do the job herself, and do it better. That maybe I'm more trouble than I'm worth.

"I'll find out more," I say.

"Yes," she says. "You better."

Chapter 1

WE WAIT UNTIL LATE that night to venture out again. The dark in Jasper Hollow is so different from the dark of other places—complete and swallowing. Anything outside the beam of our headlights is a void. It's easy to lose what's right in front of you.

I feel the impossible height of Clara Mountain sweeping high above our mud-crusted little van. As we make the climb, I'm sure Mom knows these turns and curves well enough not to send us flying into the black. I am. But I can't unclench my grip on the edges of my seat.

The warm air flows over me through my rolled-down window, thick with the smell of what I can't see—leaves, bark, and dirt. I'm more nervous than I should be. We're just going to stake out the Bowman house, see what we can learn about the family by getting a feel for how they live. Easy.

When we get close to the house, Mom pulls the van off the road, into a gap between the trees, and cuts the engine.

She turns to me and gives me a long, meaningful look, dark eyes sparking in the glow of the dashboard lights. I nod like I can read her face, but actually, I'm still trying to figure out whatever secrets she was trying to impart when she gets out of the car and disappears into the trees. I hurry to follow her.

I have to move quickly to keep the pace, never taking my eyes off her back. If I lose her here, I'm afraid I might not find her again. She told me to bring the camera with me, and it knocks against my chest with each step. She said she wanted me to take pictures of the house. She didn't give me a reason beyond "they might be useful later."

We walk in absolute silence, and after the first mile or so, I'm about to ask her if we're going the wrong way, but then the trees thin and something starts to take shape.

We duck down low, keeping to the woods surrounding the large property while we take our first good look at the place. A nervous laugh tries to bubble up my throat, but I choke it down.

If it's not a mansion, you'd only need another foot or two to make it one. It sprawls over the mountain like it grew right out of the ground, clean white with lots of tall windows bordered by shutters the same poppy-red color as the door. There are six white columns along the front, a porch that wraps all the way around, and an upstairs balcony. The flower beds are fat and happy, bursting into the yard.

It's big and beautiful, and it was built on the bones of Mom's life. We can't let ourselves forget that.

I feel Mom stiffen beside me, and I follow her gaze to the big window that looks into the kitchen. There's someone sitting cross-legged on the counter.

I pull back farther into the trees, but he's not looking at us. It's Neil. We see him from the side; he's in sweatpants, socks, and a white T-shirt, and it looks like he's watching a TV that's just out of our sight. He's got a bowl cradled in his lap, and he scoops spoonfuls of something into his mouth.

We both watch him for a few more minutes, keeping an eye on the other windows, waiting for movement anywhere else in the house. But it looks like Neil is the only one home.

I realize I'm gripping the camera with both hands. Mom is still watching the house, her lips moving soundlessly, lost in her own thoughts. I know better than to even attempt speaking to her when she's like this. So, while I wait, I decide to start taking pictures, like she told me to.

It's been a long time since I've actually used a camera, and certainly never one this nice. I can't even recall a specific time in my memory when I held one, but I must have. I know that I'm supposed to hold my eye up to the viewfinder. I figure out quickly that there's a little toggle that lets me zoom in and out, bringing Neil closer and farther away.

I frame the whole house, kneeling in the grass to get the right angle. Then I press the button to take the picture.

And then the dark fractures in an explosion of light.

The flash. I forgot about the flash.

It was so bright, I blink hard until my eyes readjust. But even when they do, I can't see Mom. She's not where she was crouched a moment ago.

I lift my eyes to the window. And Neil is staring in my direction.

"Phoenix!" A hushed snap in the dark. She's already made a break for it, but I can't tell in which direction. "*Run*."

Branches whip at my face, vines pull at my legs, and the trees whirl by so fast that all of them look the same, making me lose track of which way I'm going. I hear the crash of Mom running close by, but the churning branches hide her from me.

The toe of my shoe catches on a root and throws me down on my hands and knees, skin tearing against rocks, wind knocked from my lungs when the camera gets crushed between my chest and the ground. I gulp down air, eyes watering.

I hear the woods rustling nearby, and then the sound draws closer. I stagger to my feet, bracing for Mom to yank me by the arm and hiss something nasty in my ear for being so stupid. About how my carelessness just cost us our camera and our cover.

But it isn't Mom who pushes through the branches. It's Neil. And the air gets knocked out of my lungs all over again.

First, he asks, in a soft voice, "Are you all right?"

And then, squinting until he's sure his eyes have adjusted to the dark— "Phoenix?"

This is bad.

A photography student from Ohio State has no reason to be here. Especially not in the middle of the night. My story slips like sand through my fingers.

I open my mouth, waiting for some lie to come to me. The right words to smooth all of this over. But the only thing that materializes is a half-baked idea to buy myself more time.

I stumble, and Neil lurches forward, but I fall too fast for him to catch me. I hit the ground hard, and pain flashes through me when something cuts my cheek open, but I grit my teeth to stop myself from crying out and keep my eyes firmly closed, pretending that I've fainted.

For a beat or two, all I can hear are windblown leaves hissing and insect wings drumming, and somewhere in these woods, Mom is holding her breath.

I hear Neil come toward me. My heart pounds erratically, but I make all my muscles relax.

He mutters, "Holy shit." And then he slides one arm behind my neck and the other under my knees, and he lifts me off the ground.

I want to peek through my eyelashes so badly, but I can't risk it. The crunching sound under his shoes gives way to quiet grass, and I know he's taking me to the house. There's a hollow creaking as he climbs the stairs to the front door.

I feel Mom's eyes on us, and it takes everything in me not to jump out of this stranger's arms and run to her.

He fumbles to get the door open without jostling me too much. I hear it swing. Then he carries me inside and kicks it shut behind him, and the sound rings through me like a gunshot.

My photography student story won't work anymore. And any chances of me spying on the Bowmans from the fringes are gone.

Time for a new plan. And this one, I'll have to come up with all on my own.

Chapter 8

I FEEL THE COOL flush of air-conditioning against my skin. The smell inside the Bowman house makes me think of clean sheets, wood smoke, and cinnamon. A far cry from the van, which is usually saturated by the sour stench of dirty laundry and unwashed bodies.

Neil eases me down on the couch with a whispered, "There you go." I hear the floor creak when he steps back, probably to look me over. An incredulous half laugh escapes his lips, and I imagine him running his hands nervously through his curls.

After a tense moment of silence, he tries shaking my shoulder, gently, and says, "Phoenix?"

When I don't answer, I feel his hesitant hands on me, and I fight the urge to open my eyes just to bite him—my first reaction when almost anyone touches me. But he's only unhooking the camera from around my neck. It won't be any good to me now, anyway—I heard it crack open when I fell.

After that, he's quiet for a few moments. Then I hear him walk out of the room.

My instinct is to jump off the couch and escape while I still can. But the second he recognized me in the woods, it was too late to run. He heard my neat little cover story about being a photography student, and now, at the very least, he knows things are a hell of a lot messier than that.

If I run, that means it's over. I'd have to leave Jasper Hollow and never come back. And if I leave Jasper Hollow, if I don't help Mom get her confession, she won't want anything to do with me anymore.

When I hear Neil come back into the room, I keep my eyes firmly closed. It sounds like he's rattling through a box, looking for something. Then there's a cold swab on my cheek. He cleans my cut and then smooths a bandage over it with steady hands. He does the same for my ragged palms, and I try not to wince at the cold sting of the antiseptic.

Then his hand is on my forehead. The heel of his palm is big and rough against my skin. He takes it away, and I imagine he gauges it against the heat of his own, the way Mom and I have done for each other so many times. Then he pulls a heavy blanket over me and tucks it around my shoulders.

He crouches next to me, leaning in close. I can feel the warmth of his breath on my hair.

I hope he doesn't notice me flinch when I hear the front door open. Keys clatter into a ceramic bowl, and a girl's voice says, "Neil, you trailed in dirt again."

"I'll get it later," he calls back.

"I know you think being completely oblivious to everything around you is cute. But it's not cute."

"That's one opinion."

I can't be sure without looking at her, but from what Mom has told me about the Bowmans, this is probably Melody—Neil's sister.

The girl's footsteps come into the room. "Yeah, well—"

She must have spotted me finally. I don't know exactly how I expect her to react. But when she does, I realize how lucky I am that Neil was the one who found me outside.

"What the *hell*?"

"What?" Neil says.

She lowers her voice to a whisper, like she's afraid I'll overhear. "Who is that?"

"Oh," Neil says in mock surprise. "Her?"

The girl growls an obscenity, and Neil laughs easily. "Her name is Phoenix," he says. "I met her in town earlier."

There's a long pause. Then she prompts, "And why is she passed out on our couch with a Darth Vader bandage on her face?"

Darth Vader? The name ticks a distant memory—one of those movies my dad liked and kept saying we'd watch together when I got older.

I feel the couch sink by my head when Neil sits down beside me. He brushes tangles from my face and presses his palm to my forehead again.

"*Neil.*"

"I found her passed out in the woods a few minutes ago."

There's a beat of silence. "Well, *that's* not suspicious. Why the hell was she lurking around our house?"

"I don't know. But I'm sure she'll have a good explanation once she wakes up."

Damn, I really hope so.

"Did she steal anything?"

"No. Jesus. She's been out this whole time."

"But have you been *watching* her the whole time?" Her voice gets even quieter. "How do you know she wasn't just faking it so you'd let her in and she could cut our throats while we're asleep?"

I'd be offended by that if she weren't right about the faking part.

"Does she look like a murderer to you?" Neil says.

"Lots of murderers are normal-looking people."

Neil scoffs. "I think she's a little better than normal-looking."

Did he just call me hot?

My stroked vanity waits for the girl to disagree, but she fires back, "Murderers can be *attractive*, too."

Attractive. I've always suspected it myself but never had any-body confirm it. Mom isn't too forthcoming with compliments.

I can hear the dismissive shrug in Neil's voice. "She looks harmless to me."

Idiot.

"Idiot," the girl snaps, and I hear her footsteps retreating.

"What are you doing?"

"Calling Mom."

"She should be home any minute."

"We could be murdered by then."

Neil sighs. "Stuff like that doesn't happen in Jasper Hollow."

"Exactly," she snaps. "That's what you always hear about on the news. *Sleepy little town, never had a problem before.* And then two kids with promising futures and nice smiles turn up dead. I'm telling you, Jasper Hollow is overdue for something."

They're both quiet for a moment. Then she adds, "Don't you give me that look."

He laughs again and adjusts the blanket around my shoulders.

"I'm serious, Neily." I can't see her, but a picture of her is starting to come together in my mind, both hands on her hips, staring Neil down with sharp eyes. "One of these days, trusting every person you meet is going to get you into trouble."

Get in, get out. That's what Mom always told me before I broke into a house. But I've been here twenty minutes, and instead of coming up with any ideas, all I can think about is how pissed she must be right now about me getting caught.

Neil and the girl took their argument to the next room, and their voices are too faded for me to make out now. Once I realize I'm alone, I risk opening my eyes.

I'm on a dark-gray couch. The walls are cream-colored. The ceiling is high, and wooden beams stretch across it like the house's rib cage. The second-floor hallway overlooks the living room, the railing polished the same deep brown as the wood floor.

Neil left the bowl he was eating from earlier on the coffee table, and it's full of cornflakes that have turned to mush, floating on top of the milk. I sit up to peer down the front hallway, and there are shoes lined up along the wall, all different colors and sizes.

The house isn't messy, exactly, but there are magazines and blankets tossed all over and a leaning tower of DVDs on the table. There are black marks on the couch from where people have put their feet up—some of them probably from me. Neil didn't think to take my boots off.

It's nicer than most places I've stepped foot in, but I'm still thrown off. I don't know what I was expecting. The outside is definitely grander than the inside.

I notice too late that the voices in the other room have gone quiet. When I look up, the girl is standing in the doorway to the kitchen.

Her arms are crossed over her chest, and her eyes are as sharp as I imagined. Sharper. She has the same golden hair as Neil, and it tumbles over her shoulders in thick curls.

Now I'm certain that this is Melody. The resemblance to her brother is strong, and they look around the same age, like they should—they're twins.

Beautiful is almost the right word, but not quite. *Beautiful* is for soft things, like flowers, and I've never seen a flower look so menacing. Her face is hard, her eyebrows narrowed, and her jaw clenched. She might be a sculpture—the kind that makes you reach out and run your thumb over the cheekbone without thinking—if it weren't for the flush of blood under her skin.

The way she looks at me makes me want to bare my teeth. But I have to stop myself, because I'm not supposed to scare them. Yet.

"Should I warm up some stew?" Neil calls from somewhere behind her. He pauses, waiting for his sister's answer. When she doesn't give one, he decides, "I'm warming up stew. She might be hungry when she wakes up." I hear the clang of pots getting moved around in a cupboard.

Melody's eyes don't leave mine. "She's already awake."

Neil appears beside her in the doorway to see for himself, and a big grin breaks over his face as he wraps his arm around his reluctant twin's shoulders, herding her closer to me.

"Welcome back," he says. "Now, please, tell my sister you're not a murderer."

If I really had been passed out and hadn't heard them talking about me, I would have been jarred by that statement. I'm still a bit jarred anyway.

I'm about to speak when Melody steps between us and says, "Why were you sneaking around in our yard?"

I'm still working on an answer for that, so I don't give her one.

That's when she notices the camera where Neil left it on the side table. And her already suspicious expression hardens even more. "What the hell is that?"

"Mel—" Neil tries to intervene.

"What the *hell* is that?" she snaps again. "Were you taking pictures of our house?"

Neil grabs her by the elbow, trying to calm her down, but she yanks herself away, throwing up her hands. "Neil, in what world is a stranger lurking around our house with a camera not *really freaking alarming*? The way I see it, she's either another one of Dad's crazy superfan stalkers, or she's trying to snap a few candid photos of us to sell to *People* magazine. Or she's just a flat-out creep trying to get pictures of us undressing." She turns back to me, pointing an accusatory finger. "Neil won't call the cops on you, but I will. All right? Don't think I won't."

"Melody—"

"Well, she's not speaking up to defend herself. Don't you think that's suspicious?"

"Maybe she doesn't want to talk to a stranger who just threatened her."

Melody rolls her eyes to the ceiling, taking a deep breath before she turns back to me and thrusts her hand in my face. "Fine. I'm Melody Bowman. And you are?"

I hesitate, staring at her hand for a second too long before I think to grab it. I'm almost certain this is the first time in my life anyone has ever shaken my hand.

Her fingers burn against mine. I don't know why, but I expected her skin to be cold.

"Phoenix," I say.

"Awesome," Neil says, clenching his fist like he's just won a video game. "Melody, you just made your first friend. Are you hungry, Phoenix?"

He pauses for an answer, and when I don't give one, he says, "You look hungry. Food will be ready soon." And he disappears into the kitchen.

Melody follows, snapping at his back, "I have friends."

"If you don't talk to them after school, they aren't your friends."

"Well, it's not my fault that Jasper Hollow is full of backward, hillbilly idiots like you."

Neil's deep, rumbling laugh echoes through the kitchen. "Jesus, Mel. What's with you tonight? Are you still mad about that B minus on your duck sex essay?"

She sputters for a reply. "Who the hell told you about that?"

He holds up his hands in defense. "It's not my fault that you left the evidence in a trash can in my very own house. Or that you used the word *phallus* four times in one sentence."

I can't see her face, but the clench of her fists is murderous.

He drops to his knees and grasps her ankles. "I apologize, Great Queen of Jasper Hollow."

I wonder if this is how normal brothers and sisters talk to each other.

"Neil—" she growls.

"I didn't mean to question your extended—" He coughs. "*Extensive* knowledge of the sixteen-inch penis of the Argentine lake duck."

And then I see it. There, on the side of her face, while she braces one hand on the doorframe and looks down at her brother—the corner of her mouth lifts into a smile.

But when she turns back to me, it's gone.

"I don't like this," she says.

I can tell she's about to bark more questions at me that I don't have any intention of answering when I hear the front door open again.

I tense.

A woman's voice. "Didn't I ask one of you to vacuum?"

"Cornelius," Melody says, kicking Neil's hands away from her ankles.

He springs to his feet and goes back to stirring the pot on the stove. "Well, I was kind of *busy*."

"Like you were planning on doing it anyway. I bet you were sitting on that counter watching TV before the girl showed up."

Melody's eyes go to the bowl he left on the coffee table. "And eating cornflakes!"

Neil titters from the kitchen. "Good guess."

The woman comes into the living room with a sweep of her long, printed skirt, her arms laden with brown sacks that she can't see over. She teeters under their weight.

"Melody," she commands, and Melody helps her lower them to the floor.

And then she sees me and responds with a startled, "Oh."

"Mom, this is Phoenix," Neil cuts in. Then he explains how he met me at the bakery this morning, and then I turned up in the woods outside their house a few hours later and passed out.

I brace for whatever comes next, not sure if she'll meet me with Neil's instant, naive acceptance or Melody's suspicion.

I sense a little of both as she nods, chewing over my story. But I guess some motherly instinct in her wins out, because she reaches out and does the same thing Neil did before—presses her palm to my forehead.

"How's your cheek?" she asks.

"Fine," I answer quietly.

"You don't feel dizzy at all?"

I shake my head.

She sits down beside me on the couch and squeezes my hand. "My name is Jillian Bowman," she says. "You can call me Jill."

"Phoenix," I say, though Neil already told her my name.

"Nice to meet you, Phoenix," she says with a soft smile.

I know from what Mom has told me that she's forty-three. Her eyes have all the warmth of Neil's, but they're as dark as polished acorns, like Melody's. Her auburn hair is swept back in a dark-blue bandana printed with an elephant pattern, which some-how gives her a congenial look. Like a cross between a Sunday-school teacher and a hippie.

She pauses then, indicating now would be a great time for me to fill in all the gaps in my story.

My brain has been scrambling for the right lie this whole time, and a tenuous explanation has started to come together. But I only want to tell it once.

So it's convenient that that's when the last of the Bowmans decides to walk through the front door.

He bends to take off his shiny, black shoes and put down his briefcase. He's in a dark-blue suit that fits him too well. He should be around forty-five years old, but he has the build and moves with the effortless confidence of someone half his age. His golden hair has just started to turn gray at the temples, and it makes him look like someone who knows what he's talking about. It's brushed back from his face, but a few strands have shaken free and hang in his eyes.

Now I can see where Neil got the cleft in his chin, not to men-tion the blue eyes and those big, pearly teeth.

The man walks into the living room with a bright smile. But when he sees me on his couch, the smile falters, just a little.

"Is this one of your friends, Mellie?"

"No," she says, in a way that sounds more like *hell no*.

Jill goes to him, stepping into his arms for a hug before she looks back over her shoulder at me. "This is Phoenix. And she'll be keeping us company for the evening, if she'd like."

Melody's opinion of that idea is clear when she knits her

eyebrows together and opens her mouth. But it looks like she knows better than to argue with her mother, because she closes it again.

I nod at Jill.

Her husband laughs. "Well, I'm all for a little Midwestern hospitality." Then he holds out his hand for me to shake. And I take it.

"I'm Ellis Bowman," he says. "It's a pleasure to meet you, Phoenix."

I already know his name.

This is the man who ruined Mom's life.

Chapter 9

I'VE ALWAYS KNOWN THAT Mom was haunted by something, even before she told me what it was.

At first, she only gave me vague hints into her past, making comments about how we couldn't trust anyone but each other. *And Daddy*, I used to say, and she'd respond with a sad smile and an indulgent nod. Until he couldn't be trusted anymore either, and we were on our own.

She told me the rest of the story in bits and pieces, flashes of memories that I pieced together over the years until I started to understand why we had to live on the road. Why sometimes the weight of her past sat so heavily on her that she could hardly move or speak under its burden.

Whenever she talked about what Ellis Bowman did to her, the whites of her eyes glowed an unsettling red. There was heat all over her, burning in her cheeks and flushing her neck and shoulders, glowing hot in her hands as they clutched mine. She was usually so careful to be cold and distant with me and everyone else, but when she talked about him, she was a pot boiling over.

I listened, and the more she told me, the more I felt that heat rising in my own body, her hurt and her rage becoming my hurt and my rage. And I was eager for it. *More*, I wanted to say, because in all the years I'd known her, these were the only glimpses she gave me of her heart, in all its raw brokenness. And I finally understood.

This was the reason she always held herself back from me. At first, I thought it was because there was something wrong with me. That maybe I wasn't smart or mature or interesting enough to be worth truly caring about. But it wasn't my fault that Mom couldn't love me as much as I needed her to.

It was Ellis Bowman's fault.

Until a few months ago, I didn't know she had plans to return to Jasper Hollow and confront him. For seven years, we focused on surviving.

Mom had forty dollars in her pocket when we ran away, which we only managed to stretch about two weeks. After that, we resorted to begging. We stopped after the time I asked a stranger for his sandwich and he grabbed my elbow and tried to get me into his car.

She jumped on his back and bit his ear so hard that her mouth filled with blood, holding on until he slammed her against a brick wall, and she lost her grip. He ran from us, and we ran in the opposite direction, my hand crushed in hers, and hid down an alleyway.

Most girls want their mothers to have soft skin and pretty singing voices, but I was thankful for mine—her eyes blazing fire, her grip like claws in my shoulders, her teeth stained red with the blood of a man who'd tried to hurt us. Because monsters can't scare you if the scariest one is on your side.

That's the day she told me, "We're done asking for things."

That night was the first time I stole something. I took a box of cereal from a grocery store shelf while Mom distracted employees a few aisles over with a maple syrup spill. There wasn't a strategy. I just pulled it off the shelf, walked up to the door with it folded against my chest, and then ran like hell. I kept looking back, afraid that a bunch of teenage employees in red vests would be on my tail, but nobody even seemed to notice I'd been there at all.

We perfected the art of slipping just under everyone's radar, taking as much as we could shove under our shirts and into our pockets and waistbands. And it was terrifying and empowering at the same time, how invisible I felt in those big, cold, anonymous supermarkets while we stole a month's worth of food and no one batted an eye.

Robbing houses was much harder. There were dogs to consider. Security systems with alarms and cameras. Nosy neighbors ready to call the cops. The fear that even though a house looked empty, someone's grandmother might have been asleep on the couch. But despite the risks, Mom preferred taking things from people's homes. She said she liked seeing the inside of a stranger's world. I've watched her look around someone's living room in absolute wonder, like she'd stepped inside their bodies. She liked the way their clothes carried their warmth, their unique scents, the worried edges of their sleeves. She's always coveted things that feel lived in.

But just a few months ago, we were running so low on food

that we needed to make an emergency stop at a Kmart. The plan was simple—I'd grab what we needed while she hovered nearby and kept watch, ready to distract any employees who wandered too close.

I was shoving sleeves of peanut butter crackers in my bra when, from the corner of my eye, I saw Mom sit down on the shiny tile floor.

This was not how we flew under the radar. There was already an employee who had spotted her. In a minute, he was sure to investigate.

"Mom?" I said, kneeling beside her. "Mom, what's wrong?"

She was sitting in front of the book section featuring a mix of paperback romances and thrillers and self-help. But one author's work dominated the shelves, all the books facing out, name featured in embossed letters even bigger than the titles—*Ellis Bowman*. And right next to the display, there was an obnoxiously large sign that featured one of the covers.

It depicted a table set for dinner and a man and a woman sitting down with their arms around two toddlers, a boy and a girl with blond hair, the whole family smiling. It was called *At Our Table: The Redemptive Power of Family and Food*. The advertisement said, *Special Anniversary Edition with a new introduction! Over a million copies sold!*

And Mom was holding a copy in her lap, staring down at the pages.

I knew the book well. Mom already owned one, shoved under the passenger seat in the van.

It was a memoir about a man who had an unhappy childhood with an abusive father and an alcoholic mother. He managed to escape on a football scholarship, but then his parents died in a drunk-driving accident, and he had to quit school to come back to his hometown and take care of his little brother. He got a job at the local bakery, married his high school sweetheart, and they both worked hard and saved their money until they opened their own restaurant and had two beautiful, perfect children together.

It might seem like an unremarkable story, but I could understand why it would sell a million copies. It was solid proof of what everyone dreams about—that someone who had faced adversity and been knocked down could pick himself back up. It was a promise that if you kept your head down, followed the rules, and gave it your best, you too could one day own your own business, take care of your family, and take back control of your life.

I'd seen it in bookstore windows before, on display with other bestsellers. I was sure Mom had seen it all those times too, but maybe she'd just averted her eyes. She clearly wasn't prepared to stumble upon it here. To find this new edition.

She was gripping the book so hard now, the soft cover was wrinkling in her shaking hands.

"Mom," I said again.

"I'm reading the new introduction," she said, her voice far away.

She hunched her shoulders around the book so I couldn't see it. So I waited, hovering over her, locking eyes with the nosy stock boy who was watching us. It was enough to cow him into looking away, for the moment.

Mom was icy stillness, lips parted, wide eyes scanning the pages. And then, all at once, she snapped into motion, tearing the book apart in a fevered frenzy.

I had to drag her from the store, everyone staring, but no one followed us, even though we hadn't paid for the book she destroyed, even though there were stolen crackers peeking out from the neckline of my shirt—they were probably just relieved to be rid of us. Relieved that the woman with the red, watering eyes spitting obscenities while she threw ripped pages like confetti was solely my responsibility and no one else's.

I got her back into the van and convinced her to lie down on the mattress. Her body heaved with sobs while I held her head in my lap until the parking lot outside the windows faded into night and she fell into a restless sleep.

Then I carefully pried the book from her hands. I looked at the ripped pieces of Ellis's author photo on the back of the book, and it was so easy to be hypnotized by that earnest smile. To believe he wanted a happy ending for all of us, too.

Mom had done a thorough job of tearing the book apart, but there was just enough left for me to get the gist of the new introduction—what had sent Mom over the edge so quickly.

It was about one of Ellis's mentors who was featured prominently in the original book. Pastor Mason Holland. He also happened to be Mom's dad.

And according to this new introduction, he'd just been diagnosed with stage four lung cancer.

I was sitting at Pastor Holland's kitchen table when he told me, Ellis wrote. *The way he said it, it was like he was telling me that the Browns had, yet again, not made it to the playoffs. Something disappointing but inevitable and not worth dwelling over. "It is what it is."*

Ellis went on about how Pastor Holland's bravery through his treatments has been such an inspiration to him. How he admired his unwavering faith and dedication to serving his community.

And he ended by sharing Pastor Holland's recent decision to refuse any further treatment.

I've tried talking him out of it, of course. I've begged and pleaded. But the man is as stubborn as a brick wall. And he's made his choice. So I'd like to dedicate this anniversary edition to him. To the man who lives on his own terms. Until the end.

I put the book down. And I let Mom sleep.

When she woke a few hours later, darkness pressing against the van's windows, she said, "My father is dying."

I could see the hopelessness pressing down on her shoulders. Her powerful fury of a few hours ago had dissolved into tears slipping meekly down her pale cheeks. "I haven't spoken to him in years. Not since I left Jasper Hollow. Not since Ellis turned him against me. He told my father all those lies about me."

She buried her face in a pillow, pushing herself down deep in her sadness, where I wouldn't be able to reach her.

"I've almost gone back so many times to confront Ellis," she said. "Make him tell my father the truth about what really happened. But I've never had the courage to face him. The last time I saw him—it was so awful, Phoenix. The worst day of my life. I still have nightmares about it. But now I've waited too long. My father is going to die thinking that I'm all the horrible things Ellis said I was."

I'd seen her upset before, her emotions surging so intensely that she'd scream or break things. And afterward, all her energy spent, she'd go numb. Or at least, that's how she'd look on the outside. Maybe she was just hardening against the rest of the world, against me, and retreating into herself.

Sometimes it would last for days. Other times, weeks. But at that moment—I'd never seen her this devastated. Never felt her shake so hard.

I leaned over her as if she were a child. I had realized long before that day that sometimes daughters have to take care of their mothers, even when they're not sure how. So I grabbed her narrow wrists firmly, and I said, "Stop." It must have been the way I said it, like an order. She was so startled, I think she stopped breathing. I put my hands on both sides of her damp face, and I told her, in that capable, steady voice that she sometimes used on me, the one that always made me feel safe, "Crying is not going to help us. Stop it."

Wide-eyed, she blinked until the tears quit running. And then, she seemed to snap out of it, shaking her head.

"You're right," she said. Her lips curled unsteadily into something resembling a smile. "Being sad doesn't do a damn thing for us, does it? We need to get angry. We need to fight back."

That wasn't exactly what I'd said, but I was pleased to take credit for it. Even more pleased to hear the strength returning to her voice. "Yes," I agreed. "We'll fight back."

"We're going to make sure my father knows the truth before—before it's too late," she said.

From that day on, the idea took root in her head like a weed, choking out all other thoughts and feelings and desires.

And maybe it did pull her away from me a bit more, her all-consuming obsession with the plan to make Ellis confess. More frequently, she started to lose herself for long stretches in her head, sometimes hardly uttering a handful of words to me for a week at a time. When I spoke, she didn't seem to hear, and when I touched her hands, she'd irritably wave mine away.

But I knew that if I could just ride it out, if I could just get to Jasper Hollow and give her back her life, I'd get *her* back.

On the nights she did talk to me, there was this light in her eyes that I'd never seen before. And when someone looks at you like that, like they've just handed you their last little bit of hope, you don't put it in your pocket like a river stone, taking it out every once in a while to run your thumb over when you remember it. You chain it around your neck so you can feel it beat in time with your heart, always.

Chapter 10

WHEN I SIT DOWN at the big, wooden table in the Bowmans' kitchen, Neil sets a bowl of steaming beef-and-mushroom stew in front of me. Nausea still rolls deep in my stomach, but I need more time to think over my story, so I thank him and shovel it down.

The first few spoonfuls sear my throat. It's not until the third or fourth bite that I really notice the taste. I'm used to eating from cans that have been wasting away in people's pantries for God knows how many years. But this is *definitely* not from a can.

I slow down. I feel the thickness of it on my tongue. It's been a long time since I've had anything homemade, and I have to close my eyes for a few seconds.

When I open them, they're all staring at me, Neil watching the closest. He's in the chair beside me with his elbows up on the table, looking pleased with his handiwork. Jill is on my other side, and Ellis settles in across from me.

Melody won't come to the table. She leans against the counter with her arms crossed over her chest.

"Neil would be the head cook at the restaurant, if he had that kind of time," Jill says.

"Restaurant?" I say. Of course, I already know all about it. Ellis's books have made it famous enough that it wouldn't be unusual to say I'd heard of it. But I don't want them thinking that I'm some kind of crazed fan, like Melody suggested, so I think my best bet is to feign complete ignorance.

"The Watering Hole," Jill says, a proud smile spreading on her face. "It's a restaurant we own on the Circle."

I nod, like I'm chewing on that new information.

The kitchen falls silent again. They're all waiting for me to speak.

"The stew is great," I say.

"Thank you," Neil says.

"And your house is so lovely."

Jill and Ellis glance at each other contentedly. "It's home," Ellis says.

Then they wait for more.

So I put my spoon down, push the bowl aside, and I open with something true. "I told Neil that I was in town because I'm a photography student. But I lied."

I glance at Neil, trying to gauge how he feels about my deception. His lips are pressed together, his eyes big, like he's eager for me to give him a good reason. Eager to trust me. I wonder if it's got something to do with his comment from earlier. *She's a little better than normal-looking.*

I breathe in deep, like I need to collect myself. But really, it's to cover the fact that I'm pulling all of this out of my ass as I go.

Mom has had to teach me a lot about lying over the years. It didn't come naturally to me—she said I had too much trouble keeping my feelings off my face, so she used to coach me. I can hear her voice in my head now. *Pause. Press your lips together. Look down.*

"I never knew my parents," I say. "They died in a car accident when I was very young."

The same way Ellis lost his parents, I know from reading his books. I don't dare look right at him, or it will all feel too contrived. But from the corner of my vision, I see him nod with a very serious frown.

"I've lived with my grandmother in Indiana for most of my life. We were really close. Until I came home last week from my part-time job at the grocery store, and she was asleep in her reading chair. I tried to wake her up to tell her she needed to nap in her bed. Her neck always got so sore when she slept in the chair. But when I shook her, she wouldn't—"

I pretend that the words are too horrible to say, like they've lodged in my throat.

"Oh, honey," Jill says, reaching out and covering my hand with hers.

It's jarring to me, the easy touch. Sometimes, I think Mom withholds her affection like it's a bargaining chip, and this woman gives it away to a stranger in a second. It takes me a moment to find my train of thought again.

"When I lost Grandma," I continue, "I had nowhere else to go. I had no one. I knew I couldn't afford our apartment on my own, and I just—I had to get out. Get away. So I packed a bag and took my camera. I knew it wasn't really practical, but I wanted it so bad for Christmas last year that Grandma pawned half her jewelry for it. I couldn't bear to leave it behind."

Mom knows how to cry on command. The few times we've gotten caught stealing, I've seen her sob through her apologies when I knew with absolute certainty that she wasn't sorry.

It's a skill that I've never quite mastered, though I try hard to make it happen now. I scrub my hands vigorously over my face to bring out the red in my skin, and I bite down on my tongue so hard I draw blood. I'm satisfied that I at least get my eyes to water.

"God, she was the only person on the planet who cared about me. I didn't really understand that until I was all on my own. Grandma and I didn't have a car, so I just started walking. I hitched a ride from a nice-looking lady, and she took me over the state line before she stopped in the middle of nowhere and held a knife to my neck until I handed over all my stuff. But I wouldn't give up the camera—it was the last thing my grandmother ever gave me. So I jumped out of the car and ran into the trees beside the highway before she could hurt me."

I dart a quick glance around the table. The second I said the word *knife*, I sounded too melodramatic to my own ears, but thankfully, they seem to believe it. Jill has a shocked hand over her mouth, Neil's head is tilted and his brow knitted with concern, and Ellis is still frowning and nodding gravely.

I peak at Melody still standing across the room, leaning against the counter, staring at me. And the flare of her nostrils says, *Bullshit.* Maybe she's suspicious of everyone she meets, or maybe she's just smarter than the rest of her family. Either way, three out of four is good enough for me.

"After that," I go on, "I walked. I stuck close to the highway, but I stayed hidden in the trees, and I followed that path until I saw the sign for Jasper Hollow. And—"

I look up at the ceiling, like I'm trying hard to keep the tears from leaking out of my eyes.

"And do you know what it says on that sign?"

Jill and Ellis clasp hands on the table, Neil looks about ready to burst from smiling, and Melody rolls her eyes so hard, it looks painful.

"*Welcome weary travelers*," Ellis says in a reverent whisper.

I nod, pressing my lips together and blinking hard a few times. And to my absolute delight, I manage to squeeze out a single tear that streams delicately down my cheek. "*Welcome weary travelers*," I repeat. "And I was so weary. So tired. And hungry. When I walked across the bridge and into town, I smelled the bakery right away, and I was starving. I thought maybe I could get something with the change left in my pocket, but of course it wasn't enough."

I turn a warm, grateful smile on Neil. "That's when your son stepped in to save me. You have no idea what that cinnamon roll and cup of coffee meant to me, Neil. It was the first time anyone has shown me kindness since I left home. The first time I've felt hope since—"

My breath hitches, and I briefly squeeze my eyes shut, taking a moment to collect myself.

"Since Grandma died," I finish.

"Sweetie," Jill says softly, "is there any family we can contact for you? Someone you can stay with?"

"No one."

Ellis rubs at the stubble on his chin. "Well. I suppose we should get a social worker involved."

"I'm eighteen," I lie. "And I've got nobody."

The Bowmans meet the weight of that statement with somber silence.

I shrug and say, "I guess that's why I followed Neil home. Because he's the only person who's been nice to me. I don't want to take advantage of that kindness, and I don't expect any more. I just—I don't know what to do now, or which direction to turn next. I'm so sick of feeling invisible and lost and like if I got hit by a car tomorrow, not a single person would give a—" I pause. Swallow. "Would care. I just want to feel like somebody cares."

I fold my hands on the table in front of me and press my lips together to signal the end of my story.

I don't have to wait long for a response.

After barely a beat of silence, Neil angles his chair toward his parents like he's ready to make a case for me. "Listen, you're always telling us how important it is to help people who need—" he starts.

"I think Dad and I should discuss—" Jill cuts in.

But then Ellis stands, his chair legs scraping against the floor, and the kitchen falls silent, all of us turned toward him and waiting for him to speak.

He looks down at me and says, "You came to the right town. Jasper Hollow is a community. We look out for each other. And now that you're here, we're going to look out for you. Now you finish your dinner. We'll get the guest room ready for you."

The guest room.

I thought I might guilt him into paying for a hotel room for a few nights. The most I had hoped for was a place where I could take a hot bath, meet with Mom, reconfigure the plan.

But he's inviting me to stay in his own home.

My brain is scrambling, trying to figure out what this all means. Apparently, so is everyone else in the room. Melody is the first to react, a mixture of anger and incredulity darkening her face.

Jill's reaction is subtler, but the twist of her mouth is clear. Ellis just went completely over her head, making a decision for the whole family. She won't argue with him in front of me—it's too late to uninvite me now—but she gives her husband a look that says, *We'll discuss this later.*

But Ellis doesn't seem cowed in the least, just nods at her with an easy smile when she says, "I'll get some clean sheets," and walks out of the room with a sweep of her long skirt.

Neil jumps up from his chair and adds, "Towels. For the guest bathroom." He exchanges a triumphant glance with me before he disappears down a dark hallway.

Ellis looks pointedly at his daughter, who's still leaning against the counter. They stare each other down for a moment. Then her eyes settle on mine, and I silently will her to tell him this is a bad idea.

"Mel," he says. "Maybe some of your clothes would fit Phoenix?"

With one last scowl at me, she walks out of the kitchen.

And then I'm alone. With him.

He gives my shoulder a firm squeeze with his large hand, his wedding ring glinting gold. "Mellie takes some time to warm up to people," he says. "Don't take it personally."

"I won't."

It's an effort to keep my breathing steady. I grip my chair hard and try not to turn and look out the window, where I'm sure Mom is watching.

"You don't have to do this, sir. Really. I saw an inn in town. Maybe that would be better. I don't want to put you out—"

"Nonsense. You've been through enough. We're going to make sure you're taken care of. That's what Bowmans do."

Mom and I have been on the road for almost half of my life. If I've learned anything in all that time, it's that nothing, *nothing* is free. Especially not for people like me. You either steal it, or you pay for it. And the life of a thief has its own costs. Nobody just gives you anything—you usually just don't know the price until it's too late.

Ellis Bowman wants something from me. I simply don't know what it is yet.

The plan has shifted, but my purpose hasn't. My job is to learn everything I can about Ellis Bowman and help Mom unravel him until he tells the truth. We won't leave Jasper Hollow until he admits to everyone what he did to her.

And if we make him feel as much pain and fear as she felt and get a little revenge along the way, then that's a bonus.

I look up into his face, at a smile sweet enough to end a war, and I know the truth won't come easy. He's been hiding what happened for so many years. And things won't go well for him once it all comes out.

Finally, he lets go of me, walking down the hallway after his family with his hands tucked in his pockets. Over his shoulder, he says, "You can stay as long as you need to, Phoenix."

———

Just a few minutes later, Jill is fussing over the pillows in the guest room like they'll be softer if she hits them enough. Ellis leans in the doorway and asks, "Need anything else?"

"No. This is more than enough," I say.

Jill comes at me before I realize what's happening, sweeping me up in a hug. "It sounds like you've been through a lot in the last few days," she says, her breath warm on my hair. "If something ever happened to me, I'd want someone else to step in and take care of my kiddos."

She lets me go with a timid smile, and I wonder if she feels guilty about the look I saw on her face earlier when Ellis announced I'd be staying with them. Maybe he said something to her while I was finishing my stew—persuasive as always.

"Ellis and I are just upstairs if you need anything," she says. "So is Neil. And Mel is just across the hall."

Then they both, finally, leave me alone.

I turn to take in the room. For years, I've shared an old mattress in the cramped back of a van with Mom. Now, I have my own bed, a bathroom, a dresser, and enough room to—

Well, I'm not exactly sure what people do with this much room. Eat on the floor? Do jumping jacks?

I sit down on the hardwood, feel how solid it is under my hands. How permanent. The view outside the windows won't change, aside from the color of the leaves. I close my eyes and lie down. And even though I know that this place isn't safe, it's nice to pretend, for just a moment, that this is our house. Mine and Mom's.

For my tenth birthday, she gave me a drawing of my bedroom—the one she promised I would have, though she never told me when. There was a window seat to curl up in, with a lamp to read by. There were tall shelves along the wall, filled to bursting with books, a globe, mugs full of cut flowers, frames for photographs, and my very own radio. And in the corner, a beautiful desk and a chair with wheels.

"To practice your own artwork," she whispered.

She and I both knew that I couldn't draw to save my soul. I only did it because I liked when she put her hand over mine and guided the pen so we could make things together that no one in the world had ever made before.

I loved that picture so much. Even if it was only a shadow of what I really wanted. I wish I had it now.

I didn't know then why she couldn't give me a home. I didn't know what we were running from. I didn't know there was a wound in her and that I ripped it open wider every time I asked when I would get that bedroom. I didn't understand why she tore up the picture after I asked her one too many times.

I hear someone's throat clear. My eyes snap open.

From my angle on the floor, Melody is upside down, standing in the doorway and holding the pile of clothes that her father asked her to get for me.

I refuse to give her the satisfaction of letting her know she caught me off guard. I sit up slowly as she sets the neatly folded pile on the bed.

Then she looks down on me and raises her eyebrows, waiting for my explanation.

"It's a nice house," is the only thing I offer. Then, "Thanks for the clothes."

"You're welcome."

I grab her wrist when she passes me, and she stiffens. I offer her a shy smile. "Wanna help me up?"

She does. When I let her go, she folds her arms across her chest.

"I want to apologize," I say before she can turn to leave again.

She gives a heavy sigh. "For what?"

"For barging in on your life. I never meant to cause any trouble." *Look down at the floor,* I imagine Mom coaching me. *Now back up at her, through your eyelashes. Right, just like that.* "If I could go home, I would. But I don't know where home is anymore."

For a second, I think I've got her. She bites her lip and shakes her head at the floor, and I wait for her to say she's sorry for the way she's acted.

But then her sharp eyes lock on mine, and she says, "I'm tired of people thinking they can take advantage of my family."

This time, I can't hide my reaction. I open my mouth to defend myself, but she doesn't give me the chance.

"I hear the last person who sold a Bowman photograph to the press got a pretty penny for it." She nods at the bedside table, where Neil left the remnants of my broken camera. "Maybe you thought you'd get another one. Or maybe—" She takes a step forward, bringing her face so close to mine that all she has to do is whisper. "You're here about the accident."

The accident?

"Maybe you think this will be your big break into journalism. A boost to your college admissions portfolio. An insider's angle."

"I have no idea what you're talking about," I say. Because I don't.

I tried to do more research on the Bowmans before I got here. The thing is, all the computers in the homes I broke into needed passwords. You can't use the computers at most libraries without a library card, and to get one of those, you need a permanent address. And as far as things like newspapers and magazines, if it isn't edible and won't keep us warm, then it doesn't get to take up valuable space under my shirt or in my waistband on our grocery store runs.

All I know about the Bowmans comes from Ellis's books or from what Mom told me. After the wild success of his first book, *At Our Table*, he's written ten others to date, and she made me read them all. Most of them are considered self-help, but his advice is always given through the lens of his life experience.

But now that I think about it, his most recent book hardly mentioned his daughter at all.

"If you're some upstart reporter, you can go back to wherever the hell you came from and type up a nice big article about how Ellis Bowman's daughter is a raging, heartless bitch. I'm fine with that. But Dad is done with the interviews. You will not squeeze one more story out of the accident. Do you hear me?"

We stare each other down for a few seconds. Without my permission, the corner of my mouth starts to twitch upward. Because I see it now, why she knew right away that I was up to no good.

The flint in her eyes matches my own. I know a girl with a chip on her shoulder when I see one—because I'm one, too. I can't fake nice with her.

"Are you laughing at me?" she snaps.

I shake my head, wiping the half smile off my face. "No. I just—you think someone would be desperate enough to sneak into your house to get information about your family?"

"You clearly haven't been in this town for very long."

"I'm not here to take advantage of anyone," I say. "I swear."

Melody pinches her lips together and raises her eyebrows doubtfully. But she knows that she's not going to get me to admit what I'm really here for, and I know that I'm not going to convince her that my intentions are innocent.

A stalemate. For now.

I grab the busted camera by the strap and hold it out to her. "Take it with you, if you don't trust me."

After a moment's hesitation, she does. And without another word, she turns on her heel and storms out of the room. Her door slams across the hallway.

Getting the rest of her family to trust me was easy enough. But I have the feeling that not many people have tricked Melody Bowman.

At least I'll have something to keep me busy while I wait for word from Mom.

Chapter 11

AFTER EVERYONE GOES TO bed, I crack the bedroom window and drape one of Melody's red shirts over the ledge so Mom will know where to find me.

I expect her to come right away. I pull a chair over to the window to wait for her and start to get anxious after an hour, clenching and unclenching my hands in my lap.

Maybe an animal got her.

Maybe someone found her sneaking around and she's locked in a jail cell.

Maybe she got so pissed off at me for getting caught, she took the van and left.

I debate climbing out the window to look for her, but I don't think I'd be able to find her in the dark, and if the Bowmans catch me, I'll have to come up with more lies on the spot. I've been listening hard at the cracked window, so I would have heard if she screamed. There's nothing I can do until morning.

I undress in the guest bathroom, bundle my brand-new clothes—torn and stained from when I tripped in the woods—and shove them into a trash can under the sink.

It's been three weeks since Mom and I snuck into a YMCA locker room and had real showers, so when the hot streams of clean water hit my face and wash over my shoulders, I let myself sigh. The icy pond bath of a few hours ago is just a bad dream. Black trails of dirt twine down my legs and disappear down the drain, and I stand there until my skin turns soft and starts to wrinkle. Then I stand there some more.

When I climb into bed, my skin is hot and tingly against the sheets. My stomach is full of the best stew I've ever had. The room is dark, quiet, and cool. I'm not cramped into a tiny tent, I'm not slapping at mosquitos every few seconds, and I can't smell any animal shit.

But I can't relax enough to fall asleep. I sit up in the bed with my knees drawn to my chest and pull at my hair. I breathe in and out through gritted teeth. I worry about Mom. I doubt my abilities to pull this off. I feel guilty for lying to Ellis's family. I dread the indefinite number of days I'll have to keep up the charade.

And then I do what I always do to chase away the emptiness and the loneliness and the fear. I make myself *angry*. Because anger blots out everything else, everything I don't want to feel.

All Mom has to do to set herself burning is read from one of Ellis's books, even though she has almost every line memorized. Just a few words can leave her seething. Because every book is peppered with his wisdom on what he thinks it means to be good.

I lie down in the bed and mouth some of the words to the ceiling.

We've all been in a dark place before. I can say that from experience.

Me, too, Ellis.

Think of all the things you owe the people in your life.

That's why I'm here.

Poison can come in the form of a person.

Yes. She can.

I think of Mom when she lived here, all those years ago. How young she was when all the people she trusted turned on her. How desperately alone.

But not anymore.

I fall asleep with a rage that warms me from the pit of my stomach to the tips of my fingers. It fills me to the brim and wraps me up tight, and it whispers sweetly in the dark that maybe I am a villain, but at least I'm not a victim.

*T*he few times Nina Holland has told the story of how her life fell apart, it always starts fifteen years ago, sitting under the shadow of Harriet's Oak at four o'clock in the afternoon.

She leaned back against the trunk and had her sketchbook balanced on her leg while she drew a phoenix in black ink. She'd gotten the sketchbook for her sixteenth birthday the month before.

She'd read about phoenixes in an encyclopedia of mythological creatures from the library—birds that burst into flame at the end of their lives and are reborn from the ashes—and she liked the idea. Every time life got tired, you could start over with new hands and skin and eyes, and everything from the deep-throated rumble of an engine to the rotation of the sun and moon would seem like a big adventure again.

Of course, there was the fire to consider. A horrible way to die. But then, Jesus had died in pain, too, and that pain had saved the whole world.

Nina sat facing the Watering Hole, where the kitchen door was propped open and a truck was pulled up to unload supplies. *A boy named Jameson had been carrying in big sacks and boxes for the last fifteen minutes, the root-thick muscles in his arms straining under his tanned skin, his dark hair slicked back with sweat. It was high summer and hovering around ninety-five degrees, and his T-shirt was drenched through before long, so he peeled it off. Even in the shade, Nina felt sweat dripping down her forehead and making the hair that had come loose from her ponytail stick to her neck.*

Jameson was two years older than her, recently graduated and with no other plans on the horizon. All his friends had gotten out of town as fast as they could, and Nina had heard him make vague remarks about trade schools and community colleges, but she and everyone else in town knew that he wouldn't go. Jameson Bowman leaving Jasper Hollow would be as likely as Clara Mountain packing up and moving to California.

Whenever Jameson cursed under the weight of a box and powered it off the ground, his shoulder blades moved in a way that was hard to look away from. But Nina made herself refocus on her drawing.

The encyclopedia entry on phoenixes hadn't given her much to go on in the way of appearance; her notebook was full of not-quite-right attempts, but she was certain that she'd finally gotten it the way she wanted.

But she hated to think of it framed and hung up on a wall, the way her father would insist on doing. This was something more *than anything else she had ever drawn. Something that came from a place down deep in her chest that she was usually too afraid to touch.*

She laid her arm flat against her sketchbook and started to make slow, black lines across her skin. The sweat on her arm made the ink sputter, but she pressed down harder, until it hurt.

A voice breathed hot against her ear. "Giving yourself a tattoo?"

Nina jumped, shooting a startled line of ink right through the phoenix drawing in her notebook.

Jameson sat back on his heels, a wicked grin splitting his face. She pressed the inked side of her arm against her shirt. "Just messing around," she said.

It was a widely accepted truth that he was infatuated with Nina. Older women were always giving her sly winks in church about it, telling her that he was staring at her, that he seemed to like the dress she was wearing, that the sanctuary was a lovely place for a wedding, that she would be just the girl to straighten him out.

"Can I see your drawing?" he asked, already reaching for her sketchbook, his other hand lightly grasping her elbow.

She pulled her arm back and picked up her sketchbook. "I'm meeting Dad for lunch." Then she walked fast toward the Watering Hole.

He laughed low in his throat, and then she heard his slow footsteps following behind her. Because popular opinion was that Nina only pretended to resist him because a preacher's daughter had to resist—at least at first. So long as he never gave up on her, Jameson seemed to believe, she would eventually give in to her true feelings.

The town had decided that Jameson Bowman would eventually persuade Nina Holland, and they would get married and move into the little cabin on Pearl Mountain, and she would have his children and tell them stories about how she had made their father win her over.

Jameson was handsome and nice enough. But when he left a room, she didn't feel the pull to go after him. When he spoke, she feigned interest and hoped he would tire himself out soon. When he touched her, she felt no response deep in her core that wanted more.

The truth was that the way people talked about her and Jameson made her feel like they were trying to crowd her into a gray, windowless room and lock the door.

When Nina walked into the Watering Hole, a bell jangled erratically overhead, and a man with pale-blue eyes sitting at one of the tables looked up from the stack of papers in front of him.

Ellis Bowman was Jameson's older brother, and Nina had known him all her life. Back when he'd worked at Sugar House Bakery, she was so little that her dad had to hold her up by the armpits to look through the display window and pick out what she wanted.

When Jameson walked in behind her, Ellis seemed to catch the desperate plea on her face.

"David needs help with dishes," he said.

Grumbling, Jameson obeyed, and Nina watched him walk through the swinging door to the kitchen.

When Nina looked at Ellis again, his face had softened into a smile that made her smile back.

His sleeves were rolled up to his elbows. He kept his long, thick hair out of his face with a backward Cincinnati Reds cap. He was almost ten years older than Jameson, and his good looks were never as vivid, but he had a softness that was easy to lean into. Something to bury herself in and hide.

It occurred to Nina that this was the first time she'd seen the restaurant empty since it had opened a year ago, a lull between lunch and dinner. She knew Ellis had been nervous before the Watering Hole opened, because the people of Jasper Hollow weren't known for welcoming change. Her father was the pastor of Jasper Hollow Methodist Church, and Ellis confided everything to him.

Ellis always stopped by her house after every Sunday service so he and her father could sit in the front porch rockers and talk about God, politics, and just about everything else. He was always there long enough to eat dinner with them and sometimes stayed well into the night.

Nina would sit on the porch steps and do her homework, and sometimes she'd interject once she was old enough to keep up. But mostly she just liked to look out into the dark and listen to Ellis's voice while she watched the lightning bugs—low and gentle and as soothing as rainfall on a rooftop.

She suspected the success of the Watering Hole might have something to do with her father's influence in town. But she was sure people kept coming back because of Ellis's charm. He had a knack for making anyone feel like they were just the person he wanted to see.

"I'm glad you stopped in," he said now. And even though she knew he was this friendly to everyone, the words made a thrill shiver down her spine.

She nodded at the stack of papers on the table in front of him. "What are you working on?"

Ellis rubbed the back of his neck and grinned sheepishly. "Well . . . don't tell anyone, but it's a book."

"You wrote a book?"

His blush crept quickly from the collar of his shirt to his hairline. "I guess so."

"Can I read it?"

He shook his head, his smile falling a bit. "I mean—it's a mess. I was never too hot at English. I'm no good at all those . . . rules. I feel like the stuff I've got to say is fine, but no one is going to notice the good stuff because I can't organize any of it right on the page. Not to mention that I can't wrap my head around where to put a damn comma."

Nina dared to come a few steps closer, trying to peek at the papers. She was surprised by how high the stack was. "What's it about?"

He leaned back in his chair with a sigh. "Well, just a story about my life. The hard stuff I've been through and opening the restaurant and everything in between. I just think that maybe it could help other people, you know? Inspire them. There's some advice in there, too. Some ideas I have about how to live. How to succeed and be a good man. The kind of stuff your father and I are always talking about, you know?"

Nina nodded. And she felt the blood rushing up her own neck, so she said the words before she could talk herself out of them. "I'm pretty good with commas, you know."

He tipped his head back to look at her, a grin spreading slowly over his face, and her knees turned to jelly.

"Are you offering to help me, Nina May?"

She blushed even harder when he used her middle name and felt her own face fall. He'd always called her that when she was little—he was making fun of her. Too embarrassed to say anything else, she turned to walk out of the Watering Hole.

And then he followed her and grabbed her hand, and she stopped short.

"Hey," he said, voice and eyes softening. Her hand was entirely swallowed by his, big and warm.

"I would actually really appreciate your help. Your dad keeps telling me how well you do in school. Said you won the English award the last four years in a row. He let me read one of your essays—the one about Flannery O'Connor." He laughed. "I wouldn't tell him at the time, but I had to look up three of the words you used when I got home."

He'd hurt her feelings, but he turned the tide with a few words, and warmth pulsed through Nina's blood. She smiled so wide, it made her self-conscious, and she looked down at her shoes to hide how pleased the comment made her.

"I'm—well, I'm not ready to tell anybody about it just yet," he went on. "And I figure—" He stole a glance at her face through his long, gold eyelashes. "I think I can trust you with a secret."

He paused, and she stared back at him with her lips parted.

"Please don't tell your dad. It's been real nice of him to take such an interest in my path, but I don't think being a pastor is for me. It doesn't feel quite right, you know? I feel like I can be more useful this way." He nodded at the stack of papers.

"I won't tell," Nina said.

He squeezed her hand before he let it go.

"I won't be able to pay you much right now," he said. "All the money is going back into the restaurant while we're getting it off the ground."

She was about to say he didn't need to pay her when he snapped his fingers. "I could teach you to play piano. You told me you've always wanted to learn."

She had to rack her memory for a moment—she'd said that once as an excuse for standing so close to him onstage at Sunday services while he played the closing hymn and she sang, sometimes getting so mesmerized by the deft movement of his long fingers over the keys that she forgot the words.

"I would like that," she said.

"It'll be a nice skill to pair with that voice of yours. And I'll scare Jameson off whenever you want me to," he added.

Nina tucked the heavy stack of papers under her arm, next to her sketchbook. "You know, I can be scary all by myself."

Ellis laughed. "I hate to be the one to tell you, Nina, but that pretty little face of yours isn't going to scare anyone."

Nina jumped when the bell over the door chimed behind her. Jill

Bowman's auburn curls were tied back into a bun, and there were two toddlers—one on each of her hips—trying to grab it.

Even with the extra weight and the sticky hands waving in her eyes, she managed to lean down and nibble her husband's shoulder.

"We might actually make a profit this year if you start getting the ingredients in the food instead of on your apron," she said, nodding at the stains all over him that Nina hadn't noticed.

She gave Nina a kiss on the forehead, too, and little Neily squeezed Nina's cheek with his chubby, sticky hand while he and his sister giggled.

"What have you got there?" Jill asked, nodding at Ellis's manuscript tucked under her arm.

Nina glanced at Ellis. He gave a nearly imperceptible shake of his head, and she realized that he hadn't told his wife about the book yet either.

"Just some extra sketch paper," she said.

Because Ellis was right—she could keep a secret.

Chapter 12

THERE'S A KNOCK ON my door at seven o'clock the next morning.

I got up at first light to search the woods and came up empty. No blood or footprints. No sign that Mom had ever been there at all. So I climbed back in through the window and tried to get more sleep, but I'd been lying awake for almost an hour, staring at the ceiling.

Neil lets himself into the room, fully dressed and smiling. Bright and fresh as a sunflower. I sit up and automatically smile back—as I'm quickly learning, he's got that effect on people.

"Morning. I just wanted to make sure Melody thought to give you something you could wear to church. I was going to ask her, but—well—" He lowers his voice to a whisper, like he's afraid of waking a sleeping beast. "She's not very nice in the mornings."

"And she's sweet as honey the rest of the day?" I whisper back hopefully.

He laughs that warm, room-filling laugh. "Absolutely not."

I look him up and down. He's already dressed in black pants and a white button-up shirt, tucked in. He's even got a tie.

He rubs the back of his neck. "I mean—sorry. I guess I shouldn't have assumed you'd be going. And you don't have to dress up if you don't want to. It's just that my family always does. I thought you might want to fit in, you know?"

He looks down, tapping the toe of his sock against the carpet. And all at once, I have the urge to say whatever will make him happy. It's got to have something to do with that sheepish look. I'll have to start paying attention to that so I can learn to use it myself.

I'm about to tell Neil in the nicest way I can that I'm never going to feel like I fit in inside a church when I remember what I'm here for. Blowing my cover in the woods threw me off, but getting the chance to spend time with Ellis's family has to be better than gleaning secondhand information about him from people in town. I should take advantage of every opportunity.

And if I find information that's good enough, maybe Mom will forgive me for almost ruining everything.

"I'll go," I say.

Neil's whole face splits into a ridiculous grin.

"When do we leave?" I ask.

"I'm going in early to help with some things. But everyone else is leaving in a couple of hours, so you can ride with them."

I nod. Then I look down at my lap and back up through my eyelashes, somber as I can muster, and I say, "My grandmother emailed me a few months ago with some old family recipes, and I want to make sure I haven't lost them. Would you mind if I borrowed your computer?"

I'm eager to do a little research. Maybe figure out what accident Melody was alluding to last night.

He winces. "Mine's broken right now. Spilled coffee all over the keyboard last week. Dad's using his at the moment, and Mom usually takes hers to the restaurant with her. But"—he raises his eyebrows, like he's daring me—"you could always ask Mel."

I chew on my lip for a second, weighing the risks and rewards. I decide, "I'd rather not."

"Good call," Neil says.

"I could use a library computer, if you've got a card I could borrow."

He shakes his head again. "Library is closed on Sundays."

Dammit. I hope the disappointment doesn't show on my face when I smile and say, "No worries. It can wait."

The problem is, it can't. *I* can't. I need to find something to report to Mom. Something good enough that maybe she won't hate me for my royal screwup last night.

I'm wearing one of Melody's dresses when I climb out the guest room window. The skirt probably hits her just above her knees, but it comes about halfway up my thighs. Maybe I'll drop a quarter in church so I can give the people of Jasper Hollow something to talk about for a few weeks.

The only shoes I have are the heavy, black boots I came in, but I'm sure as hell not about to ask Melody for a pair of flats. The boots are better for trekking down Clara Mountain anyway.

The church service starts in a couple of hours, but I'm not just going to cool my heels until then. I've got a job to do. Besides, if I think about it too long, being in Ellis's house makes me feel like I've got my hand in the open jaws of a wolf—at his mercy.

It takes me about an hour to make it back to the roundabout on foot, which Jill told me last night the locals call the Circle. There are already plenty of people out—opening up shops and walking their dogs around Harriet's Oak before the heat gets to be unbearable.

And then there's Ellis and Jill's restaurant, the Watering Hole, with the silhouette of a golden elephant glittering in the early sunlight above the tall glass doors. The breakfast rush has already started, and Jill is right in the thick of it, a tray balanced on her palm, her skirt dancing around her ankles, her auburn hair tied back.

She comes outside to serve the tables on the patio, and I duck through the closest door before she can see me.

The bell jangles overhead. I see the long counter with the display window, which shows off neat rows of those sweet delectables I will probably see in my dreams for the rest of my life. I'm in Sugar House Bakery again, where I met Neil yesterday.

Tim, the owner, stands behind the counter and smiles through his gray, neatly trimmed beard, his plaid shirt buttoned up to his neck and a pale-blue apron tied around him.

I know from reading Ellis's book that before he and Jill opened the Watering Hole, they both worked for Tim. Talking to his old boss seems like a good place to start piecing together his story—his real story. Not the one he tells about himself.

I approach the counter, pretending to mull over the selection. But as much as I want one of everything, I don't actually have any money.

I see Tim give me the once-over. I took a long shower last night, and I've got Melody's pretty dress on, but I know I still don't stand up to close inspection with my DIY haircut and ragged boots and crooked teeth. His smile wavers.

"Good to see you again," I say, to remind him of how nice he was to me in front of Neil yesterday and that I'm expecting that same treatment this time.

He nods. "What can I get for you?"

"Hmm," I say. "Still thinking."

I keep perusing. He doesn't volunteer any more conversation.

I look back up at him with surprise, like I just remembered to mention, "The Bowmans are *such* a nice family!"

He nods, the suspicious lines in his face smoothing just a little. "You don't need to tell me. Known Ellis and Jill since they were tots, and the twins, too."

"They offered to let me stay with them. Just out of the kindness of their hearts. You just don't see that kind of thing anymore."

I can see him becoming more animated, little by little. "Exactly. That's what sets them apart. Old-fashioned manners and hospitality have gone to hell, but that doesn't stop them."

"Right," I say, nodding, smiling. Then I lower my voice, glancing around before I say, "I was a little embarrassed to admit that I'd never heard of Ellis or his books before."

I get a conspiratorial wink from Tim. "I'm sure he didn't mind. He doesn't do it for the fame, you know. But he's already well-known in a lot of circles, anyhow. He's well on his way to becoming a household name. Right on the cusp of things."

"And yet he's still so kind." I shake my head in wonder.

"Even . . . well, even after everything that happened." I press my lips together. "He told me about the accident."

It's a risk, alluding to it when I have absolutely no idea what happened. But I'm hoping that Tim's reaction might give me an indication of what Melody was talking about last night.

His grin fades instantly when I mention it, the sudden frown on his face made even more somber by his heavy mustache. "Yes. It devastated him. The whole family. The whole town. And what's worse is how the damn papers tried to run with it and turn it into something that it wasn't."

My mouth falls open. "No. Really?"

He leans in closer. "Tried to make it sound like he was being careless."

"That's ridiculous," I say, mirroring what's plainly written on Tim's face.

"My thoughts exactly! It's complete horseshit. It was dark and rainy out, and I've been saying for years that the Circle doesn't have enough streetlights. The boy shouldn't have been out so late. Ellis did everything he could to save him, but the kid was dead on impact."

The shock on my face is real this time. It feels like all the blood has drained from my body in a rush.

The kid was dead on impact.

"Did—" I swallow. "Did the papers say outright that Ellis did something wrong?"

"Not outright, no. I just didn't like their tone. They don't know, because they weren't there. But I was. I was cleaning up shop after we closed. I was busy sweeping, so I didn't see the impact, but I heard it. Right out there." He pointed over her shoulder, toward the Circle. "I ran out to see what had happened, and . . . I'll just say it wasn't pretty. I've never seen a man so upset. Ellis sold the car not long after. Couldn't stand the sight of it."

"Understandable," I say. Then I look back down at the display case, pretending to peruse again as I process the information.

Ellis hit and killed someone with his car. A child.

Before I can press Tim for more, the bell over the door jingles and a group of women bustle in. They're all holding copies of Ellis's books. They immediately go to a corner with a bulletin board that I'm just noticing. I wander closer to see what they came to see.

The bulletin board is covered with photos of Ellis and his family. Ellis eating a cookie at the counter when he was little, his legs dangling from a stool. Standing behind the counter with a pale-blue apron tied on and a Cincinnati Reds cap pushing back his curls. Him and Neil jamming massive chocolate cupcakes into their mouths. Him and his wife and son, grinning while they crush Melody in a group hug, candles on a birthday cake lighting up her resolutely unamused face.

Below the bulletin board, there's a little round table with no chairs. A shiny, golden plaque declares, *The original manuscript of Ellis's first book*, At Our Table. And in the middle of the table, enclosed in an actual, honest-to-God glass case, is a stack of papers.

The women fawn over the pictures and take turns snapping photos of themselves with the manuscript. All I can do is watch, mesmerized.

Tim comes up beside me, crossing his arms over his chest and smiling with satisfaction. "Ellis gave it to me as a gift. He said

Sugar House was such a big part of recovering from his parents' deaths that he owed something to me. I put it on display a few years ago, and he told me no one would be interested in seeing it. But he's always been too humble."

The women chatter like birds back and forth. "Oh, he's such a family man. I've always loved how he's such a family man."

"He just seems so genuine, you know?"

"Do you think we'll get to see him while we're here?"

"I hear he still hangs out at the restaurant sometimes. Just sits and does his writing there like a regular old person."

"He's so down-to-earth! I love how he hasn't let it all go to his head."

"We'll check the restaurant next. But I want dessert first."

They all crowd around the counter to pick out what they want. Before Tim goes to take their orders, he leans toward me to whisper, "His books have convinced hundreds of people to come see Jasper Hollow. He makes it sound like a little slice of heaven. And it is, now that he's brought the money back to it. He saved this place. And just like I told the reporters—anyone who wants to talk badly about him or his family isn't welcome here."

When he leaves me alone, I drift out of the bakery in a stunned daze.

It can't be true, that Ellis saved this place. The tourism business just picked up. All these people wouldn't have come just because Ellis Bowman lives here. I know he talks about Jasper Hollow a lot in his books—about it being the perfect place for slowing down and reflecting, finding community, and raising a family. But there's no way he's fooled people thoroughly enough to make them come to this little pocket of nowhere.

But then I remember the way I felt when I looked at the cover of *At Our Table* for the first time, before I even opened it. How bright and happy his house and his family looked. How badly I wanted to climb through it like a window just to be where they were, to feel that warmth. And I'm sure I wasn't the only one.

And then I look up and realize just how thoroughly everyone in this town has been fooled. Because the sign reads *Bowman Avenue*. I'm standing on a street named after him.

Chapter 13

WHEN I PUSH THROUGH the trees and into the clearing on Pearl Mountain, I blink against the flood of sunlight, and the cabin and the pond come into focus. But the van isn't here.

Which is nothing to panic about. Absolutely nothing to panic about.

Everything looks the same as when I left yesterday. A strong breeze whistles through the holes in the cabin roof and kicks up ashes from last night's fire. No sign of a struggle, so she wasn't attacked by anything. Or anyone.

I keep telling myself that for a while, sitting calmly by the water, going back over what Tim told me.

After a half hour, I start pacing.

She probably just went to find food. Or maybe she's doing her own work for the plan somehow—some part of it she didn't tell me about. She'll be back soon.

I tell myself that she wouldn't leave me. She needs me as much as I need her.

But my own memories contradict me.

I know what it's like to be left by her. She made sure I knew. When I was thirteen, I made her angry—I don't even remember how. What I remember is that she pulled the van over on the side of the road, in the middle of nowhere, and she said, *Get out.* And I had snapped back, *Fine.* I slammed the door behind me and flipped her off while she drove away.

As the sun went down, I walked. And walked and walked. It took me nearly an hour to find a gas station and another hour of waiting until a couple went in, and I could slip in behind them and shove my pockets full of granola bars and candy while they distracted the man behind the counter.

I was feeling pretty good when I stepped out into the parking lot, the dark gathering like a blanket drawing in close. *I can take care of myself. I don't need anyone. I'm too clever to starve. Too quick to get caught.*

I walked to the cornfield across the street from the gas station and disappeared between the stalks. I sat on the ground, the corn so tall that it obscured my view of everything else and everything else's view of me. I ate a granola bar and a pack of Reese's Cups and occupied myself for a while folding and unfolding the wrapper into the vague shape of a cat—the little orange cat I'd always wanted. But then the wind swept it away, and I couldn't find it in the dark that had suddenly become impenetrable, and I lay down.

And then I learned what it's really like to be alone in this world.

I hadn't thought it was a cold night before I lay down, but it wasn't long before I started shivering, pulling my arms inside my T-shirt.

Then came the noises. The noises must have been there all along, but it had just now gotten quiet enough for me to notice—twigs snapping and wind whistling and the rustle of the corn that I was certain was the whisper of someone who wanted to hurt me, and it startled my pounding heart into my throat.

I didn't have Mom's warm hand against my back. Her promises that one day I'd have a bed, a big house, a cat that would sleep curled up on the pillow beside me. Yes, she was often cold to me, so closed off that I felt a million miles away from her. But at least whenever I woke from a nightmare, someone would be there to hold on to.

But at that moment I was alone. If I spoke, no one would answer. If I reached out, no one would grab my hand. And when I started to cry, there was no one there to hear.

Mom left me there for two days, to make sure that I had fully, thoroughly learned my lesson. I'd become convinced that she was never coming for me at all, and I considered going back into the gas station and doing a sloppy job, getting caught on purpose, just so the attendant would look at me. Yell at me. Remind me I existed, that I was real enough to be angry with. To be, for just a moment, the focus of someone's attention.

When Mom finally did come back, I wasn't angry with her for leaving me. I didn't even think to be angry. No, I jumped into the van and threw my arms around her, and I sobbed and sobbed into

her shoulder while she rubbed my back, and I whispered, *I'm sorry.*
I'll be better. I promise I'll be better.

———

By the time I hear the van creeping up the path, snapping and grinding its way through the trees, I've been lying on my side by the pond and prying at the dirt under my fingernails for half an hour, even after there was no dirt left.

I sit up and wipe my sleeve over my damp face before she can see me.

She parks the van a few yards from where I'm sitting. She doesn't hurry to get out. And when she does, she walks right past me to the edge of the water and crosses her arms over her chest.

"Mom."

She doesn't answer me.

"Mom, it's okay." My voice cracks with desperation, and I swallow to steady it. "I came up with a new story, and they're letting me stay with them. They don't suspect a thing. We can still do what we came here to do."

Still, she acts like I'm not even there. To punish me for getting caught.

She gathers a pile of clothes from the van and starts to wash them. She dips a shirt into the pond, scrubs the soap in with her fingers, rinses away the bubbles, and hangs it over a low tree branch. Then she grabs a pair of jeans and does it over again.

I watch and wait for her to look at me, and I try to pretend not to care, the way she pretends not to. But I'm having too much trouble keeping my lower lip under control.

She gets through the whole pile of clothes, then sits at the edge of the water, her elbows resting on her knees, staring straight ahead.

When she finally speaks, it's so quiet that I almost miss the words, "I don't think you understand what this means to me."

I get on my knees, my hands clenched in my lap like I'm about to pray to her. "I do. I swear I do."

"You've ruined *everything*." The last word comes out rough, and when she turns to look at me, her eyes burn red.

"No." I shake my head. "No. I tricked them. It's all going to be—"

But then she lunges for me, and her fingers are digging into my shoulders. "You wanted me to fail. You wanted to get caught so you could get rid of me."

"No! No, I—" I grasp for something to say.

"They're going to poison you against me." Her voice is a raw hiss, her eyes on me but seeing something else entirely. "You're going to choose Ellis. Everyone always chooses Ellis."

"Mom, it's not—" My voice hitches, and I fight to control it. "I know it wasn't part of the plan." I gently press one of my hands over hers, but her grip doesn't ease. "I know I messed up, and I could have ruined your only chance. But I didn't. The Bowmans are going to let me live with them. Do you understand? I'm going to get close to them, and I'm going to find out what we need to know, and I'm going to get him to confess. Okay?"

When her clutch still doesn't loosen on me, I remember my conversation with Tim and say, "I already found something. There was an accident. He hit a kid with his car. Killed him." I relay my conversation with Tim in a rush.

After an agonizing stretch of silence, she lets go of me. My shoulders ache where her nails pinched them.

Mom turns and scans the rippling surface of the pond. Her face has gone blank again.

Is she thinking or ignoring me again? In desperation, I rattle off a list of other details big and small in the hope that something will pique her interest—Jill wears long skirts and elephant bandanas. Neil is gullible and a good cook. Melody has a bad attitude. There's a baker in town with a shrine to Ellis.

When I mention that the baker has the original manuscript, she meets my gaze for half a second, and I think I've found a way back in.

But when she does finally speak, she says, "Why did you come here?"

"I thought—I thought the accident was important."

"I don't see how. You don't even have the whole story. Just scraps. And if Tim was so forthcoming with you, the details clearly aren't a secret. He said it was written up in the paper. So how exactly do you propose we use it as leverage against Ellis?"

"I just thought—maybe there's more to it. Maybe—"

"You shouldn't have risked coming here for *maybe*. You could have been caught. Your recklessness could have ruined everything *again*."

I shake my head at the ground. She grabs my chin and makes me look into her dark eyes. Her mouth is a hard line. I guess our first night away from each other didn't affect her as much as it affected me.

"You really think the Bowmans will trust you?"

I nod immediately, pushing Melody's suspicious glare from my mind.

She gives me a measured look. Searching my face for something. "You lucked into a second chance."

"I think so."

"You won't get another."

It's not a question or a guess. It's her decision—if I mess up again, she'll never forgive me.

"Now go and find me something I can use. And don't you dare risk coming here again. Do you understand me?"

"Yes."

She stands and paces away from me, back toward the cabin, and disappears inside.

That's it. I've been dismissed.

So I walk back to the broken trail between the trees.

*N*ina knew her father didn't really care all that much about the bow. He only wanted to prove to her that he was in charge, and he always had been, and he always would be.

She knew she should have just worn it without a fight. But nobody at school wore bows anymore, and when you're sixteen years old, looking ridiculous feels like a slow death.

Her father leaned in the bathroom doorway and watched her fidget with it. He said, almost sympathetically, "I know most of these kids get to run around and do whatever they want, but we've got to be better than that." He stepped up behind her, and she watched him in the mirror when he squeezed her shoulder. "We're the example."

"And the more boys I scare away, the better?"

He laughed and hugged her too tightly, and she tried not to smile, but she did anyway.

They had a car, but they walked to church, because that's what they'd done since she was old enough to make it the whole way without being *carried. Sometimes he practiced parts of his sermons on her, or they talked about school or her drawings or people in town. Sometimes they went the whole way without saying a word.*

She sat in the front pew to watch him. He carried his Bible in a tight grip while he paced the stage. He spoke with a slow voice that rose and rose until it was a red-faced shout, and then he let it go soft again for the closing prayer and held out his hand for her to come up onstage and sing the closing hymn.

Ellis wasn't at the piano today. It was an older woman who sometimes stood in for him when he was sick. Nina felt his absence like a hole in her chest. Even though she'd seen plenty of him lately—he'd kept his promise about teaching her to play piano.

They met every Thursday night, when the church was silent except for the wind that made the old wood creak. He always sat next to her on the narrow bench, nodding patiently through her botched attempts at "How Great Thou Art," sometimes putting his big hands over her small ones to show her just how to move her fingers.

Alone onstage now, her fingers twitched at her sides the whole time she sang, fighting the urge to pull the bow from her hair.

Afterward, she stood by the cookie and juice table and twisted her hands together, looking down at her black, felt shoes. She occasionally glanced up to meet the gazes of the kids she knew from school, and they didn't laugh at her, but they didn't talk to her either.

She was starting to feel sorry for herself and had almost worked up a hot round of tears when she felt someone tap her shoulder.

Ellis beamed at her. His face was lit up like Christmas, and it was the first time she could remember so much emotion being directed at her, and for a moment, she was too happy to speak.

"Where's your family?"

"Jill's at home with the twins," he said. "Neily had a fever this morning. But I had to come see you. I've got news."

"Really?"

He nodded, his grin so wide and his chest so full, it looked like it could crack open. "I did it," he said. "The book is getting published. My agent called this morning."

She laughed out loud. Tears sprang to her eyes while he clutched her hands and laughed with her.

"I knew it would be. I told you it would be."

"It wouldn't have happened without your help, Nina. Really." His voice had gotten thick, and his face was flushed. "You're the one who should be the writer, not me. You made a hillbilly from Jasper Hollow sound like someone people should listen to."

Going through his whole stack of paper with her red pen had taken two weeks, and they'd spent more than one night at the Watering Hole after he closed up, sitting at a little table in the back room with their heads bent over it and talking about changes. She told her father she'd gotten a part-time job cleaning the restaurant after closing as an excuse for being out so late.

She knew people would read the book and like Ellis because his voice was compelling. His struggles relatable. His resilience inspiring.

"Come on," he said, pulling her toward the doors. "Time to celebrate."

Nina looked over her shoulder. "My dad—"

"I just talked to him. Told him I needed your help at the restaurant while Jill's home with the twins."

She saw her father on the other side of the building, and she waited for him to stop them. He wouldn't trust any other man alone with his daughter. Not for a second. But this was Ellis Bowman, so he waved them off with a smile, and Ellis led her away.

She didn't know where he was taking her. She thought they might go to the restaurant for a celebratory coffee, but he drove past the Circle and wound around Pearl Mountain instead. He chattered the whole way with his big hands moving and his eyes wide. "It's no rinky-dink publisher either. I looked it up. It's the same place that published Billy Graham's latest book. I'm telling you, this is the start of something. It is."

She nodded and laughed, and it felt nice to be with him until Ellis took a turn that led away from the Circle. "Where are we going?" she asked.

"I thought we'd go to Jameson's," he said. "He isn't home. I just figured it'd be nice to have some privacy. I'm not ready to spill the beans to everybody yet about the book."

"Cool," she said, reflecting his casual tone, even as her heart skittered and it got hard to breathe.

Ellis had gotten married to Jill and moved out of the cabin on Pearl Mountain a few years ago, and as far as Nina knew, Jameson was the only one living there now. When they pulled into the clearing, Jameson's truck wasn't there, like Ellis had said it wouldn't be. They were truly alone.

Nina's father had warned her about going anywhere alone with a boy. He told her that boys had trouble controlling themselves around girls, that she needed to take responsibility so she wouldn't find herself in this kind of situation—in a secluded cabin, with no one else for miles around.

But she wasn't with a boy. She was with Ellis, and her father trusted him. Loved him. He's got a pure heart if one ever did exist, she remembered him saying.

"Just helped my little brother redo the roof," Ellis said as they pulled up to the cabin. "Looks nice, doesn't it?"

"Very nice."

Ellis stopped the car next to the pond and jumped out. Nina had trouble making her fingers work well enough to get her seat belt undone. He opened her door and didn't ask what was wrong with her. He just smiled, reached over her lap, and undid it himself.

He offered her a sheepish smile—one so innocent, it relaxed her just enough before she followed him into the cabin.

There was a bottle sitting in a bucket of ice on the table. He poured two tall, delicate glasses and handed one to her. The bubbles fizzed and popped in her mouth, and she fought the way her lips wanted to twist at the taste.

He laughed and said, "You don't have to finish it."

She put her glass down in the sink, and he left his empty one next to hers.

He touched her face then, and she was so surprised that she flinched.

"You're not scared of me, are you?" he whispered, leaning in close, those blue eyes pouring right into hers.

She swallowed and shook her head, grabbing the edge of the table to keep her knees steady. She breathed in deep, eyes closing, and leaned into the big palm of his hand.

Then she remembered her ridiculous bow, and she tried to grab it, but he caught her fingers. He ran his thumb over the blue velvet. Then he unclipped it, gently pulling it from her hair, and put it in his pocket.

He was gentle when he kissed her, too, careful not to scare her away.

This was the first time she'd ever kissed anyone, but she watched a couple from school once when they snuck out of the cafeteria and went to the gym, under the bleachers. That's how she knew just when to open her mouth and to tangle her fingers in his hair.

Something danced in the pit of her stomach. At first, she thought it was elation, but then it soured into something closer to fear. She'd thought about kissing Ellis before. She'd imagined it would make her feel warm and safe and loved, the way she did when she sat on the porch at night and listened to him talk to her father about the mysteries of the universe.

But actually kissing Ellis was more like jumping off a tall building— like she was falling fast toward the concrete, and there was no way to go back to the safety of the ledge now. And she felt like she was falling all alone, even though Ellis was right there, the warmth of him clutched tight in her fingers. She wanted to stop. She wanted to scream, Help me, *but she didn't know what Ellis or anyone else could do to save her.*

Then the door opened behind Ellis, and the light burst in, and she was so startled that she bit his lip.

"Christ," Ellis hissed, covering his mouth with his hand. Blood dripped down his chin.

Jameson Bowman stood in the doorway, a mix of emotions frozen on his face. Surprise. Confusion. Hurt.

Ellis turned to his brother. Nina's heart hammered, but his voice was calm when he said, "You told me you wouldn't be home until tonight."

"I wanted to see why you needed me out of the house so bad."

"Go. We'll talk about this later."

Nina waited for Jameson to say something. She wanted him to speak up, though she didn't know exactly what she wanted him to say.

But he didn't argue with his big brother. Instead, with one last glance at Nina, he pulled the door closed and left them alone.

Chapter 14

"WHAT HAPPENED TO MY dress?" Melody whispers in my ear a few seconds after I slide into the pew next to her.

I whisper back. "I fell."

"Into a dumpster?"

I get extra close, just to irritate her, and she wrinkles her nose at the smell of sweat and mud and whatever the hell else got on the dress when I trekked up Pearl Mountain earlier. But she refuses to shy away from me, even an inch.

"I'll wash it," I whisper.

"Yes," she says. "You will."

By the time I made it back down Pearl, I was already late for the church service, and I didn't even know where the church *was*. I stopped the first person on the Circle I could find to ask—a burly man standing outside of the wood sculpture shop in a pair of camouflaged overalls, expertly shaping a tree stump into a grizzly bear with a chainsaw.

He pointed to the top of Clara Mountain—the tallest of the three by far—and I bit back the urge to curse him, God, and whoever the hell decided it was a good idea to build a church at the top of a damn mountain.

There's no way I would have gotten here on foot before the service was over. Thankfully, the nice man with the chainsaw offered me a ride. All I had to do in exchange was flip through pictures of his favorite sculptures on his phone and ooh and aah over everything from life-size bears to delicate birds smaller than my thumb.

After only one morning in Jasper Hollow, I can already tell it's not quite like any other place I've been.

"We thought you came early with Neil," Melody hisses in my ear now. "You weren't in the guest room."

"I went for a walk."

She has that look from last night again, the one that says, *Bullshit*, and I have the urge to stick my tongue out at her.

Before she can start another round of interrogation, Jill, sitting on her other side, pats her leg to ask where that Whitaker girl went to college, and isn't it nice that she finally came home to visit her family?

I've been inside a handful of churches. Sometimes Mom would take me on Easter or around Christmas, but in the last few years, we've gotten bad about keeping track of the days and even worse about keeping track of our immortal souls.

This church doesn't look much different from the others, with long, wooden pews and wine-colored cushions, a dark carpet stretching down the center aisle leading to the heavy, wooden pulpit with a cross carved into it. The only difference is that it's huge.

I know from Mom's stories that it used to be just as tiny as any other country chapel, and the congregation even smaller, sometimes less than twenty people. I can see the lines in the ceiling where the original structure was expanded on both sides, enough to fit about five hundred now. Even more than that, because when the seats fill up, more people line up along the back wall.

I see some of them craning their necks, trying to get a good look at the front row, where Ellis and his family and I sit. He pretends not to notice, his arm draped casually over his wife's shoulders.

There's something else that catches my eye—a massive slab of wood hanging down from the ceiling, over the piano. Mom told me about this. Just like the sign coming into town, it reads, *Welcome, Weary Travelers*. At least, it used to, but the words have worn down to indistinct grooves. Mom said it was carved by Will Jasper himself—the town's founder—and that it's a piece of history that everyone takes great pride in. It looks like an old tabletop to me.

I'm still studying it when someone plays a scatter of notes on the piano. I'm surprised to see Neil bowing his head over the keys. And then he starts singing in his deep, grainy voice.

Everyone stands to sing along, lifting their hands to the ceiling. I glance at Melody and watch her mouthing the words. I say right in her ear, so she can hear me over the crowd, "Shouldn't the one with the musical name be onstage?"

Melody shoots me a glare and stops pretending to sing.

I've hit on something—the hard knot in her jaw makes me sure of that. And the fact that Neil is Neil. Being related to someone that perfect can't be easy.

When the song ends, Neil smiles and gives a small nod to the roomful of applause. Some people throw *amen*s and *hallelujah*s at him, and his cheeks blaze. I look past Melody and see Ellis making big, loud claps with his hands cupped. Jill puts her fingers in her mouth and whistles. Melody claps, too, and even if she is jealous, her eyes are warm on her brother.

As Neil exits the stage, a man in his thirties bounds up the steps two at a time in faded jeans.

"Welcome, welcome, welcome," he says, rubbing his hands together and smiling down at us like we're a rack of ribs. "Welcome to Jasper Hollow Methodist Church. My name is Matthew, your favorite pastor-in-training. We have an exciting message for you today about spreading the love and acceptance of Jesus Christ to everyone around you."

I sink down in the pew to get comfortable for the long hour ahead.

"But before we get started," Matthew continues, "I'd like to invite someone up here to say our opening prayer. Someone who's written a few bestsellers." There's a ripple of laughter through the crowd, and I roll my eyes, not quite internally.

"But around here, we know him for his generosity and his love for this town and his family."

Ellis stands and straightens his suit. Jill, Melody, and I shift our legs to let him pass.

"Please join me in welcoming Ellis Bowman!"

Everyone claps, so I clap, too. But Ellis pauses in the center aisle for a long moment. And then he looks down at me and holds out his hand.

I stare at him blankly. He grabs my wrist and tows me behind him to the stage.

Pastor Matthew's smile falters when he sees me, which makes it clear that I wasn't part of the plan. But he hands Ellis the microphone and trots offstage.

Ellis is no stranger to crowds. He doesn't blush like his son.

"What a pleasure it is to be here with you all." He rests his arm around my shoulders. I search the sea of people under the bright lights, and when I find Melody's eyes, I hold her gaze. She only raises her eyebrows at me—she doesn't know what's going on either.

"Before I lead us in prayer, I want to dedicate it to this young lady right here." He pulls me in closer, and I have to hold my breath and clench my teeth to stop myself from cracking my elbow against his nose.

"I won't embarrass her by making her tell her whole story right now, but suffice it to say, she's been through a lot. She's had the courage to leave her old life behind and build a new one here in Jasper Hollow. And it's a wonderful place to start, if I do say so myself."

Broad smile. Laughter and cheers from the audience.

But he gets serious suddenly, biting his lip and looking down at the stage before he glances back up at the audience, earnest as could be. Mom's taught me plenty about controlling my face when I'm about to sell someone a whole lot of bullshit, but I think even she could learn a thing or two from Ellis.

"She's not the only one who needs a new beginning," he says.

A solemn hush falls over the church. He has to be talking about the accident.

"That's why I'm proud to say that Phoenix will be staying with my family and me as she sets out on this new journey. In the short time I've spent with her, she's already taught me so much about moving forward with courage and heart. Please join me in welcoming Phoenix to Jasper Hollow, and into my family."

Family. Jesus. Nobody was tossing that word around last night.

The congregation erupts in a frenzy of applause and *amen*s. For all they know, he dragged me out of a prostitution ring or adopted me from a war-torn country or cured me of a heroin addiction.

When I find Melody's face again, her confused expression has morphed into pure, spitting outrage.

My brain is a few steps behind hers, and it takes me another minute with the hissing static of applause in my ears to figure out why she's so mad. And then, all at once, I understand.

It can't be easy recovering a public image after killing a kid, even if it was an accident. And then, like a gift from the clouds, another kid shows up to his house. One who needs help.

He could have sent me to a hotel, but he took me into his home so he could come on this stage and prove to Jasper Hollow and the rest of the world that he's still the same big-hearted gentleman he's been selling them for years. Melody said he was done with all the press and the interviews, but I've got a feeling he's hoping for a whole new round of articles in the next few days. Articles that will tip the scales of public opinion back in his favor.

He's helping me so he can use me. And honestly, the realization is almost a relief. Because this is the Ellis Bowman I was promised—self-serving and manipulative. And now, I know what he wanted in exchange for his generosity. The price is laid out clearly on the table.

And with a winning smile at the audience, I accept.

Finally, Ellis bows his head to God, and there's a shuffling as everyone else does the same. Everyone except Melody, who glares at me like this is all *my* fault.

Just when Ellis starts to speak, Neil steps quietly through the doors in the back and slides into the pew beside his sister. Completely oblivious to his father's scheme or Melody's rage or my sudden, dark urge to laugh at how this has all turned out, he gives me a quick thumbs-up before he bows his head to pray.

I close my eyes, too, and Ellis begins, thanking God for the beautiful day, this beautiful town, and beautiful new beginnings.

All at once, I feel a presence beside me, someone who wasn't standing there a moment before. I peek through my lashes.

But then I open my eyes all the way and stare.

The head pastor towers over me with a face as stiff and joyless as stone. His gray hair is combed neatly, and he wears a navy-blue suit with a jacket and tie. His eyebrows are heavy enough to cast shadows on his face, thick and dark as storm clouds. And when he speaks, his voice is a cold, quiet thunder.

"Welcome to Jasper Hollow, Phoenix," he says.

I knew I would run into him, sooner or later. But somehow, I'm still not prepared.

I thought he would have retired after the cancer diagnosis. But now that I see him in person, I can understand why even a deadly disease would have a hard time humbling a man like him. The only outward indication he gives that it's affected him at all is the cane he clutches in his right hand.

"I'm Pastor Holland," he says.

Mom's father.

Chapter 15

ELLIS INTRODUCES ME TO a lot of people after the service, too many to keep track of, but I notice a pattern of last names—the McCormicks, the Snyders, the Perkinses, the Walshes, the Whitakers, and the Corcorans. Jill tells me that they're the ones who were born and raised in Jasper Hollow, who lived here before Ellis made it popular. I notice that they all seem to carry an air of superiority toward the newcomers, even though the influx of new people is what breathed life back into their town.

"You can tell who's a McCormick by the red hair," Jill whispers to me. "The Snyders all have those bright green eyes. The Walshes—well, if you meet anyone who acts too big for their britches, they're a Walsh."

Matthew—the pastor who's training to take over Pastor Holland's position whenever he finally retires—gives me a personal welcome, pumping my hand on the lawn just outside the big double doors. He does a good job of pretending not to notice the state of my dress.

When I stepped out of the church, I could understand what possessed Will Jasper to build something all the way up here. It's the highest point in Jasper Hollow, and the other mountains roll away in more shades of green than I ever knew summer could hold. The town pools in the valley below. Looking down on the rooftops, I think it might not be so hard to have one of those spiritual epiphanies that make people sell everything they own so they can chase a space between the clouds.

But I've always been chasing something else. I look for her in the faces that mill around the church lawn, until Melody jabs me in the ribs with her elbow and I realize Pastor Matthew is speaking to me.

"What?"

"How do you know the Bowmans?" he repeats.

Ellis steps in to answer. "Neily found the poor thing passed out in the woods. Gave him quite a shock."

"Sounds like there's a story there!" Matthew says, bouncing on the balls of his feet.

Jill squeezes my shoulder and says, "I'm sure there will be plenty of time for that later. I think Phoenix is still a bit tired. We should be getting her home."

The quick look she turns on her husband is my first clue that she isn't happy with the way he hijacked the church service to show off his charity.

"Right," Matthew agrees. "Of course. Just one thing I wanted to ask before you go, Jill. Eleanor was signed up to make a hundred cookies for the Dawn Festival, but her oven stopped working. Think you might be able to step in? We're trying to finish up the funding for our mission trip to Uganda. It'd be a real big help."

Jill's strained smile gets even tighter. "You know I would love to, Matt, but I've been very, very busy with the restaurant, and—"

"I can do it."

I turn and see Melody peering over my shoulder.

Matthew raises his eyebrows. "That's a lot of cookies, Mel. Are you sure you can handle all that on your own? But I guess Neily is a whiz in the kitchen, so if he can help you—"

"I don't need Neil's help."

She made sure to smile when she said it.

Neil probably would have volunteered himself if he hadn't gone to pull the car around. The rest of us walk toward the parking lot, and Ellis puts one arm around Melody's shoulders and the other around mine. "Who's hungry?"

But before either of us can answer, we all stop short.

Pastor Holland is a lot like a wall. His broad shoulders block out the sun. "A word, Ellis," he says in his deeply resonant voice, which was perfectly suited for his lengthy sermon today. I notice that he leans a little more heavily on the cane than he did before, like it tired him out.

Ellis lets out a little sigh that I might not have heard if his arm weren't around me. Then he lets go of me and his daughter and follows Pastor Holland to the edge of the church lawn.

I climb into the back of the Bowmans' SUV behind Melody. Neil is at the wheel, and he sighs, too, putting the car in park. "Think he'll be long?"

Jill massages her temples between her fingers. "He always is."

"What are they talking about?" I ask.

"You," Melody says.

"How do you know?"

"He stared at you the whole sermon with that sour look on his face."

"Pastor Holland's face never looks anything but sour," Jill argues. But then she sinks low in her seat. "Oh, God, he's coming over here."

And then a pair of blue-black eyes peers through her window.

Jill cringes over her shoulder at Melody and me before she rolls the window down. "Hello, Pastor Holland, it's nice to—"

"I was just talking some sense into your husband," Pastor Holland says, his voice even, a slight smile on his face, like he's talking to a toddler. "I just want to make sure we're all on the same page."

"Mason, I—"

He cuts her off again with a shake of his head and a crooked finger, like he's beckoning her to a secluded corner so he can discipline her without anyone overhearing.

Jill lets out a deep breath, clearly struggling to keep her cool. "I have to get back to the restaurant, so if you're going to give me a scolding, just say whatever it is you need to say."

He glances at me again, then back at Jill. "Fine," he says, leaning his forearms on the window frame. His voice is still calm and steady, but there's redness under his skin, like something is boiling just below the surface.

Whenever he hugged me, Mom told me once, her voice soft and wistful, *his cheek against mine was burning hot. I could always smell cigarette smoke on his clothes. Even after he promised me he quit.*

That's why Mom used to steal packs of cigarettes whenever she could—just to light them. Just to sit in an empty parking lot, legs swinging out the van's open back door, and watch the red tip burn down to her fingers. She wanted to smell the smoke.

The same smell wafts through the open window when Pastor Holland leans closer to Jill. "Fine," he says again. "I didn't want to embarrass you in front of your children, but if that's the way you insist on doing things."

Ellis stands behind him, scratching self-consciously at the back of his neck. "Now, Mason—"

"Inviting a stranger off the street into your home is—quite frankly—reckless. You don't seem to know a thing about her."

Jill throws an apologetic look back at me, then gets quickly out of the car and leads Pastor Holland a few feet away with a hand on his shoulder.

But she forgot to roll her window back up. Neil, Melody, and I all glance at one another, waiting to see if someone else will push the button to give them some privacy. But none of us do.

"I understand your concern," I can hear Jill saying levelly, her back to us. "But Phoenix needed help. So we had to help her." She adds for good measure, "Aren't you the one who read the Good Samaritan story to us when I was in Sunday school?"

Pastor Holland waves her words away like gnats in his eyes. "It's a nice story, but you're missing the point. You're going to give this town a reputation for taking in strays. Do you want homeless people camping out on every corner? How's that going to affect tourism? Now, normally I'd bite my tongue—"

Neil makes a tiny, involuntary sound, almost like a laugh. I get the feeling that Pastor Holland never, ever bites his tongue.

"But this decision affects your children, too." He leans in closer to whisper the next part, but we can all hear loud and clear. "As pleasant as she may seem, you don't know what kind of influence she could be on them. And I remember having a discussion with you on being more careful about who you let the twins associate with."

And for just a second, I see his eyes flick over Jill's shoulder to Melody, who quickly averts her gaze, her skin flushing an even darker shade of red than his.

Apparently, Pastor Holland thinks she's got a weakness for bad influences.

I can see Jill's fists clench at her sides, but she says as calmly as she can, "That's enough, Mason."

Then his gaze settles on me. I don't look away, which makes his frown even heavier, but it doesn't stop him from taking inventory of me—and the look on his face says exactly what he thinks about what he sees. And as he shakes his head and starts to turn away, I can't quite make out what he mutters.

Jill grabs his tie so suddenly, his head jerks toward her, and his eyes swell to the size of quarters. And she says right in his stony face, "I don't know if you noticed, but she's a person. Not a stray. A *child*. And my decisions about my family are *mine*. Not your concern." His eyes go even wider when she jabs a finger hard against his chest. "And you are the last person who should be telling me how to raise children."

I freeze. Melody and her brother exchange a look—she raises her eyebrows, and he bites his lip.

Because of what happened with Mom? How much do her kids know?

And why is Jill going to so much trouble to defend me?

Pastor Holland's face flushes so red that it looks like he might melt with rage on the spot. Before either of them can say another word, Ellis steps between them, gently grabbing his wife's shoulders and nudging her back into the car. "Sorry," he says over his shoulder to Pastor Holland. "We're all a bit tired. I'll drop by your house later, all right?"

Neil climbs out of the driver's seat to let his dad take the wheel and gets into the back, sliding in beside his sister. Melody scoots toward me to make room for him, and the length of her arm presses against mine.

Pastor Holland is still standing there, glaring. His eyes lock with mine through the window as we pull away, and I want to say that I gave him the finger or at the very least a smirk, but I know the weight of that stare—it's the same as Mom's. And it's always been enough to stop me dead.

From the front seat, Jill starts cursing and fanning herself with the church bulletin as we start our descent back down Clara Mountain and Pastor Holland disappears behind a curve. "God. What the hell is wrong with him?"

Ellis squeezes her arm but keeps his eyes on the road without providing an answer.

"Thank you," I say.

It slips out of my mouth before I can think better of it.

Melody glances sideways at me, frowning, like she's trying to read my face.

"For—uh. For sticking up for me," I add.

Jill turns in her seat. Her cheeks are still flushed, but she manages a soft smile for me. One that takes me so off guard, I give her one back.

"Well, I can't say that I think bringing you up onstage was the right thing," she says. Ellis's jaw twitches, and he opens his mouth to argue. His wife continues before he can get a word in, "But he wasn't wrong when he said we think of our guests as family, Phoenix." She squeezes my hand. "And we protect our family."

There's a nice little warmth that pulses through my chest when she says that. But it sours quickly. Because I remember that by the end of all of this, I'm going to hurt her family very, very badly. And from what I know of a mother's wrath, I hope Jill doesn't get her hands on me afterward.

Chapter 16

WE JUST BARELY BEAT the church rush and get a booth near the back of the Watering Hole. The restaurant is a frenzy of servers in black aprons balancing heavy trays of food; people chatter inside and outside and around the doorway.

I've been in a lot of twenty-four-hour truck stop diners off the highway, but this place feels nothing like them. Maybe because everyone here is smiling. The floors are polished wood, the walls are painted floor to ceiling with colorful animals, and there's a fireplace with two big reading chairs in front of it that must be nice to curl up in during the winter. Paper birds hang on chords from the ceiling. It feels warm. Welcoming. Like Jill.

I haven't been here long, but I can already tell that Ellis has left running the restaurant to his wife—he's content to watch and write about it.

The place feels all the warmer because Melody doesn't join us. She said she was going to talk to someone named Annie about a cookie recipe. Jill tries to sit and talk for a few minutes, but she can't help herself for long. She ties her hair back in a bandana and rushes into the kitchen for her apron.

That leaves me with Neil and Ellis.

The tall windows along the front of the restaurant give us a good view of the mountains, all the way up to their foggy tips. I try to focus on them. Jill was right—I am exhausted. And I'm definitely not in the mood to pretend that I enjoy the company of Ellis Bowman.

Ellis asks me from across the table, "So, what'd you think?"

"About what?"

"Did you like the service?"

I sip my lemonade, refusing to make eye contact with him. "Neil is very talented."

Neil flushes red and stammers, "I—well, thank you, Phoenix. That means a lot." He rubs hard at the back of his neck and looks down at the wooden table, but he can't hide the pleased look that lights his face.

Ellis nods and smiles, even though I know that's not the part of the service he was asking me about.

Our waiter comes, and Neil and Ellis order. I say I don't want anything, but Ellis insists, "It's my restaurant, Phoenix. When you're here, you never have to worry about paying."

And then the man from the next booth turns around and gives Ellis a noogie.

Ellis's hands fly up to stop him, but the man chuckles in his ear and says, "Well, if you're in such a generous mood, I guess you won't mind comping my bill, too?"

The waiter leaves, and the man slides into the booth next to

131

Ellis. I glance at Neil, but his grin is genuine when he says, "Hey, Uncle Jameson."

Jameson is handsome. His dark hair is thick, his cheekbones shadowy, and the skin around his eyes just barely starting to age. His smile is sharp enough to kill.

He reaches toward me, the arm of his mechanic's jumpsuit covered in black stains. We shake hands. "I'm this gentleman's little brother, Jameson." His speech is a little hard to understand, the words heavy and running together, and it takes an extra second for me to process everything he says. He laughs when he sees my face screwed up in concentration. "You know, El used to sound like a bigger hick than I do. Before he wrote a few books and got a few *followers*. Now he's ironed himself out."

The difference between the brothers is so stark when they sit next to each other—Ellis's blond hair is shining and neatly combed, and Jameson's is brown and matted like he just woke up. Ellis's suit is immaculate while Jameson's jumpsuit looks like it hasn't been washed in a few months.

But it goes deeper. That fortune-teller I met, what seems like years ago now, might call it their *energies*. Ellis radiates ambition and power and confidence. But Jameson is the opposite—something smothers him like a cloud of smoke. Regret? Envy? Bitterness?

And I notice that Jameson was here alone. Ellis is never, ever alone. All morning, people from town have walked up to him to clasp his hand or slap him jovially on the back, ask about his newest book or his latest tour, how Jill and the kids are faring.

But not now. Once Jameson sat down with us, the constant

orbit of adoring fans always surrounding Ellis is suddenly empty. Like Jameson repels them somehow.

Which doesn't add up with Mom's stories. He wasn't as popular as Ellis, but he was liked well enough, from what I could gather. Could they be shunning him because of what happened—or what they *think* happened—even all these years later?

Maybe Mom isn't Ellis's only casualty. And maybe that's why Jameson's presence seems to make Ellis so uncomfortable.

Jameson asks me, "So, you Neil's new girl?"

Neil coughs, choking on his water.

"You would already know who she is if you'd been to church this morning," Ellis says.

Jameson stretches his arms over his head, fingers laced together. "Some of us have to work on Sundays, Ellie. Now just tell me where you picked up the pretty little lady?" He turns that sharp smile on me when he says it, like he expects me to squirm. I try to give him the same look that Melody is so fond of giving me, like she's cutting me in half with her eyes. But I must not do it right, because he only laughs.

No, this isn't quite the man Mom described to me. He'd been rough around the edges but not callous, the way he comes off now. "She fell on hard times," Ellis says. "We're helping her out." He seems a lot less concerned about bragging now than he did in church.

"Well, she's got a great eye then, 'cause Ellis is the richest man in town. And the most gullible, too."

Ellis flushes before Jameson elbows him in the ribs. "Aw, I'm kidding. Nobody gets as far as you being a sucker, huh? And nobody knows better than me what it took to get you where you are."

Ellis has gone completely stiff when Jill appears at our table, flustered but smiling, clearly enjoying all the business. "Phoenix, sweetheart, I hate to ask you this, but we're a little shorthanded. Do you think you could take a few orders?"

I'm about to tell her that I don't know the first thing about waitressing when she grabs my hand, pulls me out of the booth, and leads me into a kitchen that buzzes with voices and clattering dishes.

She grabs both of my shoulders. "Sorry. I wanted to get you away from Jameson. I hate to talk badly about family, but—well, I'll just say I would never leave Mellie alone in a room with him."

"Really?" I say.

Instead of elaborating further, Jill claps her hands briskly. "I need to get back to work. You can hang out back here until the others are ready to leave. Or—" She wiggles her fingers like they're Fourth of July sparklers. "—you can try out waitressing."

I'm about to tell her no. The way Jill's eyes spark, she reminds me of the girls who used to ask me to play with them whenever Mom took me to a park. She used to let me shoot hoops for a few hours while she sat on a nearby bench and sketched. I tried to be subtle about watching the groups of girls I saw together, playing one-on-one or chasing each other around trees or just sitting cross-legged in the grass and talking. But whenever one of them asked me to join them, I didn't even have to glance at Mom to know that I had to turn them down. *We can't trust anyone but each other, Phoenix. Aren't I enough for you?*

But now, I hesitate. She wouldn't be mad about me spending

some time with Ellis's wife, would she? That's what I'm here for. I've been keeping my distance from people all my life, but now, it's my job to get as close to the Bowmans as I can.

I shrug and ask Jill, "What do I have to do?"

Without another word, she ties me into a black apron with a golden elephant on the front, hands me a notepad and pen, and hurries me out into the dining area, where I immediately have to dodge a woman zipping past us with a full tray of drinks.

She follows me to the first few tables to make sure I don't make a complete fool of myself, but then she leaves me to it.

Some people don't give me any trouble, but others seem determined to watch me screw up. They ask for BLTs with no T or burgers with all the condiments on the side. They want no ice or extra ice. They split their checks eight ways. I have to refill one man's sweet tea four times in five minutes.

But it doesn't take me long to realize I don't need the notepad. I remember every detail, down to who wants lemon wedges and who doesn't, and people seem to be impressed enough by it that they don't mind so much that I'm not as friendly as most of the other waiters, who make jokes and ask about their families.

I don't know if *fun* is the right word for what's happening when I weave expertly around the tables and kitchen staff, pocketing tips. Whatever it is, I feel lighter than I ever remember feeling— like for the first time in my life, I'm the opposite of a disappointment. The hours slip past faster than I ever knew they could.

When the steady stream of customers finally becomes a trickle, I look at the clock and realize it's almost four. I didn't even notice when the guys left.

I find Jill wiping down a table and try to hand her my apron, but she grins at me—that trademark Bowman Grin that Melody must not have inherited—and says, "You can keep it, if you'd like a job here."

I run my thumb over the golden elephant. "Really?"

But I bite my tongue hard right after I say it. I'm lucky Mom wasn't around to hear the hope in my voice.

"I'd love to have you."

Working close to Jill would be a good way to build her trust. But something holds me back. It almost feels like taking the job would mean betraying Mom somehow.

I try again to hand the apron back to Jill. "I don't have a bank account for you to pay me."

She waves the argument and the apron away. "Your tips are your paycheck. Now what do you say to coming in tomorrow at eleven to help with the lunch rush?"

I bite my lip. Making money can't be a bad thing. And I can keep an eye on Jill and find out more about how to get to Ellis.

It doesn't take much to talk myself into it. I tuck the apron under my arm before I talk myself back out of it.

*N*ina *and Ellis met at the cabin whenever they could—sometimes five times a week, sometimes once in two weeks. From a stifling August to a damp October, they hoarded every moment they could get away with.*

But of course, her father's watchful eye made it difficult for them. For a while, their excuse was that Ellis was giving her piano lessons. But Pastor Holland grew suspicious when he asked her to play something for him on their piano at home. The notes she hit hardly resembled a song, even though she'd supposedly been practicing for months.

It was Ellis's idea to tell her father that she'd started dating Jameson.

She hated the thought of it—how the old women winked at her in church. We told you it would end up this way, *they seemed to be saying.* We told you that you would marry a man you don't love and live a life you don't want, because that's what all of us do. You thought you were better, but we've always known that you aren't.

Even though everyone else seemed immediately pleased by the idea, her father still took some convincing. Luckily, Ellis was the one person in town who seemed to have any sway over him. He came over for one of his late-night talks with her father, and they sat in their rockers on the porch while Nina listened through the open kitchen window. "He's a good kid," *Ellis told her father. "I know he's a little immature, but he's finally starting to figure himself out. I think a girl like Nina would be good for him."*

It took a few hours, but Ellis eventually wore him down. What finally convinced him was that Ellis agreed to act as their chaperone. Which also gave him an excuse to give to his wife when he left her alone with two unruly toddlers. Jameson begged me, *he'd tell Jill with a shrug.* Pastor Holland will only let them see each other if I'm there to supervise.

Ellis would roll up Nina's driveway in his pickup truck, and Nina would climb in the passenger seat, and Ellis would yell out the window, "We're picking up Jameson on the way to the theater." And her father would smile and wave while Ellis drove her off to the cabin so they'd be alone together. Even though it was what she wanted, it almost bothered her, how easily he let Ellis steal her away.

What if Jameson tells? *she asked Ellis all the time.* He won't, *Ellis would answer with a smug smile.* I told him I'd give him my old Camaro to keep quiet.

Still, Nina got more and more nervous about it every time she was around Jameson. He would hold her hand when they were together in public and buy her red velvet cupcakes from Sugar House Bakery, supposedly to keep up the illusion, but he kept asking her if she was all right. If she still wanted this.

Truthfully, lying so blatantly to her father made her feel sick and anxious all the time. The sensation of falling from a fatal height—the desperate urge to somehow go back to the safety of solid ground—still clenched her stomach every time Ellis kissed her.

But Ellis seemed to like the rush of doing something so deliciously terrifying, something forbidden.

Still, she didn't want to end things with him. Because after she let him do what he liked, he would let her decide. At home, her father dictated everything from the way she dressed, to the people she spoke to, to the rigidity of her posture in the church pew. At school, everyone drifted around her like she was nothing but a rock in a stream. But in the cabin, after Ellis had his way, she could have hers.

What she liked doing best was curling up on the couch in the fortress of his big arms and watching TV together. Like this was their house and their children were asleep in the next room. They went through piles of VHS tapes—everything from Casablanca *to* Jaws, The Wizard of Oz *to* Pulp Fiction. *And her father couldn't tell her what movies were appropriate. He couldn't tell her that she wasn't allowed to watch them until she did her chores. He couldn't tell her anything, because when she was in the cabin with Ellis, she was an adult. She was a woman. She was in control.*

On the weekends, Ellis liked to get her drunk. And one night they were both just drunk enough, and he let her draw all over him in black marker while The Princess Bride *pulsed in the background. She covered his arms with trees and hummingbirds and his legs with ocean waves and fish.*

"Draw me something I can keep," he said.

The only piece of paper she could find was an old receipt from Annie's Market. She took a marker and inked a sunflower on the back.

She tried to hand it to him, but he pouted and said, "I'll lose this."

The wine made her just bold enough to grab a frame hanging on the wall. She accidentally tore the photo as she took it out—one of Jameson's Little League baseball pictures that his dead mother had hung up.

"Poor Jameson," she said.

"Jameson who?" Ellis answered.

She put her sunflower receipt in the frame and hung it back on the wall so he could look at it whenever he wanted.

And that's how their meetings went.

Until one afternoon in early spring when she wanted to get out of the cabin. She knew that they couldn't go on a real date, out in public. So, she settled for walking with him in the woods, her arm laced through his.

But just a few minutes into their warm, easy stroll, she felt Ellis stumble and heard him curse softly.

And then he took off at a sprint back toward the cabin. Without her.

Before she even had time to call out his name, a furious humming was all around her, a cloud of wings, and she felt a sting at her temple, and then her arm, and then her cheek. Ellis had stepped on a bees' nest that had fallen from a tree.

She ran after him, swatting at her hair and clothes, tree branches whipping at her face and bare arms, until the murderous cloud was far behind her; she was panting, the stings already aching and swelling into little bumps.

"Ellis!" she called. "Ellis! What did you leave me there for?"

She almost tripped over him in the darkening clearing. He'd collapsed just outside of the cabin, and his breath came thin and wheezing. She turned him over, and his face was swollen and red. And then she remembered—her father had mentioned it in passing once—that he was allergic to bees.

He could hardly walk, and she struggled under his weight while she helped him into his truck, tears streaming down her cheeks and her heart beating so fast, she had trouble breathing.

She was in the waiting room at the hospital for half an hour before Jill ran through the doors and threw her arms around her, thanking her through sobs for saving Ellis's life. And Nina could only stand there with her arms limp at her sides, still trying to think up some lie about why she was alone with her husband in the first place.

She offered up a half-baked story before Jill could ask her. "I saw him driving up the hill to Jameson's house, and I followed him."

Jill frowned. "What for?"

"I know it'll sound strange . . . but my father told me to always follow the feeling in my gut. And I just—I felt like something bad was going to happen."

A feeling she'd had for months. A feeling she'd ignored. But Jill didn't need to know that. Just like she didn't need to know that the same feeling still roiled in Nina's stomach now.

Like her fall hadn't ended yet. Like the ground was looming larger and larger beneath her, and once she finally met it, she'd be broken into a thousand, irretrievable fragments.

———

When Ellis met her at the cabin a week later, he stood in the living room and breathed in deep, running his hands through his hair.

"I can't anymore, Nina. I'm sorry. I mean—I've got a family. And— well. Almost dying makes you look real hard at your life. I realized that Jill and the twins are more important to me than I ever thought they could be. I can't risk losing them. This has to stop before we get caught. I've got too much to lose."

Nina said nothing. She sat on the couch, looking up at him with shining eyes. And he lifted the corner of his mouth and rested his big hand on top of her head, like he'd really thought of her as sixteen this whole time.

Like he'd never put his weight on top of her.

"Now, don't look at me like that. Stop looking at me like I've ruined your life. You're not even seventeen yet, and you've got plenty of life left. It's gonna be all right." He settled onto the couch beside her. "You can't go home looking like that. We'll watch some TV until you're feeling better. I'll sit with you till you calm down."

He switched it on, and she heard the drone of a news report and watched a man on screen, but her eyes were blurred and her ears buzzed and she had to keep swallowing. There was too much going on inside her at once—a shivering in her bones and a burning under her skin.

Chapter 17

THE NEXT DAY, I have a short window where everyone is out of the house at once. Ellis is at Pastor Holland's place for coffee. Jill went right back to the restaurant after she drove me home from my lunch shift. The twins left to pick up a pizza for dinner, and with the winding roads and Neil's inability to see someone he knows and *not* talk to them, they should be gone for at least an hour. Which means it's time for me to search the house.

I don't set out looking for anything specific, just something we might be able to use against Ellis somehow. Proof that he had more to do with Mom than anyone else ever knew.

I can't resist pawing through his office first. It's just off the kitchen, tucked into the corner of the house and furnished with a soft carpet, a dark, wood desk, and big, leather reading chair. There are shelves lining the back wall, filled with copies of his books—anniversary editions and reprints and versions translated into different languages. His name flashes on their spines a hundred times over in the light from the window.

All I find in the desk drawers are pens, reading glasses, used plane tickets, and scraps of paper with scribbled notes about meetings. I try the shelves next, shuffling around stacks of books and looking under fake potted plants and behind a broken, antique typewriter.

And there it is. Shoved into a corner on the top shelf, hidden behind a hardcover copy of his very first book—an old, wooden cigar box.

I can tell the moment I pick it up and hear the contents shifting inside that it holds a deeper story than any book in this room. After I cast a look over my shoulder at the door, I gingerly lift the lid.

What's inside would look unimportant to most people. Just a collection of odds and ends—a bottle of pink nail polish and a chewed pencil that I run my fingers over like a topographical map.

And a blue, velvet hair bow.

My father made me wear it, Mom told me once. *Ellis pulled it from my hair, right before he kissed me the very first time. I never saw it again.*

It's nondescript enough—it could have belonged to Melody when she was little. And maybe it did. Maybe all these things did. But then he'd have no reason to hide them like this.

I'm tempted for half a second to think that maybe Ellis kept the bow because he cared about my mother more than I realized. But my guess is that it's probably more like a trophy to him. Maybe he takes it out when no one is looking, running his hands all over it, reliving his past transgressions like dark fantasies.

She only ever told me about the bow. The nail polish and the pencil might have been hers, too. The alternative is too horrific to think about.

That they're his trophies from other girls.

The bile rises in my throat. I swallow it back and try to shake the thought from my head. I don't have time to dwell on it.

But it sticks, and I have to sit down on Ellis's office floor until my bout of dizziness passes. The nail polish is pink, and Mom has never liked pink. And I've never seen her chew on a pencil once.

My guess is that whoever they were, Ellis was with them before Mom—assuming he wasn't lying when he said his near-death experience inspired him to focus on his family again. The nail polish in particular looks like it's been here for years, dry and flaking around the cap, the label peeling. It's a brand I don't recognize, and I've covetously scanned the makeup aisles in grocery stores enough times to know.

Which means it's unlikely that he's having any affairs right now. Because catching him red-handed, exposing his true nature without a confession, would just make my life too damn easy.

With a final shiver, I make myself get up. Instead of wondering who these objects belong to—where they are now—I decide to focus on what I can *do*. So I shove the box in the waistband of my jeans, tucking it safely under my shirt.

These things never belonged to Ellis. I'm taking them back.

———

I don't find anything else useful before Jill and the twins get home. But I do manage to convince Jill to lend me her laptop after dinner.

I get in bed with it, the screen glowing blue in the dark room, and it isn't until I start typing that I realize how rusty my computer skills have gotten. I painstakingly search out each letter on the keyboard with my index fingers until I've finally searched *Ellis Bowman*.

There are countless results about the accident, and I can see why he felt the need to do damage control. The tabloid headlines are each more inflammatory than the last—

Man Who Preaches Family Values Kills Little Boy, Self-Help Author's Careless Driving Turns Deadly, Distraught Mother from Bowman Accident Speaks Out. I click on one and read the details, filling in the gaps of what I gleaned from Tim.

It was a dark night in March, the roads slick with two days of heavy rain. Ellis and Neil were on their way home from a college visit when Ellis struck and killed a fifteen-year-old boy who was crossing the street.

Tim was quoted as a witness, though it seems he didn't actually see much. He was determined to defend Ellis before anyone had even made an accusation—*I've known Ellis more than forty years, as long as he's been alive, and I can't think of a better man.*

There had been a few other witnesses, including someone who anonymously submitted a grainy photo of Ellis's back, which is mostly blocking the view of the body. But you can tell he has his arms around the dead boy. He's holding him. He has his face turned, screaming something.

And now I understand Melody's reaction the second she saw my camera—someone had made her father's private moment of pain very public. For money.

Next, I click on the interview with the boy's mother because it's the most recent article, skimming it to see if there's any additional information that's come to light, but it's sparse—her responses are short and numb, and I suspect she just wanted the reporter out of her house. *Yes, Anderson was good in school. Yes, he had a lot of friends. I don't have any idea what he was doing in Jasper Hollow that night. I was working late. Yes, I'm sad, but* sad *is such an inadequate word for a feeling like this.*

There are plenty of YouTube videos of Ellis's speeches and interviews, and I watch a few, but I'm mostly concerned with the comments. I sift through hundreds of them. Contrary to the media's opinion, most people frustratingly seem to have only positive things to say about him. *He's such an inspiration. So real. A family man. Doesn't deserve to be persecuted by the media this way.*

But then I stumble upon a comment that makes me raise my eyebrows.

Mostly homophobic slurs that aren't worth repeating.

And there's a link.

And I find another reason for Melody's negative reaction to seeing my camera.

It's a chaste photo, really. Just someone giving her a kiss on the mouth. No tongue. But that someone just so happens to be a girl.

I may not have participated much in society for the last seven years, but even I understand the state of things—being anything but straight in a town as small as this one must have been hell. And Melody's famous dad got her some national attention, too. Now she's open to unsolicited opinions about her life from all over the world.

I remember what I realized earlier, that Ellis had hardly mentioned his daughter in his last book, and I wonder if this is why. If he was ashamed of her.

And despite myself, that makes my heart break a little for the Bowman with a chip on her shoulder.

Chapter 18

ON FRIDAY AFTERNOON, I hear a frenzy of beeping timers, whirring mixers, and running water coming from the kitchen. The Dawn Festival is tomorrow, which means Melody has one night to make the cookies she promised Pastor Matthew.

Neil warns me not to go in there. "She doesn't want any help," he says. "I tried to step in anyway, but—you know that look she gives sometimes? The one that feels like a knife between your eyes?"

He doesn't need to say any more. She's been banging dishes around and cursing under her breath all afternoon, so I think it's safe to say she's in a shitty mood. And she barely tolerates me when she's in a good one.

All week, she's been trying her damnedest to pretend that I'm not even here. She always keeps to the opposite side of the room whenever we're forced to be in the same place. She answers when I speak to her directly but uses as few words as possible, and she's careful to avoid eye contact.

You like school okay?

It's school.

What do you like to do?

Swim.

Got any friends?

I asked that one during dinner last night, just to get her to look at me, and when her eyes snapped to mine, I thought she might launch herself across the table and strangle me. And when she didn't answer, both her parents spent the rest of the evening naming every person who had ever been remotely nice to her while she glared at me with enough intensity to disintegrate a small animal.

I can't imagine why she's not the most popular girl in Jasper Hollow.

I peeked into her room this morning while she was eating breakfast, just to get some insight into who she is. It was neat. Sparse. The only thing I could discern for certain is that her favorite color is green. Green like pine needles. It's the color of her curtains, the blanket on her unmade bed, and even the dress hanging from her closet door.

I don't know what color I expected her to like. Not green.

After Melody scared him off, Neil goes to his room to play video games. Jill and Ellis stay up for a little while longer, watching movies while Jill has her head on a pillow in Ellis's lap, but they turn in before ten o'clock so they'll be well rested for an early morning.

After they go up to bed, I hang out on the couch for a few more minutes, watching a game show.

Something feels off, but I'm not sure what. So I turn down the volume and listen.

And then I realize that the noises from the kitchen have stopped, which must mean Melody has finally finished her cookies. But when I peek into the kitchen, she's still in there, sitting on a stool at the counter with her back to me, her head clenched in her hands and her fingers tangled in her curls.

Every inch of the counter is covered in dishes caked with sticky dough. Stray globs have fallen on the floor, which is littered with eggshells and smears of damp sugar. The sink is a pile of metal trays, mixing bowls, and soap bubbles.

I watch her for about a minute before I convince myself to step into the kitchen.

Melody is peering down at a tray in front of her like it's the gaping mouth of hell. When I peer over her shoulder, I see a swirled mixture of dough and melted chocolate chips. And I realize that this ugly, soupy mess is supposed to be a fresh batch of chocolate chip cookies.

An eggshell crunches under my boot, and Melody's head snaps up. She shoots a glare over her shoulder at me, but it's less like a knife between the eyes and more like the growl of a beaten dog.

She coughs and turns away from me. "I screwed it up."

I'm terrified that she's going to start crying. "I—I'll go get Neil."

But before I can escape the kitchen, she snarls, *"Don't.* Tell. Neil."

I want to say that it doesn't matter—lots of people are shitty bakers. But her shoulders are rigid, and that's enough for me to see that it matters to her.

She stands up so fast that her stool would have toppled over if I didn't catch it, but she doesn't seem to notice. She goes to the sink and starts scrubbing furiously at the crusted dough on the inside of a mixing bowl.

"I followed the fucking recipe every fucking time, but I'm the only one in this family who can't fucking bake, and now I have to tell Pastor fucking Matthew that nobody's going to fucking Uganda because *I fucked up the fucking cookies.*"

Her hands are shaking so hard, she drops the bowl in the sink and soapy water sloshes over the counter and down the front of her shirt, but she just picks it up and scrubs harder. I have to pull it from her hands and set it aside to get her to look at me. She turns her eyes on me like that beaten dog again, like she can't decide if she wants to bite me or limp away to lick her wounds.

I grip her shoulders. She's wearing a pale-blue tank top, and my thumbs rest in the hollow dips of her collarbones.

"You fucked up," I tell her. "Now it's time to unfuck it."

Her voice is as quiet as I've ever heard it, her eyes red-rimmed when she says, "But I don't even know what went wrong."

"You're sure you didn't forget to put anything in?"

The look she gives me narrows to that knifepoint that Neil told me about. "You think I forgot it *three times*?"

"Let me see the recipe you used."

She grabs a piece of paper from the counter, stained with drips of vanilla extract. Someone scrawled directions on it in blue pen.

"Where did you get this?"

"Annie. She owns the grocery store on the Circle. And she makes the best chocolate chip cookies in Jasper Hollow. Ask anybody."

"I'll take your word for it." I scan Annie's recipe. When Mom and I still lived in my father's house, we used to make chocolate chip cookies once a week. Every Thursday night. They were his favorite. Butter, brown sugar, eggs—

"Flour."

"What?"

"She forgot to write down flour. Why didn't you look up a new recipe?"

Melody snatches the paper from my hand. "I did. And all the other recipes used flour, but I thought—I don't know. I thought it was Annie's secret ingredient or something."

I stare at her for a few beats. "You thought her secret ingredient was . . . the lack of an ingredient?"

Her temper flares bright in her cheeks, and she hisses, "If you're going to be an ass about it, then get out."

I shrug. "Fine."

She didn't mean it—I can see the regret instantly change her face. She opens her mouth, then snaps it shut.

I wonder if this girl has ever been able to say *I'm sorry* in her life. I almost want to help her through it, like if I pressed my fingers to that hollow dip at the base of her throat, I could soothe the tightness there. *It's okay, Melody. Everyone is wrong. Everyone's a goddamned idiot, not just you.*

Instead, I leave her to finish her cookies all by herself.

Chapter 19

THE KNOCKING HALF AN hour later cuts through a thick, warm kind of sleep. I bury my face in the pillows and grumble, "Too late to ask for help, Mellie." But the sound comes again, and I realize it's not coming from the door.

I look up at the window and see a pale face with dark eyes peering through the glass.

I scramble to slide it open, and I reach for her, but Mom steps just out of my grasp to stand to the side of the window. "In case anyone comes in," she whispers.

The humidity has made her hair tangle and curl like vines around her face. She claws the mosquito bites running up and down her arms when she says, "Tell me everything."

I don't want to admit that I haven't found out much in the past few days, so I focus on the church service. "Ellis brought me up in front of everyone to brag about how he's letting me stay with him. Good PR after the accident."

She nods, grim. "Sounds like Ellis."

I hesitate before I tell her the next part. "I met Pastor Holland."

She's stuck in a thoughtful silence for a few moments after I mention him. "How did he look?" she asks.

I pause to think over my answer, but her gaze sharpens on me, cutting out the truth. "Like he's trying to look strong. But after the service, he was tired. Like he'd run a mile."

She nods. I expect her to ask me more about him, but she moves on quickly. "Does Ellis still play piano at the church services?"

I shake my head. "His son does now."

"Interesting," she whispers.

I wait for her to share what's so interesting about it. But instead, she gets lost in thought, muttering to herself. As she starts to turn away from me, I grab her wrist.

"What are we going to do?"

She stares down at my hand gripping her arm until I let go.

"*You* are going to wait," she says. "Let me worry about the rest."

"But I can help—"

"You need to be patient," she says, her tone hovering at the edge of her own patience.

"Is this because I got caught in the woods?" I say. "You don't trust me anymore."

Mom closes her eyes. Takes a deep breath, in and out through her nose.

"Fine," she says. "If you want a job, then you can look for something that might remind Ellis of me. Something no one else will recognize but him. Something we can plant to scare him."

A pleased smile flushes my face when I remember. "I already have something."

I reach under my mattress and come back to the window with the blue velvet bow I found in Ellis's office.

She stares at it in my hand for a long time, her face wiped blank, and for a moment I worry that maybe it isn't the same bow she told me about. Then, slowly, she takes it from me. And with shaking hands, she pins it in her tangled hair.

I wonder if I shouldn't have given it to her. If I've pushed her even further back in time, further away from me. But then she reaches through the window and gives me a tight hug.

"Thank you," she whispers.

I bury my face in her hair.

"Keep looking for more," she says. "Just like—"

Both of us freeze at the knock on my bedroom door.

I hurry to slide the window shut and dive into bed, and by the time I look back at the window, Mom is gone.

"Yeah?" I say.

Melody takes that as an invitation to come in. The room is dark, but the light from the hallway shines in her hair. "I thought I heard voices," she says.

"I talk in my sleep sometimes."

As soon as it's out of my mouth, I realize that there's no way I look like I was just sleeping. My cheeks are hot, every muscle tense.

She stares at me for a minute. My heart pounds so fast from almost getting caught that I can hardly breathe, so I say, "*What*?" with a little more venom than I mean to.

"I—" she says.

She pauses. Tries again.

"Well, I'm here because I'm just—"

For a moment, she looks like she's about to bolt, taking a step away from me.

Then, resolute, she comes all the way into the room and blurts, "I'm sorry."

The apology tumbles out of her so quickly, I almost don't catch it. Like holding it in her mouth burnt her tongue, so she needed to get it out as fast as she could.

"For being a bitch to you," she goes on. "I was tired. I'm so tired, I can barely think."

"Hmm." I nod. I should say more, but I have to take a deep breath to slow everything down in my head—to remind myself that even though we were half a second from disaster, it wasn't a disaster.

But Melody must think I'm still mad at her, because she sighs, shutting the door softly behind her. "Okay, so it's not just about tonight. I've been an asshole since you got here. I know. And I'm sorry about all of that, too."

"You're just saying that because you want my help with the cookies."

She takes a minute to answer, her lower lip caught between her teeth. "Maybe that's part of it," she admits. She looks down at the floor, the heel of her sock grinding against the wood. "The other part is that I've been thinking about the way Pastor Holland treated you at church the other day."

She clears her throat before she sits down on the edge of the bed, as far away from me as she can be without falling off. But she meets my eyes in the dark when she says, "He's a sad, hateful bastard. I probably shouldn't say that about a sick person, but it's true. My dad says that he's got nobody anymore, so he's used to doing things his own way. But that doesn't mean he's allowed to treat you like shit, and I don't want to be a sad, hateful bastard like him. So maybe I shouldn't have decided you were up to something the minute you got here. Because that's exactly what Pastor Holland did when he found out about you, and now I just feel—sorry."

If I were really a lost girl the Bowmans took in, the girl they think I am, this would be some kind of defining moment. Like I'd finally been accepted into the family.

I'm not lost, and I'm not interested in being a Bowman. But she does look exhausted, her voice thin and shaky with it. So I take pity on her.

I get out of bed and walk past her, toward the kitchen. "You're lucky I have a soft spot for girls with bad attitudes."

She snorts but doesn't try to argue with me.

"Does this mean we're friends now?" I ask over my shoulder.

This is when somebody like Neil would say, *I'd like that.*

Melody answers with just enough bite. "I never said that."

I can't stop myself from laughing. I bark so loud that she hisses at me to shut up or I'll wake the whole house. Which makes me laugh even harder.

*A*fter Ellis decided he didn't want her anymore, Nina cried for weeks in her locked bedroom and in the bathroom at school. She sniffled at the dinner table and wouldn't touch any food. And despite her father's numerous attempts to discern exactly what the problem was, he still had absolutely no idea.

Then one night, when she refused to eat her spaghetti after the third time he'd asked her what was wrong, he slammed his fist down on the table and told her, "That's enough."

She looked up at him through her wet lashes.

"I'm going to guess this is about that Bowman boy."

Her throat felt like it had been squeezed shut. He knows he knows he knows.

"You should have listened to me. You should have stayed away from dating just a little while longer. This is the kind of hurt I was trying to protect you from, you know."

No, she realized. There was no way he knew. Not about how far she'd gone or who she'd gone there with. Because if he did, he wouldn't be giving her the soft look he was giving her now. He thought she was upset over Jameson.

He took her hand across the table, and that made her cry harder. So he went to her and put his big arms around her, and she squeezed him back and said, "I'm sorry, Daddy."

"We've all done things we aren't proud of, sweetheart. Just be thankful this wasn't a mistake you can't come back from."

"I'm sorry," she sobbed again into his shoulder.

"Stop that. Stop that right now."

He held her for a long time, until he finally coaxed her into eating her dinner. Afterward, he talked her into leaving the house, and he even managed to make her laugh once on the way to Annie's Market to get a tub of mint chocolate chip ice cream. They ate at a picnic table in the Circle, nestled safely between the mountains and the warm night, watching the stars that watched over them.

Her father took her out for ice cream once a week after that, even after the weather turned cold. He would stay up late in the living room with her every evening so they could watch TV or read or talk. When she asked him about it, he said, "I've heard that it's a bad idea to leave someone alone when—when they're having a hard time."

She smiled at that. She liked his company.

Finally, she began to see it—she didn't really want Ellis. It became so clear to her, now that he held her at a distance. He'd never been the man she thought he was, the man everyone thought he was. He'd lied to his wife about where he'd gone on the nights he was with Nina. He'd lied to Nina when he told her he loved her. He lied to the whole town every time he walked into church with his beautiful little family, everyone admiring the perfect life he'd built.

Nina had fallen in love with the man Ellis Bowman pretended to be. But that man had never existed, or he never would have been with her in the first place.

Once she understood that, moving on was easier. She went back to her old life, to listening to her father practice his sermons, and writing essays that her English teacher told her would make her shine at whatever college she chose, and drawing mythical birds that were too magnificent to be real.

She'd been heartbroken for a little while, but the world had not quite ended. Her father still loved her, and her life was still waiting to unfold in front of her, and she was going to be just fine.

Until the day it occurred to her that maybe she wasn't.

That something was different.

Off.

That night, she told her father she had a headache and went to bed early. Then, when she was certain he'd gone to his own room, she snuck out her window and walked to Annie's Market just before it closed.

She went directly to what she needed. And then she hid the little box behind her back when she went to the register. Annie gave her a familiar smile, and when Nina leaned in to whisper something to her, Annie leaned in, too.

"You can't tell my dad what I'm buying."

Annie laughed, but Nina didn't.

Annie asked, "Why not?"

Nina put the pregnancy test on the counter, and Annie's hand went over her mouth, muffling a strangled sound that made Nina's stomach turn.

"It's not for me," Nina said quickly. "Do you remember my cousin? The one who came with me to church last week? She begged me to get this for her. She was too embarrassed to get it herself."

"But she couldn't be older than—"

"She's seventeen. And she wants to keep it a secret until she's sure. If my dad finds out, he'll tell her parents, and she'll never forgive me. Can you promise me you won't say anything?"

"She should really talk to her parents."

"She will. When she's sure. Do you promise?"

Annie hesitated before she nodded.

Nina went home with the box shoved down the front of her jeans. Her father was already in bed, but she didn't take it out until she was in the bathroom.

She stayed there for an hour afterward, crying quietly and pulling her hair and biting at her knuckles until they bled. She threw up only once, and it settled her stomach just enough for her to gather the box and the stick and sneak out into the woods. She buried them far away from the house.

Chapter 20

MELODY AND I BAKE until three in the morning, and it feels like my head has just touched the pillow when there's a soft knock at my door. Apparently, the Dawn Festival really starts *before* dawn.

Neil pokes his head through the door with his customary smile and a soft greeting. "Hey, there," he says, like he's waking an infant from a nap.

I press my bare feet to the cold wood floor. "Give me five minutes."

We're on the road in ten, brown sugar still crusted under my fingernails. Everyone is quiet in the car, all of us muffled by the thick fog of sleep. But some silences are more content than others. Melody sits beside me with her tangled curls scraped up into a ponytail, scowling out the window at all the shadowed trees that zip past.

Neil gives me a whispered rundown of how the Dawn Festival works. First, everyone sits in church to listen to the story of the founding of Jasper Hollow. It's usually Pastor Holland's job, but it's one of the few duties that he's begrudgingly passed on to Pastor Matthew, his trainee. Then everyone goes outside to watch the sun rise over Mattie Mountain, just as Will Jasper supposedly saw it when he decided to build his church. The festival part starts later, down in the Circle, with a Ferris wheel and booths for food, games, and crafts.

Even with the building's expansion, the church is still only big enough to cram less than half the people inside. The ones left on the church lawn don't seem too put out, though. Their folding chairs and picnic blankets dot the hillside in the dark, lit just enough by string lights draped between the trees. They all chatter and laugh and shout hello to their friends, louder than anyone ought to this early in the morning.

I expect to join them on the grass because we're one of the last families here, but Ellis walks us right up to the door, where Pastor Matthew clasps his hand and leads us to reserved seats. I should have known Jasper Hollow would make sure its favorite citizen had an honorary place in the front row.

But then I see who's saving the seats, and I understand why everyone else steered clear.

Pastor Holland shakes Ellis and Neil's hands, hugs Jill and Melody, and pretends that I don't exist. He sits at one end of the family, and I sit at the other. Which suits me fine.

Just a minute later, Neil trots onstage to take his place at the piano, and the whole room quiets when he brushes his deft fingers over the keys. Pastor Matthew takes the microphone and says, "Good *MORNING!*" so bright and loud that I grit my teeth.

Neil sets the tone with a hopeful melody while Pastor

Matthew tells us about the day Will Jasper first came here with his family in 1851, not a possession to speak of besides his tool chest and a dream to build his own church. He was scouting out the perfect spot when he crested Clara Mountain—*right where you sit today!*—and saw the sun rising over Mattie.

"Rumor has it, he threw down his hat, dropped to his knees, and didn't rise again for an hour." Pastor Matthew points to the slab of wood hanging over the piano and adds, "The very next thing he did was carve out this sign."

I feel Melody's head nod against my shoulder, her breathing slow and her hair tickling my neck.

I shrug her off. "If I have to stay awake through this, so do you."

She stifles a yawn and rolls her head back against the pew. "I've heard this story before. Seventeen times, to be exact."

Then she leans toward me and adds in a whisper, her hot breath grazing my ear, "They never tell the whole thing, anyway. I did a research report about it once. See, I read Will Jasper came here because he owed some money to people in Virginia. He did build the church, but the strangers who passed through for a visit said his sermons were . . . unusual. He'd roll his eyes up in the back of his head and say God was talking through him. And once, God told him to walk right up to a man, put his hands around his throat, and tell him to leave town before the next sunrise or be damned."

I gasp, like we're gossiping about someone we know.

"The man skipped town that night. And Will's sweet little wife, Harriet, hung herself from the oak tree in the Circle the very next day. He was her lover."

"Jesus. Really?"

"It gets crazier," she says. "Some men came from North Carolina not long after, claiming Jasper robbed a bank. He ran away before they could get their hands on him. No one ever heard from him again."

Pastor Matthew is still going on in the background of our conversation, talking about how Ulysses S. Grant may or may not have stayed at the Dusty Rose Inn on the Circle. (The messy signature scrawled in the guest book makes it hard to say for certain.)

"Maybe you should tell everyone the rest of the story," I whisper back to Melody. "It's a lot more interesting."

"People around here don't care much for the truth."

Matthew goes on cheerfully, "The town's construction was all planned around the favorite tree of Mr. Jasper's beloved wife, Harriet. And that's how we got our Circle. They started with a general store." He points to Annie, who grins and waves her hand high. "The same building where Miss Annie's grocery store is now. Then the blacksmith's, where Sonny sells his baskets today. And the schoolhouse—"

Suddenly, Melody surges to her feet beside me, hissing in a breath between her teeth.

Someone else screams.

And the sign Will Jasper carved falls from its cables and makes a bone-shaking crash when it splits the piano down the middle.

The discordant, high-pitched ring of the snapped piano wires keeps sounding long after the crash, the background noise to hundreds of people swarming, screaming, running for the door like they're afraid the whole roof is caving in.

Melody, Jill, and Ellis have already rushed the stage before I've stood around blinking long enough to understand what just happened. Through breaks in the crowd, I see Neil lying flat on his back on the stage, his father kneeling over him, cupping his son's face in his hands.

But then, Ellis laughs. Nervous and unsteady, but a laugh. And he helps Neil to his feet, slowly, clapping his shoulder. Neil brushes off wood splinters before he waves his hands at the crowd to let them know he's okay. The whole room breaks into applause.

I remember last night. Mom at my window—when she asked me if Ellis still played piano at the church. I told her it would be Neil this time.

We aren't here to hurt anyone but Ellis. Neil was never in any danger. I knew he would be all right.

But I still have to press my hand over my chest and wait for my heartbeat to slow down.

As the crowd disperses and I get closer to the stage, I see something scattered on the floor under the remnants of the crushed piano—hundreds of white sheets of paper. I push my way closer, snatching one up from the ground.

In thick, black marker, large enough to cover the whole page, it reads, *Tell the truth.*

Underneath that, there are typed words. I read a few paragraphs before I realize what I'm holding. It's a page from Ellis's first manuscript. The one that was in the glass case at the bakery.

Which means Mom must have broken in and stolen it last night.

And there are also red pen marks scattered throughout—Mom's notes from when she was helping him revise the book. There are phrases scribbled out, overused words circled, little encouraging notes to counteract the harshness of the red ink. *Interesting! Haha! Like this section!* The lengths Mom went to, trying to protect his feelings.

But the marker doesn't care about the fragility of his feelings.

When I look up from the page, I see Ellis bending down to pick up a piece of paper for himself.

I see the ink bleeding through the back. Mom wrote the same phrase on every single piece of paper, to make sure he'd see it. *Tell the truth.*

I watch his face as he looks it over. It must take him no time at all to recognize his own words. To realize what he's holding. And just a few seconds more to get at least an inkling of what it means.

His son was almost killed.

The sign falling might have been written off as an accident. But someone clearly planted the manuscript.

And who would have a reason to hurt a Bowman?

I'm sure Ellis has more than one enemy. But there's only one whose handwriting is on the paper he's holding.

He glances around to see if anyone else saw the papers yet, and I'm quick to hide the one in my hands behind my back.

He snaps into action, gathering up the scattered manuscript while everyone else is busy fussing over Neil or pushing toward the exit. Because if anyone else suspects that the sign falling wasn't an accident, they'll have questions. Who'd want to hurt a family so perfectly kind? So absolutely innocent?

They might start to suspect that Ellis isn't so innocent.

His wife notices him with the stack of papers before he can hide them, and he mutters, "Just some old programs," before he disappears backstage with them, where I'm sure he'll do a thorough job of disposing of them, because that's what Ellis does with all his dark secrets. Buries them.

But he didn't do a thorough enough job burying Nina Holland.

I wish she could have been here to see his face, the moment he saw those words—*tell the truth*.

His eyes popped so wide. He looked as gaunt as a skeleton in the dim light of the sanctuary.

Like deep down, he could feel that the secrets he buried so long ago were rumbling closer and closer to the surface.

Mom told me she wanted to scare him. Haunt him.

And by the look I saw on his face, I'd say that for the first time in a long time, Mom is finally getting what she wants.

Chapter 21

"THE TIMING WAS JUST too perfect to be a coincidence," Melody says. "Right in the middle of the Dawn Festival? While the whole town was there to see it?"

Jill brought blankets for us to stretch out on and watch the dark sky. She and Ellis are on one, while I'm wedged between Neil and Melody on the other. Neil's ankles are crossed, and his fingers are laced behind his head like he wasn't just a few feet from getting his skull smashed in by a giant hunk of wood.

"So, what are you saying, Mel?" he asks. "Someone's out to get me?"

It sounds so ridiculous, even Melody can't argue—because it's Neil, and no one could hate him, no matter how hard they tried. And because this is Jasper Hollow, and nothing so heinous has happened here since Will Jasper skipped town. As far as anyone knows.

Pastor Holland brought his own lawn chair, and he's slumped in it right next to where Ellis is stretched out. The pastor is rolling his cane in his hands. "It's because Matthew hasn't been checking those cables, like I told him to," he grumbles.

"I'm just glad no one got hurt," Jill says, squeezing her son's elbow.

"Exactly," Ellis says. "Exactly right. Let's focus on that."

He insisted on going up to the church attic himself to investigate. The bolts that held the sign's cables in place were drilled through the attic floor. "Both bolts had come loose," he said. "It was only a matter of time. I thought the sign had been looking a bit crooked lately." Once he said it, everyone else nodded along and said they thought so, too.

Who knew that Ellis himself would be our greatest ally in covering our tracks?

And that's that. Ellis has given his verdict on the situation, and everyone has accepted it as the truth and is ready to move on. Pastor Holland starts criticizing the sermon Matthew is supposed to give to the youth group this week.

"I had to bully him into letting me look over his notes, and let me tell you, it's a good thing I did. You'd think he could manage something as simple as the story of Jonah." He keeps muttering, mostly to himself, about how misguided young pastors are these days while Ellis, Jill, and Neil get into a discussion about the metaphorical meaning of a man getting swallowed by a whale. Still, Ellis is tense all the while, darting furtive glances at the shadowed trees around us, like Mom is hidden somewhere in their depths, watching him.

And she probably is.

Melody is quiet beside me. I nudge her with my elbow. "Chill," I advise her. "Nobody would want to hurt your brother on purpose."

She chews on her lip. "I wouldn't say nobody," she whispered. "But he's a teddy bear."

"Most of the time," she agrees.

I wait for her to elaborate. She sighs. "Don't make fun of me."

I raise my eyebrows, intrigued.

"So I was really into *Lord of the Rings* when I was a kid," she says. "And I got a pair of elf ears for my tenth birthday."

She looks pointedly at me, daring me to laugh. I determinedly keep a straight face, but at the same time, I make a note to scour her room later for evidence of this elf obsession.

"I wanted to wear them to school once. Dad warned me not to, but I told him I could hide them under my hair. But of course, this idiot named Trey Parks teased me all day, and I snapped and yelled at him in the hallway. Something like, *Touch them again, and I'll shove them up your ass.*"

"Did he touch them again?" I ask.

"He tried to. But Neil punched him out cold before he could."

"Really?"

I never would have expected Neil to be capable of something like that. He's strong enough to hurt somebody, sure. I just didn't think he had the stomach for violence.

"I know," Melody says, reading my face. "I couldn't believe it either. Dad was proud of him for defending his family, though. He talked the principal into letting him off with a week of detention instead of suspension."

"So . . . what? You think this Parks kid is out to get him?"

Melody shakes her head. "No, he moved away years ago. I'm just saying, don't assume that just because he's usually so nice that he hasn't made any enemies."

She's quiet for a few beats, and I can see that she's dwelling on it. But even though it's unlikely that she'd guess who was really behind it, I don't want her thinking it was anything but an accident, so I change the subject.

"Ellis and Pastor Holland are close?" I ask her.

She shrugs, her shoulder brushing mine. "I guess so. Mom says Dad had a hard time when he was younger, and Pastor Holland was there for him a lot."

"A hard time?"

"When his parents died. They were both killed in a car accident when he was in college."

"Jesus," I say, pretending I don't already know.

"Yeah."

The others aren't paying attention to us, but it feels like something that should only be talked about in whispers.

"Dad was nineteen," she goes on, staring up at the sky, which has gotten just a pinch too bright to see the stars. "Uncle Jameson was nine, so Dad had to drop out of college and come back to take care of him."

I read about it in his book. I'll admit, whenever I really think about it, something like pity starts to open up in my chest. He grew up dirt poor, and the football scholarship was his bright, shining opportunity to get out, make something of himself, be more than his parents. And it was all ripped away in a second.

But it doesn't take much to strangle my sympathy for him. All I have to do is think about his nice, big house, with the shiny floors and fresh paint and things, things, things that fill up every room. Things that Mom paid for with everything that ever mattered to her.

I have to remind myself of that more often. Because you have to nurture hate just as much as you nurture love. Keep it thriving.

"That's when Pastor Holland stepped in," Melody says. "He got him a job at the bakery and dropped in all the time to check on him. Helped him out with money, too, probably. And they talked a lot."

"Nice of him."

She shrugs. "I guess he thinks of Dad like his son."

I dig my nails into my palms. "Because he never had any kids of his own."

Melody pauses for a moment before she says, "I think he had a daughter. But Mom's never told me what happened to her. She says it makes her too sad. She must have died, somehow."

"Have you asked your dad about her?"

"He changes the subject every time I bring her up. It must be sad for him, too."

For a moment, I don't trust myself to speak. I swallow a few times, trying to calm the angry heat that clenches and unclenches my fists.

When I drop my head to the side to look at Melody again, her face is cast in the gray blue of the brightening sky. Her eyes are closed, and she breathes in deep through her nose; I think it's because she likes the mountain smell—dirt, trees, wind, and hidden creeks. I've seen her do it before. She's always just a little less tense when she's outside. Maybe that's why she likes the color green so much.

And somehow, I've forgotten what I was mad about.

I shake my head to clear it, trying to get back on track.

I remember what Mom told me last night. *Look for something that might remind Ellis of me.*

"Has your dad always lived in Jasper Hollow?" I ask Melody, offhandedly.

"Born and raised," she says without opening her eyes.

"The same house?"

"No. He grew up in a little cabin on Pearl."

"Yeah? Is that where Jameson lives now?"

"No. It was destroyed in a storm. There's no one there."

"Hm." I pause. "Did your dad keep anything from it?"

She opens one eye to look sideways at me. "Like what?"

I shrug, trying to look like I only have a casual interest in the conversation. "I don't know. Keepsakes. I just think it's cool to have your family history all right here, you know? I think that would be nice."

"I don't think he kept a thing. He's never gone back, as far as I know. He wanted to leave that part of his life behind."

"You think?"

"I know. He talks about it in one of his books—*Leaving the Past Behind.*"

"Oh," I say. I hope the disappointment doesn't show in my voice.

Then, a few seconds later, Melody adds, "Jameson kept a few things."

My heart flutters in my throat.

"But nothing sentimental. Things like the couch and the dining table. Maybe even the pots and pans. I don't know. It's been a million years since I've been to his house."

"Why? Does he live far?"

"No. He's over on Mattie Mountain." She yawns. "I just think he's a creep."

I chew on that information for a few minutes. Before I can come up with another response, the rim of the sun peeks over the tip of Mattie Mountain, and Jasper Hollow greets the day with thundering applause. They clap and whistle, keeping it up for a long time, until the sky blazes with light. Everyone except Melody.

Our all-night baking session must have finally caught up with her—she's curled up on her side next to me, her breath coming slow and warm through her parted lips, whispering against my cheek.

While everyone else welcomes the morning, celebrating Will Jasper like he wasn't a thief, a liar, and a fraud, Melody Bowman falls fast asleep.

———

We go back to the house after sunrise to squeeze in a couple of hours of sleep before the festival starts at nine. At eight thirty, Melody loads the cookies into her father's car to take to the Circle. I carry out the last box, and after I stack it with the others in the trunk, she says, "You can sit in the church tent with me and help me sell these things. If you want to."

Her cheeks bloom pink, and she has a hard time meeting my eyes.

I smile. "Are you asking if I want to hang out with you?"

Her blush burns brighter. She slams the trunk shut and storms past me. "Well, I said you don't have to."

"Mel."

I don't know why I called her that. No one calls her that but Neil. I wait for her to whirl on me and say something snarky, but when she turns to meet my gaze, she doesn't say a word.

"I would," I say. "But I think I'll head to the festival a little later."

"Oh."

"I'm just really tired. From last night. You know."

"Right."

No matter how stiff and emotionless she manages to keep her face, I can't help thinking that I've hurt her feelings somehow. Like she doesn't ask for things often and it's hard for her to do it.

She walks back into the house without another word. I sigh and follow her in.

Half an hour later, I watch through a window while the Bowmans climb into Ellis's car. The second it pulls away, I grab the keys to the twins' Jeep from the bowl by the door.

———

When I get to the clearing on Pearl Mountain, the van isn't there. I yell for Mom. I'm certain she's nearby, ready to hear all about exactly how Ellis reacted to her little stunt. But I don't find her.

That shouldn't make me worry. I shouldn't feel the panic spreading though my chest and down my arms, making my fingers go numb.

She told me not to come looking for her, that she would find me, but she won't be angry. I'll tell her about the haunted look on Ellis's face. *And* I think we can find something useful at Jameson's house. That will make her happy.

"Mom?" I yell again, heart skittering.

The sun is high above me, and the heat is everywhere, even under the shade of the trees. I'm pacing, my teeth grinding, sweat dripping down my back. I taste salt on my lips.

I try not to think about Jill, who always tells her kids where she's going, and when, and why. The way they don't even listen anymore, but she tells them anyway.

I need to stop comparing them. Mom's had a hard life. I shouldn't expect so much from her.

Should I?

Once she gets her revenge on Ellis, this will all be over. Once her father knows the truth, she'll let go of her pain. And then she can be everything I need her to be. I just have to be patient.

No one else has to be patient. No one else has to do this.

I pull at the ends of my hair, trying to clear that foreign whisper in my head.

I pause midstep next to the pond, my eyes on the spot where Mom and I built the fire our first night in Jasper Hollow. It looks like it hasn't been touched in days. I scan the dirt under my feet and don't see any fresh footprints but mine.

I'm searching the clearing for any sign that she's been here recently, the panic rising like a fist in my throat, when I find the piece of paper under a rock on the cabin's front porch.

It says, *I told you not to come looking for me again.*

I read it over and over, until I get it through my head that I won't find her here. Her hiding place has changed.

She didn't trust me enough to stay.

No—she knew me well enough not to stay.

I crush the piece of paper in my fist, the realization sinking in that until she decides to come for me, I'm completely on my own.

*N*ina had been learning about Hell since she was old enough to understand what pain was.

Her father preached about it often. He did whole sermons on the meaning of eternal suffering—of the burning that doesn't end. He'd slam his fist over and over again on the pulpit, red-faced and spitting his words. "Pain that lasts forever. Do you know how long forever is? We've all said it before, but do we really know what it means? Forever is longer than it would take one man to drink up the ocean. Forever is more time than it would take to count every speck of dirt on every mountain in the world."

Hell was his favorite topic. Nina shouldn't have been surprised that he preached about it the Sunday after she found out she was pregnant with a married man's child.

Ellis had been listening to her father's sermons even longer than she had. While they were seeing each other, she'd wanted to ask him if what they were doing meant they were doomed to suffer. But without really *being aware of it, she'd always believed that nothing Ellis did could ever be so wrong. He was a good man—her father said so all the time. People like Ellis didn't go to Hell. As long as she was with Ellis, she would be safe.*

But he had left her, and she didn't feel safe anymore.

She'd lain awake every night since she found out she was pregnant, forming a plan in her head. She would walk to the next town over. It would take more than an hour, but that was the closest place with a bus that would take her to Columbus, where she could go to an abortion clinic. She'd looked up the address on a computer in the library.

The problem was that she knew she'd need money. She didn't know how much, but it had to be more than the hundred dollars her aunts and uncles had sent her for her birthday. She was still trying to think of a way to get more.

But now, sitting in the pew closest to the front, looking into her father's bloodred face, she knew she wouldn't do it. She was going to have the baby she didn't want, and Ellis didn't want, and her father didn't want, because she was terrified of what her eternity would be like if she didn't.

Ellis sat two rows behind her, and she tried to catch his eye over and over again, but he stared straight ahead at her father the entire service. He had his arm around his wife, and his son sat on his knee. Jill held little Melody close to her heart.

After the service, Nina tapped Ellis's shoulder before he could step outside the wooden double doors. He ignored her, but his wife noticed and said with a warm smile, "How are you doing, sweetheart?"

"My dad needs a box from his office taken to the car. I was wondering if Ellis could help me. It's heavy."

Ellis wouldn't meet her gaze, busying himself wiping Neil's runny nose. "I've got to help Jill with the kids."

But Jill was already pulling Neil out of his hands. "Nonsense. I've got these two." She slipped out the door before her husband could argue. So Ellis followed Nina down the hallway, into her father's empty office.

When she told him, he grabbed the edge of her father's desk with white knuckles. For a full minute, he didn't speak—just swallowed over and over again, staring down at his hands with a horrified look on his face, like they'd just been cut off.

When he finally spoke, he said, "Are you lying to me?"

"Why would I do that?"

He bit his bottom lip and ran both his shaking hands through his hair.

"Are you—are you going to go through with it?"

Her father's Hell sermon must not have scared him the way it scared her. Maybe he thinks I'll be the only one punished.

"Yes," she said.

He dropped to his knees in front of her. He took both her hands in his and looked up into her eyes and begged her, "Please don't tell anyone it's mine."

For a moment, Nina was too baffled to reply. "Who else's would it be?"

He shook his head. "It doesn't matter. Tell them it was someone you met on that church retreat you went to. Tell them . . . tell them he forced himself on you."

She ripped her hands from his. "No. Someone could get in trouble."

"Then just don't tell them anything. Don't say who it was."

She pulled nervously at the ends of her hair. "But—"

181

"*Nina.*"

His voice shook, and he looked almost like a child, staring up at her with shining eyes. Like she held the weight of his entire world in her hands.

"*Nina, you can't tell anyone. Please. I have a family. I have to take care of them. Jill would never speak to me again. My career, all that work we did on the book. Jesus, I'll lose everything. Do you understand that?*"

"*Ellis—*"

"*I'll pay you. I'll pay for whatever it needs. Just please, please promise me you won't tell anyone.*"

She'd felt a sick, constant churning in her belly ever since she took the pregnancy test, but she forgot about it for a moment now. Just long enough to feel the ache in her chest for him.

Even if the life she knew was over, that didn't mean she wanted to destroy his.

She nodded. "Okay."

Ellis surged to his feet and took her in his arms, crushing her to him, his chest heaving. She could feel the dampness of his tears on her hair. The intimacy of it made her squirm. She kept her arms stiff at her sides.

She walked home, hoping the redness would leave her face by the time she made it there. But every time she let herself think about anything, a fresh bout of tears scorched her cheeks.

Her father was sitting in the rocker on the front porch when she crested the little hill just before their house, still in his church clothes. He smiled and waved at her, but as she came closer, he saw her hair sticking to her damp cheeks.

He tried to lift her face with his hand, but she couldn't look at him. He tried to ask her what was wrong, but she wouldn't answer. So he wrapped her up in his big, sun-browned arms. She buried her face in his shirt, and he smoothed down the back of her hair with his rough hand. And she knew that she would hide there forever, tucked away in his arms, if he'd let her.

Until a man drank up the whole ocean or counted every speck of dirt on all the mountains in the world.

Chapter 22

I WILL NOT CRY. Tears have never saved anyone. I'd choose anger over tears every time.

But I can't get angry with Mom for leaving me either. She told me to stay away, and I didn't listen. This isn't her fault. It's Ellis I should be angry with, for making all this necessary in the first place. I tighten my grip on the steering wheel and focus on him until my eyes dry up and blood burns in my cheeks.

The street that goes to the Circle is blocked off for the Dawn Festival, so I park the Jeep as close as I can before I get out and walk, head down.

I've been picking up as many shifts at the Watering Hole as I could get ever since Jill gave me the job, but I'm not scheduled to work today. Jill said she wanted me to enjoy the festival, and when I come through the glass door, she tries to turn me out. But then she sees my face and says, "What's wrong, honey?"

I don't answer her. She frowns, a concerned little line creasing between her eyebrows. But she doesn't argue when I tie on my apron.

In the restaurant, I find a third option for coping with being deserted—one other than tears or anger. I take orders and get people what they need and clean up spills and carry out heavy trays and pour refills. I work nonstop, always moving, and for a while, I'm entranced by the rhythm of that motion, of fulfilling promises, of receiving tangible rewards in the form of crisp dollar bills stuffed in my apron pockets. This is the only place in Jasper Hollow where I feel absolutely capable. Until I'm jarred right out of that beautiful rhythm with one hushed word.

"*Melody.*"

Whispered like something dirty. Something that doesn't belong in polite lunch conversations.

The girl who said it is part of a group in the big corner booth. They all look around my age, and one of them is wearing a Jasper Hollow High School T-shirt. And the way they glace toward the front of the restaurant, to make sure Jill is out of earshot, makes me pretty sure I know exactly which Melody they're talking about.

I grab a rag and start wiping down the empty table next to them, close enough to hear their lowered voices.

"Somebody should really warn the girl living at their house about her," one of them says.

Giggles. Are they talking about me?

"They were pretty cozy together this morning at the ceremony. Maybe she doesn't *want* to be warned."

More giggles. My heart rate picks up.

"But . . . how do you *know*?" another girl asks.

"Didn't you hear about the party last summer? At David Cochran's house?"

"That was before I moved here."

The next girl who speaks does it so quietly I almost don't catch her words.

"Melody got caught kissing a girl."

"Janie McCormick's cousin," another one pipes up. "She was visiting from Chicago. I hear she works at a gay bar. They have tons of them there."

Some of them bite down on their knuckles to keep from laughing too loud. I stop pretending to clean the table.

"They were right in the middle of the kitchen. They didn't even try to hide it."

"Melody always seemed like such a *normal* girl, you know? Like, she's got a temper, but I thought she was a good person. I just couldn't believe it. Especially when her dad is such a good guy, you know?"

"Do you think she's, like, a full-blown *lesbian* or she just wanted to try it?"

"I don't know, but I'm on the swim team with her, and I swear she was checking me out when we were changing after our meet in Lancaster. My mom took it to the school board and everything, but nobody wanted to kick her off the team because they were *so* worried about winding up on the news for being homophobes. A bunch of PC bullshit. Now I have to change in a bathroom stall."

That one's voice holds something in it that makes me remember what Jill said to me not long ago. *If you meet anyone who acts too big for their britches, it's a Walsh.*

The girl pulls out her phone and adds, "At least I made some money off the picture," and she pulls it up to show everyone around the table so they can giggle some more.

It would be satisfying to go over there and slam my palm on the table hard enough to rattle the silverware. To see how fast all their bluster gets sucked out of the room when they realize that someone was actually listening to them.

I'd love to lean in so I'm eye level with the Walsh girl—whose eyes happen to be the same shade of blue as the toilet water at the Bowmans' house—and say, *I think she hasn't looked at you once. In fact, I know she hasn't. Because a girl like Melody would never settle for a bitch like you.*

I'd like to watch her squirm like she was choking on a chicken bone. Her cheeks flaming hot enough to fry eggs on.

But I know better. People like me don't have the luxury of boldness. I've built my life on subtlety. Invisibility. I've got too many secrets to risk causing a scene.

So instead, I walk calmly back to the kitchen and grab the carafe from the coffee maker. And with a furtive glance around to make sure no one is paying attention to me, I use an empty cup to stir in a generous helping of dirty dishwater. I fish out any noticeably large bits of chewed food that get mixed in.

And then I go back to the girls' table, and with a smile, I refill their empty coffee cups to the brim.

———

When the sun slips behind Clara Mountain, the lights from all the shops come on and spill into the Circle, mingled with the twinkle of string lights and the bluegrass twang of a local band called the Jasper Hollow Bullfrogs.

The dancing starts when Neil kicks off his shoes and spins a little girl around in the grass under Harriet's Oak. She'd been crying over not winning a prize at the ring toss booth, but now the tears are dry on her face, and her laugh echoes in the night. Other kids drag their parents onto the makeshift dance floor. Girls grab their boyfriends, wives rope in their husbands, and then the Circle is a riot of dancing feet and twirling skirts.

I've just finished up a busy shift. And I'm still hurt and confused by Mom abandoning me, but the hard work has numbed my mind just enough to get caught up in the fun. Melody seems content to stand on the fringe and watch, but I grab her hand and drag her right out into the middle.

She refuses to dance at first, her arms crossed firmly over her chest while I twirl around her. I've never really learned how to dance, but I've also never really learned how to be embarrassed about it. She bites her lip, fighting hard to keep the sour look on her face, until I link my arm through hers and spin us until she's too dizzy to care much about being embarrassed either.

When I let her go, she steadies herself with her hands on her knees, her head down. I hear her laughing, but it's when she looks back up at me, hair springing loose from her braid, that my breath catches.

Because she gives me my very own, first-ever, pearly white, mile-wide, Melody Bowman smile.

The feeling that thrills through me then—it's like my veins are made of light bulb filaments, pulsing with enough electricity to make me glow.

I grin even more than Neily does for the rest of the night. Most of it, anyway.

Except for the part where I see Tim, the baker, working his way through the crowd, followed by a couple of stern men in sheriffs' uniforms, asking people what they know about the manuscript someone stole from his bakery late last night.

—

The Bowmans and I don't leave the Dawn Festival until long after dark, our skin glowing warm from the sun and our feet aching in that satisfying way that comes from walking miles and miles, even if it was only in circles around a restaurant or up and down the crowded streets of a small town. Melody sold all her cookies, Neil spent the afternoon catching up with friends over cold apple cider, Jill's restaurant was packed from open to close, and I made over a hundred dollars in tips.

We meet Ellis back at the house. He left the festival hours earlier, claiming he didn't feel well. But whatever ailment he had has miraculously cleared up, and he's all smiles, sitting down at the table with his family over glasses of lemonade while they recount stories from the day, their laughter echoing through the big house's halls.

But what I see later that night tells a very different story.

I'm lying awake when I hear someone creeping down the stairs. I sneak out of my room and down the hall, and I peer around the corner and through the kitchen. I see Ellis's open office door.

His back is to me. But I can see he's holding a piece of paper. One of the manuscript pages.

Tell the truth.

He walks to the window, his socks completely silent against

the carpet. And he stares out for a long, long time. I angle my head to get a look at his face.

He does so well, hiding his fear in front of others. Just like he's hidden everything else. But it's naked in the moonlight—in his wide, searching gaze as he scans the dark trees outside of his big, beautiful house that once felt so safe and now probably feels more like a giant target.

He looks for her, his hands white-knuckled on the windowsill. But Nina Holland won't be found until she wants to be found.

Not even by me.

*N*ina knelt on the floor of the Walsh Clothing Company men's department and shoved as many T-shirts as she could into her backpack. Her stomach strained against the top she was wearing. She got it for being a vacation Bible school counselor the summer before, and it was the only one she had that came close to hiding how swollen she'd become.

The teenage boy who worked at the register snuck up behind her. He grabbed her wrist before she even knew he was there.

Of course, he knew her. He sat behind her in geometry. She let him copy her notes once after he'd been out sick for an entire week. But that wasn't enough to keep him from taking her to his manager.

They called her father at work, and he was there in ten minutes.

He yelled at the manager first for taking the word of an idiot cashier. Then he accused the cashier of stealing the shirts himself and trying to frame his daughter for it. Then he watched the security tape in absolute *silence, a burning shame crawling up his neck and weighing down the corners of his mouth.*

Nina wanted to drop at his feet and beg him to let her start her whole life over. But she just stood beside him with her hands clenched together and her eyes on her tennis shoes.

He dragged her out to the car by her elbow. The manager called after them that they wouldn't be welcome in the store again.

The yelling started the moment the doors closed. "What the hell were you thinking?" and, "You just can't get it together, can you?" and, "How am I supposed to lead a congregation if I can't keep my own daughter under control?"

"Daddy, I—"

"I just don't understand why. If you wanted a bunch of T-shirts, I'd have gotten you some. Hell, you could have borrowed some of mine!"

He didn't pause for her answer. He hardly seemed to take a breath the whole ride back to the house. By the time he parked in the gravel driveway, his face was red with the effort of expressing his absolute disbelief about everything.

So instead of waiting for him to pause, she just came out and said it, right in the middle of his sentence.

If he hadn't been looking right at her, he might not have noticed that she'd spoken at all. Whatever he was about to say was lost forever. He fumbled for a moment. And then he could only manage, "What?"

"I'm pregnant."

She watched his face. His eyes were locked on hers. The red of his skin got deeper, and it spread from his neck to his hairline. His arms and hands glowed hot, and his chest heaved, and she waited for a bout of screaming louder than any hellfire sermon he'd ever given before.

But he didn't say a word.

He breathed in and out, looking down at his hands knotted around the steering wheel, the skin stretched taut over his knuckles. Then he got out of the car and walked away, toward Clara Mountain.

Nina jumped out and yelled after him, "Don't leave! Please! I need you!" But he didn't turn around or give her an answer.

He was gone for hours, and he didn't come back until long after Nina had gone to bed. But she thought maybe that was for the best. Of course he needed time on his own, to come to terms with it.

But he didn't speak to her the next day either. Not when she ate breakfast with him. Not when she asked him questions. Not even when she cried and grabbed his hands, begging him to say anything. He didn't look at her or acknowledge her for the entire day. Or the next.

He pretended she didn't exist for a week.

He left for work before she woke up for school and stayed there until late at night. And when he did come back, he went straight to his room and locked the door behind him. Even when she sat outside on the floor and begged him to come out. She would spend whole nights whispering through the wall that she was sorry. That she was scared. That she couldn't do this alone.

On a Friday, she skipped school and walked all the way up Clara Mountain in a misty drizzle. She pushed open the heavy doors of the church. A maintenance worker was standing in the lobby with a toolbox, staring while Nina walked past him, her long, black hair sticking to moon-pale skin.

She knew that everyone in Jasper Hollow would know by tomorrow that she'd gone off the deep end. The maintenance man would tell everyone the way her wet dress clung to the hard lump of her belly, and no one would believe him at first, but word would spread like a brushfire anyhow, and soon, there would be no denying it.

But none of that mattered now. She knocked on her father's office door, and when he opened it, she threw herself into his stiff arms and begged him to please, please, please forgive her.

She was relieved beyond words when he patted her back twice before he gripped her arms and made her let go of him. Then he eased her down into a chair and put his coat around her shoulders. He pushed a wet curl out of her face before he said the first words he'd spoken to her in several days:

"I think you're going to have to go away for a while."

Chapter 23

AFTER ALL THE FESTIVITIES yesterday, I'm exhausted. I trudge through an eight-hour shift at the Watering Hole, through customer meltdowns over slightly burnt toast and watery sodas, through scraping unidentifiable substances off the bottoms of tables and reciting the day's specials so many times that I'm pretty sure I'll be chanting nonsense about chicken chopped salad and broccoli soup in my dreams tonight.

When the clock ticks down the last seconds of my shift, there's a palpable feeling of release, a satisfying sigh that sweeps through my body.

I did it. And I've got a pocketful of tips to show for it.

Normally, Jill drives me home when I'm done, but she presses her keys into my hand instead and says, "I'm going to stay behind to help with the dinner crowd. Do you think you could do me a favor?"

Black Cat Lake is around the backside of Mattie Mountain. I ease Jill's minivan off the street onto a dirt road that winds somewhere cut off from the rest of the world by crowded trees and jutting rocks that surround the glassy water. I park just off the path and step out of the car.

Melody is giving swimming lessons at the lake today, but she forgot her gym bag with her suit in it in her mother's car, so I told Jill I would bring it to her.

I walk toward the lake with the bag slung over my shoulder. A group of girls stands talking at the end of a dock that stretches far out into the water, a mixture of high schoolers and little kids there for swim lessons. I notice a few from the restaurant yesterday—the ones I served dishwater coffee—and I have to suppress a smile.

Everyone is in a swimsuit, except for one girl, who stands a little bit apart and pretends to be very, very interested in the dirt under her fingernails.

The others look at her every so often and whisper to each other, like they're observing an open-heart surgery through a glass window. And it isn't going well.

When Melody spots me, she looks embarrassed for half a second, taking an involuntary step closer to the group. But it only takes a moment for her eyes to settle into their customary glare before she stalks toward me.

"I thought Mom was coming."

"It's pronounced *thank you*. What the hell is your problem, anyway?"

As of yesterday, I thought we had a truce. But she looks even more pissed at me than usual.

Melody grabs my hand, yanks me toward the path, and drags me behind her Jeep.

Then she pulls her shirt up over her head.

Her flat stomach stretches, revealing a groove at the center of her torso, the soft outline of muscle. Her bra is pale pink against the honey gold of her skin. I watch her slide out of a pair of denim shorts and drop them on the ground.

She holds her hand out to me, and for a moment, I'm too startled to understand what she's waiting for. Impatient, she snatches the gym bag from my hands.

"Turn around," she orders. Still in a slight daze, I do.

"Lou at the gas station told me he saw you drive my Jeep past the Circle yesterday," she says. "Toward Pearl."

When I went to see my mother. It's the last thing I expected her to say, and I'm not ready for it. If I had a quick answer, she might have believed me. But I pause for a few seconds before I say, "I went on a drive to clear my head. I didn't know I needed to fill out a report for you."

She finishes changing quickly, then grabs my shoulder and turns me around, her face very close to mine. I can feel the heat rolling off her. "You're lying to me," she whispers.

When I can't come up with an answer, she walks away from me. "We'll talk about this later."

I follow her onto the dock, the boards making hollow sounds under my boots. "Let's talk about it now."

"Go away," she says, without turning around.

I grab her elbow. "Mel, I—"

She whirls and shoves me. "I *told you*—"

But that's all I hear before I trip backward and plunge into the lake.

Mom and I ran away from my father's house the summer I was supposed to start swim lessons. After, we only waded into the shallow edges of ponds and creeks long enough to rub the grime from our bodies and let it float downstream.

In other words, I have absolutely no idea how to swim.

I pride myself on being good in a crisis. On my ability to stay calm and think quickly and save myself. But it's hard to stay calm when there's water burning up your nose and stealing the air from your lungs in a plume of rippling bubbles. I flail and thrash and try to claw my way up, but I don't know where *up* is, and I'm terrified that I'm just pushing myself deeper.

Then I feel strong arms lock around my waist, and through the murky lake water, I see a glint of gold hair. Melody pulls me against her chest and kicks for the surface, effortlessly, like she doesn't even notice my fingernails hooking into her back.

When we break through, I cough up water. My first breath is painful, too deep, but I keep heaving it in. I don't let go of Melody until my hands are braced on the edge of the dock. I lift myself out, water streaming from my clothes. Her hand is on my back, pushing me up.

I crawl away from the water on my hands and knees. The girls swarm me, all their frantic words streaming together. *Oh my God are you okay what happened did she push you can you breathe do you need to go to the hospital?*

Melody hauls herself out of the lake and hurries over to me, squeezing the back of my neck. "Phoenix? Phoenix?"

I throw my elbow into her chest, and she falls back onto her butt with a surprised *oomf*. Then I push myself to my feet and storm down the dock, back to Jill's van.

My clothes cling to my body. The breeze makes my teeth chatter, my hair sticks to my neck, and my socks squish inside my boots.

"Wait," Melody calls, running after me. I yank on the handle of the minivan's door, but it doesn't budge. Locked. I fumble in my wet pocket.

Melody grabs my elbow. "Shit, Phoenix, I didn't mean to knock you in, I swear."

I laugh without humor and throw my hands up. "They're gone."

Her brows furrow in a way that might have been cute, if I weren't so ready to strangle her. "What's gone?"

"The keys. They were in my pocket. And now they're probably at the bottom of that goddamn murder pit you call a *lake*."

Chapter 24

WE DON'T GET BACK to the house until a good three hours later, because that's how long it took Melody to find her mother's car keys. She dove into the murky lake water again and again, long after everyone else had gone home, while I sat on a rock under a tree, a safe distance from the water, and sulked.

I can tell when we walk into the kitchen that Jill must have already gotten about a dozen phone calls from concerned parents. She's waiting for us at the table over a cup of coffee.

Jill just crooks her finger at her daughter and walks up the stairs to her bedroom.

Melody gives me a long look, her eyes hollowed out with exhaustion, before she follows her mother. The second the door closes behind her, I creep up the stairs, just far enough to make out their voices, muffled through the door.

"Did you push her?"

"No. I mean—she grabbed me, and I—"

"Were you fighting?"

"Not fighting. I wouldn't call it fighting."

"What were you *not fighting* about?"

I hold my breath, waiting for her to rat me out—to tell her mother that someone saw me driving the Jeep where I wasn't supposed to be. But she stays quiet.

"Whatever it is," Jill says in a low, steady voice, "you need to work it out."

"But—" Melody starts to argue.

Something makes her shut up. I can't be sure what, but I picture the look Mom has given me a hundred times, so poisonous that it never fails to make me bite my tongue.

I hear Melody walk toward the door, and I hurry back down the steps, flitting down the hall to my own room, settling into bed with my back against the headboard like I've been here all along by the time Melody knocks on my door.

I ignore her, but she comes in anyway.

Melody's hair is still damp, her cheeks flushed red from a sunburn. She doesn't seem to know what to say. I watch her with my lips pressed shut.

I'm angry. Which is ridiculous. I've done a lot worse to other people than she did to me. Sure, she almost killed me with one push, but I'm the one who's got it out for her family in the first place.

Maybe it's got more to do with the fact that she saved me. Maybe I'm mad at myself because of the way I clung to her.

But she doesn't know that. She stutters for a moment before she gets out, "I'm here to—"

"Apologize?"

"Right. I'm sorry."

"I don't care."

She crosses her arms over her chest. "I didn't think you would."

"So you only came in here to make your mother happy."

"No. I really am sorry. And—and I want to make it up to you."

My hands still burn hot. But I wait for her to explain.

"Forgive me, and I won't ask again about where you went in the Jeep."

I scowl. "I told you, I went for a drive to clear my head."

"And I told you that's bullshit."

"Well, unless you can prove it, I've got nothing else to say to you."

She catches her full bottom lip between her teeth. "Then what do you want from me?"

Before I can bite back a reply, Neil pokes his head in the room. "Make her give you a foot massage," he says. "Mel is grossed out by feet."

"By *your* disgusting feet," Melody says, shoving his head out of the room and slamming the door shut. She turns back to me. "Whatever the hell you want. Whatever will make you stop being mad at me."

I think that over for a few seconds before I say, "You know, I don't think I've ever had a foot massage in my entire life." I point one of my toes at her. "Do they really gross you out?"

She makes a face but moves to sit down on the bed. "As long as yours aren't as hairy as my brother's."

"Aren't you supposed to use lotion?" I tilt my head at her expectantly, just barely suppressing a smile.

She growls but goes into my bathroom and comes back out

with a tube that she squeezes into her hand. She settles in at the end of the bed, legs pretzeled, and takes both of my feet in her lap.

The lotion is cold, but her hands are warm, her fingers pressing firmly into the soles of my feet.

"How is that?" she asks.

I tilt my head back against the headboard. "I should have started making people do this for me a long time ago."

Her mouth quirks. We're both quiet for a few minutes. I close my eyes and feel her thumbs move in little circles over my skin. I wasn't lying when I said I'd never had a foot massage before, and I wonder vaguely if it's normal to feel like you're turning liquid under someone's touch. Her hands warm my blood until I'm boiling, and somehow, I can't quite remember what I was angry about.

My eyes open again to watch her hands work up to my ankles, and then she's rubbing slow, firm circles into my calves. "Does that feel good?" she asks. And maybe I imagine it, but her voice sounds a bit breathier than it did before.

I try to answer, but I can't make words take form, because she's moving higher now, gently tickling the backs of my knees.

She has to feel it—the way my skin burns under her fingers. And it has nothing to do with anger at this point. She gets on her knees now to lean over me, her touch light as a breath, tracing over my thighs. She catches her lip between her teeth, and I can see the flush in her own face.

I hold my breath, waiting for her to go higher.

But then she looks up at me, and something about meeting my eyes makes her embarrassed all at once. She pulls back her hands. "I—I'm sorry."

"Mel—"

I reach for her, but she's already pushed herself to her feet and she's striding toward the door.

"Wait," I say, but she's gone.

I sigh and flop back against the pillows.

She's going to hate you when she finds out why you're really here.

Mom would be angry if she found out what you're feeling right now.

There's still work to do.

Very good points. But I'm having trouble concentrating on anything but the way my skin feels where Melody touched it, so warm and sweet that it's almost an ache.

Chapter 25

A FEW DAYS LATER, I'm at the Watering Hole, sitting at the counter and catching my breath after the lunch rush with one of Jill's fluffy *pan au chocolats*, renowned all over Jasper Hollow as better than anything you could find in Paris—even though there probably aren't many people from Jasper Hollow who have wandered past the borders of Ohio.

"The secret," Jill whispered to me when she handed me the plate, "is extra *chocolat*."

I glance over my shoulder every few minutes at Ellis, who's been here since we opened, tapping away industriously on his laptop. But I doubt he actually gets anything done. He's here for the people. His people.

Everyone who comes through the door seems to think they need to stop and talk to him. Some of them only nod hello, but most of them slide into the booth across from him to shake hands and exchange news about their families. More than half the conversations end in tears, people telling him about their sick mothers or lost jobs. Ellis nods sympathetically, clasps their hands, and offers wisdom in the form of inspirational quotes and anecdotes.

He's careful to keep a somber look on his face, but I know he loves it. Every second. It's one thing to know he's got the world eating out of his hands. It's another to see it in action.

He works here often, when he's not out of town for speaking engagements and interviews and meetings. I used to watch him carefully whenever I could, trying to see if he would give me anything to use against him—furtive exchanges, secret touches, or hushed arguments. But I always came up empty.

I asked Jill once how she felt about it, and she only shook her head with a half smile, not looking up from the dish she was scraping clean. "As long as he sits next to the front window, where people can see him. He draws in a good chunk of business."

But I've seen her peering over his shoulder sometimes, when he spends too long with the women. To my frustration, he never gives them any special treatment, but they definitely seem to think *he's* something special. When they let their eyes linger too long, or their voices get too husky, or they lean in too close, Jill makes sure to stop by to run her fingers through his hair and ask, "Need another coffee, dear?"

Between clients, Ellis gets a phone call, and I'm trying to eavesdrop when a storm cloud blows through the door.

Pastor Holland usually doesn't miss a chance to complain to Ellis about something going wrong in the world, but when he sees Ellis is busy, they exchange a short nod before the pastor shuffles to a booth in the back, leaning heavily on his cane. He hunkers down with a copy of the *Jasper Hollow Weekly*.

As it happens, the clock above the kitchen door just ticked down the last few seconds of my break.

I retie my apron around my waist and walk over to him. "Good afternoon, Pastor Holland."

He raises a thick, black eyebrow at me, his frown heavy. "Good afternoon."

"What can I get for you?"

Asking is only a formality. One of the boys in the kitchen got started on his black coffee and two eggs over medium the second he walked through the door.

"Black coffee," he says. "And . . . ," he ponders, chewing his lower lip. "Two eggs, over medium."

I nod and turn to go.

"Shouldn't you write that down?" he says.

I tap my temple. "Don't worry. Got it all up here."

"Hmm," he grumbles. "Well, I want sausage, too. Links, not patties. And bacon. Extra crispy."

"Got it." I take another step away.

"And some biscuits. With apple butter."

"Done."

"You're still not writing it down."

"Still don't need to."

He adds a glass of water with two lemon wedges, a slice of blueberry pie with whipped cream, and a hot fudge sundae with no more and no less than one tablespoon of fudge.

I clink every plate down on his table after it comes out of the kitchen, and he combs it all over with a critical eye.

"Something wrong?" I ask.

I don't try to hide the satisfied smile that curls my lips when he can't find any mistakes to complain about. I nailed it, and he knows it.

I tap my temple again. "Told ya. All up here."

All he can do is glower at me like I've spoiled his appetite. I'm about to let a snide comment slip out when someone latches on to my shoulders from behind.

Ellis is shaking me, laughing, but when I look back at him, there are tears streaming down his face. "Jill!" he calls. "Jill! Get out here!"

His wife runs out of the kitchen, breathless, sprigs of auburn coming loose from her bandana. Ellis sweeps her up in his arms, laugh booming, her shoes a foot off the ground. She giggles and teeters when he sets her down again, and he turns to the dining room to address all the people staring at him.

"I just got a call," he says. "And I'm glad you're all with me to hear the news." He takes a deep breath, his grin stretching impossibly wide. "You're the people who've known me since I was only a kid digging for worms at Black Cat Lake and climbing Harriet's Oak, dreaming of nothing more than speaking and being heard."

I wonder if anyone else sees the lines around his mouth, from years and years of smiling—the marks of years of nothing but good news.

They're all beaming at him like he belongs to them. Like he's their golden boy, up on the stage, winning a spelling bee.

Ellis pauses, taking it in, and I grip the edge of Pastor Holland's table to keep myself from choking the information out of him.

"Let me tell you," Ellis says. "The world is gonna hear us now."

Us. They love that. They're already clapping and whistling and stomping their feet.

Before the anticipation reaches a fever pitch, Ellis holds his hands up for silence, and the room obeys. Not their golden child. Their king.

Finally, he announces, "I just found out I'm getting my own TV show!"

That's enough to whip the crowd into a frenzy, but he hurries on before they can drown him out. "And we're filming the first episode *right here in Jasper Hollow!*"

The room erupts. The tables shake with pounding fists, and the cheering is a roar that vibrates my skull. Pastor Holland has gotten to his feet, hollering through cupped hands, and then he's laughing, tears shimmering on his face. Ellis goes to him first— after he kisses his wife—and they hug each other.

I storm out of the Watering Hole, into the glaring sun of the Circle, but not a soul seems to notice.

Chapter 26

TO CELEBRATE ELLIS'S LATEST step toward conquering the world, he makes dinner reservations at a fancy restaurant an hour from Jasper Hollow. So fancy, I have to wear a dress.

Melody brings me a navy-blue one and hangs it on the knob of my open bedroom door. She's already wearing hers—her favorite color, dark green. The hem brushes her ankles, but halfway down her thigh, the fabric becomes sheer enough to see through. My eyes graze the ghost of her strong legs.

"Are you okay?" she asks me.

I've been in a foul mood all evening, pacing my room, growling obscenities into pillows, and even kicking the mattress every once in a while. I'm sure she heard me from across the hall.

"I'm fine," I say.

"Are you sure?"

Ellis is about to get richer from every lie he's ever told, and Mom is nowhere to be found. I've been lying in bed for the last half hour with the afternoon light slanting in, pulling my hair and trying to think of a way to stop feeling so powerless.

"I'm sure."

"If you're upset about Pastor Holland coming with us to dinner, you don't have to talk to him. I'll talk to you. And so will Neily," she adds. "We can pretend he isn't there."

I smile. "Thanks. I'm just tired from work."

"Oh."

She doesn't leave the doorway. Like she's got something else to say but doesn't know how.

"Well." I crawl out of bed. "I guess it's time to get dressed."

"Right." She shakes her head like she's trying to shake a thought. "I—"

She turns to leave, but then she comes back and holds something out to me.

I take it from her and turn it over in my hands. It's a metal feather, dull gold. A hairpin. "You can't wear an old piece of ribbon to a restaurant like this," she says, trying to sound snooty.

I smirk and touch the silky, red ribbon I've been wearing to keep my hair out of my eyes. "And why the hell not?"

"Because you just can't."

If I didn't know her, I'd say her cheeks redden because she's irritated by how clueless I am. But I'm almost certain that it's because she's completely mortified that she just gave me a gift.

I untie my ribbon and stand in front of my bathroom mirror. "Where did you find this?"

I've never used pins in my hair. But as soon as I think it, I realize that's not quite true—my dad gave me a set of purple flower clips in second grade that I wore every day for a year.

But I've never paid attention to how girls older than ten are supposed to wear them. Melody watches me make a few botched attempts before she comes up behind me and takes it from my hand. "Let me." She brushes my hair out of my face and arranges it into a neat little twist. "It was in an antique shop on the Circle. I got it for fifty cents. Not a big deal. I just—well, when I saw the feather, it made me think—"

"Of me."

"Of your name."

"Right."

"Right." Done with my hair, she drops her hands. "Get dressed. We're leaving soon."

She turns to go again, but I catch her wrist.

"Thank you, Mel," I say.

I notice in that moment when the light comes through the window and hits her face at just the right angle, her brown eyes flash the same shade of green as her dress.

"You're—" Her voice cracks, and she has to swallow. "You're welcome."

Then she pulls away from me, and I'm alone.

———

I can't remember the last time Mom and I ate inside a McDonald's, let alone a real restaurant. And I've never been within spitting distance of the kind of place Ellis takes us to.

The round tables are all draped with wine-red cloths that brush the shining wood floor like the hems of ball gowns. The walls are aged brick, and glittering chandeliers drip from the ceiling. A woman in the corner plays a sleek, black piano while waiters flit around the room in pressed white shirts with collars and red ties that match the tablecloths. It seems like one of them was hired for the sole purpose of brushing crumbs off people's tables.

I'm always on the other side of the window when it comes to elegant places like this. But somehow, here I am. And I didn't even have to sneak in. I almost want to be excited.

Our waiter starts reciting some things from the menu too fast for me to keep up. And Melody just kicked me under the table for the third time. After the fourth, I turn to her and snap, *"What?"*

With an exaggerated sigh, she takes the cloth napkin folded on the table in front of me, unfurls it, and places it in my lap. I glance around and see that I was the only one who hadn't done it yet.

"Oh," I say.

"It's pronounced *thank you*," she whispers with a half smile, which I mirror.

"I guess I deserved that."

But I can't even fake a smile once Ellis starts talking.

"We've been trying to get the green light on the show for months, but I didn't want to tell anyone until it was a sure thing. We've already got a name and everything. *By Example*. You know, like leading by example? It's perfect, isn't it? I think it's just perfect. I'm supposed to travel around the country and interview people who are overcoming the odds and doing positive things. You know, like blind people learning to paint and prisoners training service dogs. Real uplifting stuff."

Jill chokes on a sip of her water when he mentions traveling around the country—apparently, he hasn't run that by her yet. But Pastor Holland hangs on every word.

"Tell us about this first episode," he says. "The one you're filming in Jasper Hollow."

"Well, it's really going to be something. We want it to be an annual thing, where people from all over Ohio can come and celebrate."

"Celebrate what?" Neil asks before he shoves half a buttered roll in his mouth.

"Letting go. Moving on. Leaving the past behind to start working toward a brighter future. I'm going to give a speech, maybe sign some books—"

"People will come from all over Ohio for that?" I blurt.

He chuckles, leaning back in his chair. "Well, I'm always flattered by the support I get. I mean"—he glances at Jill—"remember how many tickets sold for my last tour? I was just blown away. It was a real blessing, but I'm not sure what I've done to deserve it."

I don't think I ever fully understood the term *humblebrag* until just now.

"It's going to be a kind of ceremony," he goes on. "Once it gets dark, everyone is going to line the streets with candles. They'll all get little slips of paper to write down one thing they want to let go of, and then they'll burn the papers. It's symbolic, you see? And that's when I'll give my speech. I think all those candles will look real nice on camera, don't you?"

It's a good thing someone interrupts before I can tell him a better place to put his candles for the camera.

A man in a black suit pumps Ellis's hand with both of his, and after a minute, I figure out that he's the owner of the restaurant and that they've known each other for years. When Ellis tells him the news, the man claps his hands and whispers something to a passing waiter. A minute later, a complimentary bottle of champagne arrives at the table. And then the adults are toasting and laughing and exchanging news.

I zone out because it's the only way to keep myself sane. Somehow, the conversation must have turned to the piano, because the owner asks Ellis, "When is the last time you played?" And then they go sit on the bench together and pound out an upbeat duet, Jill and Pastor Holland standing on either side of them, laughing and clapping.

"This is unnatural," I say to no one in particular. "Isn't this unnatural?"

"He's good at making himself at home." Melody shrugs and takes a sip of her water. "People like him. They can't help it."

Neil looks over the menu, like he hasn't even noticed that his father is serenading the whole restaurant. "You should get the filet," he says to me.

I find it on my own menu. *"Forty-five dollars?"*

He looks embarrassed all of a sudden.

"Is it a giant steak?"

"No. You get two sides with it, though."

"I don't think those are included in the price," Melody says.

"Oh."

"Quit bitching and order it," Melody snaps, cutting herself a piece of bread. "You aren't paying for it."

I glare at her for being a spoiled, rich brat. But she's right. So I order the filet. And mashed potatoes, green beans, and crab-stuffed mushrooms.

I glance at the piano to make sure the adults aren't paying attention before I filch Ellis's half-empty glass of wine and refill it from the open bottle on the table. Melody gasps and snatches for it. "You can't—"

I hold it out of reach and warn her, "Touch it, and I'll tell your mother you pushed me into that lake on purpose."

I'm bluffing, and she knows it. But she doesn't want to risk causing a scene and ruining her dad's big night. So she settles back in her chair with a scowl and looks the other way.

I guzzle the first glass without pausing for breath, getting a dry burn down my throat. It's not bad, but honestly, I miss the cheap stuff I'm used to—the kind they sell for eight dollars a bottle at Kroger that tastes like juice.

I pour another glass, then offer the bottle to Neil, and he shakes his head at first, but then he agrees to just a sip.

"Neil!" Melody hisses, but he does it anyway, and the way his face screws up at the taste makes me laugh.

"Bitter."

"Maybe you've got to be a little bitter to enjoy it," I say.

"Or twenty-one," Melody grumbles.

"Christ. I don't know anybody who needs a drink more than you do."

It must have come out meaner than I meant it to, because she looks at me like I've slapped her. "You think I'm too uptight."

"It was a joke—"

"You think I'm boring."

"When the hell did I say that?"

She stares at me for a long moment, biting her lip. Then she grabs the glass from my hand.

"Mel, hold on—"

She tips the wine down her throat, emptying the whole thing in a few swallows. Her mouth pinches at the taste, just a little, but she fights to hide it, her eyes on mine the whole time. A challenge.

She moves to pour another glass, and I stop her with my hand on her wrist. "One is plenty."

"You've had two."

"This isn't the first time I've had a drink."

"Mel, maybe you shouldn't—" her brother starts.

"If Phoenix can take it, so can I," she says, pouring another glass.

Melody is a handsy drunk.

She keeps hugging her brother and braiding and unbraiding my hair. I'm in the middle of asking her how she's feeling when she nods very seriously, tracing the cusp of my ear with her finger. Neil laughs, and she turns to him and does the same thing to his nose. When she starts running the smooth curve of her knuckle over my bottom lip, I have to take both her hands and force them into her lap, because after nearly an hour, the adults are walking back toward us.

I already hid the empty wine bottle under the table.

Ellis orders another, and he and his wife have a glass each, but when the waiter tries to pour one for Pastor Holland, he holds his hand over it and says, "A man's judgment is poor enough without it, don't you think?" Which sends Melody into a fit of giggles so intense that Neil and I both have to kick her ankles to make her shut up.

Jill rolls her eyes at Pastor Holland and signals for the waiter to top off her own.

Neil stands suddenly, loosening his tie, and announces, "I'm going to the bathroom."

The adults hardly notice him, busy laughing at something Ellis just said. He's at the height of his charm right now, telling jokes and talking with his hands, captivating people from a few tables over who seem to recognize him. I'm the only one who sees Neil walk in the opposite direction of the bathroom.

He slips out the front door just as a man is about to walk through it, but Neil takes him by the shoulders and pushes him back. He nods his head reasonably, calmly, while the man tries to shove him off.

I glance at Melody, who's too busy playing with the springs of her mother's curls to pay attention to me, or her brother, so I sneak quietly from the table.

When I step outside, the man is pacing the parking lot, rubbing the stubble on his face and muttering something, listing to one side like he's drunk. The valet politely pretends nothing is happening, standing behind his little podium while he watches from the corner of his eye.

"I'm sorry, Uncle Jameson," Neil says. "I think Dad just wanted a small, quiet dinner tonight, that's all. I don't think he meant to leave you out. Really."

"He's a spineless goddamn *son of a bitch*," Jameson growls, shoving Neil. "He wouldn't be here if it wasn't for me, you know that?" he says, pounding his chest with his fist. "Ask him what I've done for him. Ask him!"

"I will, Uncle Jameson, but you need to—"

"Get in your car," I say. "I'll drive you home."

Both of them turn to look at me where I stand on the sidewalk, my hands braced on my hips.

"You don't have to do that, Phee," Neil says at the same time Jameson sneers, "Shut up, bitch."

Neil shoots a glare at him. "I'll take him home," he says.

I shake my head, walking toward them. "You need to go back in there and be with your family."

Neil dips his mouth toward my ear and whispers, "I don't think that would be . . . safe. He's pretty drunk."

I laugh. "You don't need to worry about me."

He shrugs, offering a lopsided grin. "Maybe not. But I need to be the one to take him home."

After a moment, I nod. "Okay. I'll stay with him while you go tell your parents."

I watch Neil jog inside, and the second the door closes behind him, I hold out my hand to Jameson. "Keys," I say. Jameson eyes me for a moment before he looks at the restaurant again—through the glass window, at his brother and his beautiful family, celebrating yet another victory while Jameson is stuck on the outside.

I snatch the keys from his pocket while he's distracted, and then I grab him by the wrist and tow him to the car.

"He wouldn't be here if it wasn't for me," he says again. The anger in his voice has faded.

"I know he wouldn't," I answer, softly.

We pull out of the parking lot before Neil ever makes it back.

*T*he baby was born in the quiet hours of the morning, a few days after Nina's seventeenth birthday. He weighed just over eight pounds. He had a tuft of soft, black hair and a small birthmark on his left cheek the size of her pinky nail. Nina named him Bailey.

His grandfather didn't come to see him. Her father had sent her to live with Aunt Janet and Uncle Arnold months ago. They both stood over her bed with fidgety smiles, hands clasped behind their backs and their eyes averted. But they relaxed when it was their turn to hold the baby. They huddled over him and poked at his puckered mouth and made soft little noises.

Nina didn't know exactly what she was supposed to feel about the baby, the little bundle that had caused her so much trouble, but she found it impossibly easy to smile at him, so pink and fragile in her arms.

But he wasn't enough to dispel the sourness that had clung to her since her father had made her leave home. Since her pregnancy had started showing.

She'd never gotten used to the staring or the whispers, people saying, So young *and,* What a shame. *Even the nurses hissed into each other's ears. Nina made her face blank, but she couldn't make herself feel blank.*

For the first two weeks after her father sent her away, she'd called him every day, even after it became clear that he wouldn't answer. Then she settled for leaving him messages—about how Aunt Janet and Uncle Arnold spoke to her like a stranger at the bus stop. About how she felt so sick all the time and her whole body hurt. About how scared she was because she'd heard how painful having a baby would be.

God, it had hurt. Even more than she had expected. And maybe her father being there wouldn't have made it hurt any less, but she would have liked it if he'd been there to hold her hand and let her cry.

But he hadn't said he would send her away forever. He just didn't want the people she had known all her life to see her that way. He'd been trying to protect her, she knew. And now that the baby was here, he'd let her come back. She was certain. Looking down at her child, she knew that this is what she must have looked like to her father the first time he held her.

He wouldn't abandon her. No matter what she did, he couldn't do that.

She used the hospital phone to try to call him, but this time, a cold, anonymous voice informed her, The number you have dialed has been disconnected.

She tried again three more times. Listened to the same recording three more times.

Then she tried calling the church. It was Sunday, and he always got there early. But one of the female volunteers answered.

"Can I speak to Pastor Holland?"

There was a long pause on the other end. "Is this Nina?"

Nina cleared her throat before she answered, "Yes."

"It's Jill. Jill Bowman. It's so good to hear from you, sweetheart. I've been so worried. How are you doing?"

With just a little hesitation, Nina told her that she'd had the baby. Jill congratulated her, sounding sincere, asking a million questions about what he looked like and how big he was.

"Is my dad there?" Nina asked.

Another long pause. "I think he just needs a little more time. I'm sorry, Nina."

Nina swallowed, afraid she wouldn't be able to speak.

"Ellis has tried talking to him about letting you come home," Jill continued. "Many times."

"Oh."

"Your father hasn't budged yet, but he's going to keep trying."

Nina knew she was supposed to say thank you, but she still couldn't bring herself to speak.

"It's just—well, honestly, I feel kind of responsible. Ellis feels awful. We should have kept a tighter leash on him."

Nina stuttered, "On—what?"

"You know," Jill said, her voice dropping to a whisper. "On Jameson."

"Jameson," Nina repeated, still not understanding.

"Right."

Jameson.

"Ellis told me everything, sweetheart."

Nina knew that couldn't be true. If Ellis had told her everything, they would be having a very different conversation.

"What exactly did he say?"

There was another pause, and Jill sounded embarrassed when she spoke again. "He said he caught you and Jameson in the cabin. And, when pressed, Jameson came clean to your father."

Nina felt as if she were choking.

"He should have known better, Nina. And we're going to make sure he pays some kind of child support."

Jameson? Jameson?

"Ellis and I will keep talking to your daddy. I've been praying for you every night, Nina. I hope you've been praying, too."

"I have," Nina whispered. "Has—has Jameson told anyone else?"

The beat of silence that followed told her he'd already lied to everyone in Jasper Hollow.

She called him next. She was so angry, her body shook with it, and it scared her, how everything she felt now seemed to be too big for her body, like if this went on much longer, then she might just shatter to pieces. She thought of how much everyone would love that, if they overwhelmed her out of existence, and it made her anger burn even hotter.

When Jameson answered the phone, she could hardly speak. She could only say, "Why?"

Jameson sounded self-conscious on the other end, like that one word was enough for him to feel the rage and the hurt boiling inside her. He was probably running his fingers through his hair, the same way his brother did whenever he was nervous, Nina thought. "Ellis said this is the best way to protect you, Nina," Jameson said. "To protect both of you. He told me your dad would never let you come back if he found out you were sleeping with a married man."

"But it's a lie," Nina growled. "My father won't forgive me if I keep telling lies."

223

"You think this is easy for me?" Jameson said, his voice cracking with desperation. "Everybody hates me now for knocking up the preacher's daughter. I'm doing this for you!"

"You're doing this because your brother told you to."

"This is the only way to keep his family together and maybe convince your dad to let you come back home. Don't be so stubborn, Nina. Just let me help you. Just let me take care of it, and everything will be fine."

Chapter 27

I'M NOT SUPPOSED TO be here.

I know I'm not supposed to do anything until I hear from Mom. But Melody told me at the Dawn Festival that Jameson kept some things from the cabin, which might mean he could have something useful. And if I've already gotten it for Mom by the time I see her again, then maybe that'll soften the blow when I tell her Ellis's latest good news.

Jameson is sullen the entire way back to Jasper Hollow, slumped against the door, only speaking to me when we start winding up Mattie Mountain and get to a fork in the road, and I ask him, "Right or left?"

"Left," he mumbles.

I lower my window to let the warm night and pine-spiced air roll over us.

Jameson's house is a remnant of the old Jasper Hollow, before Ellis *saved* it. The Jasper Hollow from Mom's stories. The windows are boarded over. Every inch of the yard is covered by rusted frames of old cars, stripped of their wheels and most of their paint, weeds sprouting from their busted windshields. A foldout chair sits on the sagging porch, surrounded by an army of empty brown bottles—enough alcohol to send most people to the hospital, but he managed to drive all the way to the restaurant just to cuss out his brother.

He rolls out before I even put the truck in park, landing on his knees in the gravel, then draws himself up with all the dignity he can muster and staggers toward the front door. I follow him in.

The phone is already ringing. Jameson ignores it, flopping down on the couch and closing his eyes. After three more rings, it cuts off, but it starts up again a minute later, and Jameson growls, *"Make it stop."*

When I answer it, Jill is on the other end, sounding worried. "You made it all right?"

"Just fine."

"He didn't bother you, did he? I really wish you had let Neil go."

"No, I'm fine. No issues."

"We're on our way, but we're stuck in traffic. It might be another hour before we can pick you up. Are you sure you'll be okay?"

"I'm fine, Jill. Really. Thanks."

When I hang up, Jameson is snoring, half on the couch and half off it. I poke his shoulder to make sure he's really sleeping before I start looking through his things.

His yard tipped me off, but a few seconds of looking around the inside of his house confirms it—Jameson is a hoarder. He's got five mismatched lounge chairs jammed into his living room, even though I'm pretty sure he doesn't get many visitors. There are towering stacks of newspapers and catalogs. A bike in the kitchen with a twisted wheel. Boxes full of baseball cards, Little League trophies, and old clothes. A litter box in the hallway, even though I haven't seen any cats. A cabinet with a shotgun.

The place is cramped and cluttered and dirty. The exact opposite of Ellis's. I'm sure people shake their heads and wonder how two brothers could wind up living such different lives. But I might understand it a little better than most.

This is how I think it is for Jameson—he had his path laid out before him when he was a teenager. He was never as smart or ambitious or athletic as Ellis, so he had no real future prospects aside from staying in Jasper Hollow, marrying a nice girl—maybe even the preacher's daughter. He'd get a decent job at one of the local places because even though no one liked him as well as his brother, they liked him well enough.

But when he took the fall for Ellis, this town that had been his home no longer welcomed him.

Ellis should be grateful, but it was clear at the Watering Hole that he can hardly stand to look at Jameson. He can't hide his brother away in the little box where he kept Mom's bow, a memory that he can take out only when it's convenient. No, his brother is a living, breathing reminder of his shame, parading right out in the open, even if no one else recognizes it.

Jameson has no friends left. No family. Just this mess of a house. I understand what it's like to want to build the life that you think you deserve. To surround yourself with useless things, just to feel like you have a place in the world. To take ownership of what little you can.

Unfortunately for me, all this junk makes it really, really hard to figure out what I need.

Look for something that might remind Ellis of me, Mom had said. The manuscript had the desired impact on Ellis, but she wants to take it a step further. I suggested using the bow somehow, but she's decided to keep that for herself. So I need to find something else in this mess that we can use.

My heart starts beating too fast to think clearly, a combination of nerves and rising panic that this was a wasted risk.

When Mom finally comes to me for news, all I'll be able to tell her is that Ellis is about to be a whole lot richer, that there's no fix for the way he hollowed her out, that I can't save her.

I start pulling on closet doors, rifling through shelves of medicine, towels, and blankets. Then I open one near the front of the house and meet a wall of dark that sparkles with floating specks of dust, and when I step into it, I nearly trip down a flight of stairs.

It's a basement. I put one foot on the first step and wince at the way it creaks. But I can still hear Jameson snoring in the living room, so I hurry down the rest of the way.

The floor is concrete and sheeted in a thick layer of slippery grime. The only light is a single, naked bulb hanging from the ceiling. The small space is cluttered with boxes, crates, and trash bags. Immediately, I start digging.

I don't have all night to look, so I go through everything with frantic speed, holding up objects to the dim light and tossing them aside. There's an assortment of car parts, old appliances, broken furniture, and boxes of magazines and stained paperwork. I don't bother to put anything back where I found it—it's so chaotic down here, I doubt Jameson will notice what I've displaced.

Jill said that traffic might give me an hour before they get here, but that's not a guarantee. Each minute that slips past, my hands get slicker with sweat and my heartbeat crawls up my throat. I come up with excuses that I can give if anyone catches me down here, but not one of them is convincing.

I notice that the things closest to the stairs appear to be the least worn. It would make sense that the stuff near the back wall would be the oldest, and the last time Jameson had anything to do with Mom was years ago, when they were teenagers. I focus there.

Stacked under a few crates is a box so aged that it looks like it'll fall apart at the seams if I try to pick it up. I rifle through and find that it's full of framed photographs. Some black-and-white wedding pictures of people I assume are his parents. Some school portraits of Jameson and Ellis.

And then I find something that makes me take a breath so sharp that I suck in dust and have to swallow down a coughing fit, eyes watering.

It's a drawing of a sunflower on the back of a receipt. I'd recognize Mom's artwork anywhere.

It's still in the frame. I pick it up, gently, reverently. She only told me about it once, in a story about how she and Ellis had gotten drunk and she'd drawn this for him, not long before their relationship ended.

But Jameson is the one who ended up keeping it.

I don't have time to consider what that means, because then someone says from right behind me, "You aren't supposed to be here."

For a second, I can't breathe. Then I turn and wrap Mom up in my arms.

"Quiet. *Quiet,*" she snaps. She grabs my shoulders, nails pinching, and holds me away from her. Her eyes are too sunken, her cheekbones too sharp, her skin so pale, it looks gray. There seems to be less and less of her every time we meet, and I wonder if there's going to be anything left by the time this is over.

"Are you eating enough?"

"Don't worry about me," she says in a hard voice that isn't open for discussion. I close my mouth. "This isn't the time to be losing your head."

"You left me."

She sighs. "It was only a few days, darling."

"But—"

"You need to trust me. That's the only way we can make this work."

She looks into my face for a long moment, pressing her lips together like she wants to say something else. But she doesn't.

"How did you know I was here?" I ask.

"I told you I'd be watching. And I also remember telling you not to do anything like this without talking to me."

"But you said—"

She turns her sharp eyes on me again. "Stop pretending you did this to help. You did this to prove something."

I look down at my boots and bite the inside of my cheek.

But then I square my jaw and meet her eyes. "Ellis is getting his own TV show," I tell her.

I can see the way she flinches, like someone shoved a knife between her ribs. I knew it would hurt her, and I planned to be more tactful about it, but maybe there's a tiny bit of me that still resents the way she abandoned me.

She shakes off the information, saying, "We'll talk about this later." Then she shifts her focus to the framed drawing in my hands. Her breath catches when she sees it, like she wasn't quite prepared. She reaches for it with unsteady fingers, like she's reaching toward the girl she was when she drew it. But she stops just short.

"We need to get out of here," she says.

I follow her up to the main floor. Mom pauses at the top of the stairs, listening for the steady rattle of Jameson's breathing. Then she walks slowly, quietly, to the front door. I glance at Jameson when we pass through the living room, still sprawled on the couch, his head hanging over the armrest and his handsome face turned to the ceiling, his mouth open vulnerably.

Mom gets the front door open quietly but not soundlessly, and I look over my shoulder again. When I'm certain we haven't woken him up, we both step carefully onto the front porch. Mom pulls the door closed behind me, and then we're free.

She brought the van with her—I can just barely see the back end of it through the branches, where she hid it in the trees. I'm looking at it when I take my first step down the stairs.

My foot lands just half an inch too far, and my heel comes down on the edge of the step.

I slip.

I fling my hands out to steady myself, and Mom rushes forward to catch me, her arms around my waist. She steadies me, and I manage not to fall.

But I drop the drawing.

The frame hits the edge of the bottom stair, and the glass shatters.

Loud enough to wake Jameson.

Mom says, "*Go.*"

The glass in the frame is mostly destroyed, but the sunflower drawing is still stuck inside, so I scoop it up, and we make a run for the van. We're just a few yards from it when I hear Jameson's door bang open.

I fling the van's back doors wide and toss the drawing in, and I'm about to jump in after it when Jameson yells from his front porch, his voice numb with shock, "Nina?"

He recognizes her.

Shit shit shit shit shit, he recognizes her.

The van's wheels are already spinning, and I have to throw myself in before I'm left behind. The tires catch, and then we're tearing back down the mountain, and I wrench the doors closed behind me.

It takes me a few tries to crawl to the passenger seat because I slam into the walls every time we hit a sharp turn.

A horn blares. I whip my head around and see Jameson's truck catching up to us, swerving around a curve.

"*Shit,*" I hiss.

Mom is already going as fast as she can without sending us over the side of the mountain, and maybe we'll be able to stay ahead of him for a while longer, but once we get to town, someone is bound to notice and call the police. And once the police get involved, this is all over.

"Mom?"

She keeps her eyes on the road. Thinking.

"We have to stop," I say. "He recognized you. We have to talk to him. Maybe we can convince him not to tell anyone. It's our only option."

She doesn't answer.

"Mom—"

Then she takes a sudden right and slams on the brakes.

"What are you doing?"

The nose of the van is up against the mountain, the tail still sticking out into the road.

The street behind us lights up, Jameson coming on fast.

Then Mom steps on the gas.

The van hurtles backward, and I slam forward, busting my forehead against the dashboard. The flash of pain between my eyes is enough to blind me for a few seconds. But I hear everything.

The van rams into Jameson's truck, and the sound is so loud, it fills my skull. The windows shatter, metal screeches against metal, and the whole world quakes around me. The last time I heard this sound was when we crashed the van through my father's garage door, the night we ran away.

I reach for her, because I'm certain that we're about to plunge over the edge.

But we don't. Jameson does.

We slide to a stop, and there's a flash of relief as the van stills, but then I can hear Jameson's truck rolling down the side of Mattie Mountain. On and on and on. And there's nothing for Mom and I to do except stare at each other and listen. The lights from the dashboard shine in her blue-black eyes.

When it's over, I step out of the car, legs trembling so hard, I fall. The first thing I see is the guardrail, split like a rope. By the time I crawl to the edge and peer down, Jameson's car has settled on a ridge.

The boy who kept Mom's drawing all those years, crushed like a tin can.

"Phoenix. Phoenix, get back in the car."

Mom's hands are on my shoulders, hauling me up. She shoves me into the passenger seat and slams the door. Then, just like that, we're on our way back to Jameson's house.

"I told you," Mom says. "I *told you*. You should have waited for me. I could have gotten it myself. This didn't need to happen."

If I open my mouth to answer her, I know I'll lose it. And I can't cry yet. If the Bowmans see tears on my face when they come to pick me up, they'll want to ask Jameson what he did to me.

Mom parks in front of his house—dark and silent, the front door still hanging open.

"Phoenix."

I look away from her, biting my trembling lower lip. Clenching my shaking hands.

She grabs me by the shoulders, gripping hard, like she's trying to wake me up from a dream. "Phoenix. Can you do this? I need to know if you can do this. Tell me the truth."

I nod.

She hugs me. I squeeze her middle, locking my hands behind her back, trying to keep the whole world steady.

"I'll check in on you soon," she says, smoothing her fingers over my hair. "It won't be much longer now."

"Until we go home?" I can't help it—my voice cracks on the last word.

She presses her forehead to mine, and her palm is cold when she cups the back of my neck. "Until we go home."

Chapter 28

THE BOWMANS PULL UP to Jameson's house just a few minutes after Mom drives away. I'm hugging myself, the wind whipping my hair and goose bumps rising on my legs. Jill rolls down the window, and I manage a smile for her. It's almost a relief, seeing her face. Not because it makes anything better, but because the concerned look she gives me feels like getting tucked into bed. *I know you're tired. Rest. I'm here.*

"Everything okay?" she asks.

I nod. "Just fine."

"No trouble?"

I shake my head. "He's inside. Asleep."

I climb into the back seat, where Melody has her head pillowed on her brother's knee, his jacket pulled over her shoulders.

"I'm sorry," I say. "For taking off without you."

He shrugs, mouth quirking. "Just glad you're okay," he says in a whisper so he won't wake Melody.

Ellis turns in the driver's seat to look at me while I pull my seat belt on. "Thanks for taking care of my idiot brother, Phoenix," he says. "I owe you one."

He eases his SUV down the mountain, back toward the house. Neil puts on a pair of headphones, and I can faintly hear his music. I lean my head against the window and close my eyes, pretending to sleep so Ellis and Jill won't ask me any more questions.

I hear Jill whisper from the front seat, "If Jameson had done something to her—"

"He wouldn't," Ellis said.

"What makes you so sure? After how he treated Nina?"

I peek through my lashes to see Ellis's hands tense on the wheel.

"That was all consensual," he said.

"As far as we know. None of that ever added up to me. She never seemed all that serious about Jameson, even when they were dating."

"You don't have to be serious to accidentally get pregnant."

"I know it. It's just—she worshipped her father. I never would have guessed that she'd so boldly flout his rules. And then everything that happened after, the way she—" Jill bites her lip, unable to finish the thought. "I've just always thought that there was more to that story."

She doesn't know how right she is.

It's all making sense to me now, the way Jameson seemed to repel everyone around him. If Jill thinks he forced himself on Mom, she probably isn't the only one.

Which means Ellis has stood by all these years and—to save his own skin—let everyone believe that his brother was a rapist.

The fortune-teller told me she could sense the pain in my mother. And I think I could sense it in Jameson, too. I just didn't recognize it for what it was until this moment.

It's not good to live with that burrowing in your bones, she told me. *It rots you. Turns you mean.*

Maybe that's what had happened to the boy from Mom's stories. Maybe that's why his smile had become so sharp, his every word a thorn. Because when people treat you like a monster for so long, sometimes the only thing to do is act like one.

I hold it together until we make it back to the house. I wait until after Ellis hugs all of us good-night, thanking us for celebrating with him. After I help Neil guide his sister to her room, tuck the blankets in around her, and brush a stray curl behind her ear. After I squeeze Neil's hand and tell him I'm sorry again.

I wait until I close my bedroom door behind me, shut off the lights, and crawl into bed before I press my face into my pillow and cry like I'm a little girl again, the way I used to when Mom tolerated that kind of thing, before it ever occurred to me that I had to pretend to be strong.

My breath catches when the door opens suddenly, light from the hallway flooding in. I sit up and wipe at my face with the backs of my hands.

Melody leans in the doorway. "Phoenix? What's wrong?"

"Nothing. Go back to sleep."

She comes all the way into the room, closing the door behind her, and climbs into my bed without an ounce of the hesitation sober Melody would have. I feel her hand on my wet face. "Liar."

I try for a laugh, but it comes out more like a sob.

"Tell me what's wrong."

"I'm just a little homesick."

It's the easiest lie because it's not exactly a lie.

"Oh." She leans back against the headboard. "Do you miss Indiana?"

For a second, I've got no idea what she's talking about, until I remember that that's where I told the Bowmans I used to live. With my fake, dead grandmother.

"Maybe homesick is the wrong word. I don't know what I mean."

"Do you miss a person?"

I shrug, settling in beside her. "Maybe."

"Something else?"

My chest aches thinking about Jameson, but there are a million other thoughts buzzing in my head, like moths pinging against a porch light, weaving in and out of each other so fast that you can't tell one from the other.

I need to see Mom again. I need to sleep in a bed that's mine. I need to feel, for once in my life, like I'm exactly where I should be. Like there's a safe space to curl up inside, where no one can hurt me. And where I don't have to hurt anyone else.

"I guess I miss something I've never really had, if that makes any sense."

She rests her head on my shoulder. "It doesn't."

I smile, letting my eyes close. "I guess you wouldn't get it. You've got your big house. Your nice family. Your perfect town."

I was mostly teasing her, but I can just make out her scowl in the dark. She fidgets against me, like I've cut through her pleasant

238

buzz, and her usual cat-drenched-in-water mood peeks through. "It's not all pretty views and quaint festivals."

"What? You're too good for small-town life?"

She doesn't answer for a while, so long that I think she's fallen asleep. But then she says, "Pastor Matthew started working at the church last summer, getting ready to take over for Pastor Holland when the time comes. Just a few days after a certain party that I'm sure you've heard all about by now. A party that was everybody's favorite topic for a while, like there isn't any hunger or genocide going on in the world to keep them occupied. And that Sunday, you know how Pastor Matthew started off his illustrious career as the spiritual guide of Jasper Hollow?"

I wince before she even says it.

"With a two-hour sermon on the dangers of letting teenagers stray too far from their parents, the decision-impairing qualities of alcohol, and the sanctity of marriage between a man and a woman."

"Ouch."

"I wasn't drunk. That's the only way anybody could make sense of it—by assuming I was too drunk to know what I was doing. But I knew."

I nod, her curls tickling the bottom of my chin.

"I could feel everybody I've known since I was a baby staring at me the entire service. Like my old violin teacher has any business thinking about my sex life." She lets a long breath out between her teeth. "*That's* small-town living."

I don't have any idea what to say to that. All I can offer is, "You're going to college in a couple of months."

"Yeah," she says. But she doesn't sound too reassured.

"You don't want to go?"

She thinks about it for a long time before she says, "I do. I hate this town. But that doesn't mean it's going to be easy to leave behind."

"Why not?"

"Because Mom helped Neil and me plant cucumbers in our backyard when we were eight. We've never been able to grow anything else, but we have cucumbers every year. And—well, there are a lot of cucumber plants in the world that probably look a hell of a lot better than ours, but there's only one cucumber plant in the entire world that Mom helped Neil and me plant when we were eight." She glances up at me, her eyes shining in the dark. "Does that make sense?"

I give her a soft smile before I answer, "No." She laughs and buries her face against my shoulder.

We stay like that for a while before she whispers, "I hope you find a place where you feel at home someday."

"Thanks, Mel. I hope you do, too."

She curls her body against mine, and I want to lean into the warmth of her, but I make myself pull away. "We need to get you back to your room."

"But I want to sleep with you."

Her curls tumble over her shoulders, and I can almost feel how soft they would be tangled in my fingers. I can just make out the fullness of her lips.

I feel a shiver down my legs. "Not tonight."

She pouts, letting me take her hand and pull her to her feet. "Why not?"

"Because you're drunk, and you'll be mortified about it in the morning."

"Yeah? What the hell do you know?"

I know that even if she weren't drunk, this would be wrong. Because she thinks she's started getting to know me, that she's learned enough about me to decide she likes me. But it's all based on lies.

She crawls into her bed like a headstrong child, pulling roughly at the sheets and settling back into the pillows with a *hmph*. I tuck the comforter around her shoulders.

"Sober Melody wouldn't just crawl into bed with me like that," I say.

"Even if she heard you crying?"

"Even then, I think."

She turns onto her side, facing me. "I'm not so sure about that. I have secrets, too, you know."

I giggle. "Oh, yeah?"

But she doesn't crack a smile. Instead she says, very seriously, "Really. I've got one so big, it could ruin everything."

I'm about to remind her that the whole lesbian thing isn't exactly a secret, but then she says, "I'm not even sure if it's true."

I frown. "What do you mean?"

She clamps her lips shut.

"Melody . . . is the secret about you?"

Her mouth still sealed tight, she shakes her head.

My heart pounds harder. "You can tell me. Is it your mom? Your brother? Your—your dad?"

She shakes her head again. "I don't want to ruin everything."

"Mel—"

But she's got both her hands over her face now, and I'm afraid she's going to start crying. And if I know anything about drunks, it's that most of them don't know how to cry quietly. I shush her and run my hand over her hair, before she can wake up the whole house. "Okay, it's okay, we'll talk about it tomorrow."

I coax her into closing her eyes, running my fingers through her hair and whispering snatches of songs. When her breathing finally evens out, I shut off the light, and with one last look at her, the moonlight coming through the window and playing on her blond curls like they're ripples in water, I go back to my own room. Alone.

When I close the door behind me, I press my back to it and slide down to the floor, threading my fingers through my hair until I feel pinpricks of pain all over my scalp. And, unbidden, a handful of lines from Ellis's books pop into my head. Believe it or not, he's written a lot about feeling guilty.

Forgiving yourself is vital to making things right.

Learn from the past, then let it go.

No one is entirely innocent.

But I know those were only words he used to comfort himself. If he really knew anything about life, he would have written something more like this:

There is no outrunning it. There is no reasoning with it. There is no begging it for mercy. Punishment always comes, even if there's no one left to give it.

Chapter 29

THE NEXT MORNING, I'M drawn out of bed and into the kitchen earlier than usual by the smell of the mushroom omelets Neil is cooking. Jill has the morning off from the restaurant, but she's never content with standing still. She washes the dishes as Neil finishes with them. Melody and I set the table while the air thickens with the heat of the stove, the sizzle of butter in the pan, and the smell of breakfast. Ellis sits at the table with coffee and a copy of the *Columbus Dispatch*, reading aloud snatches of the article that ran today announcing his television show. I tune him out.

Whenever I imagine the home Mom and I are going to make for ourselves—and I've imagined it a hundred times over—I always picture a kitchen. Never one as nice as this, but with the same sounds and warmth and feeling, both of us bustling from the cabinets to the counter to the table, weaving around each other with plates of homemade food piled high, brushing hips, talking easily. The kind of kitchen where the clatter of plates and the jingle of silverware and the rhythm of laughter all knit together to make a song that's better than anything on the radio.

It's a simple thing, but sometimes, it seems like too much to hope for.

When the food is ready, we all sit down at the table. While we're eating, Jill starts telling stories about how well I'm doing in my job at the restaurant. She tells me how many customers have said nice things about me, how efficiently everything runs when I'm there, and despite myself, I feel my face flush with pleasure. Ellis is sitting beside me, and for just a moment, he covers my hand with his and says, "I'm glad you're settling in so well, Phoenix."

His hand is big and warm, and instead of the sickness I usually feel when he gets anywhere near me, there's something else that jolts through me. Something that scares me.

For a moment, with my hand engulfed in his, I feel safe.

I wonder if my own father used to hold it that way. He must have. Even though I'd forgotten, my hands remember. Even after I'd done my best to scrub my memory clean of Jonah, the landscape business owner in Virginia, there's a part of me that misses having a dad. The kind of dad Ellis pretends to be.

I look up to meet his gaze. But all at once, the warm look on his face morphs into surprise. Alarm.

"Watch—" he starts to say.

I turn my head to see what made his eyes get so big all at once.

And I duck and cover my eyes just in time.

There's an explosion of shattering glass and rushing air, and for half a second, I wonder if this is what it was like to be inside

Jameson's car when he rolled down the mountain, right before the frame crushed him.

Chairs clatter to the floor and dishes break. I glance up to see what crashed through the window.

The broken picture frame with the sunflower drawing.

It swings at the end of a thin rope, suspended at the apex of its arc, frozen in the air for just a second. It hovers a few inches above Jill's head.

Then the frame swings back out, spinning, toward the trees. The other end of the rope is tied to the branch of a big maple in the front yard.

Jill stands slowly, in shock, turning to look out the gaping hole where the window used to be. And then the frame swings back toward her.

Ellis tackles her just before it hits her. I hear the broken glass scatter where they land and see blood seep across the wood. Melody, crouched beside me, sees it, too. She scrambles to the floor, crawling toward her parents.

Neil gets there first, lifting his mother to her feet. Melody helps her father, grabbing his hands. I watch, opening my mouth and making noises that aren't quite words, like my tongue has been cut out. I shake my head, hurrying to the cabinet under the sink, where they keep the first aid kit.

The frame has lost momentum, spinning on the end of its rope like a tire swing. Neil tries to get Ellis to sit down so he can bandage him up. His sleeves are shredded, blood dripping down his forearms, but he brushes his son off and runs for the front door.

Melody's hands are shaking so hard that she can't get the

bandage unwrapped for her mother. I take it gently from her, peel the wrapper apart, and smooth it over Jill's bleeding forehead. While I do, I watch Ellis out of the corner of my eye.

He runs into the yard, and instead of going to the frame, he looks up, searching wildly for whoever is hiding up in the trees. Mom might still be crouching somewhere in the branches—it's the only place she could have let go of the frame from.

I hold my breath while he searches, weaving between the trunks, trying to see through the leaves. But she must be long gone, because he turns away in frustration.

"I'm fine, Mellie," Jill says while Melody tries to wash the blood off her mother's hands. Tries and tries, but she's still trembling hard all over, and she keeps dropping the washcloth, until her brother takes it from her and tells her, "I've got it. It's okay. Everyone's okay." But his own voice cracks.

Melody turns to me, her breath hitch, hitch, hitching. I gather her to me, holding her head against my shoulder. While her tears soak into my shirt, my eyes flick back to Ellis.

He grabs the frame in both hands to stop its spinning. And he's staring at it. Holding completely still, like his feet have grown roots that could hold him there forever.

He's staring at the sunflower Mom drew.

I see a flash of red writing in the frame that wasn't there before. I can't read it from this distance, but my guess is it's the same as what was on the pages of his manuscript.

Tell the truth.

If he had any doubts before, he has to know now.

She's back. And she's not leaving him alone until he gives her what she wants.

And he knows exactly what she wants. What she's always wanted.

Melody isn't holding back now, sobbing hard, eyes pressed to my collarbone, her arms tight around me and her fingers digging into the small of my back. I pat her between the shoulders to a steady rhythm and rock her back and forth like she's a child I'm trying to put to sleep.

The blood is already soaking through the bandage on Jill's forehead. Neil pulls a chair up beside her, holding a pair of tweezers, and sets to work on picking tiny grains of glass from the cuts on her palms. "I'm sorry," he says every time she flinches, his face wet and his voice thick. Like this is all his fault.

Jill keeps her lips pressed tight against the pain, only opening them long enough to reassure him, "I'm okay."

Nothing is going to stop me from ruining Ellis Bowman's life. But watching his wife and his son and feeling the way his daughter's whole body shivers against mine, I wish I could do it without ruining anyone else.

*I*n the time since Nina's father had sent her away to have her baby, the Bowmans had moved. She went to their old house first, on Mattie, and found it inhabited by a new family. But she knew exactly where to look next. Ellis had always told her it was his dream to rebuild in the same exact spot where Will Jasper's house had been, before it burnt down.

"Mr. Jasper's always been an inspiration to me," he told her once while they were talking over book edits at the restaurant after hours. "He built a whole town from nothing. He made himself into what he wanted to be, whatever it took." He'd tilted his head toward the tall restaurant windows, to the Circle and Harriet's Oak and the mountains. "And what a beautiful life he made."

Nina chugged up Clara Mountain in her aunt's rust-colored Pinto. She'd left Bailey with her aunt and uncle for the afternoon, telling them she was spending her day at the library to study for a history test.

Honestly, she was failing all her classes at this point. Even art. It was *hard to focus on things like formulas and poems, things that hardly seemed real to her, when the life in front of her eyes was collapsing.*

She knocked on the front door of the Bowmans' new house, the paint so fresh that she was surprised it didn't turn her knuckles poppy red.

Jill looked startled when she opened it, but she recovered quickly, squeezing Nina in a quick hug and waving her inside. "Ellis is getting ready to leave on a little business trip," she said, leading her to the kitchen. "They're interviewing him at a radio station in Columbus. Can you believe it? Who knew one little book could get so much attention?"

The twins were on a blanket on the kitchen floor, bigger now, hitting each other with stuffed animals. Both of them looked more like Ellis than Bailey did, with their yellow hair curling around their plump cheeks.

Jill was pouring Nina a glass of lemonade and asking her questions about her baby when Ellis walked in, pulling on his suit jacket. His hair was still wet from the shower, and he took a long drink of the coffee that Jill handed him.

"Have you seen my—" he started to say to his wife. But then he saw Nina sitting at his kitchen table and dropped his mug.

He caught it before it hit the floor, but he yelped, hot coffee scorching his hands, and dropped it again. It shattered, and the twins squealed with delight, like he'd done it just for them.

Jill rushed to soak a rag in cold water and wrap it around his hands. "Are you okay?"

"I'm fine."

Nina had been so angry since she'd talked to Jill on the phone, she didn't know if she'd even be able to form words when she saw Ellis. But now, she found a cold calm inside her, and she said, "I came to talk to Ellis about my father. Alone."

"Of course," Jill said, even though Nina had been telling, not asking.

Ellis nodded for a moment, chewing on the inside of his cheek. Not looking at Nina. But he clearly couldn't think of a way out of it, so he walked to his office without a word, and Nina followed.

He shut the door behind her and let out a deep breath. "Nina—"

"Don't. Just shut up."

To her surprise, he did.

He looked down at her with his big, blue eyes, and for a moment, she faltered. But then she said, "You're going to go to my father's house right now, and you're going to tell him the truth."

Ellis shook his head. "I don't see how that's going to—"

"It's the only way he'll let me come home. If he knows it wasn't Jameson. You're his favorite person in the whole world." Her voice wavered when she said it, but they both knew it was the truth. "If he knows that we did this together, maybe he'll think about forgiving us both."

"Maybe," he said. "But maybe not. Maybe you're trying to make me destroy my family for no reason. Have you thought of that?"

She clenched her jaw. "This isn't all my fault. You were part of it, too."

"Nina—"

"Does Dad still invite you over for chili every Wednesday night?" she asked quietly. "You sit in the backyard, don't you? Right under the shade tree, at the picnic table."

He ran both hands through his curls so hard, it looked like he'd pull them out.

"While I'm stuck at a house with people I hardly know, going to school with strangers. Raising our—"

He coughed to cover up the last word.

"You know I can't tell him," he said.

"Why not?"

"Because he'll be out for blood, Nina. I don't care how much you think he likes me. He'll ruin me."

"He wouldn't," Nina argued.

"You should hear the things he's saying to everyone about Jameson. He's convinced the whole town to freeze him out. And Jameson's not even married. Doesn't have children. Isn't twelve years older than you. I've been to your house so many times to beg him to stop, and he won't listen."

"And you don't feel bad letting your brother take the fall for what you did?"

"Of course I feel bad. But he doesn't have half as much to lose as I do. If your father finds out I was involved, there won't be any way of talking him out of it. My reputation will be destroyed. The restaurant will fail. The book will tank. I've got two kids to feed, Nina. Even if Jill gets her job back at the bakery, do you really think that'll be enough? And do you think—"

He choked on the words and had to start again.

"Do you think she'd ever speak to me again? Do you think I'd have a family, after everything's said and done? I just don't think you understand what you're doing, Nina. I really don't, or you wouldn't be asking this of me."

"You already took my family from me," she said.

"Jesus. Wake up, Nina. You're better off without Mason. He's a controlling, judgmental son of a bitch, too saintly for anybody to please. All right? You needed to get away from him anyhow."

Her hands curled into fists. "Don't talk about him like that."

"Move on. Take the baby and get as far from Jasper Hollow as you can and start over."

"He's my father. I need him to know the truth."

Ellis's brow furrowed. He looked into her face for a long moment, like he felt sorry for her. Like she was a backwoods lunatic. Like he didn't owe her a damn thing.

"I'm not telling him."

"Then I'll walk out that door and tell everybody in the Circle."

Ellis fell into his office chair with a sigh. "Nobody will believe you."

"They will after you take a paternity test."

"And why the hell would I do that?"

"Because I can ask a court to make you do it, if that's what I want."

Ellis's fidgeting hands froze in his hair. He looked up at her to see if she was bluffing, but it was true. She'd looked it up on a computer in the library.

He dropped his hands into his lap and looked away from her, out the window. "I need to think about this."

But she knew he was only saying that to make her go away. If she gave him more time to think, he'd find a way out of it. So she stood in front of his office door with her arms crossed over her chest, caging him in. She made herself stand very tall, the way her father always told her to do when she sang in church. If you want people to listen to you, really listen to you, you have to look like a force to be reckoned with. Even if you don't feel like one.

Jill knocked on the office door and told Ellis he was going to be late for his interview. But he didn't answer, and she went away.

"Fine," he said finally, his voice rough, like she'd strangled the word out of him. "But you need to give me time to talk to my wife about it first. I don't want her to find out from anybody but me."

"Tell me when you'll talk to him. Exactly when."

"Jesus," he said, clutching his head between his hands, speaking to his lap. "I'll tell Jill everything when I get back tonight. I'll speak to your father in the morning. If that's what you really want."

Nina nodded. She kept standing very straight, even though her knees wanted to buckle.

Tomorrow. She was going home tomorrow.

Chapter 30

WHILE MELODY AND I sweep glass off the floor and Neil and Jill duct tape a blue, plastic tarp over the gap where the kitchen window used to be, Ellis shuts himself up in his office. I hear the click of the lock behind him.

I linger in the doorway of the kitchen, the one closest to his office, and I can just make out his harried whispers. "Jameson, I know you're there. Pick up the goddamn phone."

Pause. Nervous knuckles rapping on his oak wood desk.

"*Jameson.*"

The phone slams against the table. Ellis growls, probably racking his hands through his pretty curls.

He dials the number again. Waits.

He thinks Jameson is ignoring him. But I know better. The phone is ringing in an empty house.

"I'm not messing around, little brother. I've tolerated you thinking you could hold this thing over my head long enough.

You don't have any power over me. Do you hear me? You don't want to play this game with me. You'll lose."

He's trying to delude himself into thinking that this is a prank Jameson is playing on him. That the girl he knew wouldn't be capable of something like this. But I know he doesn't really believe that.

He dials again. Mutters curses that I'm certain he'd never use in public. Fear has a way of corroding people down to their cores—to the truth of them.

Something slams against the office wall so hard, the house rattles.

"Honey?" Jill calls.

When he answers, he's restrained his fury just enough to sound normal. "I'm—I'm all right, sweetheart. Everything is all right."

A few minutes later, he storms through the kitchen, glass crunching under his shiny leather shoes, and hurries out the door, toward his car. Jill tries to run after him. "Ellis? Where are you going?"

He only pauses long enough to call back to her, "Don't tell anyone about this until I get back."

"But shouldn't I call—"

"*No* police," he says. A little too forcefully. Police would ask too many questions. Police would dig up secrets.

He swallows before he adds, "I don't think it's necessary yet. It was probably just a bad joke. I think—well, I know Jameson's still pissed at me about not inviting him to dinner, and I wouldn't put something like this past him. Don't call anyone until I talk to him."

"But what if—"

But Ellis has already ducked into the car and slammed the door. He peels out of the driveway and disappears down the mountain.

———

Ellis isn't home for dinner. We eat sitting on the living room floor, leaning our elbows on the low coffee table.

It's subtle, but I notice all of them glance at the windows every so often. I didn't realize until now that there are so many, giving us a view of the light dimming over the mountains, muting the colors like a veil.

Melody watches the table, like she knows something she isn't saying. But even if she has a guess about who's really responsible, there's no way it's the right one.

We wash the dishes after dinner, and Neil makes sure the tarp he put over the broken window is still secure. By full dark, Ellis still isn't home.

When I slip off to bed, Jill is pacing the living room, calling Ellis over and over again, leaving him messages. "I'm worried, Ellis. Even if it was Jameson, he really could have hurt someone. If you aren't home by midnight, I'm calling the police."

I slide my window open, waiting for Mom to come. I know she'll want to talk. But when I stop to listen, I hear something that makes me freeze.

Someone's cell phone ringing.

And then Ellis's soft curses as he picks his way through the dark woods. "Dammit, Jill." He pushes a button, and the rings go silent.

He must not have been able to find Jameson. So now he's searching the woods for Mom.

I kneel in front of the open window, mostly out of sight, and peer over the ledge to watch him stumbling through the trees that rock and hiss with the wind.

He looks like a man half-wild, his hair sticking up like he's been pulling it, his expensive shoes caked in mud, his shirt untucked and torn open at the collar, his voice a scratch against the wall of shadowy trees. "Nina. *Nina*."

He stares into the twined branches, which look like a maze of claws and teeth. If Mom hides inside it, she doesn't answer.

"Come on. Come talk to me."

The woods regard him coldly.

"I know you're here," he growls. "You wanted me to know, didn't you?" He throws his arms wide. "So come out and talk to me. Tell me what you want."

He knows what she wants—the truth.

"I can help you," he says. He ventures farther into the trees, reaching through the black like he'll snatch her by the hair and drag her into the glow of the house's lights. But he keeps his voice as soft as a lover's. "We can keep all this between us. I'm not mad. You know I'd never be mad at you. I just don't want to hurt Jill. I know you don't want to hurt her; she was always so good to you. Come on, Nina. Please. Just let me help you."

She won't risk talking to him, even if she wants to. But Ellis and I wait for an answer.

He listens for a full minute, walking deeper into the woods with the same terrifying quiet of a snake before it strikes.

Then he takes off into the shadows. He must have heard

something. I push the window open further and grip the frame, listening hard, trying to decide whether or not I should run after him.

A few minutes later, I hear a cry, and I almost throw myself toward it. But the voice isn't Mom's. Ellis curses, emerging from the trees alone. "God*dammit*, Nina!" He slams his fist into a tree, once, twice, then presses his forehead to the trunk and moans.

A strong wind sweeps over Clara Mountain, the leaves and branches churning into a frenzy of sound. The gust catches a shovel leaning against the house, near my window, knocking it over with a clatter.

Ellis whips his head around in my direction, and I dive out of sight, skitter across the floor, and slip into bed.

Did he see me?

I close my eyes and listen.

Heavy footsteps approach the open window, twigs snapping like little bones in their wake.

I make my breathing slow and deep. And no matter how much I want to, I don't let my eyelids flutter to steal a look at his face. I wonder if this is the moment—when he'll finally figure out that I am part of his problem.

And I know what Ellis does to his problems.

But after a few tense, silent moments, his phone rings again. And this time, he answers it.

"David?" he says. A name I don't know.

I hear his footsteps retreating from my window. Faintly, I catch him saying, "I'll be right there." And then he's too far away to hear.

I can't seem to make myself open my eyes—I'm trapped inside

myself, my heart ricocheting in my rib cage, my whole body shaking under the covers.

It takes me an hour to calm down, but not enough to fall asleep. So I just lie there, still waiting for a dream to steal me away or to wake up and realize that this world was the nightmare all along.

Then I hear a voice at the window that makes my eyes snap back open.

"Phoenix."

I bound out of bed. "You can't be here. He's looking for you. You need to hide."

Mom shakes her head, completely calm. "Phoenix. Do you trust me or not? Do I need to keep explaining myself to you?"

I bite my tongue.

"You have to keep it together. All right? Can you do that?"

I nod.

She wants to know how the Bowmans reacted to the chaos she—we—created. I tell her that even though Ellis suspects her, he did his best to convince his family that it was a prank Jameson was playing on them. I say that they're all still on edge.

"No one got hurt," I add.

Her face is blank again. I can't tell how she feels about that information. At best, she's trying to stay focused. At worst, she doesn't care.

"I'm working on the next part of the plan," she says. "I'll let you know when it's ready."

"It?"

Then I hear the front door open. Ellis's voice echoes through the house. "Jill?" he says. "Jill?"

His voice sounds off. Something is wrong.

Mom smiles a smile so chilling, I flinch away from her. And without another word, she turns and runs.

I make myself walk slowly to the living room. Jill is already there, gripping her husband's arms. "What is it? What's happened?"

I see Jill sweep her gaze over the room—over Melody in the kitchen doorway and Neil coming down the stairs and even me standing behind her. Taking inventory, making sure the important things are safe.

Ellis leans against the wall. His eyes are red but dry. His hands are unsteady. The tremor in his voice might be grief, but if my money were on it, I'd say it's got more to do with fear.

"I—David called and told me to come—"

It takes a few attempts for him to get the words out. But once he does, there's no mistaking them. And no going back.

"Jameson is dead."

Chapter 31

THIS TIME, ELLIS CAN'T talk Jill out of calling the police.

She sends us to our rooms to get dressed while we wait—it's half past midnight, and we're in our pajamas. I take my time, going to the bathroom to splash water over my face, trying to get a grip like Mom told me to.

When I come back out, Ellis and Jill are nowhere to be found, probably up in their room arguing. I debate eavesdropping when I see Neil and Melody are sitting next to each other at the kitchen table, their backs to me. And I hear Melody whisper to her brother, "Phoenix might have been the last person to see Jameson alive."

Of course Melody was the one to make that connection. She doesn't miss much.

I pause, then press my back against the wall beside the kitchen, out of sight.

"You think she had something to do with it?"

Melody is quiet for a moment. But then she says, "No.

Jameson was drunk. Really drunk. It was probably his own damn fault. An accident, like Dad said. But—"

"What?"

"I mean, she shows up here out of nowhere and all of this bad stuff starts happening. It would be naive to ignore that, right?"

Right.

"You really think she'd want to hurt us?"

She sighs. "Look, I don't want to believe it either." After a long pause, she adds, "Unless you think it's—"

"No," Neil says. "No."

Whatever she was about to say, it upsets him. He starts crying, quietly.

"I'm sorry, Neily, I just—"

"I can't listen to this right now," he says. "Uncle Jameson is *dead*, and you want to start throwing around accusations? Now?"

She shifts her chair closer to him, putting her arm around his wide shoulders.

"I can't believe this is even happening," he says. "This kind of stuff shouldn't happen."

"I know," she says.

———

Two policemen show up at the house a little while later—Officer Perkins and Officer McCormick.

They don't bother to question us separately. They sit beside each other on the living room couch while the rest of us pull in chairs from the kitchen. Officer Perkins tilts his head toward the broken window. "What happened there?"

Ellis waves his hand dismissively. "We think Jameson did it

this morning. He was really upset with me, you see. I saw him last night, and he was drunk out of his mind. Probably kept drinking through the night, came here, and on his way home he—he must have crashed."

The officers nod along, like it all makes perfect sense. Nobody would ever accuse Jameson of having good judgment, Perkins and McCormick included—they went to high school with him.

"Sounds about right," Perkins says. "We figured he was hammered and got himself into an accident. We sent some guys over to look at the car, and they found glass from Budweiser bottles."

"We'll still have to do a full investigation, either way," McCormick cuts in. "Gotta cross our t's and dot our i's, you know."

Ellis nods, putting his arm around his wife and pulling her closer. "You do what you have to do. Just make it quick. For my family's sake."

Ellis handles most of the talking, giving the officers a rundown of what happened that night—we went to dinner, Jameson showed up drunk and angry, and I drove him home.

That's when Officer McCormick turns to me.

"What happened when you took him home?"

I shrug. "He was quiet most of the way. He walked himself inside. I went in for a minute and watched him collapse on the couch. I thought he was asleep, so I went outside to wait for the Bowmans to pick me up."

"Why did you wait outside? Did you feel threatened by Jameson?"

"Not exactly," I say. "It's not the most welcoming place." I give a little shiver, playing into their image of Jameson. Not the boy who kept the sunflower drawing but the man who took advantage of the preacher's daughter and has been an angry, brute drunk ever since.

"Did you notice any glass on the stairs by the front door when you walked outside?"

Glass. From the shattered picture frame.

I don't miss a beat. "I did. I didn't know why it was there at the time. But if Jameson is the one who smashed the picture frame through the window, maybe he broke it on his way out of the house."

Ellis is quick to pick up the thread, nodding vigorously. "Makes sense."

"Picture frame?" Perkins says. "You didn't mention that before. Can we see it?"

After just a moment's hesitation, Ellis goes to his office, where he stashed it. But when he brings it back out, it's empty—no sunflower drawing or *Tell the truth* note.

"Not sure what the significance was to him," Ellis says. "Maybe he just grabbed the first thing he could find."

Perkins and McCormick look it over with narrowed eyes, nodding.

For a moment, I think I'm off the hook, but then McCormick asks, "What did you say your last name was?"

I clear my throat. "Mallory."

"How long have you been staying here with the Bowmans?"

"A month or so."

"And how did you come to live with them?"

I give them the same sad story I offered the Bowmans—dead parents and dead granny. Sniffles and eye rubbing and lip biting.

"What was your grandmother's name?"

"Gloria Mallory."

Actually, that's the name of an old woman in Indiana who died about a month ago. The night I borrowed Jill's laptop, I took the time to search through some old obituaries for a name I could give to back up the story I'd made up, in case anyone asked. Gloria had a granddaughter named Julie, so if Perkins and McCormick dig that deep, I can tell them that Phoenix is just my nickname.

If they dig deeper than that, I'm screwed.

"We've loved having her," Jill cuts it, like she feels the need to defend me.

"Truly," Ellis says. "She's really finding her place here."

I feel my face heat.

"They've done so much more for me than I ever expected," I tell the officers. "They've treated me as a member of their family when I needed one most, and if there's anything I can do to help the investigation, please, let me know."

Chapter 32

THE FUNERAL HAPPENS THREE days later, in the church at the top of Clara Mountain.

The body was mangled beyond recognition, so Jameson's casket stays firmly closed at the front of the sanctuary. But his face is everywhere—hanging on the walls, propped on tables in velvet frames, and printed on programs that get passed around. A big projector screen behind the casket runs a slideshow.

Every inhabitant of Jasper Hollow steps foot in the church at least once throughout the day, probably less because they'll miss Jameson and more because he was Ellis's brother. There's a strange note of relief to the whole thing, like everyone knew Jameson was born to self-destruct and they can breathe easier now that the other shoe has finally dropped.

"At least he didn't take anybody else down with him," I hear Jeffery, the owner of the Dusty Rose Inn, say. People nod, eyeing the closed casket like they think the corpse will pop out at any moment, bones splintered through rotting skin, rictus smile spread over knocked-in teeth, broken fingers reaching out to drag them all to hell.

"Glad he never married," Annie from the market says. "No kids to leave behind."

"Well, there was the one," Jeffery says.

She shakes her head, mouth pinched tight. "No, don't bring that up. I don't want to think of it, poor thing."

There's one person who is noticeably absent—Pastor Holland. He claimed he wasn't feeling well and left officiating duties to Matthew. There are whispers about that, too.

"Probably can't wait to dance on his grave," Tim from the bakery says. "But can you blame the man?"

Ellis insists that I stand next to the casket with the rest of the family to accept condolences. I shake hands with strangers and let God knows how many of them hug me. I have trouble figuring out how sad I'm supposed to look, because on the one hand Jameson was part of the family I've been inducted into, but on the other, I only met him twice.

Not to mention, I'm the one who got him killed.

Melody stands beside me, and she seems to enjoy the whole thing even less than I do. She hugs people with her arms stiff and her back rigid. Her body doesn't seem to fit quite right with anyone else's.

Neil, of course, is another story. He knows everyone by name and embraces every last one of them like he's never been so happy to see anybody in all his life. He cries a lot, but a few people manage to make him laugh, too.

Throughout the day, I hear Ellis deliver hundreds of prepackaged quotes about grief—giving in to it, moving past it, learning from it, growing through it. "I smell another book," Melody scoffs quietly at one point so only I can hear. She looks guilty immediately, but when I laugh, she offers a small smile in return.

I watch the slideshow of pictures to pass the time. Most of them are of Ellis and Jameson, fishing and riding bikes and graduating from high school. Their father is in a few of them, too, always in a stained white shirt tucked into muddy jeans. The man who gave Ellis his blond hair and Jameson his good looks.

When I glance over at Ellis again, he's telling an old woman, "My brother has been struggling with depression for quite some time. The alcohol didn't help any."

"You think he did this on purpose?" the woman asks.

Ellis shrugs, a thoughtful sadness weighing on his face. "Mrs. Johnson, I'm sure that question will haunt me for the rest of my days."

He inhabits a lie like a second skin.

Melody catches me staring at her father, and our eyes lock for a moment—until someone stumbles into her, accidentally splashing the front of her dress with punch.

The woman who spilled it, a pretty redhead, dabs frantically at Melody's chest with a folded napkin. "I'm so *sorry*, Melody, I—"

Melody steps back, covering her chest with her hands. "No, I—it's fine. Don't worry about it."

The woman frowns at Melody as though she doesn't like her tone. But Melody isn't looking at her anymore. Her eyes flick to a group of girls nearby, and I recognize some of them—the ones making fun of her at the restaurant.

I clear my throat and meet their gazes with a glare, and they all turn away.

"Really, it's fine," Melody says again to the redhead, then brushes past her, head down and cheeks flaming, toward the bathroom.

But she needs to be up onstage in just a few minutes to say the opening prayer before her father gives the eulogy, so I grab her elbow and pull her the other way.

"What are you doing?"

"Bathroom line is too long. We need to switch dresses." I'm wearing one of hers anyway.

We duck down one deserted hallway and then another. I pull a door open at random, and we slip inside. It's a Sunday school classroom. The walls are bright orange and covered in pages ripped from coloring books. On the back of the door, there's a massive poster of Jesus sitting under a tree, barefooted children clamoring to get close to him. The caption reads, *The kingdom of Heaven belongs to such as these.*

I pull my hair over my shoulder and turn my back to her. "Unzip me."

When nothing happens, I glance back at her. She's biting her lip. "Someone could come in."

"So?"

She widens her eyes at me.

I sigh. "Keep your back to the door, and they won't see anything good. Now hurry up."

After another pause, I feel her grab my zipper and yank it down along the column of my spine. I do the same for her, and we both slip quickly out of our dresses and trade.

When I'm done, I start to ask her to zip me back up, but she's still trying to pull her dress on. I watch her sharp shoulder blades move under her honey-gold skin, skin that I know is warm to the touch. The top of her sheer underwear rests just above the dimples on her lower back, a pattern of lace roses—the same shade of red as the wine she got drunk on a few nights ago.

When the dress finally slides down over her body, she smooths her hands over the skirt and turns in time to catch me watching her.

Before I can avert my eyes, she steps close to me and circles her fingers around my wrists.

"Phoenix?" Her eyes are intent on mine.

I stare back, like I've got no other choice.

"Do you care about me?" she whispers. "Even a little bit?"

My laugh is unsteady. I try again, and it comes out too harsh. So I settle for swallowing before I give her a nod.

"I care about you, too," she says. "And if you really care about me, you'll tell me if you had anything to do with the bad things that have been happening."

I hesitate. Mom would throttle me if she could see the way I hesitate. I've been lying without a problem for weeks, but for some reason, the next words that come out of my mouth are the thinnest, most unconvincing words to ever pass my lips.

"I had nothing to do with it."

But that's all it takes. Melody's eyes soften, and then she puts her arms around my neck and pulls me to her. Her body isn't stiff, the way it was when she hugged everyone else in the sanctuary. It relaxes into mine. When I hug her back, she breathes in deep and rests her forehead against my shoulder.

She believes me. And I know it's not because she's gullible or naive.

She believes me because she wants to.

*N*ina woke up the morning after she spoke to Ellis feeling better than she had in a long while.

He was going to tell her father the truth. She was going home.

She lay in bed and looked up at the ceiling of her uncle and aunt's house, and she breathed easy. The window was open—she didn't remember leaving it open, but she was glad she had, because it let the spring air filter through. She decided there was nothing better in the world than a mouthful of Ohio air. It felt like healing. Like she'd had little punctures all over her body for months, and just letting the coolness coat her insides was everything she needed to knit them back together.

Then she glanced at the clock and saw that it was nine, and her heart shot into her throat. She sat up so fast, her vision blurred and she had to bunch her hands in the sheets to steady herself.

Since Bailey was born, he'd never let her sleep past six in the morning. Like clockwork, he always roused her with a wail that let her know it was time to roll out of bed, pluck him from his crib, and sit in the old rocker by the window to feed him.

When the dizziness finally lost its grip on her, she hurried to her son's crib and peered inside.

She almost screamed.

But maybe she'd slept through his crying and her aunt or uncle had taken him out of the room to calm him. She ran to the kitchen, where they were both sitting down to breakfast and reading the paper. Bailey wasn't with them.

She checked their bedroom. She checked the living room, the dining room, the bathrooms, and under all the beds, tables, and blankets. She ran out the front door and circled the whole house, even though he couldn't have gotten out there on his own—he was hardly strong enough to hold up his own head. The more places she looked, the harder it became to breathe. When she got to her bedroom window, she stopped breathing altogether.

On the ledge, there was a dark smear of blood.

Bailey wasn't lost. He was gone.

Gone, gone, gone, gone.

And Nina knew who took him.

Chapter 33

"I ONLY NEED ONE thing from you," Mom whispers to me through my bedroom window.

Just a few hours ago, I watched Jameson's body lowered into the earth while Neily sobbed into my shoulder because he couldn't face it. Melody held her mother's hand, and Ellis had his arm over his wife's shoulders, squeezing her close.

It's dark now, crickets chirping like this is any other night. But Ellis has been locked in his office all evening, muttering to himself or into a phone.

"I hope you're being careful," I say to Mom.

She raises an eyebrow. "I'm still alive, aren't I?"

"He wouldn't kill you. Would he?"

She shrugs. "He'd have to. If he turns me in to the police, they might start digging in places he doesn't want them to."

A new fear tightens its fingers around my throat.

"It's what I'd do, in his shoes," she says. "Nobody notices when somebody like me disappears."

"I would notice," I say, the hurt raw in my voice.

She waves the words away like they're nothing but smoke.

"Tomorrow," she says, "I need you to unlock Ellis's office window."

I frown. "That's all?"

"Close his curtains over it so he won't notice. If he locks it again, it won't work."

"What happens if he locks it? Can't we just wait another day?"

"This is . . . time sensitive."

Her heart is so full of twists and turns, it's a maze that I think even she doesn't know the way through. I want to grab her and shake her until she tells me what she's planning. I want to tell her that she can trust me.

But then Melody's face flashes in my mind. *Do you care about me?*

I shake my head clear.

"What time does Ellis start working in the mornings?" she asks.

"Seven. Sharp."

She nods. Then she squeezes my hand. "It's almost over," she says. Those blue-black eyes searching mine. Like she glimpsed something in me that worries her. "Okay?"

I squeeze her hand back and nod.

I creep to Ellis's office after everyone else has gone to bed.

I glance at Melody through her cracked door on the way; she's sleeping hard, her face pillowed against her elbow. She has her soft, green blanket wrapped around her like a cloak.

I tiptoe down the hall and through the dark kitchen and then push the office door open as quietly as I can. I unlock the window and close the curtains over it, just like Mom told me to. The warm breeze makes them shiver, phantoms made of cream-colored lace.

It was so easy, but I have a feeling that tomorrow isn't going to be.

I don't sleep that night. The hours creep along, a cycle of closing my eyes and trying not to think and opening them to stare at the ceiling. A pattern of wishing morning would come and praying it never does.

When my window grays with light, Jill is already stirring. For someone who wakes up early almost every day, she isn't a morning person. She scrambles to shower, dress, eat, and get out the door to open the Watering Hole, all in under half an hour. I trace her movements with my ears, lying completely still in bed.

When I finally hear Ellis roll out of bed, his footsteps thumping softly through the ceiling, I close my eyes tight and curl in on myself like I'm bracing to get punched in the gut. I listen to him walk down the stairs. I hear the drip and steam of the coffee maker.

I listen to the door to his office swinging open—

But it's not the office door. It's mine.

I probably look like a spooked animal when Melody pokes her head in. "Hey," she says, hair disheveled, her voice still thick from sleep. "It's supposed to be a nice day. I thought it might be a good time to teach you how to swim. I promise I won't try to drown you again. And—"

"Great idea," I say, climbing out of bed and pushing her back toward her room. "Get dressed." Maybe if we hurry, I can get her out of the house.

But I'm too late.

I'm watching her face when it happens—the confusion that furrows her brow for a split second when she hears her father scream.

It's probably a sound she's never heard before. I wonder if she'll even recognize it. Then the horror and dread set in, and I know she does. I say her name, but she's already running out of the room. I follow and hear Neil rushing down the stairs. "What's happening?"

I stop when something black and small zips past my ear. There's another, crawling across the kitchen wall. Melody grabs the handle of her dad's office door. "*Stop*," I say, right before she swings it open.

A swarm of bees billows through, and then they're everywhere.

I hold up my arms to cover my face. They stick to my skin, even when I stomp my feet and try to shake them off. I call the twins' names, my hand pressed over my mouth so nothing can get inside. I get just a glimpse of where they're all coming from; on the office floor, there's a burlap sack with a wooden box inside, coated in broken honeycombs. Mom must have thrown it through the unlocked window.

"Go!" Melody shouts over the furious buzz of thousands of wings, shoving me toward the front door.

I tumble onto the front lawn, slapping at my skin and rolling in the grass to crush the little bodies that cling to me, shaking corpses loose from my shirt. But Melody doesn't come out behind me. It's another agonizing stretch of seconds before I see anyone else, but it's Neil, backing out of the house. He's dragging his father, gripping him under the armpits.

He hauls Ellis down the steps and lays him out flat in the grass. His eyes are closed. There are red welts starting to swell all over his body. Neil holds his fingers over the still lips, and his voice cracks with panic when he says, "He's not breathing."

And that's when I remember a story Mom told me about the time she and Ellis were walking together in the woods and he stepped on a hive.

He's allergic to bees. I'd forgotten all about that.

But Mom never forgets anything.

Melody bursts from the house at the same time Neil shoves his phone into my hands. "Call nine-one-one," he says and starts pumping his father's chest.

Melody drops to her knees by Ellis and stabs a needle into his thigh.

I hold the phone to my ear, watching the tear tracks on Melody's face, glistening under the rising sun. But I haven't dialed the numbers yet.

I should let him die now. Mom won't get his confession, but at least she'll have her revenge so her blue-black eyes can stop looking so haunted. I want the people who love Ellis to mourn him and move on. I want to hold Melody's hand at the funeral and let her believe that I had nothing, absolutely nothing to do with her pain.

Mom would be saved, and Ellis's family would be safe. If he died right now, I could have both.

I could have both.

But I know that isn't true. I'd never be able to look Melody in the eyes again. Mom would never forgive me if I ruined her chances at getting the truth from Ellis's own lips.

And besides, watching Neil do CPR on his dad while Melody sits helplessly on her heels—it feels like someone is digging around in my chest with a hot poker. Nailing my hands to the wall. Pulling a rusted knife, slow and deep, across my skin.

The kind of pain that leaves you gasping and seeing stars. The kind of pain you'd do just about anything to stop.

So I call 911.

Chapter 34

WHEN JILL HURRIES INTO the hospital waiting room, Melody and Neil run to her, and she crushes them both in her arms.

She kisses the tops of their heads and tells them, "I'm proud of you. Both of you."

It feels like an intimate moment, so I avert my gaze.

I stay in one of the hard, plastic chairs we've been waiting in for the last hour while she fusses over their stings, running her finger over the little red bumps on their faces and arms. She even comes to me to tap the one on the tip of my nose.

"Thank you for staying with them, Phoenix."

"I—" I shake my head. "Do you want me to get you anything? I could take the car and get you guys food."

I'm halfway out of my seat, but she puts her hand on my shoulder, easing me back down, saying, "That's all right." She adds in a whisper, "I think Neil and Mellie will want you here, if you don't mind staying a little longer." She swallows hard, eyes glistening.

"I'm just—I'm so sorry I wasn't there. I—" She can't finish, and the twins converge on her, holding her up. I look away again.

I slump in the chair, chin dipped to my chest, and pretend to sleep. I *am* exhausted. But it's the kind of tired that makes you feel thin, hammered out, beyond sleep. The kind that makes you paranoid. I jump at every sound, and I wait for the suspicion to creep into the others' voices. For someone to say, *He never leaves that window unlocked.*

A nurse walks in thirty minutes later to tell us that we're allowed to see Ellis. We follow her, hurrying along sterile hallways to keep up with her clipped pace.

But I'm not quite ready to see Ellis. No one notices when I stop just short of the door and let it close. I lean against the wall and watch the speckled tile between my boots, straining my ears, but I can't make out any words. They're probably holding him and telling him they love him. I don't want anything to do with that anyway.

I start pacing, which turns into wandering until I find a vending machine. I'm digging in my pocket for change when someone says behind me, "You're still here?"

I turn to see Pastor Holland leaning heavily on his cane, a little out of breath. His storm-cloud eyebrows are narrowed at me.

"They asked me to stay."

His frown deepens like he's disappointed but not surprised. I watch a bright-red vein fracturing the white of his left eye when he tells me, "The Bowmans are a good family."

He doesn't say anything else, but I know what he wants to add. *You need to leave them alone.*

I'm here because of you, I want to say. *Because your daughter still loves you, for some unfathomable reason. Because all she wants is for you to stop being so stubborn and love her back.*

Instead, I repeat slowly and clearly, "They asked me to stay."

He breaks the stare with an irritated sigh before he walks toward Ellis's room. I wait a few minutes before I follow.

When I round the corner of the hallway, Pastor Holland has already disappeared behind the door, but there's someone sitting outside. Neil has his back against the wall, knees drawn up to his chest, his eyes closed.

The memory of him from a few hours ago, hands pumping frantically against his father's chest, is impossible to shake.

Neil doesn't look up when I walk toward him. He doesn't even seem to notice I'm there when I sit down. He doesn't stir until I press my shoulder to his. And then, he just leans into me.

"This wasn't your fault," I whisper.

When he speaks, we're huddled so close together that I can feel the deep rumble of his voice. It's so intimate, I might as well be pressing my fingers to the soft spot on his neck, counting out the thrum of his heartbeats.

"I'm angry," he says quietly.

"You have every right to be," I say.

He laughs without humor. "You don't understand. I'm so—I'm so fucking pissed off. It scares me, how pissed off I am. I feel like my chest is going to bust open."

I'm taken a little off guard at the rage I feel in his voice—the way he shakes. I've never seen Neil angry. I suspect it takes a lot. But he's been through more than a lot in the last few days.

And as sweet as he's always been with me, I'm relieved he doesn't know that the girl who caused his family's pain is right beside him.

"I know exactly how you feel," I say.

Chapter 35

JILL SAYS SHE'LL STAY at the hospital. "The rest of you need to go get some sleep."

"No," Neil says, standing next to his father's door with his arms wrapped around himself, like he's been cut down the middle and might spill open if he lets go.

Melody stands across from him, pinching her lips together. "I'm tired," she says, glancing at her mother like she wants permission. Jill nods her approval.

Melody presses her car keys into my hand, then turns and walks down the hall. I guess that means I'm going with her.

I follow her out to the parking lot. When I pull the Jeep onto the road, the sun is hanging low in the sky. We've been at the hospital almost all day—the clock on the dash says it's six in the afternoon.

It's a thirty-minute drive back to Jasper Hollow; the closest hospital was in the next town over. The radio is off, and the silence is uncomfortable. Melody's jaw works, like she's chewing over something, but she keeps her eyes straight ahead and her mouth clamped shut. I roll down my window and rest my elbow on the frame, letting the wind curl through my fingers.

"How's your dad?" I ask.

She takes so long to answer, I think she'll ignore me. But then she whispers, "He'll be fine."

I nod.

I don't speak again until we clatter over the wooden bridge into town and I realize we probably shouldn't go back to the house. It might still be crawling with bees—or worse, cops.

"Should I—"

"Pull over here," she says.

We're still a mile from the Circle, nothing around but Pearl Mountain and the trees.

"But—"

"Just pull over," she says.

So I do.

She doesn't speak for a minute. Just keeps staring straight ahead. But I can tell she's working up to it, so I cut the engine and wait.

"I think I know who did this," she says finally.

My fingers curl tight around the steering wheel.

"Mel—"

"I got an email from a boy. About a year ago now. His email address was just a bunch of random numbers and letters. And he didn't say what his name was."

She pauses, like she's still not quite ready. A thousand questions rise in my throat, but I grit my teeth against them.

She swallows before she plows on. "He said he thinks he's Dad's son."

I open my mouth.

Close it.

My vision swims, like I've been spinning around in circles. My body goes weak. I stop breathing.

That night, in her room, when she got drunk and shivered under the covers. *I have secrets, too, you know. I've got one so big, it could ruin everything.*

"Which is crazy," she says. "It's crazy, isn't it? Dad wouldn't—"

She might shake her head, but I'm having so much trouble focusing my vision, I can't be sure.

"What did the email say?" My voice wants to quiver. It's a fight to make it sound the way it should.

"He told me that someone was dropping off money in his mailbox every year on his birthday. No note or anything, just his name written on the envelope and a hundred dollars in cash. Nobody ever saw who did it. Except last year, when he stayed up all night and watched. He saw a black SUV pull up around midnight, and then he borrowed his mom's car—his adoptive mom's—and followed him all the way back to our house."

I rake my fingers through my hair and fight the urge to squeeze my head between my knees.

Melody swallows hard and looks at me, waiting for me to tell her it's ridiculous.

"That's not enough to go on," I say.

"Right," she says, nodding. "I didn't believe it either. And neither did Neil."

"You told him?"

"I showed him the email. He told me not to worry about it. People try to get to Dad all the time. Use him, because of his money or his influence or whatever."

"You never told your dad?"

"Just Neil. I didn't talk to Dad because I was afraid—I was fucking terrified that he'd tell me it was true. So I just tried to ignore it and hoped that would make it go away and we could go on living the way we always had. But then another email showed up. He said he wanted to tell people."

"Who?"

She shrugs. "The media. Everyone, I guess. He didn't think it was fair that my dad was lying to the world about him. He said Dad's entire career was based on *lies*." Her voice catches. She swallows again. "But he wanted to know how Neil and I felt about it first, because he knew that once he did it, it would make our lives chaos. He said he'd give me a chance to talk him out of it."

She shakes her head at her lap.

"The thing is—I wasn't sure I *wanted* to talk him out of it. I didn't think it was true. But what if it was? That would mean that Dad had been lying to everyone all this time. It would mean he'd been lying to *us*. I freaked out. I didn't know what to do. So I talked to Neil, and he said I should just ignore it. That it was all a bluff to blackmail us somehow, and as long as I didn't take the bait, it would be okay. And he was right—whoever it was, I haven't heard from him since. I thought it was all over with. But what if all the weird things that have been happening lately are because of him? What if this is his way of making Dad pay for lying about him all these years? Maybe we should tell the police—"

"No police," I say, too quickly.

"Why not?"

I come up with an excuse quicker than I knew I could. "You don't know if your dad did anything wrong. It wouldn't be right to tell anyone about it until you're sure."

"But how do we find out for sure?"

"Do you know where we can find him? The kid who emailed you?"

She shakes her head. "He never gave me any information about him."

I shrug, like my heart isn't trying to pound out of my chest and my brain isn't swirling and she hasn't just told me that maybe Mom and Ellis's son is still alive somewhere. Mom looked for him after he disappeared. But there was no trace of where he'd gone, and the blood on the windowsill made her think—

"Then there's nothing we can do right now but wait," I say. "Just let the police continue with their investigation, and if it leads back to this boy . . . we'll deal with it then. I'm sure Neil is right— it'll all work itself out."

She doesn't look very convinced. But she can't offer a better solution, so she just chews on her lip and grabs my hand. It takes everything in me to try to keep mine from trembling. But I don't know if she'd even notice, since hers is shaking so hard.

*N*ina rang the Bowmans' doorbell less than an hour after she realized her baby was missing.

She had told her aunt and uncle that she was going to take Bailey for a drive and walked past the couch in the living room, where they were watching television, with an empty bundle of blankets in her arms. She held her finger to her lips, like the baby was sleeping and she didn't want to disturb him.

It was warm and bright out, the sun bearing down on her while she stared at the Bowmans' red door, and she felt her whole body flush the same shade, and even her vision started to heat to a desperate, angry red. When no one came after she rang the bell, she pounded on the door with both fists and kicked it with her untied sneakers.

When Jill finally opened it, Nina shoved past her and started searching the house—the bedrooms first. She tore apart blankets and sheets, flipped over mattresses and chairs, and ripped the clothes from every closet. She turned over couches and opened cabinets and pulled down shower curtains. She chanted, "Where is he, where is he, where is he," and Jill followed her from room to room, voice quivering from confusion and fear, saying, "Tell me what you're looking for, Nina. I can't help you unless you tell me."

Nina ran into the nursery when she heard crying, but it was only the twins, with their soft cheeks and golden curls, just like their daddy's.

There was one room left—Ellis's office. He sat at his desk, still in his pajama pants, reading glasses crooked on his face. He had the nerve to look surprised to see her, like he hadn't heard her tearing apart his house.

"You goddamned coward," Nina said, launching herself at him across the desk, grabbing him by the front of the shirt and shaking him hard. "You tell me where he is."

He raised his eyebrows at her and frowned, a perfect mixture of confusion and concern and pity for the wild-eyed girl whose face was red as blood, spit dripping down her chin from screaming at him.

He pushed her back firmly by the shoulders and got to his feet. "I don't know what you're talking about, sweetheart. You know I want to help, but you're going to have to calm down and explain—"

"You know what I want. You fucking know what I want." She pounded at his chest and screeched, "Give him back! I won't tell anyone; just give him back! He's mine, Ellis, he's mine!"

"Nina," he yelled over her, "I'm sorry, I can't help you. You need to leave before I call the police."

He exchanged a look with his wife over Nina's shoulder, one that said, Poor girl, and it made Nina lift her hands to scratch his pretty, blue eyes out.

He wrapped his arms tight around her, the way he used to at the cabin, but now every part of him that touched her felt like it was burning. He carried her to the couch in the living room, but she'd flipped that over while she was searching, so he held her down on the carpet while Jill talked quietly into the phone. But she wasn't talking to the police.

Nina had her forehead pressed to the carpet by the time her father arrived, sobbing quietly. She didn't remember when she'd stopped fighting Ellis, when he'd let go of her, or when she'd decided that there was no point in looking for Bailey anymore.

Her father crouched down beside her and rested his big hand on the back of her head, and she felt her whole body relax. She was just a child herself, she remembered. She still needed him. He had to see that.

She sat up, and her father brushed back the tangles of hair that stuck to the tears on her face. He wouldn't quite meet her gaze, though. He looked around the wrecked room, shaking his head. "Now, look what you've done here. You're making yourself look like a crazy person. I don't know what you think you're doing."

It was the first time she'd heard his voice in months, his real voice and not just the recording on his answering machine. All she wanted was to plunge into his arms. But she had to tell him.

She opened her mouth, but she hadn't spoken the words out loud to anyone, and she choked on them. She buried her eyes in her fists and moaned.

"Come on," her father said, softer now. He wrapped his fingers around her bone-thin forearms and ran his rough thumbs over the soft insides of her wrists. "Don't be that way. Let me see my girl's face again. Will you let me look at you? Where's the little one who caused all this trouble, huh? When does his grandpa get to hold him?"

Grandpa.

She felt her chest crack open, and everything important, everything that made her Nina Holland, leeched out—Sundays at the little church on Clara Mountain, and quiet mornings sitting on her front porch with *her legs dangling while she sketched the trees, and eating ice cream at the picnic tables in the Circle, and riding her bike around and around in the dark while her father talked to Annie after she closed her grocery store because he was trying to flirt, but he sounded more like he was interviewing her for a talk show.* What do you like to do for fun? What's your favorite food? If you could go anywhere in the world, where would it be?

She knew that what she said next meant that she would never be able to go home again.

"He's gone."

Her father stared at her, waiting for her to say more. When she didn't, he said, "Gone? Gone where?"

She looked around the room for Jill—the one person who had been nice to her through all of this. But she'd disappeared into the nursery to comfort her own children, who were crying because Nina had scared them with all her noise.

Why did she always have to do the hardest things alone?

"I don't know," she whispered.

"You don't know," he repeated.

She pointed at Ellis. "But he does."

Ellis had his back pressed to the wall, as far away from her as he could get, like he was locked in a room with a rabid dog pulling on her chain. "I have no idea where he is, Nina."

"Why would Ellis know?" her father said.

"Because he's his baby, too." She tried to make the words sharp, to make them wedge like a knife in Ellis's chest, to cut to the human part of him that would feel wrong about what he'd done.

But he didn't even need to speak to deny it. He just gave her that look again—pity for a girl who'd gone completely out of her mind.

Nina hurled herself toward him, teeth and claws bared, but her father grabbed her around the waist and threw her to the floor so hard, it knocked the air from her lungs. She gasped while he pinned her to the carpet by her shoulders. "What did you do?"

His whole face had turned a dark, terrifying red. His hands quaked against her, like they wanted to rip her to pieces.

"Daddy—"

"Tell me what you did with the baby!"

"I didn't—"

He crushed her shoulders so hard, she yelped. "What did you do with the goddamn baby? Where are you hiding it?"

"I didn't hide him! Ellis did!"

He leaned down close to her face, so close she felt his breath right between her eyes when he yelled, "Did you kill him?"

"No! No, I—"

Then Ellis was there, one hand on her father's chest and the other on hers, trying to push them apart. "That's enough. That's enough! You both need to calm down."

He flinched back when she slashed her nails across his face. "Liar!" she screeched. "You liar!"

But his carefully crafted expression never faltered—confused, concerned, innocent, innocent, innocent. He pressed his hand to his cheek, and his fingers came away dark with blood. Nina reached to claw him again, to peel that look right off his face, but her head jerked violently backward when her father grabbed a handful of her hair.

He yanked it up so hard, she screamed, but he kept pulling, dragging her to the door.

She cried and begged and tried to loosen his fingers. She could hear

Jill yelling, "Let go! You're hurting her!" But her father ignored them both.

Nina latched on to the frame of the front door. "Tell him, Ellis, please!"

Ellis was still on the floor, on his knees, and he held his head in his hands. "This isn't about us," he moaned, though it wasn't clear if he was speaking to Nina or his wife.

Her father tore her loose from the doorframe and threw her down the front porch steps. She fell on her hands and knees in the grass. She heard Jill yell her name, but her father must have pushed her back into the house, because the door slammed shut, and Nina was alone.

She closed her eyes. She dug her nails into the dry grass. She tried to remember how to breathe without choking. There was blood dripping down her chin—she had busted her lip on the stairs.

Nina's life had just ended, but the sun shone bright and cheerful over the mountains, and black birds spun lazily in the sky.

She let herself feel the crack that had shaken her down the middle. She let herself scream and pound the dirt. Scream until her voice was a raw scratch in her throat. She knew they could hear her, but it wouldn't matter if she cut herself open and bled out on the lawn. They wouldn't listen. They wouldn't help.

Then she made herself be quiet and think about what to do next. She could go to the police. They'd have to open an investigation for a missing baby.

But then she'd have to go to court against Ellis. He was older and better connected. He spoke with more confidence and wore nice suits that his wife ironed for him every morning. He had enough money to build a beautiful house, and all Nina had now was the change still *jingling in her pocket from filling up the gas tank with money her aunt had given her.*

She had already learned the hard way that telling the truth isn't enough to protect you. That what really happened matters a lot less than making everyone choose your version of what happened. And the only version anyone would see would be a pastor's daughter who got herself pregnant, desperate for someone to blame.

Ellis had already turned the people she loved against her, so she knew she didn't stand a chance at getting any judges or juries on her side. Ellis would convince them that Nina had killed Bailey, and she'd go to jail for a very, very long time.

No, she decided. Maybe her life was already over, but she wasn't going to die in a concrete box while Ellis walked free in her town, prayed at her church, breathed her Ohio air.

All she knew was that she had to go—not where, or for how long, or what to do when she got there. Just that she wasn't welcome here anymore.

So, with a deep, steadying breath, she pushed herself to her feet and staggered to the car.

Chapter 36

JILL CALLS MELODY'S CELL just as we're driving into town, about to hit the Circle. Melody listens for a couple of seconds before she puts it on speaker.

"—and I don't know if I'm going to be able to stop myself from strangling him this time," Jill is saying. "I really don't. Promise you'll hold me back."

"Depends on what he's done," Melody says. I glance at her, and she mouths, *Pastor Holland*.

"Listen to this. Just *listen to this*. I already made arrangements with Sherry Snyder for us to stay at her place—she called as soon as she heard what happened. She's got three extra rooms, now that her sons have all moved out. She gets so lonely, and she said it would make her feel useful again. How sad is that? So I accepted the offer, and she even volunteered to stop by our house and pack up some clothes and things for us, and Pastor Holland was already there. Loading up bags for us *into his trunk*."

"Bags of what?" Melody asks.

"Clothes."

"Clothes? He had his hands in my underwear drawer?"

"I don't know, Mellie, and I don't want to think about it. The point is, he told Sherry that we're staying with *him*. And Sherry tried to explain that I'd already made plans, thank you very much, but he told her to *tell Jill that the plans have changed*." She pauses, to let that sink in. "Can you believe that?"

Melody gasps in outrage.

"*Yes!*" Jill says. "That's what I said! And I was about to call him and give him what for, but your father begged me not to. And under any other circumstances, I would tell him he's out of his damn mind, but I don't want to stress Ellis out anymore. And I only agreed on the condition that the second Pastor Holland so much as gives Phoenix a dirty look, we're out of there. Do you hear me, Phoenix?"

"Got it," I say. "Thanks, Jill."

"Neil and I will be there tonight. Be safe, both of you."

"Wait," Melody says before her mom can hang up. "Is Dad coming with you?"

"I wish he were, sweetheart. They're going to keep him another night."

I turn the car toward Pastor Holland's little house at the bottom of Clara Mountain.

I park in the gravel driveway. While we're climbing out of the car, a screen door slams shut, and Pastor Holland comes out to greet us. To greet Melody, at least. He hugs her and ruffles her hair with familiarity and leads her inside, ignoring me entirely.

I guess that means we're going by the If You Don't Have

Anything Nice to Say rule. Which is fine by me. I follow close behind them and only growl a little when he lets the screen door bang shut in my face.

The truth is, even if he threatened to gut me in my sleep, I wouldn't ask Jill to find me another place to stay. I've wanted to see the inside of this place for years.

It was already a hundred years old before Mom left. The wood floor is uneven, and every step creaks. The doorways are framed in the same shade of dark wood as the stairs and railings. Everything is just like Mom described, down to the red paint on the walls and the big, plaid armchairs in the living room.

I run my fingers over a drip of purple nail polish dried onto the arm of the couch.

Pastor Holland already has dinner cooking, the smell of mashed potatoes and gravy thick in the air. He stands at the stove, stirring a pot, and says, "I've got the guest room set for your parents, and I've got blow-up mattresses for you and Neil in my office." He pauses and then, without looking at me, adds, "And she can sleep on the sofa bed."

I assume *she* means me.

"I can't sleep in the same room as Neil," Melody says, grabbing a stack of plates to set the table. "He snores."

She turns to me, handing off some silverware, and asks, "Can I share the sofa bed with you?"

"Fine by me," I say, pulse quickening, voice going a little unsteady.

I glance at Pastor Holland to see if he has a problem with it, but he doesn't say anything.

Neil gets home before Jill. He says she's talking to the police again and didn't know how long she would be, so she'd find another ride home.

The four of us have a tense dinner at the small kitchen table, where Pastor Holland talks around me and Melody gives short answers to all his questions, either in protest of him being an ass to me since we got here or because she flat-out dislikes him. Neil breaks a sweat trying to carry the conversation on his own.

I'm too distracted to focus on the words anyhow. I'm sitting across from Pastor Holland, and even though he does his damnedest to avoid looking at me, I stare right at him.

We used to sit across from each other every morning for breakfast, Mom told me, more than once. When she was really missing home. *Seven a. m. sharp, no matter what day of the week it was.*

I got irritated with him once because he was so focused on his newspaper that he couldn't hear a word I said. So I used my spoon to shoot bits of cereal into his scrambled eggs, and I thought he had no idea. But then I flicked one too hard, and right before it hit his head, he looked up and caught it in his mouth.

She'd always laugh at that point in the story, drawing her knees up to her chest and resting her chin on them. *He'd never been so satisfied with himself in all his life, I'm sure. He threw both his hands in the air and said, "Bet you didn't see that coming, huh? Nothing gets past your old man!"*

I put a piece of corn on my spoon, pull back the tip, and let go. It zips across the table and hits Pastor Holland squarely on the forehead.

He looks at me for the first time since I got here, his eyes big. Shocked. He blinks.

Then the front door opens, and Jill's voice sings, "Hello?"

She sweeps in, curls springing loose from her bandana and half-moons darkening the skin under her eyes, but she smiles, goes around the table to kiss Neil, Melody, and me on the tops of our heads, and even spares a kiss for Pastor Holland's cheek.

"He's doing well," she says, before anyone can ask. "He should be out of the hospital by tomorrow morning."

Pastor Holland jumps up from his chair to make her a plate. "We would have waited on you, but we weren't sure what time you'd be back."

Jill drops into the chair next to mine, rubs her temples, and tells us what the cops know.

"They found a burlap sack in Ellis's office. There was a wooden frame with a hive in it. They think whoever did this stole it from Jack Larson's bee farm."

I twist my hands together in my lap, imagining Mom's pale face covered in red, swollen stings. She probably got more than I did. I wish I knew where to go and check on her, but at the same time, the thought of our next meeting makes my stomach knot because I know that when I see her, I'll have to talk to her about Bailey.

"Any ideas about who did it?" Melody asks.

Jill shakes her head. "They just say they've got *leads*, but they can't tell me anything until they look into them. Which I think is a load of horseshit." Pastor Holland clears his throat at her language, but she ignores him. "Dave just doesn't want to admit that he's got nothing."

I decide that now would be a good time to set up the sofa bed. I rinse my dishes in the sink and pat my hands dry on the front of my shirt, walking toward the living room. The voices of the others fade behind me. But then a cracked door off the front hallway catches my eye.

It's the only room that isn't painted red. This one is wallpapered floor to ceiling with a pattern of black birds.

There isn't much inside—just a bed with frilled white blankets, a wooden dresser, and a little table with a lamp on it. But I know this was Mom's room. She must have traced these wings with her fingers a thousand times. They're shaped the same way as the ones on her phoenix tattoo.

I pull open one of the dresser drawers and take a sharp breath when I see that there are still clothes in it. I pull out a pale-pink sweater—a stale, untouched smell wafts out, but it's still soft. Small.

All at once, I feel surrounded by her in a way that I haven't since I started living with the Bowmans. But it won't be long before we're together again. The police went easy when they questioned me. I know it's only a matter of time until the evidence speaks for itself. This has to end soon, whether that means getting a confession out of Ellis or getting out of Jasper Hollow before we end up in handcuffs.

The thought of all this being over in a few days hits me so hard, I have to sit down on the bed.

"I had a daughter."

I jump back to my feet when I hear Pastor Holland's voice from the doorway.

He takes a tentative step into the room, his gaze on my hands. I'm still holding Mom's sweater. He takes it from me gently, folding it and returning it to the drawer.

"Where is she?" I ask, so quietly, I don't know if he'll hear.

"I don't know," he says, his whisper matching mine. "I wonder about it every day."

I clear my throat. Shake my head. "I'm sorry. I shouldn't have been snooping."

I start to walk past him, but he grabs my wrist hard enough that I feel his bones grind into mine. "I'd like to talk to her again."

I pause. It's like he's giving me a message he wants me to pass along.

I flicked the corn at him to remind him of her, if only for a second. I thought she would flash in his mind and then he'd move on, leave her behind like he did so many years ago.

That couldn't have been enough to connect me to her.

But he's still looking at me like he's staring at a ghost.

I wonder if he's got me all figured out or if he's just got a feeling. Maybe he's trying to get me to say something to prove I know his daughter so he can send the town out to hunt her down.

But he kept her clothes. After all this time, he's left her room just the way it was. Like he's still waiting for her to come back. Maybe—

Now isn't the time for this. We're too close to the truth.

But I can't stop myself from asking, "What would you say?"

The floorboards in the hallway creak, and Pastor Holland drops my wrist half a second before Melody appears at the door.

She casts him a wary look—the same one she used to give me when I first got to Jasper Hollow. Except now she's using it to save me.

"Can I borrow you?" she asks me.

With one last glance at Pastor Holland, I follow her out of Mom's room.

Chapter 37

NEIL AND JILL WASH dishes after dinner, and I hear the murmur of their voices while I help Melody stretch a sheet across the sofa bed's thin mattress.

She's already changed into a pair of plaid pajama shorts and a T-shirt with the sleeves cut off. Pastor Holland went to bed early, so I don't feel too embarrassed about wriggling out of my jeans in the middle of the living room and slipping on black athletic shorts.

I climb into bed without another word. Melody switches off the light and then slides in beside me. We twist and turn until we're settled in. The bed is tiny, but we both do our damnedest to stay at the edges, leaving a sliver of space between us.

Dishes clatter while Neil and Jill put them away, both of them humming different songs. I smell smoke when one of them blows out the apple-scented candle on the windowsill. Then they switch off the kitchen lights, and Jill leans over the back of the sofa to ruffle our hair and say good-night. Neil flicks both our ears. Then they go to their rooms, and we're alone.

I don't know how long we both lie there, staring at the ceiling, our bodies rigid beside each other.

I'm too aware of her—the rise and fall of her chest and the way she taps her long fingers lightly against her rib cage. I almost don't notice the pulse of light in the corner of the room.

A lightning bug. It found its way in somehow and doesn't seem too concerned with finding its way back out. When it flashes again, it hovers closer to the bed. Again, and it lands on my arm.

I've lived outdoors for a long time, but I've never warmed up to bugs. And ever since that day at the Bowmans' house, the hissing, stinging, furious cloud of bees overtaking me, I'm even less tolerant than I used to be. I lift my hand, ready to smash it, when Melody whispers, "Don't."

I let my hand drop back to my side. But then the bug crawls along my arm, and I start to squirm.

"Don't be scared," she says quietly, propping herself up on her elbow to peer across my stomach at the slow progress of the little light.

"How do you know I'm scared?"

Melody murmurs so softly, it's like she's trailing the tip of her finger along the cusp of my ear. "If you weren't afraid, then you wouldn't need to kill it."

It's a dare. I can see a smile tugging at the corners of her mouth in the dark. I bite my lip. "Fine."

We both watch the lightning bug drift from my arm to my stomach, and slowly, so slowly, crawl up. It trails over my rib cage then in the dip between my breasts, so weightless that I don't really feel it until it crosses from my shirt over to the bare skin of my chest. Its little legs are a tickle, an itch, and I grit my teeth against the squeal rising up my throat. The closer it gets to my face, the harder my heart pounds.

I finally lose control of my urge to smash it when it makes its way over my collarbone and starts to climb up my neck. I lift my hand, but Melody gets there first.

Her palm is a cup against my throat, the lightning bug trapped inside.

She's leaning over me now, her other hand braced beside my head on the pillow. Her curls graze my cheeks.

This is the part where she's supposed to realize she's too close and pull away from me, turn her back, and pretend to go to sleep. But instead, she shifts again, and her stomach grazes mine. I can feel her shake against me.

"Are you scared?" I whisper.

She dips her face toward mine, and I feel the soft tip of her nose trail over my burning cheek. Her breath mists against my ear when she whispers, "Always. But I'm trying to be brave."

I make a sound when she touches me, a little gasp, before I can stop myself. My hands itch to reach for her, but I clench my fists and keep them at my sides, because—

I can't remember why, just now. Her lips are grazing my jaw, and without my permission, my back arches, and I suck in air between my teeth. My pulse flutters against my throat, but then I realize that it's the wingbeats of the lightning bug under Melody's hand, and an intoxicating mix of fear and want and heat surges through me so hard, it leaves me dizzy.

Still, I won't let my hands pull her closer. I'll control myself, and she'll chicken out, and we can go back to the way we were.

She draws back, and I hold my breath, waiting for her to avert her eyes, to go back to her side of the bed, to let me stare at her shoulder blades, moving with her slow inhales and exhales, so I can want her all night from a safe distance.

Melody takes her hand off my neck, and the lightning bug floats up above our heads, flickering and weaving around the ceiling like a drunken star.

And then she dips her head again and presses her mouth to mine.

She's terrified. I can taste it on her lips, but she kisses me anyway, and God, it makes every wall in me crumble. Every door fly open. Every tether snap.

She breaks the kiss for half a second, and I breathe her name before I clutch her around the waist and crush her to me.

We go slowly at first, getting used to the warmth and shape of each other. I've imagined holding her like this more times than I'll ever admit, but really holding her is another thing altogether. Then Melody slips her tongue tentatively between my lips, and I open them to her, and there's no going back after that.

I can't do everything that I want to do with her, not right in the middle of Pastor Holland's living room. But just kissing, just feeling the silk of her bare stomach under my hands—it's enough to drown in.

This moment with her isn't like the stars aligning—it's more like they've been knocked out of place, like they're ricocheting against each other and spinning out to infinity.

And it might keep me reeling forever.

———

Hours later, Melody and I sit on Pastor Holland's front steps with mugs of coffee, wrapped in a blanket and leaning against each other, watching the dark sky lighten to a gray dawn. Clara Mountain looms cold and beautiful to one side, and the town sleeps to the other.

My whole body aches, in a good way. Melody's hair is soft against my cheek when she leans her head on my shoulder. She yawns and seems content just to be here and not think.

I want to lean into this moment, too. But the guilt is too much to ignore—that I'm lying to her, and if she knew the truth, she would hate me. I let myself lose sight of that last night.

My mind goes racing through scenarios. Maybe the plan could change. Maybe there's a way to get Ellis's confession and show my real self to Melody without scaring her away forever.

Maybe there's a future where I can make Mom and Melody happy at the same time.

I go over and over the possibilities. But I keep coming up empty.

I could have more, I tell myself, trying hard to believe it. *I could have them both.*

But I know it isn't true. Because Melody knows who she is, even when the world tries to tell her over and over again that she doesn't. Melody knows what's best for her, and once she finds out who I am, she'll know that it's not me.

Mom has so many memories about better times, before she got involved with Ellis. I've listened to her agonize over her choices, obsessing about how if she'd done things differently, she never would have had to leave Jasper Hollow.

And even as it's happening, I know that this morning with Melody will be one of the moments that I'll come back to. Dwell over. Wish I could relive so I could make the right choice.

You would think that having this awareness would mean I had the power to change it. To choose Melody now, instead of spending the rest of my life regretting that I let her slip away.

Maybe if I were as sure of myself as Melody, I could.

When people talk about loving someone, they only ever tell you about moments like this, sitting on the porch with someone warm at your side, watching the sun come up. But that's never been what love is like for me. Because in my experience, love cares a lot less about what I want and a lot more about what it needs to keep breathing. It's never felt like a choice to me. It's always been a demand—a pair of blue-black eyes asking a question that isn't a question, knowing that *yes* is the only answer I've ever been able to give.

Maybe that isn't love. Maybe one day, I'll know how to choose a lifetime of moments like this for myself.

But today, all I know how to do is choose wrong.

Chapter 38

JILL IS UP BRIGHT and early, even though she took the day off from the Watering Hole. Today is the day Ellis comes home.

The whole family piles into the car while I watch from the kitchen window. I lied about having a headache to get out of it at the last minute. I keep the heating pad Jill warmed up for me pressed against my temple until her van is completely out of sight.

Pastor Holland stayed behind with me. He said he was feeling a little tired. At first, I thought it was an excuse not to leave me alone in his house, that he'd pegged me for a thief—which I can't be all that offended about, because he wouldn't be wrong. But when I walk past his room, I can hear him snoring softly.

After everything Mom told me about him, and getting to know him a little myself, I figure that Pastor Holland isn't normally the type with the patience for naps. She told me he used to wake up before the sun every morning, reading his Bible by lamplight and scratching out notes with a pencil for his sermons.

When he wasn't planning for Sunday, he still kept busy, praying over sick parishioners in the hospital, officiating their weddings and funerals, and counseling them through their divorces and their grieving and their doubts.

Aside from the cane and the dark circles always under his eyes, he's hidden his sickness well. But when he sleeps, he can't hide the toll it's taken on him—the way his skin hangs from his gaunt cheeks, the way the lines on his face have deepened so much that there's more shadow than skin. His dry, cracked lips are parted, and his breath wheezes through. The movement of his chest under the blanket is barely perceptible.

I'm glad Mom doesn't have to see him like this up close. But at the same time, I'm angry, so unbelievably pissed off, that whatever precious time he's got left, she doesn't get to spend it with him. All because he was too thick-skulled to listen to her.

I turn away from the cracked door and head to the guest room, where Jill slept last night. And just like I'd hoped, her laptop bag is with the rest of her things that Pastor Holland brought from the house. I sit on the bed and power it on. I remember the password from when she let me borrow it a few weeks ago.

Melody didn't give me much to go on to find the boy who emailed her a year ago claiming to be her brother. But I have to try, because if it's true—if he is Ellis and Mom's son—then we don't need Ellis's confession. All we have to do is get Bailey's DNA tested, and then there won't be room for any doubt.

And then maybe the stubborn man asleep in the next room will have no choice but to admit his daughter was telling the truth.

The boy who emailed Melody said that he was determined to reveal that he was Ellis's son. Maybe he did but no one believed him, so the story never caught traction. It's a long shot, but I search *Ellis Bowman son*.

Hundreds of pictures of Neil come up. Videos of him playing football, and articles about how proud of his dad he is, and how he can't wait to follow in his footsteps. *He never got a chance to finish a season with the Buckeyes, so I'm really excited for the opportunity. It feels like I'm carrying both of our dreams on my back. And it's an honor.*

I scroll through page after page. The media likes Neil—the way his good looks match Ellis's so well and how bashfully charming he is on camera. There's a lot to sift through.

But then a link catches my eye. A video.

It's titled, *Chillicothe Woman Claims Ellis Bowman Killed Her Son on Purpose.*

With a glance down the hall to make sure Pastor Holland hasn't woken, I press play.

There's a woman sitting on a couch. The caption underneath identifies her as *Mother of boy killed in Bowman accident.* The clock on the wall behind her head says that it's noon, but she's still wearing her pajamas. The pants are striped pale-blue and white and covered in stains, like she's had them on for a few days. At first, I thought her hair was wet, but then I realize it's slick with grease, matted on one side, like she was just sleeping on it.

The man interviewing her believes she's crazy. I can tell by the pitying look on his face—he's only here to get a headline, not the truth.

But I don't think she's crazy. I think her grief has driven her to the brink, kept her from showering or doing laundry or cleaning her house. Her eyes are clear when she tells the news crew,

"Anderson wouldn't have snuck out without a reason. And he had no reason at all to be in Jasper Hollow."

In the interview she did that I read a few weeks ago, her son had just died. Her responses were numb. But this video is from barely a month ago. She's had time to think.

"He got good grades. He stayed out of trouble. He was smart, and he had plenty of friends, but not a one in Jasper Hollow that he ever told me about. He didn't even have his learner's permit yet, so he had to break the law to drive my car over there alone. And anyone who knew Anderson could tell you he was a rule follower down to his bones."

"Why do you think he went to Jasper Hollow?" the interviewer asks her.

"Ellis Bowman lured him there," she says, matter-of-factly.

"But what reason would he have to do that?"

She shrugs. "That's my question. What's a good reason for killing someone's son?"

"What makes you think he did this on purpose?"

"You've seen the video," she says. "The video speaks for itself."

The feed on the screen changes—suddenly, I'm looking at a grainy, nighttime video of the Circle. By the angle, I'd say it's security footage from Annie's Market.

It's mostly deserted, only a few people closing up businesses for the night. I can just make out Tim at the bakery across the street, sweeping the floors.

And then I see a shadow move beneath Harriet's Oak. I can't make out his face in the dark, but it has to be her son, Anderson. He walks toward the road. Steps into it.

Then the street is flooded by headlights, and he turns toward them, almost as though he's expecting them.

"The car speeds up," his mother's voice says in the background.

It all happens so quickly, it's hard to say for sure.

"Ellis never even swerves," she says, more quietly.

She's right. The nose of Ellis's SUV never changes course, up until the final moment—

The video cuts out just before contact. Too awful for TV.

Ellis probably argued that he just didn't see Anderson until it was too late. That he didn't even have time to think of swerving. That it was dark, that the rain reflecting off the pavement played tricks with his eyes.

When the feed switches back to Anderson's mother, she's holding something in her hands. A picture frame, with a photo of her son.

"I adopted Anderson when he was just a baby. After my divorce, I wasn't sure I'd ever have children, so he was an answer to so many prayers. He was my absolute—" She swallows. Closes her eyes for a moment. "My absolute favorite person. And nothing is ever going to bring him back. But he deserves the truth. Everyone deserves the truth."

I pause the video. And I stare at the photograph in her hands.

It looks like a school photo. He's wearing a collared shirt, trying hard to sit up straight, smiling self-consciously.

He has black hair.

A tiny birthmark on his left cheek.

And blue-black eyes that I would know anywhere.

The room swirls, and I have to grab the sheets of Jill's bed to steady myself. To get a grip long enough to figure out what all of this means.

Anderson was Mom's son.

He's the one who contacted Melody.

Ellis found out, somehow, that Anderson was planning on revealing the secret he'd worked so hard to keep.

So he killed him. Murdered him. His own kid.

And now I have to tell Mom that the child she thought died years ago actually died years later, while we were far away, plotting our revenge.

Bailey took his last breath long after we gave up on looking for him.

Chapter 39

I'M SITTING ON PASTOR Holland's front porch when Jill's van turns into the driveway, gravel popping under the wheels.

I'm ready to pretend that nothing has happened. I took time to splash cold water on my face over and over again to compose myself. To remember that I already knew Ellis was a monster and it's the reason I'm here in the first place. Time to focus on what I can do to make him pay.

Ellis gets out of the car, slowly, but he's steady on his feet. If I didn't know he almost died yesterday, I would have thought he was just tired. He grins when he sees me, walking toward the porch steps with open arms.

I walk down them to meet him. And as I stand in his embrace, time does that cruel thing where it slows down when all you want is for it to move along, the seconds sounding off in my head like the maddening drips of a leaky faucet. *Ping. Ping. Ping. Ping.*

Fuck. Fuck. Fuck. Fuck.

Then another set of arms locks around us, squeezing us even tighter together—Neil. He's got the infectious joy of a golden retriever, clearly so happy to have everyone together again that he can't contain himself.

"Gentle!" his mom shouts when Ellis feigns a groan, and then they let me go and both of them are belly laughing, reflections of one another.

"Glad you're back, Ellis," I say, but he won't let me off that easily. He slings his arm around me as we walk up the porch steps.

"You been taking care of my family?" he asks.

A memory from last night flashes through my head—his daughter's hair tangled in my hands, her lips warm on mine—and I have to bite back a smirk before I answer, "Of course."

We all turn at the sound of another car pulling into the driveway, parking behind the van. A delivery truck.

A man in a brown uniform jumps out and jogs over to Ellis with a clipboard.

"I went to your house first, Mr. Bowman," he says, "but Dave Perkins said you were staying here for a while."

Ellis signs the clipboard and passes it back to him. "Thanks, Ronnie. What do you have for me?"

Ronnie proceeds to unload twenty massive boxes that he can hardly fit his arms around. Neil helps him, and they carry them to the porch. Ellis pulls out a pocketknife to slice one open, and we all peer inside.

The box is filled to the brim with more black boxes, and printed in shiny silver foil on the tops, it says *By Example*.

The candles for the ceremony. With everything going on, I'd managed to completely forget that filming for Ellis's show starts in two days.

Chapter 40

THE NEXT MORNING, ELLIS comes to breakfast smiling. He kisses his wife, helps set the table, and trades sections of the paper with Pastor Holland. If it weren't for the dark circles under his eyes, it might have been easier to forget his frantic wandering through the woods a few nights ago. The fear in his voice as he called Mom's name. I wonder how he slept last night. If he jumped at every sound, wondering if Mom would climb through the guest room window and finish the job the bees couldn't.

Neil and Jill talk with him animatedly about preparations for the ceremony, everything from food to sound equipment to the construction of the stage that will be right in front of Harriet's Oak, where he'll make his speech. Until Ellis interrupts to ask, "You all right, Mellie?"

She's looks up from her plate, which she hasn't taken a single bite from. "Just tired," she says.

She has trouble holding eye contact with him. Like it hurts

her. I told her not to worry anymore, but I knew that she wouldn't be able to let go of her theory about the boy who emailed her having something to do with all the bad things that have happened.

And she's not too far from the truth.

Ellis frowns at her for a few seconds, then nods. "Hopefully the police will let us back into the house soon," he says. "You'll feel better when you can sleep in your own bed."

When he finishes the cheese and bacon omelet that Neil made for him, he announces he's going for a walk to get some air. But he waits until he gets to the door, his hand on the knob, before he pauses, turns back to us, and says, "Mason, why don't you join me?"

He planned for Pastor Holland to come with him all along. His voice is too light, and he tilts his head too far to the side. His lies are usually so seamless—this is a slipup that proves that Mom is getting to him. But I think I'm the only one who notices.

My heart leaps in my chest, and I hope I do a better job of masking my thoughts than Ellis does.

This is it. The plan worked. He's finally going to confess the truth to Pastor Holland. All we had to do was send him to the brink of death.

Pastor Holland grabs his cane, then picks up his jacket, looks confused for a second, and puts it back down, probably remembering that it's ninety degrees out. He hasn't been quite right since our conversation in Mom's room.

He follows Ellis out and pulls the door closed behind him. It takes every ounce of control in me to wait a full minute before I stand up from the table and announce, "The orange juice has pulp."

Jill blinks. "Yes?"

"I don't like pulp."

"Well, I suppose I could—"

"I'll get it."

I hurry out the door before Neil or Melody can offer to come with me.

Ellis and Pastor Holland haven't gotten far by the time I step outside, but I can't get close enough to hear what they're saying without drawing their attention. From ten yards back, it looks like they're just passing small talk back and forth. Pastor Holland points out things in town and shakes his head, while Ellis nods along.

The sun is already a pulsing, vengeful thing, probing light and heat into every shadow, laying Jasper Hollow bare. A sun that makes liars sweat more than usual—Ellis rubs it away from his forehead with the back of his arm, and I can already feel my shirt sticking to my shoulders. But it's not my turn to confess.

It's only a ten-minute walk from the house to the Circle. They find an empty bench under Harriet's Oak. I have to take a wide arc around them so they won't see me. The bench faces away from the tree, so I press my back against the trunk to listen.

Then Ellis asks Pastor Holland with an inflected casualness, "When's the last time you heard from Nina?"

Pastor Holland doesn't answer. Not for a long time. So long, I'm about to peek around the tree to make sure they haven't gotten up and walked away.

"Why?" he finally asks.

"I just wonder about her sometimes. Don't you?"

I can't help myself—I peer around the tree. I can see the side of Pastor Holland's face. He stares at Ellis like he knows there's more to this. He waits for Ellis to get around to what he brought him out here to say but looks uncertain about whether or not he really wants him to get there.

"What was it?" Ellis says. "Fourteen years ago now? Fifteen?"

Pastor Holland grunts.

Ellis's voice comes out strange when he starts his next question. He has to stop himself, cough, and try again. "What would you say to her?"

"What do you mean?"

"If you saw her again."

It's the same question I asked him in her room the other night.

"Why would I see her again?"

"I'm not saying you would. It's just a hypothetical, that's all. I just wonder."

Pastor Holland heaves a deep breath, in and out. "Maybe you should think more on what is instead of wondering about what's not."

"Humor me."

"I'd call the police."

My back goes rigid against the oak. I dig my fingers into the bark.

Ellis fumbles for a response. "On your own daughter?"

"Yes, on my own daughter," Pastor Holland snaps, like he would have yelled it if he weren't worried about drawing attention. "After what she did, I don't see how I could do anything else."

Ellis furrows his brows. "It was a long time ago, though. She was only seventeen."

"You're talking like she got caught drinking or skipping school."

"Look, I know—"

"She's dead, for all we know. Long dead. Doesn't make any difference to me whether she is or not."

Even Ellis flinches at that.

This wasn't how he talked to me last night. His face wasn't closed off like a brick wall. His voice didn't have that edge. So either he was acting for me, or he's acting for Ellis.

He can't mean it. A father couldn't mean that. No one could look at Mom in the face—at her blue-black eyes that see everything—and turn her away.

But he had. Both of them had.

There's a long pause that stretches for a minute or two, nothing but leaves rustling and birds chirping. I wait for Ellis to go on.

Tell him she didn't do it. Tell him it was you. I clench my fists, itching to wrap my hands around his throat and squeeze the words out of him. *Save yourself. Save your family. Please.* I'm not above hurting him, and I'm not above begging him—whatever will make him speak.

"You're finished with her then?" Ellis asks finally. "Nothing will change that? Even if—"

"I told you, I'm not interested in hypotheticals," Pastor Holland says.

"Well. All right, then."

The way he says it, it's like that's the end of it. Like he's hoping Mom is listening, hoping she'll see that no matter what Ellis tells him, her father will never change his mind about her. That there's no point in a confession.

My hands pulse, wanting to do something. Wanting to tear Ellis Bowman apart and put him back together the right way, but I wonder if all the pieces are even there. Men like him look so much like everybody else, but there's something vital missing, deep down. Something that's supposed to tell them that the rest of us weren't put on this earth to be their collateral damage.

I think about rounding the tree, blowing my cover, telling Ellis what I really think of him—anything to release the pressure of rage boiling under my skin. Then Pastor Holland says, "The last I heard of her was about seven years ago. A call from the police."

"The police?" Ellis whispers.

"Mm-hmm. From Virginia. They were asking me if I knew anything about where they could find her."

"What for?"

"Said she kidnapped a little girl."

I breathe out slowly. But then I can't seem to remember how to breathe back in.

"Though I expect she isn't so little anymore. A teenager by now. If she's alive."

Air. I can't get air.

"They made me speak to her dad. His name is Jonah. *From father to father*, he said. *If you know anything about where I can find my baby girl, please tell me.*"

I'm choking on nothing. My airway constricts, like I'm breathing through a straw.

My father looked for me?

"Told me he was dating Nina for a while, but he broke it off, and then she just lost it. Stole the girl in the dead of night, and he hasn't seen either of them since."

"Horrible," Ellis mutters.

I stagger a few steps from the tree, even though I know I'm supposed to stay hidden, but my feet won't do what I tell them to. I reel to one side and then the other, throwing out my hands for balance.

Kidnapped.

Pastor Holland pauses for a long moment before he says, "How much do you know about Ph—"

"Phoenix?" Ellis says.

He's spotted me. I hear him jog up behind me, over to where I've staggered to my hands and knees. I'm coughing hard, trying to remember how to use my lungs.

His hand is on my back, his face close to mine. "I think you're having a panic attack," he says.

"Orange juice," I say between gasps. "I just wanted—orange juice."

He rubs his big palm between my shoulder blades. "Deep breaths, Phoenix. Just breathe." But his hand on me just makes the panic pound harder against my chest. I try to crawl away from him, but he grips my shoulders.

I can't move. I can't breathe. I can't—

I lock eyes with a woman sitting on a bench a few yards away. Her black hair tucked into a knit cap. Her blue-black eyes frozen wide. She's usually so good at controlling them, never giving anything away. But now, they tell me everything I need to know.

I remember that night, when blood ran down her chin from her busted lip, bright red against pale white. I thought my father

323

hit her. That's what she wanted me to think so I'd go without a fight.

But she did it to herself.

My father never wanted us to leave.

He wanted *her* to leave.

And she took me with her.

Her face wavers in my vision, Ellis's concerned voice falls away, and I drown in the cool, black depths behind my eyelids.

*N*ina Holland turned her back on Jasper Hollow all those years ago, when it turned its back on her. Even though it felt like closing the door on her own heart. Even though it went against every instinct in her.

Her father had been planting the seeds all her life. He taught her that a place can matter to you just as much as a person. That Jasper Hollow was where she grew up, surrounded by the beauty and the wildness of God's creation. She would grow old under the watchful gaze of Clara, Pearl, and Mattie—the mountains that were larger-than-life, larger than any of her little pains. She would be buried in the same cemetery as the mother who died before she knew her but whose photograph had smiled on her benevolently from the mantelpiece since she was a baby.

Those seeds had flowered by the time they were pulled out to their roots and tossed into the wind.

She left Jasper Hollow because it was the only way to keep surviving. But as soon as she did, she wasn't certain she wanted to survive anymore.

Her life became a blur of movement. Going forward for the sake of going forward, because it was all she could think to do.

Finding a job was a challenge because she couldn't share her real name. She was afraid she'd be recognized and dragged to jail. Arrested for being a baby-killer. Maybe torn apart in a cell by women desperate to see their own children again. She took under-the-table work from an untrustworthy man with a barrel chest and bad breath and a mean streak, cleaning tables and floors and dishes at a seedy bar. He didn't pay her enough to find her own place to live, so she sometimes huddled in the corners of shelters or shared cramped apartments with other girls who couldn't reveal their real names either.

Sometimes there were customers who would tell her that they liked her hair. Her hair had been Ellis's favorite thing about her. She always made sure to keep it washed, would choose shampoo over food if she had to, because as long as it shined and looked soft, she could often find a man willing to take her home, who would tuck her into his arms and distract her from the dark gathering at the corners of her mind. She let them do what they liked to her, as long as they let her sleep over when they were done.

They never kept her around for long, even the kind ones. She didn't blame them. She was too hollowed out, too silent and insubstantial and blank for anyone to fall in love with.

There was a bald man one feverish night who kept buying drinks and giving them to her, and she threw back all of them because she liked how they numbed her. He told her he was a tattoo artist, and he thought she was so beautiful that it would be his honor to give her one for free. She knew it wouldn't actually be free, that he would demand something from her afterward, but she didn't care. She did the phoenix sketch for him on a napkin, to be his guide. I want to start all over, *she'd told him.* I want to burn down to ash and come back as something new.

Just a few weeks later, she met Jonah. He had soft, brown eyes and an easy smile, and he owned a landscaping company. And maybe he could see how run-down she was, how lost. Whatever the reason, he asked her while she cleared the dishes from his table, "Would you be interested in coming to work for me?"

She learned how to use a lawn mower. She tended dying trees, planted flowers, weeded flower beds, and lugged heavy bags of mulch in the summer heat. It was hard work. But he paid her well, and he was never mean, and he helped her find her own little apartment where the landlord didn't ask too many questions.

He waited a full year to ask her on a date. Five months more to bring her to his house.

She didn't love him. She didn't have it in her to love him. But she faked it well enough because anything was better than being alone with the memories that clawed at her insides.

And then she walked into his kitchen for the first time, and she saw his little girl sitting at the table. Her eyes were deep brown, like his. Her hair a tangle of curls. Her gaze quick and sharp.

Nina didn't know what it was. Maybe because the girl was around the same age as her son would have been. Maybe because the girl reminded her of herself, when she used to sit at her own father's table, legs too short for her feet to brush the tiled floor. Maybe it was all out of her hands, beyond anything logical—one soul calling to another. Either way, she felt a sudden, tiny pulse in a heart she'd thought long dead. She smiled, and the girl smiled back.

From that day on, Jonah's daughter was her little shadow. She always wanted to be near her, always had her hand bunched in Nina's shirt like she was afraid that if she let go, Nina would disappear in a cloud of smoke. She was in awe of Nina's drawings, of the way she dressed and braided her hair. She always wanted to be in Nina's lap, transfixed as she traced the lines of the phoenix tattoo on her forearm with her little fingers.

When the girl looked at her, Nina didn't feel like a failure or a killer or a whore, or any of the other cruel names her father gave her the day he threw her out of Ellis's house.

She took a special delight in all the times Jonah opened his arms to his daughter and the girl ran to Nina instead. She felt a deep, euphoric joy that she didn't even know she was capable of anymore the first time the girl called her Mom.

———

Of course, it couldn't last. Nina had learned that nothing good could last.

Jonah told her she was an empty cup. That he had tried for three years to reach her, but there was nothing inside her—or if there was, he couldn't find it. Couldn't find her. He said he kept her around so long because he knew that his daughter loved her. That Nina loved her, too. He said he'd done everything he could to fix her, but there was nothing else to be done—she needed to work out her problems on her own.

It wasn't unexpected. They'd been fighting about so many small things lately, as insignificant as who would pick up the groceries. She was numb to the whole conversation until he said that she couldn't see his little girl anymore.

"You can't take her," Nina had said. "She's mine.*"*

She couldn't leave behind the first bit of light that she'd been given since she'd been thrust into the pitch dark of the world.

She couldn't go back to being alone.

She couldn't lose her child. Not again.

That's when she started to beg and plead. To bargain. "I'll be better. I'll try harder. I won't turn away from you anymore."

But it was too late. Jonah wouldn't change his mind.

So she took a deep, steadying breath, and she said, "All right. I'll leave in the morning."

He offered to sleep on the couch for the night so she'd have the bed to herself. She acted hurt and said she couldn't stand to sleep in the room they had shared.

He said he was sorry, and she believed him. He said he would help her find another job, and she thanked him. And then they went their separate ways.

She lay down in the living room with her eyes wide open, listening hard for an hour, two, until the house was silent and she was certain that Jonah had fallen asleep. All the while, she worried at her lip, biting until blood dripped red down her chin.

Then she went to her little girl's room. She gripped her by her thin shoulders and shook her awake, and she told her, "We need to go. Now."

Chapter 41

I BLINK AWAKE TO Melody's face leaning over me, what feels like days later. The sunlight slants through the window. Her eyes are shadowed, and it makes them a liquid brown that comes to life when she tilts her head one way and then the other, and for a moment, I'm contentedly mesmerized.

And then I remember that I passed out. Why I passed out. And I sit up so fast, Melody and I almost smack foreheads.

Kidnapped. Mom kidnapped me.

I must look like I'm about to spiral out of control again, because Melody grabs me gently by the shoulders and eases me back down on Pastor Holland's couch. "You were out for almost an hour. Don't rush it."

Jill runs in from the kitchen when she hears her daughter's voice and announces to everyone else in the house, "She's awake!"

A man I don't know emerges from behind her. He introduces

himself as Dr. Whitaker and waves a flashlight in front of my eyes while the Bowmans and Pastor Holland huddle around to watch.

I sit through a lengthy examination on the couch. Dr. Whitaker asks me questions about dizziness and head trauma and family history. I try hard to seem conscious and alert, but it's not easy. Because over his shoulder, through the window to the backyard, something bright flashes at the edge of the woods, like someone is signaling with a hand mirror.

Mom. She wants to talk. And she's not subtle about it. She's desperate enough to be careless.

But I can't slip away. Not with Jill's watchful, worried eyes on me the rest of the day, checking in every ten minutes to ask if I feel dizzy or if I need an ice pack or if I want to lie down. I have to wait until long past dark, after everyone else falls asleep.

———

It's almost two in the morning when I step into the woods. She's waiting for me in the deep shadow of a bent oak tree.

Neither of us speaks for a long time. I take inventory of her—bone-thin, every inch of pale skin covered in red bee stings, deep pits dug out of her cheeks and beneath her eyes. She watches me from under the thick fringe of her black lashes, her eyes half-wild.

"Why the hell are you looking at me like all of this is my fault?" I say.

Her hands clench into fists. "Why did you keep me waiting for so long? I was worried."

"I didn't want to blow our cover. Which makes one of us," I snap.

"You're abandoning me, aren't you?" she says quietly. "That's

331

what you're going to tell me? I always knew you would. Just like everyone else."

"Yeah, well, unlike everyone else, I've got a pretty damn good reason." I step closer to her, and she's startled, her eyes darting away like she's afraid of me suddenly, but I get right in her face. No more evasion. No more riddles and mazes.

"I've always been on your side," I tell her. "I believed you when no one else did. So why did you lie to me?"

"I was afraid you wouldn't want to come with me. That night."

"So what?" I said. "You didn't think that maybe there was a good reason for that? That maybe I would have been better off with him, living a normal life?"

She swallows. Blinks. A shiny film covers her eyes.

"No," I say. "Of course you didn't. Because it's never been about what's best for me. It's always been about you."

I start to turn away in disgust, but she stops me with her hands on my shoulders. "He was taking you away from me, Phoenix, and I couldn't let him do that. I couldn't. You're mine. A man could never understand what a child is to a mother." She shakes her head again, muttering now. "Ellis never understood that either."

"So you did the same thing he did? Kidnapped someone else's kid?"

"No," she says fiercely. "No, no, no. It's different."

"I don't see how."

"You were mine. You loved me."

"I didn't know you. I *don't* know you." I start to back away from her. "After everything Ellis put you through. You *stole* me."

"You don't understand," she says, desperation thinning her voice. "You're supposed to be the one who understands."

I take another step back. "I can't do this. I have to—"

"You *promised*," she growls. "You promised to help me. You think the girl changes that?"

I flinch. Did she watch Melody and me through Pastor Holland's window? The thought makes me feel violated in a way I never have before. Since the day we met, Mom and I have shared everything from food, to blankets, to dreams. But the thought of her spying on me and Melody makes it feel like maggots are burrowing under my skin. Like no part of me is really mine.

"I've protected you," Mom says. "You loved me *first*."

She waits for me to answer, but I bite back the words that rise in my throat. Because if I let myself speak, it's going to be what I know will hurt her the most. *Not now. Not like this.*

"She's just like him," she hisses. "They're all like him. She's going to use you until she gets bored of you, and then she'll leave you in the dirt. You'll have no one. Do you understand what that means? Do you know what being alone *really* means?"

Don't say it. You can't take it back once you say it.

"She's a liar. She's a *Bowman*. I thought you were too smart to let her get to you. I thought I could trust you, but you were so much weaker than I thought. Even after I told you the truth about that family, you let them fool you. I should have known—"

"Bailey is dead."

She flinches. Swallows.

Then she says, "I told you that. There was blood—"

"No. He didn't die that day. He died a year ago."

She shakes her head. "I don't know what you're talking about."

So I explain it to her—the cold, hard truth. The emails to Melody, his plan to reveal who his father was, the accident. The video of him turning toward the headlights in his last moments. The photograph his new mother held of him while she cried.

Mom blinks, a dazed look on her face, like she's just run into a wall she didn't know was right in front of her.

"You mean—" But she can't finish her sentence.

"I mean," I say, "that Ellis didn't kill him the night he took him from his crib. He put him up for adoption. I mean that Bailey was less than an hour away from Jasper Hollow for thirteen years. I mean that when you ran away, you left him behind. And now it's *too late to get him back*."

For the span of a few seconds, the whole world is poised on the edge of a blade. Teetering back and forth between the moment I spoke and the moment Mom understands everything I said.

It lasts long enough for me to regret what I've done. I take a step toward her, reaching out like I can pull the words back.

Her lips open in a silent cry that she doesn't seem to have the strength to give. Before she collapses, she hooks her arm around my neck, and we both fall to our knees in the dirt.

For weeks, Mom has been getting weaker, thinner, ignoring my offers to bring her food or give her money. But no matter how frail she looked, her bloodshot eyes still glowed hot, like what was left of her heart was a coal-powered engine.

But all that heat drains from her in an instant. She is boneless in my arms, and the only sign that she's still alive is her muttering, too low and weak to understand, the erratic beats of broken wings.

"Mom—Mom, I'm sorry. I shouldn't have said it."

I wanted to hurt her, but now that I've done it, I feel the pain in my own chest. The shaking in my own hands. The dizziness in my own head. *Make it stop, make it stop, make it stop.*

"I'm sorry, Mom. Talk to me. Look at me."

I was all self-righteous bluster a few seconds ago, but that's shattered now. Maybe other people can turn it off like a switch, the second someone they love stops deserving that love. But Mom is sewn into my fabric. Trying to pull out the stitches is like ripping myself to ragged pieces. And the longer she lies limp in my arms, the more I feel the tearing.

I know that I should hate her. Be scared of her. Run away from her. But in my life, *should* has never meant a thing. All that's ever mattered is what *is*.

She doesn't cry or scream or wail. She just shuts off. The muttering has gone silent. Her eyes are dry and blank as a corpse's.

"Come back," I say, my voice breaking, my body trembling enough for the both of us.

I draw her into my lap and rock back and forth with her until the sun starts its climb behind Mattie Mountain and the night sounds go quiet with the dawn.

I'm sweating, but Mom is cold, and I rub down her arms with my palms to try to warm her.

"You've still got me, okay? You've always got me. Just like I promised." I clutch her close to my heart, vision blurry with tears.

It's like talking to a stone. I might as well be the only person in these woods. *Do you know what being alone really means?* she asked me.

"It's better to be angry, remember?" I say. "Angry is always better than sad. Let's be angry together. Come on. Come back to me. Tell me how to fix this."

When her eyes finally, finally come back into focus, a relieved sob shakes me. I pull her in tighter.

She presses her cold lips to my ear and tells me what she needs me to do.

Chapter 42

I WAKE UP ON the morning of filming for Ellis's show with Melody's head burrowed against my collarbone and her arm curled around my waist. Her eyelashes flutter against my cheek as she dreams.

Neil is already in the kitchen, making a large breakfast for the big day ahead. And I shouldn't, I know I shouldn't, but I wonder what he would do if he were me.

I imagine going into the kitchen and asking him, *Is it ever right to do something wrong?*

Maybe he'd laugh at me or look at me with disgust. Maybe he couldn't even begin to understand. Maybe I'm the only person in the world who has ever been torn this way.

But I've never pretended to be as good as everyone else.

———

We each have a job to prepare for the ceremony. Jill left the house at five this morning to ready the Watering Hole for the surge of out-of-towners. Neil runs around the Circle with a clipboard, making sure all the trucks and booths and speakers are where they're supposed to be. Melody and I take Pastor Holland's truck and load up boxes packed with candles. And Pastor Holland follows everyone around and intimidates them into working faster, because intimidating is what Pastor Holland is best at.

Ellis's signing starts at noon, but he walks around the Circle all morning having earnest conversations with the people who have come from all over to see him—as earnest as any conversation can be when there's a cameraman recording the whole thing. He puts his arm around their shoulders, leans in close when they talk, and does an excellent job of pretending he cares more about what they have to say than about how well the angle highlights his jawline or the way the sun makes the distinguished threads of silver in his hair shine.

By the time the signing starts, it's ninety degrees, but it feels more like a hundred with all the bodies packed into the Circle. They crowd around picnic tables and shop doorways, taking hundreds of pictures of the place they've read so much about, holding their phones high above their heads to try to capture shots of Ellis at the head of the line, which snakes all the way down Bowman Avenue to the base of Clara Mountain.

I notice there are a lot of kids here, twisting around their parents' legs and swinging on the low branches of Harriet's Oak. I watch them, clenching and unclenching my slick hands.

But no one is going to get hurt today but Ellis. Mom promised me that.

Melody and I set up tables and make neat stacks of candles, then help pass them out and answer questions. Throughout the day, people recognize her as Ellis's daughter and ask to take pictures with her. They say things like, *I bet Ellis is a wonderful father. You are so blessed. What a perfect place to grow up in.*

She does a good job of answering the way she's supposed to, smiling when it's expected, pretending not to mind all the strangers touching her like they have a right to her.

I'm just a girl trying to help the day go right—that's what I tell myself to calm the sick nerves in my stomach. I pass out more boxes, help organize the signing line, carry trays of food from the Watering Hole out to picnic tables in the Circle. The sun starts to slip toward Clara.

I keep busy, and just like the rhythms of my job at the restaurant, it calms me and keeps the time from being unbearably slow.

It's four o'clock by the time I take a break, sitting at a picnic table with a glass of lemonade that Jill brought me. I'm taking a sip when I see the hand mirror flashing between the trees down the road, where the asphalt curves and disappears around Pearl Mountain. The signal.

I knew it was coming, but I still choke on the lemonade, coughing, eyes watering.

Then I feel a strong hand pound my back. I glance behind me to see Neil, frowning down at me, eyes full of concern. "You all right?"

I nod. "Fine."

He's already changed into his clothes for the candle lighting ceremony—we're all supposed to be onstage with Ellis for his speech. I twirl my finger in the air. "Let's see you."

He smirks and gives me a full turn. I whistle and bare my

teeth like I'll eat him for dinner, which makes him tut in disapproval. "Girls are aggressive these days."

"Always have been," I say. "We're just less interested in hiding it now."

Neil laughs, the deepest, most honest, most beautiful laugh I've ever heard. I have to swallow hard to force down everything that wants to rush to the surface, but he still notices, and the frown returns. "What's wrong?"

"Do you—do you think you could take a walk with me?"

He doesn't ask me why. He doesn't hesitate a second before he holds out his hand to pull me up from the picnic table. And then he follows me away from the crowd, toward the trees, where the signal came from.

For the first minute or so, I can't speak. Neil ambles patiently beside me, his hands in his pockets.

I clear my throat, reaching for something to say. Anything.

"I made out with your sister."

He stammers, "I—uh—well, congratulations."

"Thank you."

"I mean, I knew you liked each other. I knew that from the beginning—"

"How the hell could you know that?"

He shakes his head, smiling. "I probably knew how Melody felt before *she* knew. At least, before she'd admit it to herself. Maybe it's a twin thing." He shrugs. "You, I wasn't as sure about. But you seemed to enjoy irritating her even more than I do."

Somehow, even with the sick churn in my stomach and heaviness in my lungs, he manages to make me laugh.

We walk in silence for a few more moments, drawing closer to that dark spot in the trees. We round the bend in the road, out of sight from the Circle. "You don't think there's something wrong with us?" I ask.

"No."

"But your dad—"

"He'll have a problem with it. I mean, I hope you guys tell him someday. Really. And I'm sure, eventually, he'll get used to it and we'll all live close together and have really awesome barbeques at each other's houses. But it won't be like that at the beginning." He drapes his arm over my shoulders and squeezes. "He'll come around, though. Because we're a family, and Dad and I won't ever let anything change that. And until he remembers it, you can have awesome barbeques with me."

God, Neily's head must be a nice place to live. I have to look away from him to get my trembling mouth under control and swipe my forearm over my burning eyes.

And that's when I hear the noise beside me—a hollow crack.

Neil falls.

Mom stands over him, holding a rock.

Bring me one of them, she whispered to me last night, in the woods while I held her. *I'll let you decide which.*

Every time I tried to even think about giving Melody over to Mom, my heart stuttered in my chest and all I could think was, *No.*

As fierce and brave as she is, Neil is stronger. If something goes wrong—

But nothing is going to go wrong. We're going to get our confession, and Melody will end up hating me, but she'll be safe, and so will Jill and Neil. Mom promised.

I scramble into action, taking his ankles while Mom lifts him under the arms, and we carry him into the woods where the van is waiting, back doors flung open. Once we get him inside, I help her bind his hands and feet with rope.

He lies so still that I hold my hand over his mouth, just to make sure he's still breathing. Then I brush a curl back from his forehead, slowly, trailing my fingers over his skin like he'll be able to feel everything I want to say. *You'll be all right. If you knew the whole story, I think you'd understand.*

And then I glance up and notice it, balanced there on the dashboard—a small, black handgun.

"Where did you get that?" I whisper, like it'll go off if I disturb it.

"I took it from Jameson's house. After the Bowmans picked you up that night."

The night we killed him.

When I look back at Mom, her eyes are narrowed at me. But she doesn't say a word more. She just slips a knife into my palm.

I watch her drive Neil deep into the woods before I walk back to the Circle alone.

Chapter 43

"WHERE'S NEIL?"

It took less than an hour for Jill to notice. She raises her hand to her teeth to bite her nails but remembers her fresh manicure and drops it.

I've changed into a dark-purple dress with short sleeves. Not one of Melody's this time, but something that Jill picked out just for me. And now I have to look her in the eye and say, "Maybe he's still helping with the food."

We're standing by the stage under Harriet's Oak, and the Circle is swarming with even more people, a wall that's impossible to see through. We ran out of candle boxes hours ago, and Annie's Market sold out of lighters not long after.

Melody breaks through the crowd and hurries toward us. The sun set a few minutes ago, and the dusk makes her pale skin take on the blue-gray glow of the moon. "Have you seen Neil?"

I shake my head, fiddling with the feather pin in my hair.

"He better get over here, or we'll have to start the speech without him," she says, glancing around.

"He wouldn't miss Dad's speech," Jill says.

Melody grabs my hand and tugs me toward the crowd. "We'll go look for him."

Volunteers are instructing people to line up on both sides of Bowman Avenue. Everyone takes the slips of paper from their boxes to write down whatever it is they want to be rid of. *Jealousy. Fear. Anger. Uncertainty.* Some show each other and laugh. Others guard their words carefully with cupped hands.

Melody scans all the faces in the crowd, and I pretend to look too, until Jill comes to collect us. "It's too late. We'll have to start without him." She's forgotten all about her manicure at this point, gnawing at her jagged nails, her gaze fluttering nervously over the shifting sea of faces.

I start to walk with them toward the stage, but I stop and clutch my stomach. "I don't think I should go up there."

Melody slides her hand around the back of my neck, frowning. "You okay?"

"I'm not feeling great. Maybe stage fright. I don't want to ruin your dad's big night by throwing up on TV."

Melody looks like she wants to argue. I know she's nervous to go up without me. But she purses her lips and nods, squeezing the back of my neck before she turns away from me to follow her mother.

———

The moon crests over the treetops just as Ellis climbs the steps to the stage in front of Harriet's Oak, the mountains cast in deep blue. The applause echoes, punctuated by whistles and shouts. Jasper Hollow is full to bursting with pride. Everyone looks so happy, with broad grins and flushed faces.

A row of spotlights mounted in the grass is bright on Ellis. There's nowhere to hide, and for once, he seems to feel it—he blinks a few times, holding up his hand to shield his eyes, until he remembers people are watching. Remembers to smile.

Under the direction of volunteers, everyone settles into their places, lining up along the street with their candles in hand. But I stay focused on Ellis. He glances behind him at Jill and Melody. From where I'm standing, I can see him mouth, *Neil?*

Jill shakes her head helplessly, lips pinched tight.

By the time Ellis turns back to the crowd, his smile is back in place. He clears his throat before he lifts his microphone to his mouth. "Welcome."

I creep slowly around the base of Harriet's Oak to the back of the stage, careful to keep out of the light.

"We're here today because we are human. And humans are, as we all know from a young age, imperfect creatures."

I press my hands to the warm bark at the back of the tree and peer around it. Waiting.

"*Knowing* that we are imperfect is another part of being human. And striving to be better—well, that's the most important part of us, isn't it?"

Even though it's all been said before, and probably been said better, everyone watches Ellis in rapt silence.

Candles start to glow to life in the crowd, flickering in their hands, casting their faces in yellow. Their eyes and cheeks look hollow, and I watch the street transform into an army of skulls.

345

I can see Melody on the stage in front of me, just a few feet away. I want to reach out and take her hand. I want to pull her from all of this and run. Run until we're in a place where no one has ever heard of Jasper Hollow and Ellis Bowman is nothing but a face on a dust jacket.

But I don't.

Because I promised to help Mom, and no matter what she's done, I won't be another person who's lied to her.

Because even though I want Melody, I can't let myself be with her when she doesn't really know me.

Because no matter how much I care about her and Jill and Neil, Ellis deserves this.

Because everyone deserves the truth.

"We're here because we all have something we'd like to let go of. Something that we've been holding on to for so long, it's affected the way we live, from the choices we make, to the people we let into our lives, to the way we love the people closest to us."

Everyone's gaze is intent on Ellis, but I'm staring in the opposite direction. That's why I'm the only one, at first, who sees someone slip through the line of people and stand right in the middle of the road. A person without a candle, just a dark smudge moving down an avenue of light.

I creep closer to the stage.

"I'm here to tell you that it's okay to forgive yourself. It's okay to let it all go. I know you've been holding that pain close"—he clutches his chest, voice rising, cheeks flushing, something taking over—"to punish yourself. But that won't make it better. It won't change what happened. All you can do is change *right now*. It's time to start over." He stalks from one end of the stage to the other, his voice rough with emotion. "It's time to wipe the slate clean. You don't need anyone's permission, but I'm giving it to you now. Forget about what you've *done* and focus on what you'll *do*. Forget whatever is causing you pain. Take the past and *burn it*."

Every muscle in his body strains with his desire to force the words into being true. His fist is high in the air, punctuating his words.

But no matter how hard Ellis wants to forget the past, the past will never forget him.

Suddenly, he's stone-still. Staring.

The dark shadow comes into focus. Tall, with wide shoulders and gold hair that dances like its own flame in the guttering candlelight.

Neil.

Jill and Melody rush toward him. I can't see Ellis's face from this angle, but his whole body goes slack with relief. "Son," he breathes, reaching a hand toward him to beckon him up onstage.

But then he realizes that something is wrong—Neil isn't smiling. He always smiles when he sees his dad.

He shuffles forward. His strides are short and awkward because of the rope knotted around his ankles. His wrists are bound behind his back. And he keeps glancing behind him.

As his son moves closer, it becomes clear that there's someone following him.

And slowly, Ellis falls to his knees.

"No," he says. But he's dropped his microphone, so Jill, Melody, and I are the only ones who hear.

And Mom. She's close enough to the stage now to reach around Neil and grab the microphone Ellis dropped.

She presses it to her lips and says, "Everyone on the ground. Or I'll start shooting."

There's a moment of confusion, people glancing at each other, whispering. And then Mom turns to the side so they can all see Jameson's gun pressed to the center of Neil's back.

Chaos breaks in the Circle, some people taking off back toward their cars, some dropping to the ground and covering their heads, and others just freezing on the spot.

Then a shot rings out, and everyone drops flat on their stomachs.

Mom has the gun pointed straight in the air but settles it back between Neil's shoulder blades. Her voice comes calmly over the speakers. "Just stay calm and listen closely, and everyone will be fine."

I climb quietly onto the stage, right behind Melody. Her body is tense, her eyes trained on my mother, and she doesn't hear me sneak up on her. But just before I can grab her, a low branch of the oak tree tangles in my hair. And when I yank it free, my feather pin comes loose.

It clatters to the stage. The sound makes Melody flinch. And then she turns to me.

Our eyes meet. She frowns, brow furrowing. Confused.

I'm frozen. For a few seconds, I forget what I'm supposed to be doing. Because her confusion is about to become understanding. Once I do what I'm about to do, she'll know she was right about me from the beginning.

There's no going back now. I remember who I am and what I promised. And I hold my knife out.

The original plan was to hold it to her throat, but I can't bring myself to do it now. I just hold it between us and warn her, "Don't move."

"Phoenix," she says.

It comes out hard. Cold. The way she spoke to me the first night we met.

Everything that's happened between us is suddenly wiped away. We're strangers again. Enemies. The thought makes me sick to my stomach, but I hold the knife steady.

The Bowmans are all staring at me. And I tell them, "Do what Nina says, or I'll kill your daughter."

I won't. But they don't know that—they don't know anything about me anymore.

Mom guides Neil up the steps of the stage, moving slowly so he doesn't trip over the rope around his legs.

"Where is Pastor Holland?" she says into the microphone.

After just a moment's pause, one of the people on the ground pushes slowly to his feet with the help of his cane. Everyone watches as he approaches the stage, staring into the face of his daughter for the first time in fourteen years.

Mom keeps her face blank as she watches his slow progress up the stairs. She doesn't say a word to him. Instead, she turns back to Ellis and says, "You know why I'm here."

Her voice echoes from the speakers all down the street, soft and grainy, the way she used to talk to me years ago, at my father's house. When she'd crawl into my bed at night and tell me stories about birds reborn in fire.

Ellis is still on his knees, both his hands in the air, tears streaming down his handsome face, glittering under the harsh spotlights. "Nina—"

"*Louder,*" Mom snaps, thrusting the microphone toward his face.

He clears his throat and leans in. "Nina, I know we have a lot to talk about."

Nina. Nina Holland. The name ripples in whispers through the crowd. They recognize her. They remember her.

"But you need to leave my family out of this," Ellis says. "They've done nothing to you."

Mom laughs, low and dangerous. "If family means so much to you, why did you think it was okay to take away mine?"

Ellis pauses, thinking before he answers. His eyes dart to Neil and then to the crowd before they settle on Mom again. "I know you lost your son," he says. "And I understand that was very hard on you—"

"I know what you're doing," she growls, jabbing the gun so hard into Neil's back that he gasps, and Ellis flinches. "You want everyone to think that the grief drove me insane. To discredit me so everyone will take your side. But I have to tell you, that really isn't necessary. Everyone always believes you over me. My own *father* picked you."

Pastor Holland takes a sharp breath in but doesn't argue.

"That's why I went to all this trouble," she goes on. "He needs to hear the truth from your mouth. Because it's never meant anything coming from mine."

Whatever happens here, the whole world will know about it by morning. While most of the camera crew abandoned their equipment, I spot a woman hidden between Sugar House Bakery and the post office, crouched with a cell phone to her ear, probably talking to the police. And her camera's still rolling.

"Tell him what really happened," Mom says. "Tell everyone what you did."

Ellis casts his eyes in every direction but hers, looking for some way out of this, when he remembers me.

"Phoenix," he says. "Please, talk some sense into her. I know—" He swallows. "Whatever she's told you about me, it isn't true. But if you don't believe me, then think about my family. Please. They've been good to you, Phoenix. They have nothing to do with this."

All eyes are on me now. Even Mom slowly shifts her gaze in my direction.

I keep my eyes firmly on Ellis's when I say, "Everyone will be safe if you tell the truth. Just tell the truth."

He shakes his head, staring down at his fisted hands. "I—I don't know—"

Another shot rips through the Circle, greeted by more screams.

The bullet went straight in the air, but then Mom jams the barrel hard under Neil's chin. "Last chance, Ellis."

"No! No, don't hurt him. Please, Nina, just—"

"*Now*, Ellis," she growls.

"I did it, goddammit! Now let go of my son!"

The Circle is completely silent. Like the only people here are the ones on the stage.

At the very least, Jasper Hollow is listening. Even if they don't believe it yet. But all that's ever really mattered to Mom is making one person believe.

Pastor Holland has been completely still and silent this whole time, lips parted, eyes wide on his daughter.

"What did you do?" Mom's whisper echoes through the speakers.

I watch her face, expecting her to smile, or at least show some sign of satisfaction, now that she's getting the thing she's longed for all these years. But the set of her mouth is grim.

"I took your son from you. Kidnapped him." Just a few minutes ago, he was polished for the camera. Now, he runs his hands through his hair, making it fall wild and stick to the sweat and tears shining on his face.

"Why?" Mom's voice is so quiet now, it's hard to make out, even with the microphone.

"Because I didn't want anyone to find out he was my son, too."

I watch Pastor Holland's face to see what the words do to him. His eyes get even wider, but he doesn't say a word. He doesn't move toward Mom or away from her.

Then I look at Neil. He stares hard at his dad, jaw clenched.

Ellis goes on, like now that he's started, it's a relief to throw open the floodgates and release everything he's been working so hard to hold back.

"I did it myself," he said. "Snuck through the window while you were sleeping."

"The blood," Mom hardly manages to choke out.

"I cut his hand and dripped his blood on the windowsill. I thought it would make you think—I thought it would stop you from looking too hard, if you thought Bailey was dead."

Mom pauses for a long time before she asks her next question.

"Is he dead now?"

When Ellis looks back up, his eyes pass over Mom's and lock on Neil's.

"Yes," Ellis says.

I already told Mom. But hearing it straight from him, she feels the pain of it all over again. The sound that rips from her, it's like the words were a hot brand pressed to her skin.

Her legs are trembling so badly, she looks like she'll fall. "Why?"

Ellis looks down at the stage for a moment, like he's gathering himself. Or trying to get his story straight. The stage rings hollowly when Mom stamps her boot and says, "*Tell me why.*"

"Because he found out that I was his father. He said he wanted to tell everyone the truth. I told him to meet me in Jasper Hollow, just to talk. But I just—I lost it. I couldn't risk letting him walk around with the information that could ruin me. I'm so, so sorry, Nina. I let this thing get out of hand, and I didn't know how to stop it without hurting more people. Without hurting my family. I—"

When Mom fires the gun, the microphone amplifies the sound with a high-pitched ring—a scream that mingles with a hundred others.

Ellis collapses on his side, gasping, his whole body writhing against the pain. The bullet pierced a hole through his left arm. He clutches at it, blood seeping through his shaking fingers and making a dark puddle on the stage.

This isn't about revenge, Mom told me over and over. *It's about getting the truth.*

She has the truth now. But that didn't stop her from shooting him. And it doesn't stop her from aiming the gun again, this time straight between his eyes.

Neil lunges toward them but trips over the rope tied around his legs and hits the stage hard. Jill screams, scrabbling toward her son on her hands and knees to cover his body with hers. And Melody—

Maybe she knows that I would never hurt her. Maybe she doesn't. Either way, she ignores my knife and tries to step between the gun and her father.

But I yank her back and step in front of Ellis myself.

Mom's finger tenses on the trigger at the same moment I come between them. Half a second later, and the bullet would have blown through my stomach.

"What are you doing?" Her voice is an impatient growl. She doesn't lower the gun.

"You don't have to do this," is all I can think to say.

It's not that Ellis hasn't earned the bullet.

It's Jill, all the times she defended me against Pastor Holland. It's Neil, on the ground and fighting hard to unbind the ropes and get back to his feet to save his father. It's stubborn, self-righteous Melody who just heard her dad confess to murder and was still ready to take a bullet for him.

"Mom. You got what you wanted. He told the truth. It's time to go."

But she keeps the gun pointed at me.

"Move," she says.

"Mom," I say again. Trying to remind her of who she is to me. Of what I need from her. I reach toward her, trying to tangle my fingers in the loose fabric of her black dress.

"*Move*," she says again, voice scratching.

"I'm asking you not to do this."

She tries to lunge past me, but I tackle her at the same moment the gun goes off again.

I sit on her stomach while she writhes under me, screaming and clawing at my face. I try to pin her arms down, but I freeze when I feel the cold barrel of the gun buried in my stomach.

"Get *off me*."

"It's me," I tell her, though my voice is so broken by now, so exhausted from trying to hold myself together all this time, I don't even know if she understands what I said.

She screams, pressing the gun up hard through my ribs like a punch, pushing the air out of my lungs until I'm gasping. "Why did you stop me? *Why did you stop me?*"

I can just make out the faint blare of sirens in the distance.

I grab her by the shoulders and shake her hard, her bones so close to the surface that they're sharp under my hands. "We have to go. I'm not leaving without you. I promised I'd never leave you, didn't I?" I peer down into those eyes. Those eyes that look black until she lets you get close enough to see the blue. The whites are shot through with red veins. Her grip on the gun shakes. I know she's tired, too.

The sirens are getting louder.

I press my forehead to hers. "Come on, Mom. Choose me. For once in your goddamn life, choose me."

I feel the pressure on my stomach ease, just a fraction. When I draw back, she's frowning up at me.

"I'm still here," I whisper.

She stares at me, lips parted, like she's looking at someone she's never seen before. Or maybe like she's found something she didn't know she'd lost.

The girl she drew once, with a pair of blazing wings.

And then the grief breaks over her like a wave. The gun clatters to the stage beside us, and she wraps her arms around me, shaking so hard that I can barely lift her up, even though she's lost so much weight. "My baby," she mumbles into my hair, and I don't know if she's talking about me or Bailey, but it doesn't matter.

Now that she doesn't have the gun, half the people have started rising from the ground, confused, some of them already running for their cars. I can see red and blue lights flashing against the dark trees, coming around the corner. We have to get out of here. I half drag Mom toward the edge of the stage.

Then another voice comes from behind us. And it says with a chilling calm, "My dad didn't kill Bailey."

I turn to see Neil. The ropes that tied him lie at his feet.

He's holding the gun Mom dropped.

"I did," he says.

"Neil?" Melody says, standing behind him.

"I'm sorry," he says. "I had to do it. I had to protect my family. And that's why I have to do this."

He points the gun between Mom's eyes and pulls the trigger.

Chapter 44

A WHITE VAN THAT'S seen better days. A bird carved into the passenger door with the tip of a key. Curly fries bought with cup-holder change. Long games of Monopoly with more pieces missing than found. Learning to whistle and snap my fingers. Learning to drive. Learning to slip my hand into someone's pocket without a soul noticing, without a soul getting hurt.

Reading to each other from books found in donation boxes. Painting her nails by firelight, amazed by the steadiness in her hands, the shape of her fingers, callused like an artist's. Imitating the way she drew pictures, just so she would keep drawing them. Picking her bouquets full of the most beautiful weeds I've ever seen.

Jim Croce and radio talk shows and radio static. Fingers and hair, breath and thoughts entwined. Warm soup on cold nights. Walking under twinkling skyscrapers so tall, they disappear in the clouds. Wandering dark fields in the middle of nowhere, the sky a sheet of black silk, a thousand holes poked through it and flashes of Heaven peeking through.

Warm, cold, rain, shine, night, day, asleep, awake. Up in the stars and drowning in the ocean.

The wildflower she picked and carried home.

Chapter 45

MOM'S BODY FALLS INTO mine, and we both crash into the stage.

It all happened so fast, I didn't even have time to scream.

She's facedown beside me in a pool of spreading blood, and I reach for her, frantic, turning her over to see for myself.

Her blue-black eyes stare back at me.

Then they blink. And she says, "Phoenix?"

And then I look beside her and see another limp body. And I understand what happened.

Pastor Holland has Neil pinned under his tall, broad frame. Neil struggles to get free, the gun knocked from his hands.

As Neil pushes and scrambles, Pastor Holland doesn't move.

The blood pooling on the stage is coming from the hole at his temple.

When Mom sees it for herself, she throws up over the edge of the stage, into the grass. She grips the boards like the earth is tilting around her.

My ears are ringing, as though a bomb just went off. I hardly register all the people running for their cars and yelling for each other. I don't have time—the sirens are so close.

I grab Mom around the waist to haul her to her feet, and then I reach down to grab the gun from where Neil dropped it.

Melody's hand gets there first.

She snatches it away from me. But she doesn't point it at me—just holds it out of reach, while she stares me down.

Even after everything that's happened, everything I've done to her, she still says, "Go."

And I know that's the closest thing I will ever get to forgiveness from Melody Bowman.

Without another look back, I drag Mom off the stage—carry her almost, because it seems like she doesn't have control of her legs anymore. I hardly even notice Ellis when we stagger past him, passed out from the pain of his gunshot wound.

But Mom is awake for every second of her pain. She screams like every inch of her is on fire—bursting blood vessels, blistering skin, crackling bones, and smoke-filled lungs. She screams like someone will listen and put out the flames. She screams and screams, but there's nothing I can do to stop the burning.

I force her into the van, which she parked behind Sugar House Bakery so we could make a quick exit. Then I jump into the driver's seat and hit the gas, and just as the Circle fills with police cruisers, we speed off into the dark, leaving Jasper Hollow and all the wreckage in our wake far, far behind.

*N*ina Holland's favorite memory of her father, the one that she held close to her heart all those years away from home, was a quiet one. Before everything that happened. She was in eighth grade, and she had a D- in Mrs. Snyder's Algebra I class. And she had finally worked up the courage to show her father her interim report.

It was a Sunday morning, and they always got to the church before the sun came up on Sunday mornings. The window showed it was still dark outside his office—the tiny, green-carpeted room down the hall from the sanctuary.

He was looking down at his sermon notes when, without a word, she placed the yellow slip of paper right in front of him.

She held her breath with her hands knit tight together as he picked it up. Looked it over. Lifted his eyes to her.

And he said, "Let's take a walk."

He put one hand on her shoulder and the other in his pocket, and they walked down the quiet hallway, past the empty sanctuary, out the big double doors, and onto the church lawn.

She had a million arguments on her lips, ready to throw up like a shield. But she forgot every one of them when her father stopped on the lawn and turned to her. His face looked even more severe than usual in the pre-dawn shadows, and she braced herself for whatever he had to say next.

But he didn't say anything. Instead, he took off his jacket and spread it out on the dew-covered grass. And he sat down on it.

She stared at him in stunned silence—her tall, dignified father, sitting on the ground.

He spread his coat out and patted the space on it beside him. And she took that as her cue to sit down, too.

"Mrs. Snyder called me last Friday," he said.

She swallowed. "You've known all week?"

He nodded.

Great. Now she'd be in trouble for keeping it from him for so long, too.

But he put his arm around her then. She was so nervous about his reaction that she hadn't realized how cold she was. Not until he tucked her close to his side and melted the chill with his warmth.

He said, "I want you to remember something. It's a secret that all parents have. And I'm only ever going to say it this once, and if you ever bring it up again, I'm going to deny it. All right?"

She nodded gravely.

He pulled her in tighter and spoke right into her ear, even though there was no one else around to hear him.

"I am your father. But I'm also a person. Just a person. Which means that sometimes I don't know what's best for you, and sometimes I make the wrong choices, and sometimes I'm a bad father. Do you understand what I'm saying?"

She nodded again, though she wasn't entirely sure she did just yet.

"You didn't show me your grade for a week because you were afraid I'd get mad. Really mad. Is that right?"

"Yes," she whispered.

"I'm sorry that's what you've come to expect from me. I'm sorry that I can't always be better for you."

"I forgive you," she said instantly, burrowing her face against his shoulder.

He rested his cheek on the crown of her hair. They sat there together and watched the sun crest over Mattie Mountain, their own little private Dawn Festival.

"I just need a little more time to come around than most people," he said. "Never give up on me, and I'll never give up on you."

"I won't," she whispered back. "I promise."

Chapter 46

I DRIVE.

That's what we used to do, before Jasper Hollow. We drove. Wandered. Did our best to outpace our demons, until the day we decided to run toward them.

Did we beat them? I don't know. The truth is out. Pastor Holland learned what really happened to Bailey, who his daughter really was, before he died. Maybe she was right and that's all it took for him to forgive her. For him to realize that he loved her enough to take a bullet for her.

But then I remember that night in her bedroom, where he kept all her clothes neatly folded, when he told me, *I'd like to talk to her.* And I wonder if he already knew that he loved her enough.

There's no way to ask him now. The truth shifts and dissipates like smoke.

Mom lies on the mattress in the back, staring blankly up at the ceiling. She hasn't said a word since we drove away from Jasper

Hollow. I keep the van's radio on, turned up—the only bit of privacy I can offer her.

But I'm glad she's asleep when one of the stations shares some breaking news.

Neil confessed to the whole thing, right on camera while the police put him in handcuffs.

He was going to spread lies about Dad. I had to stop him. So I told him to meet me in Jasper Hollow, just to talk. Dad and I were coming back from a college tour—he didn't know a thing about it, I swear—and I was driving. He insisted on switching seats and telling everyone he was the driver, but it was me. Anderson started walking toward us, and I stepped on the gas, and—

I turn the radio off.

———

I don't have any particular direction in mind, and I pay more attention to the time than the miles. Getting through each hour is an accomplishment, because I've always heard grief gets better with time. I cling to the idea that every minute between us and that gunshot is a minute closer to Mom feeling okay again.

I try not to think about what I'd be doing right now if I were still in Jasper Hollow. About my apron from the Watering Hole, recently washed and folded neatly in the top drawer of my dresser.

I drive through the next day and deep into the night, little stars flaring to life above the infinite road. The sky is so wide here that it seems to curve at the edges, like we're trapped under an empty bowl. I drive until I'm too tired to go any farther. Then I pull off the road, far into an abandoned field, grown over by dandelions that dance in the warm breeze.

I put the van in park and cut the engine. Then, without looking back at her, I say tentatively, "Mom?"

She doesn't respond. I didn't expect her to. Lost in her head—and I worry that maybe this will be the time that she never finds her way out again.

Instead of joining her in the back, I decide to give her space and sleep outside in the balmy night. I don't bother with the tent. I just grab a blanket and find a soft patch of dirt to spread it over.

If the inside of the van felt too cramped, out here, the world's too big. Too much empty space to fill with thoughts, about what Melody is doing, and how Jill feels about me after everything, and whether or not Ellis and Neil are in jail. About what life will be like for Mom and me from now on.

Then I hear the back doors of the van swing open and shut. And a few seconds later, Mom settles down beside me on the blanket.

I let my head fall to the side, and I meet her wide, shining gaze. We stare at each other for a long time.

She reaches for me. I reach back.

We don't say a word. Just hold on tight, rocking each other through our griefs—hers for her father, mine for our perfect life in a warm house with a little orange cat. I don't know how long we stay like that—until we both fall asleep, swept up in our own dreamless oblivions.

We wake with the sun the next morning, and Mom says, "I'll drive."

Though I have no idea where we're supposed to go from here. After everything, we're on the run again.

We'll never have the life we've been chasing. That realization crushes me.

I know we've crossed too many lines to ever really deserve it. But now, I'm not sure that anyone does.

Chapter 47

TWO DAYS LATER, MOM parks the van on a quiet suburban street. Just a few driveways down from a little green house with a basketball hoop in the driveway.

We watch it for a couple of hours, the way we used to before we broke into a place. Only one person lives here, and he doesn't come back from work until dark. He walks to the front door with his shoulders slumped, like he's got something heavy slung across his back.

The house is just a place to come back to. The grass is overgrown and uneven and sprouting through cracks in the driveway. The siding could use a power wash and paint job. The garage door hangs crooked on its tracks.

But the basketball hoop has been taken care of. The weeds pulled around the base and the backboard scrubbed to a shine.

The man has focused much less on taking care of himself. His hair and beard are long and unkempt, his clothes hanging on his wiry frame. He eats his dinner standing at the kitchen counter and then tosses the balled-up wrappers in the trash. He braces his elbows on the counter and holds his head in his hands for a few minutes.

The lights in the kitchen switch off, and the man goes to the living room to watch TV. He falls asleep in a recliner with a *Seinfeld* rerun on in the background.

"You're the one leaving me," I say to Mom quietly, my eyes still trained on the man. "You always said I'd be the one to leave you."

"Not forever," she says.

"I just don't understand."

She squeezes my hand until I meet her gaze. "You deserve to know him," she says.

Tears prick at my eyes. "You sure you just don't want me around anymore?"

She grips my hand tighter. "You've always tried to do what's best for me, and now it's my turn to do what's best for you. Even if it hurts me."

I stare hard at the man, motionless in his recliner.

"What if he turns me away?"

"He won't."

"But—"

"I'll wait here for tonight. You can come back out if he won't let you stay. But that isn't going to happen. Okay?"

I press my lips together. Nod.

We make our last hug short and tight. She kisses my forehead. And then I get out of the van.

I don't let myself look back as I walk up to the door.

I knock three times.

There's a pause. I imagine him grumbling as he pushes himself up out of the recliner. His slow shuffle to the door.

Then he opens it. And he stares at me, waiting for an explanation, like maybe I'm selling insurance or Girl Scout cookies.

I open my mouth, but I can't think of one to give him. All that time in the car, and I couldn't come up with a single plan beyond knocking on the door.

And then he steps forward, into the porch light, and stares hard into my face.

After a moment, tentatively, he says, "Lily?"

Lily. A nervous laugh escapes my mouth. No one has called me that in years—not since Mom and I ran away and she gave me a new name. I almost forgot it ever belonged to me. I don't know how I feel about it right now. I may not be Lily anymore, but I'm not sure that I'm Phoenix either.

"Dad?" I say.

I brace myself for questions. Maybe anger at me and at Mom. The only thing I'm really hoping for is that he'll let me in and that maybe he'll have something in the fridge that hasn't expired.

But then he staggers forward, wraps me in his arms, and crushes me to him. At first, I don't have any idea what to do in response, because I didn't do anything to earn this. Nothing except come back.

Hesitantly, I hug him. His whole body shakes, and his tears dampen my hair. "Lily," he says. "Lily. My Lily. God, I thought—"

He can't talk anymore, so he just holds on to me harder.

A lot of thoughts tumble through me, too many to latch on to more than this one—I don't know this man. But something looms larger than anything else, swelling above the chaos in my head.

It's the same feeling I had with Mom when she used to stroke my hair while I rested my head in her lap. The same feeling I had with Melody, the night we danced and she smiled at me for the very first time.

Mom and I tried so hard for so many years to belong somewhere in the world, but in this moment, I think that maybe this feeling is all that's ever mattered. Like if tomorrow the oceans dried up and the mountains fell and the world decided to collapse in on itself, knowing each other was enough.

Home is a place where I am enough.

Acknowledgments

This book took me nearly a decade to complete, and in that time, I complained about it to *a lot* of people. I forced friends to read pages, polled my softball teammates on plot decisions, pestered coworkers to help me figure out names for fictional places or landmarks, and asked just about everyone to brainstorm titles with me. If I have ever bugged you for an opinion on this book, thank you for putting up with me.

To my agent, Victoria Doherty-Munro—thank you for being my champion. I'd be lost without you. Thank you for answering all my anxious questions and always understanding my stories even better than I do. And thank you most of all for taking a chance on me.

To my editor, Allison Moore—you made my dreams come true, and I'll be forever grateful for that. Thank you for reading my story about girls with bad attitudes, deciding that it was something that should be unleashed upon the world, and for giving me the notes that made it better.

To everyone at Bloomsbury who got this book into readers' hands, specifically: Danielle Ceccolini, Donna Mark, Jeanette Levy, Oona Patrick, Diane Aronson, Nicholas Church, Melissa Kavonic, Lex Higbee, Faye Bi, Phoebe Dyer, Erica Barmash, Cindy Loh, Mary Kate Castellani, and Manu Velasco.

To Nicole Rifkin, for the stunning cover.

To Brianna Bourne and all the other 21ders who helped me navigate the ups and downs of being a debut author.

To my bookshop friends, old and new—bosses, coworkers, and customers. Thank you for letting me share my favorite books with you, and for sharing yours with me. I hope this one is a worthy addition to your shelves.

To my Author Mentor Match mentor, Lauren Karcz, for reading an early draft and offering me the feedback I needed to take the story to the next level.

To all my teachers at Zane Trace and Franklin College who encouraged, shaped, and supported me—especially Kathy Carlson, Katie Burpo, Susan Crisafulli, Richard Erable, Emily Stauffer, Tyler Wertman, and Theresa Colopy.

To Gunner Barnes, for the author photo, and for teaching me how to pump gas that one time.

To the Davis and Byard families—it takes a village to raise a writer, and I'm so thankful to all of you for being part of mine.

To Weston, for all the history lessons, debates, and games of make-believe in the backyard, and to Emily for teaching me that every house needs a gnome (and also for being the best sister-in-law ever).

To Afton, for being my favorite shopping buddy and confidant. Nobody makes me laugh quite as hard as you do.

To Aubri, for reminding me what it's like to be a teenager and for handling the challenges of growing up so boldly. And also for reminding me every chance you get that I am absolutely not cool.

To my grandma, Patty Byard, for loving books even more than I do. I hope you love this one!

To my parents. Dad, for teaching me to "just keep swimming" no matter what, and also for asking me "So how's that book coming?" pretty much every day since you found out I wanted to be a writer. Mom, for reading to me so many nights and for teaching me that the best stories are the ones you share. I fell in love with books listening to your voice. And to both of you, for believing in me, and for showing me the meaning of unconditional love every single day.

To Merlin and Lilly, the best writing buddies a girl could ask for.

To anyone I forgot to mention (typical Brooke), I'm so sorry! I'll catch you in the next one!

And to Quinton—you clumsy, handsome man. I got my first offer for this book the same week we went on our first date, so I think that makes you my good luck charm. Thank you for convincing me to take risks, and for being my safe harbor in the storm. For pushing me into the unknown, and welcoming me back home with open arms. Most of all, for being you, and for letting me be me.